THE
WEDDING NIGHT
THEY NEVER HAD

JACKIE ASHENDEN

THE ONLY KING
TO CLAIM HER

MILLIE ADAMS

MILLS & BOON

First Published in Great Britain 2021
by Mills & Boon, an imprint of HarperCollins*Publishers* Ltd,
1 London Bridge Street, London, SE1 9GF

www.harpercollins.co.uk

HarperCollins*Publishers*
1st Floor, Watermarque Building,
Ringsend Road, Dublin 4, Ireland

The Wedding Night They Never Had © 2021 Jackie Ashenden

The Only King to Claim Her © 2021 Millie Adams

ISBN: 978-0-263-28260-3

08/21

MIX
Paper from
responsible sources
FSC™ C007454

This book is produced from independently certified FSC™ paper
to ensure responsible forest management.
For more information visit www.harpercollins.co.uk/green.

Printed and bound in Spain
by CPI, Barcelona

Jackie Ashenden writes dark, emotional stories, with alpha heroes who've just got the world to their liking only to have it blown wide apart by their kick-ass heroines. She lives in Auckland, New Zealand, with her husband, the inimitable Dr Jax, two kids and two rats. When she's not torturing alpha males and their gutsy heroines she can be found drinking chocolate martinis, reading anything she can lay her hands on, wasting time on social media or being forced to go mountain biking with her husband. To keep up to date with Jackie's new releases and other news sign up to her newsletter at jackieashenden.com.

Millie Adams has always loved books. She considers herself a mix of Anne Shirley—loquacious, but charming, and willing to break a slate over a boy's head if need be—and Charlotte Doyle—a lady at heart, but with the spirit to become a mutineer should the occasion arise. Millie lives in a small house on the edge of the woods, which she finds allows her to escape in the way she loves best: in the pages of a book. She loves intense alpha heroes and the women who dare to go toe-to-toe with them. Or break a slate over their heads...

Also by Jackie Ashenden

The Italian's Final Redemption
The World's Most Notorious Greek
The Innocent Carrying His Legacy

The Royal House of Axios miniseries

Promoted to His Princess
The Most Powerful of Kings

Also by Millie Adams

The Kings of California miniseries

The Scandal Behind the Italian's Wedding
Stealing the Promised Princess
Crowning His Innocent Assistant

Discover more at millsandboon.co.uk.

THE
WEDDING NIGHT
THEY NEVER HAD

JACKIE ASHENDEN

MILLS & BOON

When the wind stops and, over the heavens,
The clouds go, nevertheless,
In their direction.
—*The Death of a Soldier* by Wallace Stevens

PROLOGUE

PRINCE CASSIUS DE LEON, second in line to the throne of Aveiras, sat in his limo after a hard night's partying and contemplated his choices. Outside, four women waited, all beautiful and all eager to be his companion for the night.

He wasn't going to rush choosing one, however. He liked to take his time when it came to deciding on his bed partners, because there were many important things to take into account.

Would the delicious brunette with the hot, dark eyes turn out to be passionate or shy? Would the curvy redhead with the infectious smile let him lead the way? Perhaps the tall, Amazonian blonde would be more demanding than the other brunette, the one with the dirty laugh, but did he feel like 'demanding'? Or did he want someone more low-key?

It was a difficult decision; he didn't like to disappoint and someone was going to have to miss out. Though… maybe not. He could have all four. He was, after all, feeling quite energetic tonight.

At that moment, the door to the limo opened and a fairy got in.

Cassius blinked.

No, not a fairy, but a tiny, fragile-looking woman wearing the shortest, most clinging black mini-dress in the history of creation. She was very pale, with long, silvery white hair that hung to her waist, and she stared at him from under lids heavy with garish blue eyeshadow and lashes gone spidery with inexpertly applied mascara. Her eyes were a luminous grey and the biggest he'd ever seen.

He blinked again.

No, not a woman. A girl. A teenage girl.

Cassius frowned. What the hell was a teenage girl doing climbing into his limo? It wasn't entirely unheard of, but his staff was usually better at weeding out people who shouldn't be approaching him.

'Your Highness,' the girl said earnestly. 'I'm sorry. I know this is quite rude, but…um…well… I really need you to ruin me.'

Cassius blinked a third time. 'What?'

'I need you to ruin me. Quite urgently, in fact. Tonight.' She glanced nervously out the window. 'Right now, if possible.'

It was true that his reputation as a notorious womaniser was well-earned and he was famous for never saying no to anything that might prove to be enjoyable. However, that did not extend to teenage girls. And, if this one thought he customarily ruined teenagers, then his reputation was even worse than he'd thought.

Won't your father be proud?

Cassius did not appreciate this thought so he ignored it.

'First things first,' he said, giving her a narrow stare. 'How old are you?'

'Twenty.' Her grey eyes shone. 'I'm not a child.'

He sighed. 'Of course you're a child. And, sadly for you, I'm not a pervert. Get out of the limo, little one. I have actual women to see tonight.'

The sprite frowned then reached into the tiny silver mesh bag slung over one narrow shoulder, pulled out a pair of glasses, rubbed the lenses on her dress then put them on her pert nose.

'Look,' she said very seriously, 'You don't have to do anything to me. I only need everyone else to think that you have.'

Cassius knew he should open the limo door and get one of his guards to get rid of her, and he couldn't think why he wasn't doing so now, especially when he had several delicious beauties all ready and waiting for the crook of his finger. But he was curious about, not to mention intrigued by, her boldness. It took guts to climb into the limo of a prince of Aveiras, automatically assuming he wouldn't simply throw her out.

He stretched out his legs and shoved his hands in his pockets. 'I assume you're going to tell me why you need everyone to think I've taken a sudden liking to teenagers?'

Her forehead creased. 'I'm not a teenager. Anyway, the reason is that my parents want me to marry this horrible, abusive man. But, if word gets out that I've spent the night with Prince Cassius, he'll know I'm not a virgin any more and he won't want me.'

Cassius waited for her to offer more, but she didn't. So he opened his mouth to issue a gentle but firm refusal when she added, 'The man is Stefano Castelli.'

Cassius closed his mouth.

Stefano Castelli was the head of one of the old aristocratic families. He was fifty if he was a day, childless since his wife had died some years before, and he'd made no secret of the fact that he was in the market for a new wife to deliver him heirs. What he did keep secret was the rumours of his…unorthodox sexual tastes. The man was a monster and, if this child was given to him in marriage, she wouldn't stay a child much longer.

'What's your name?' he asked, curious, because if an arranged marriage was on the cards she must come from one of Aveiras's aristocratic families.

'Inara Donati.' She gave him an owlish look. 'Well? Will you help me?'

He hadn't heard of the Donatis. Then again, he'd never paid attention to the interminable lessons about royal protocol his father had put him and his brother through when they'd been children which, among other things, had required memorising the list of important Aveiran families.

Perhaps the Donatis were part of the nouveau riche who were desperate to claim links to the aristocracy in order to bolster their own social standing. Aveirans were notoriously snobbish when it came to their lineages and arranged marriages were common. Though they didn't usually start them off that young.

Whatever the case, if what she said was true—and she probably wasn't lying—then marrying off this child to Stefano Castelli was nothing short of criminal.

Cassius seldom stirred himself for others, because he was nothing if not committed to his life of supreme self-indulgence, but he didn't like that thought. At all.

'I need more information,' he said. 'Your real age, for example.'

She looked irritated by this. 'I don't see how—'

'If you please,' Cassius commanded.

The girl pulled a face. 'Okay, fine. I'm sixteen.'

It wasn't illegal to be married at sixteen, not if you had your parents' permission, or in this case your parents' insistence.

'I see,' he said carefully. 'And why are they so set on the marriage?'

'Because the Castellis are an old family and my parents want to be part of the aristocracy.' Inara fiddled with her bag. 'Is that all?'

'What about other family members who could help you? Or friends, perhaps?' It was a perfectly reasonable question, but he thought he knew the answer to that already.

She shook her head. 'I'm an only child and no one will stand up to my father.'

A difficult situation. Even more difficult when her parents had a legal responsibility for her until she turned eighteen.

You could help her, though. No one will say no to a prince. And perhaps this is your chance to show your father what you're made of.

Cassius didn't care what his father thought of him, but the old man had been on his back about his behaviour recently and it was getting tiresome. Because, while it was true that when his brother ascended the throne Cassius would be expected to be his right-hand man, Cassius wasn't going to be king himself, so why should he have to conform?

Still, this girl had come to him for help, and she was looking at him as if he was her saviour. This was something of a novelty, when his family tended to view him as the disappointment he was, while his lovers were only hungry for the pleasure he could bring them.

No one looked at him as though he could save them, as though he was the answer to all their prayers.

He liked it.

Except...being this girl's saviour would be difficult. She was under age, and therefore still under her parents' guardianship, and, though he might be able to find her a refuge, if her parents claimed her he wouldn't be able to stop them. No one was above the law, not even royalty.

There was the police, but the filing of reports took time, as did investigations into abuse allegations, and that was probably time this girl didn't have.

He could ask the King for help, of course, but his father never looked kindly on his activities. Besides, a small piece of him didn't want to ask his father for help anyway. A small piece of him wanted to save this girl himself.

Yet how? If he could somehow become her legal guardian, that would be ideal, but also impossible, considering her parents were still alive.

The girl frowned at him. 'It's easy. All you have to do is keep me for a couple of hours and everyone will think—'

'Everyone will think that my tastes run to under-age girls and, while it's true that I don't care much about my reputation, I care enough not to want rumours like that attached to my name.'

She bit her lip. 'Oh. I hadn't thought of that.'

'Clearly.' He kept his tone dry. 'Also, I'm afraid that, while virginity might be valued in some circles, I'm pretty sure Stefano Castelli wouldn't care if you were one or not. He just wants heirs.'

Her forehead creased, a line appearing in the smooth skin between her brows. She looked…anxious. No, more than that. She looked scared.

'Then what should I do?' Desperation suddenly glowed in her eyes. 'I could leave the country. I could—'

'Where would you go?' he interrupted gently. 'You have no passport, I'm assuming, and no money. And, even if you did, the courts would soon make sure you were sent back to your family.'

She took a soft breath and looked away, blinking hard. It was obvious she was trying hard not to cry. 'Then,' she said in a shaky voice, 'I suppose I have no choice. I'm sorry, Your Highness. I'd better go.'

But Cassius had already made a decision. She was distressed and in danger, and she'd come to him for help. Not to his brother, the noble heir who could do no wrong, but to *him*.

To her he wasn't the dissolute, no-good second son. To her he wasn't a careless, self-centred playboy prince.

To her he was a hero…her potential saviour.

So that was who he'd be.

'Wait,' he said, his brain moving at lightning speed, sorting through all the most likely options and then discarding them.

There was only one way he could think of to become her guardian. Only way to save her from marriage to a monster and to keep her parents happy at the same time.

He'd marry her himself.

It was a shocking decision that would likely appal his parents, and there'd no doubt be a scandal. But that was too bad. He'd never be the kind of prince they wanted him to be and he'd long since given up trying.

He'd be a hero for this girl instead.

And as for her parents, well, they'd probably be delighted to have a prince for a son-in-law instead of some minor lord.

He'd offer her the protection of his name and, in essence, she'd be his ward. He'd look after her until she reached her legal majority.

Two years. That was all it would be. And then they'd divorce and she'd be out of her parents' clutches for ever.

It was unorthodox, certainly, but the main thing was that she'd be safe. And *he* would be the one to save her.

She was looking at him with big eyes, as if her entire existence waited on his next word.

Which it did.

'There is one way I can help you.' He met her gaze very directly. 'But I'm afraid you might not like it.'

'It can't be any worse than having to marry Stefano Castelli,'

'That depends,' Cassius said. 'How do you feel about marrying me instead?'

CHAPTER ONE

'His Majesty has arrived, Your Majesty.'

Inara looked up from the email she'd been in the middle of excitedly typing to a colleague in Helsinki and blinked at Henri, her elderly butler. 'What? Already?'

Used to her absent-minded lapses when it came to time, the butler inclined his head. 'Indeed, Your Majesty. He's in the lavender sitting room.'

Inara's heartbeat accelerated. The lavender sitting room wasn't the tidiest room in the Queen's Estate and she knew her husband valued order. Henri and his wife Joan kept the estate in reasonable order, but it wouldn't be up to the King's standards.

How awful.

Inara felt her face get hot. She shoved back her chair and stood up quickly, her heart beating even faster. Even now her palms felt sweaty and her breath was short.

It was always this way whenever he visited. Five years she'd been married, and she was still as in love with him as she'd ever been, while he still barely acknowledged her existence.

No, that was a lie. He used to visit her regularly, shielding her from the scandal that their marriage had caused, then making sure she'd been looked after as the years had gone by. 'The Prince's Forgotten Wife', the press had dubbed her, which was fine. She didn't care.

He'd protected her from her parents with his name and his power, allowing her to finish school and attend university, pursuing her interest in mathematics. Most of the time he left her alone, though he'd used to visit for dinner or sometimes lunch, a breakfast here and there, and they'd talk, discussing all manner of subjects.

She'd loved those visits. She'd had him all to herself.

Then, two years after their marriage, his entire family had been killed in an accident and he'd become King. And the visits had stopped.

Inara wiped her hands on her dress unthinkingly. 'Oh dear, I know I left about a thousand teacups in there, and I—'

'It's all tidy,' Henri interrupted in that fatherly way he had. 'Don't fret, Your Majesty.'

Inara gave him a grateful smile then half-raised her hand to her hair, wondering vaguely if she should do anything about it, before lowering it as Henri gave a small shake of his head.

No time to change or fuss with her appearance. The King didn't like to be kept waiting.

Inara moved around the side of her desk and into the wide hallway that ran the length of the little manor house. She'd moved here from Katara, the capital, when Cassius had ascended the throne. The traditional holiday estate of the queens of Aveiras, it was buried deep in the countryside amongst farmland and ancient forests, and she loved it for its isolation and privacy. Here, she was away from the city and its frenetic pace that disturbed her thinking, and away from the glare of the press and the eyes of the world that always made her feel small and plain and inadequate.

Cassius had only visited her a couple of times since he'd

been crowned, preferring her to come to the city whenever there were royal duties to carry out as his queen. It made her wonder why he was here now.

Her stomach twisted in a sudden attack of nerves, but she swallowed it down. She didn't want anything to ruin her joy at seeing him.

The door to the sitting room was open, so she went right in. Her husband stood before the fireplace with his back to her, a tall, broad statue in a dark suit. His hands were clasped behind his back, the royal seal of Aveiras gleaming on the middle finger of his right hand, his plain gold wedding band gleaming on the ring finger of his left.

Even with his back to her, he dominated the room.

Inara's chest tightened, her stomach doing its usual swoop and dive, like the starlings over the south field in the evenings.

It was always the same whenever she was in his vicinity. She got hot and jittery, and her brain wouldn't work. She also couldn't stop staring at him.

She tried to hide her reaction to him, because she wasn't sixteen any more, but she suspected he knew anyway. He was an experienced, much older man and, regrettably, not stupid. However, he never mentioned it, for which she was grateful, pretending not to notice her stutters and her sweaty palms, and coolly tolerant of her lapses into vagueness.

Really, it was a blessing she only saw him occasionally.

Inara pushed her glasses up her nose, took a breath and opened her mouth to welcome him.

'How are you, Inara?' he asked before she could get words out. He kept his back to her, his gaze on the watercolour of a vivid lavender field that hung above the fireplace and gave the room its name.

His voice was deep and cool, flowing over her heated skin like river water on a hot summer's day.

'Oh…um…good.' Distractedly, she rubbed her hands down the sides of her cotton dress. 'I've been chatting with Professor Koskinen in Helsinki about a theory I've been working on. It's really interesting. I've had look at some of the—'

'I'm sure you have.' He continued to examine the painting in front of him. 'But I'm afraid I'm not here to discuss your theories.'

Stop babbling and start acting like a normal person.

Inara closed her mouth hard against the urge to chatter, her joy at seeing him fading somewhat. 'Why are you here, then?

Slowly he turned around to face her and Inara's heart clenched like a fist.

Cassius de Leon, King of Aveiras, was quite simply the most beautiful man she'd ever met, and she lost the power of speech whenever he was near. At six-four, he towered above most men, and was built broad and muscular, like a mediaeval warrior. His hair was coal-black and his eyes were dark amber, his features possessing a fierce, compelling masculine beauty that captivated everyone he met.

When she'd first met him, he'd been a notorious playboy with a wicked streak a mile wide, and a charming smile that had granted him access to bedrooms and hearts all over Europe and beyond.

Those days were over, however. Now, that charm rarely made an appearance, and wickedness not at all. There was only a steady, cool authority that made most of his court, not to mention parliament, cower before him.

The notorious playboy prince was gone, leaving in his place a rigid and unbending king.

The King who was her husband.

Inara gritted her teeth against the urge to kneel before him that always gripped her whenever she was confronted with him. She'd done so once, the day of his coronation, and he'd told her to get up. Queens didn't kneel, so she'd tried not to give in to the urge.

That didn't stop it happening, however.

With difficulty, she met his gaze.

'It's quite simple,' the King said. 'I'm here because I want a divorce.'

Cassius was expecting his wife to nod in her usual absent-minded way and tell him that a divorce was fine, before offering him a cup of tea and launching into a conversation about whatever thing was holding her interest at that moment. Six months ago, when he'd last visited, she'd been talking about dark matter and he'd been lost within minutes.

To be fair, that might have had more to do with how she'd been wearing a ridiculously filmy white shirt through which he'd been able to see her lacy bra, and he'd been far too distracted for his own good.

Another reason—as if he needed yet another—why a divorce was a good idea.

Except this time Inara didn't nod in her usual absent-minded way. Her pretty elfin features went pale and her small, perfect rosebud of a mouth opened in what looked like shock.

'A…divorce?' Her voice, usually sweet and clear, now sounded husky.

She looked as if he'd stabbed her and he wasn't quite sure what to make of that. They'd agreed they'd divorce when she legally became an adult at eighteen, but then his brother and his parents had died, he'd become King and everything had gone to hell in a handcart.

A divorce had been the last thing he'd wanted to think about and it had been the last thing the country had needed after the shock death of its king and heir. Stability and normality was what Aveiras had needed so that was what he'd delivered.

But three years had passed since then and, now the country had recovered, it was time to shore it up by producing an heir. His ministers were very insistent about it and he couldn't argue with them. Cassius was the only surviving member of his family so securing his legacy with children—and lots of them—was imperative.

He needed a woman who could be a real wife to him, who could provide him with the heirs he required and who could take her place at his side as a proper queen. Someone who could meet heads of state and hold her own at royal functions, who had the authority, grace, and dignity of Aveiras's previous queen, his mother. And, most importantly, someone who was not the teenage girl he'd married when he'd been young and stupid, still thinking that he could be somebody's saviour. That saving her would prove that he wasn't as selfish as his father had always believed him to be.

Inara's misty grey eyes were huge behind the lenses of her glasses, her fingers curled into fists. She wore a loose, white cotton dress that was as filmy as the shirt she'd worn the last time, and the material was transparent enough for him to see her underwear. Her knickers were lacy and dark-blue, her bra lacy and purple.

He shouldn't be looking. His days of being led around by his baser appetites were over and done with. They'd died along with his brother.

Inara's hair was in its usual messy tumble of silvery white curls that hung to her waist and it looked as though she hadn't brushed it. Some of it was tied back from her face with a rubber band. She had a small blue line across one pale cheek, as if she'd accidentally drawn on herself with a pen.

Definitely not queen material.

No, she never had been. And when he'd married her that had been the last thing on his mind.

'But I…' Inara began, still sounding husky. 'Um, I mean, c-can I ask why?'

Of course there would be questions. He'd expected that.

He stared at her impassively. 'To be blunt, I need heirs. And I'm sure you can understand why. Also, Aveiras needs a queen who takes an active interest in the country and who supports me in my duties as King.'

'Oh,' Inara said faintly. 'I…s-see.'

She was still very pale, which was odd. The plan had never been to stay married, and besides, he knew that she didn't like living in the city. That she didn't like being Queen, full-stop. So surely she should be pleased at this news?

'You can keep the Queen's Estate, if that's what you're worried about.' He glanced around the room, noting that, while it had certainly been dusted well, there was still a lot of cheerful clutter everywhere.

The Queen's Estate was a pretty place, but it reminded him too much of his mother, so if Inara wanted it she could have it.

'Or you could take your pick of any royal property, if you prefer,' he went on when she didn't say anything. 'You'll also be given a monthly stipend that should keep you quite comfortable.'

Still she said nothing, continuing to look at him as if he'd hurt her.

'Your life won't change,' he said gently, because her colour hadn't returned and it concerned him. 'You can stay here and continue with your research. You don't have to move if you don't want to. And you won't have to come into Katara any longer.' He paused. 'You'll be free, little one. The way you always wanted to be.'

Yet the shocked expression on her face lingered, and after a moment she looked away, clenching and unclenching her hands.

She definitely was *not* pleased by the news, and he still couldn't understand it. When he'd offered her the protection of his name that night in the limo five years earlier, she'd been wary, and rightly so. She'd wanted to escape a marriage, not jump head-first into another one.

His parents had been horrified, as had the majority of the country after news of the marriage had come out. They hadn't seen him as the saviour he'd hoped they would, and it didn't matter that he'd done it to protect someone else. It had been a scandal attached to the family name and how could he be so selfish? What was one girl compared to the dignity of the crown?

They were right, of course; he hadn't married Inara to save her. He'd married Inara to save himself in his family's eyes. Still, what was done was done, and he'd stubbornly stuck to the story he'd told himself: he'd saved an innocent teenage girl from the clutches of a monster.

However, the necessity of the marriage hadn't existed for three years. He should have started divorce proceedings earlier, but assuming the duties of a position he'd never wanted, and had never envisaged taking on, had consumed most of his time.

'If you're worried about what will happen to you,' he said into the growing silence, 'Then you needn't—'

'I'm not worried about what will happen to me.'

Cassius stared at her.

She kept her attention out of the window, her hands

still clenched, her knuckles white. She'd never interrupted him before.

He frowned. 'What's wrong, Inara?'

Agitation poured off her. She'd always been bright and sparky and interested, with a magpie mind that darted here and there. He found her intellectual, yet quirky and amusing, and he enjoyed his visits to check on her progress.

She hadn't seemed to care that he was a prince or a king. She'd been interested in his opinions, not because he was a royal, but because she seemed genuinely interested in him. And she didn't always agree with his views; she was quite happy to argue a point, which he found stimulating, as hardly anyone argued with him any more.

She looked at him all of a sudden, her pointed chin firming as if she'd reached a decision about something.

'No,' she said flatly.

Cassius wasn't sure what she was talking about. 'No? No what?'

Inara's chin came up. 'No, I'm not giving you a divorce.'

CHAPTER TWO

INARA HAD NEVER said no to him, not once. In all the years she'd been married to him, she'd done everything he'd asked. Refusing him wasn't something she'd ever contemplated. He'd saved her from the marriage her parents had tried to force her into and, even though some of the things he'd asked her to do after he'd become King had been annoying and anxiety-producing, she'd done them without hesitation or complaint.

She owed him and, though he might not have said that explicitly, she was fully aware of her debt and was happy to pay it.

So she wasn't sure why she said no now.

She'd always known their marriage wasn't going to be for ever, that eventually he'd gently but firmly disentangle her from his life. She'd expected it at eighteen, but then the royal family had all died in a helicopter crash, leaving Cassius to ascend the throne, and all the divorce plans had fallen by the wayside.

For the past five years she'd been his wife in name only, and she'd been happy. She'd lost herself in the research her parents had never allowed her to undertake, as they didn't view it as helpful to their social-climbing interests, content with burying herself in the glory of numbers and intellectual discussions via email with other researchers and experts.

Sometimes Cassius visited her, and she lived for those visits, yet dreaded them at the same time.

Lived, because she got to see him.

Dreaded, because he treated her the way he had always treated her: as if she was still that sixteen-year-old girl who'd crept into his limo one night.

Even so, she was happy. And a divorce wouldn't change things, as theirs wasn't a proper marriage in the first place. How could it be, when she'd been a child bride and he a notorious playboy prince?

He didn't love her. He didn't want her. He'd married her to rescue her and, now that she was safe, there was no reason for their marriage to continue. None at all.

Yet everything in her rebelled at the thought.

Cassius stood like a statue, a dark, still point in the bright, pretty room. The walls had been painted a parchment colour, and there were watercolours on the walls, all of them echoing that lavender shade, as did the soft velvet of the couch. The furniture, which she'd ordered herself, was as delicate and pretty as the art on the walls, but suddenly all of it seemed flimsy and insubstantial next to him.

His expression hadn't changed, yet Inara was sure that the late-summer sunlight flooding into the room had dimmed and the temperature had dropped.

'Excuse me?' His deep voice was mild. 'Did you just say no, you're not going to give me a divorce?'

He was always composed. Always controlled and cool. He never got angry, never lost his temper. But he never smiled either. He used to smile a lot…

Inara took a slow, steady breath. She should nod her head and give in, tell him that of course he could have a divorce. That he could go and find some other woman who could do all the things he'd said. Who could give him children, support him as a wife should and be the kind of queen Aveiras deserved instead of the absent-minded, overly intellectual, socially inept mess that she was.

She'd always known she didn't have what it took to be a queen, just as she'd always known he'd never feel for her what she felt for him. So, really, she should step aside and let him find someone else to make him happy. Or at least happier than he was.

But you don't want him to find another woman.

That was the problem. She didn't.

'Th-that's right,' she said, annoyed with herself for stuttering. 'I mean, you have a wife already, Your Majesty.'

Cassius's expression remained inscrutable. 'A wife who calls me "Your Majesty" is not the kind of wife I need.'

She blushed. How ridiculous to have called him that. Before he'd become King, she'd called him Cassius, and had had no problem with it. It was only after his family had died that he'd become so reserved and distant, and calling him Cassius had felt too…presumptuous.

'Fine.' She gave him a steady look. 'You already have a wife, *Cassius.*'

'But you're not really my wife, Inara.' His voice, again, was gentle. 'That was something forced on you, so why wouldn't you want to be rid of me as soon as you can?'

She could tell him the truth—that she was in love with him. That she'd loved him for years and, now that the reality of losing him for ever was staring her in the face, she couldn't stand it.

But what would he say? What would a man like him, a king, want with the love of the girl he'd once rescued and married out of pity?

How can you lose him when you never had him in the first place?

She unclenched her fingers, stretching them to relieve some of her agitation. 'I've enjoyed it, though.'

'Again, what part of your life is connected to mine? Apart from legally?'

She tried to think. 'You…come and visit me.'

'Occasionally, yes. But occasional visits are not enough, and I think you know that.'

Of course she knew that.

'Well…why can't I h-help you out with all those things?'

He frowned. 'Why would you want to do that?' He said it as if it was the most mystifying thing he'd ever heard in his life.

Inara found it irritating. He'd never been quite this patronising before. 'It just seems a little… I don't know… pointless to go looking for someone when I could, you know, do what ever you need.'

'But I didn't marry you for that,' Cassius said patiently. 'I married you because you needed protection, nothing more.'

'Yes, I know that, but—'

'I will be needing heirs, little one. You do know how children are conceived, don't you?'

The use of his old pet name for her was both irritating and comforting at the same time.

'Yes, of course,' she said testily. 'Believe it or not, Cassius, I'm not sixteen any more. And even when I was sixteen I knew how children were conceived.'

The calm expression on his face didn't change. 'Then you'll understand why it's impossible for you to continue being my wife.'

A needle of hurt pierced her; she was so stupid to think he might want her. She'd left herself open for that, hadn't she? Not that she'd truly thought he would, but a part of her had nursed a faint hope.

'I didn't think I was that unattractive,' she said before she could stop herself. 'But I suppose if it's impossible then I must be.'

'Of course you're not unattractive,' Cassius said. 'But it's not about your attractiveness or otherwise. It's about the fact that I still see you as a sixteen-year-old girl.'

It didn't come as any surprise. He'd always thought of her that way and she knew it.

You haven't done much to change his mind, though, have you?

No, and she hadn't because she…well…she just hadn't. She'd pushed it out of her mind, not wanting to think about when the day would come that he'd need heirs, a proper queen, a life…

A divorce.

But that day was now here and she couldn't ignore it any longer.

You need to do something.

Yes, but what?

'I'm not a sixteen-year-old girl, as I've already pointed out.' She tried to sound as cool as he did. 'I'm twenty-one.'

'Be that as it may, you are still not a suitable prospect for queen.'

Inara took a couple of steps towards him, annoyed now. 'That hasn't been a problem for the last three years. What's changed?'

His amber gaze flicked down her figure and then up again, lightning fast, but there was no alteration in his expression. 'I've been advised it's past time for me to start a family. Aveiras needs heirs, and the sooner the better.'

She understood. The country had lost nearly its entire royal family in one fell swoop, so naturally parliament would want to safeguard the royal line. They'd also want a queen who lived at the palace and took part in royal life, not someone who preferred an isolated country manor and spent most of her time studying arcane mathematical problems.

No, everything about this made logical sense and, given that the pathways of her own mind tended towards the logical, there was no earthly reason why she should refuse to give him the divorce he wanted.

Except that the part of herself she'd never understood and had never wanted to think about too deeply, the part that had fallen desperately in love with her husband, didn't want to.

Her heart wanted to be his queen. It wanted to give him heirs. It wanted to be by his side and support him. It wanted do all the things he'd just said and more, and it was furious he'd even consider choosing someone else.

But what could she say? How could she argue? He still saw her as a child and, as long as he did, nothing would change his mind.

The fizzing happiness of his presence began to recede, a flat feeling stealing through her.

He'd never been a man who changed his mind once he'd made a decision, not even when he'd been that laughing, charming prince, and she knew there was no point arguing with him.

'Fine. I suppose it doesn't matter what I say.' She clasped her trembling hands in front of her. 'You've obviously made your choice. I don't know why you bothered coming here at all, in that case. You could have just sent me an email.'

Another frown flickered over his perfect features. 'An email? You really think I'd ask you for a divorce via email?'

'You haven't visited me in nearly six months. And you've already made up your mind. You could have just sent me an order; you didn't need to make the trek all the way out here.'

Cassius's gaze sharpened. 'You're upset. Why?'

Shock pulsed down her spine. She'd forgotten how perceptive he could be—when he deigned to notice, that was.

But she couldn't tell him the truth. He'd look at her with distant, condescending pity and tell her gently once again that any kind of relationship between them was impossible. The thought was unbearable.

'I'm not hurt,' she said, forcing away her anger and the small, sharp pain of rejection. 'I'm only…shocked, I suppose. It's quite sudden.'

He gazed at her, still frowning, and she thought he might push it, but as he opened his mouth to speak someone said, 'Your Majesty, we have an issue.'

Inara turned to see one of the uniformed palace aides standing in the doorway to the sitting room.

Cassius straightened. 'What is it, Carlo?'

'There's a mechanical problem with the helicopter. A part needs to be replaced, and we can get it, but it won't be here until after dark.'

If this annoyed him, Cassius didn't show it. His expression remained opaque. 'How long will it take to fix?'

'A couple of hours.' Carlo looked apologetic. 'I'm terribly sorry, Your Majesty, but—'

'It's no problem,' Cassius interrupted. 'I'm sure the Queen won't mind if we stay here the night.'

Inara blinked. 'You want to…what?'

'Flying at night can be an issue and safety is of prime concern to me.' He nodded at Carlo. 'Tell the pilot not to rush. We'll leave first thing tomorrow morning.'

Wait. What was he suggesting?

'T-Tomorrow?'

He glanced at her. 'We'll stay here, obviously. There should be room for everyone.'

Already unsettled, his casual arrogance was a further irritation to her. Sure, he was the King, and casual arrogance was part of the job. And, yes, technically, although it was known as the Queen's Estate, the manor was owned by the crown, thus him. But, still, she'd been living here for three years and she'd come to think of it as hers. He couldn't just arrive, demand a divorce then decide to stay the night, as if having the house full of his presence for the next twelve hours wouldn't be an issue.

Except...how could she argue? He was the King and this, despite all her protests, *was* his house.

Yes, and you're the Queen. Don't forget that.

That was true. She was. Maybe not for too much longer, but she was still the Queen now.

Inara raised her chin and stared at him in what she hoped was a haughty fashion. 'Actually, I'm not sure. I'll have to check.'

Another flicker of expression crossed his perfect features, but whether irritation or impatience she couldn't tell. 'No need. Henri is still managing the house, I imagine? I'll inform him. It's only me, Carlo, the pilot and a couple of my guards.'

Already he was looking away from her. Already he was dismissing her as if her feelings and her opinions were of no consequence.

As if *she* were of no consequence.

It reminded her too much of her parents and the way they'd controlled every aspect of her existence when she'd been young. She hadn't been a daughter to them, only currency. A way to buy themselves more social standing, not a person with hopes and dreams of her own.

Hurt buried itself inside her, making her ache. If she'd needed any more proof that he didn't care about her, then this was it, wasn't it?

What do you expect? He asked you if you were upset and you told him you weren't.

It was true, and she had no one to blame for that but herself.

Inara opened her mouth to tell him that she would have appreciated being asked first, but he'd already moved past her and was issuing further orders to Carlo, leaving her standing there, gaping silently after him.

Cassius entered the small library and stopped, surveying it with some disapproval. The room bore the signs of recent cleaning, yet there were still stacks of papers and books scattered over various surfaces. The sideboard had on it some dead flowers in a vase and what appeared to be several tea cups with different levels of tea in them.

A woollen garment of some kind—a cardigan?—had been thrown carelessly onto one of the leather arm chairs that stood beside the fireplace, and now half of it was trailing on the floor. A single slipper had been kicked under the chair. A few pens sat on the mantelpiece above the fire, along with yet more tea cups.

A disgrace. Was his wife the culprit or did the fault lie with the staff for not cleaning properly? Not that he could blame the staff, given Henri and Joan were getting on in years. However, had Inara always been this untidy or had he never noticed? It had been six months since he'd last been here, after all.

A thread of something that he refused to call shame coiled through him. It was ridiculous to be ashamed that he hadn't visited her. She might legally be his wife, but there was nothing between them beyond that. He visited her out of a sense of duty, that was all, and, although she was always pleased to see him, she'd never said that she wished she saw more of him. In fact, the few times her presence had been required for any kind of state function in Katara, she'd appeared uncomfortable, awkward and downright miserable, which had led him to believe she only liked to see him when he was scheduled to visit.

Certainly her obvious displeasure with him today had confirmed that theory. True, initiating divorce proceedings wasn't a happy subject, but he hadn't thought she'd be quite so upset. And he definitely hadn't thought she'd care about him staying.

Apparently, he'd been wrong about both of those things.

Cassius stepped into the room and closed the door behind him, going over to the arm chair that didn't have the cardigan draped over it and sitting down. A large glass of brandy had been set on the table beside the chair—good brandy too, from the smell of it.

He stared at the glass for a long moment.

Alcohol was something he only touched sparingly these days, as he did with most of his old indulgences. He wasn't twenty any more and he had a country to run. His days of drinking in bars and partying in nightclubs were over.

Perhaps he should have asked Henri for some tea instead. Yet the chair was comfortable and he was tired, and the last couple of months discussing budgets and taxes had taken it out of him. Numbers weren't his thing. In fact, being a king in general wasn't his thing—he'd been brought up as the spare, not the heir—and it had taken him a good two years of hard work to get a decent grasp of what was expected of him.

Caspian should have been King, not you.

Yes, he should. But Caspian was dead and Cassius was all Aveiras had left.

The silence of the house settled around him like a balm. He was rarely alone these days. There were always people wanting something from him—a signature, an opinion, an order or even simply to be in his presence.

He found it tiring.

'Are you sure you don't want the crown, little brother?' Caspian had asked him one day. 'It's not too bad once you get used to carrying the weight of an entire country'.

Cassius had shuddered with distaste. 'I'll stick with carrying the weight of my own reputation, thank you very much. Which, luckily, is exceedingly light.'

He hadn't known then he'd end up stepping into his brother's shoes. Or that he'd end up carrying the weight of that crown, and all alone. But he hadn't had a choice, and he wouldn't let his family down—not again.

Cassius picked up the brandy glass and had already taken a few sips before being fully conscious of having done so. The alcohol sat warmly in his stomach, the taste rich and heavy on his tongue. He shouldn't indulge—control in all things was important—yet it seemed a shame to waste such a good vintage.

He only had time for a couple more sips before the library door opened suddenly and he looked up to find his wife standing in the doorway, staring at him.

It was late and he hadn't seen her all afternoon. She'd vanished after he'd finished sorting out the arrangements for himself and his staff for the night, and she hadn't been around when Henri had served dinner in the little dining room.

He'd made some enquiries as to her whereabouts, but Henri had only shaken his head and said he didn't know where Her Majesty was.

Cassius had told himself it didn't matter where she was, that he didn't care, but he couldn't shake the feeling that somehow he'd upset her.

She hadn't received the news of the divorce well. No matter that she'd told him she wasn't upset, he'd seen the shock in her eyes, and the hurt too.

She didn't look pleased to see him now, her pretty mouth firming as she spotted him sitting in the armchair.

She'd grown up into a lovely woman, which wasn't something he'd wanted to notice in his visits over the years, yet he'd noticed all the same. Once he'd been a connoisseur of women, and adult Inara was definitely a woman he'd have made time for.

If he'd still been the charming, feckless prince he'd once been, of course. But he wasn't. He had a duty to uphold, so he'd left that prince behind the moment he'd found out his family had died.

He hadn't taken a woman to his bed since and it wasn't because of a shortage of offers: he had more seduction attempts and frank invitations now he was a king than he'd ever had as a prince.

But his baser appetites had died along with the callow youth he'd once been, so he'd ignored every single offer. A king should be above reproach, as his father had always taught, an example of good leadership, and a new woman in his bed every night wasn't an example of good leadership.

Besides, as King he couldn't be seen to be unfaithful to his wife, even if they'd never consummated their marriage. Not that he'd found abstaining a hardship. Grief had killed any hint of the rebel in him and that was probably a good thing.

Yet he couldn't help noticing again that the white cotton dress she wore was just as see-through now as it had been earlier that day, his attention drawn to the pink glow of pale skin and the lacy shadows of her underwear.

Something stirred inside him. Something he hadn't felt for a long time.

'Sorry,' Inara said stiffly. 'I didn't realise you were in here.'

He recalled that she wasn't a woman who hid her feel-

ings and it was obvious that right now she was very annoyed. Hostile, even. He wasn't used to it from her and he
found he didn't much like it.

'If I'm intruding you only need say,' he said formally.

'It's fine.' One small hand gripped the door handle. 'I'll
leave you in peace—'

'Oh, come in,' he interrupted, feeling suddenly impatient, knowing he'd have to have this discussion with her
at some point so he might as well have it now. 'We need
to talk.'

'Do we?' She pushed her glasses up her nose with one
finger. 'I think you said all you needed to earlier today.'

Cassius leaned forward, clasping his brandy balloon between his fingers. He nodded at the chair opposite him. 'Sit.'

'I'm not one of your staff, Cassius. I don't appreciate
being ordered around.'

He'd become used to people jumping every time he
spoke. And maybe it was the brandy relaxing him but,
instead of feeling irritated at her refusal, he was almost
amused instead.

She hadn't been impressed with him even at sixteen,
that night she'd appeared in his limo, even though he'd
been a prince and she the under-age daughter of an unimportant family. She'd been suspicious of his marriage
proposal, had asked a great many questions and had then
insisted on him putting it in writing and signing it even
before they'd got out of the limo.

It appeared she still wasn't impressed with him, even
though he'd been King for three years.

'Please,' he added.

She wrinkled her nose, pursed that pretty mouth, finally
let out a breath and let go of the door handle, coming over
to the arm chair opposite and sitting down on the cardigan
still half-draped over the seat.

'You're sitting on….' He gestured.

'Oh.' She frowned then wriggled half off the seat, pulling the cardigan out from underneath her. 'Oh, there it is. I've been looking for that for ages.'

Watching her fuss with the cardigan was soothing, though he wasn't sure why. He took another sip of his brandy, his attention caught by the way she lifted the long, silvery waterfall of her hair off the nape of her neck so she could drape the cardigan around her. It was a deft, practised movement, her curls silky-looking as she shook her hair out over her shoulders.

She was still rather fairy-like, her features elfin and delicate, the shape of her slender and fragile.

She continued to fuss around with the cardigan, then adjusted her glasses, before smoothing her dress in small, agitated movements.

She's nervous…

He frowned. Why would she be nervous? Was it him? They'd known each other for five years and, although it was true he hadn't seen much of her the past couple of years, surely he was still familiar to her?

Or maybe it wasn't so much him as the topic of conversation: the divorce he'd asked for.

It mattered to her, as he'd already realised.

That was puzzling.

'Tell me,' he said after a moment. 'What's bothering you about this divorce?'

Her gaze dropped to her lap and she smoothed a non-existent crease in the fabric of her dress. 'Nothing. It was a shock, that's all.'

He didn't think that was all it was but, given how nervous she seemed, he decided not to press. 'And so you give me permission to start proceedings?'

'Do you need my permission?' She didn't look at him. 'You can do whatever you like. You're the King.'

'Yes, but you're still my wife.'

'No, I'm not. I might be your wife legally but I'm not in any other sense.'

Cassius watched her, caught by the strange, sharp note in her clear voice. If he hadn't known any better, he would have said that she sounded hurt, though he wasn't sure why that would be. Did she want to be more to him? If so, she must know how impossible that was. She was not in any way the Queen Aveiras needed and, as the country already had a king they hadn't asked for, he wasn't going to foist an unsuitable queen on them too.

That wasn't the legacy he wanted for the family he'd lost.

'That's true,' he said gently. 'So won't it be a relief to you when you're not my wife at all?'

She looked up, the colour of her eyes silvery behind her glasses. Idly, he noticed that her irises got darker closer to her pupils, the grey turning into charcoal. Her lashes were also darker, the contrast startling with her pale hair and skin.

'Why do you keep patronising me?' Her stare was very direct. 'You don't have to soothe me like a child. If you want to divorce me, divorce me. What does it matter if I agree to it or not?'

The feeling that had woken up inside him when she'd come in gripped him tighter. But he continued to ignore it, because he hadn't felt it for years, and he shouldn't be feeling it now, especially not with her.

Not when that way led back to the prince he'd once been and the choices he'd made that had changed his life for ever. He'd never be that prince, that careless man, again.

'I know you're not a child.' Absently, he cupped the brandy balloon between his palms, swirling the liquid, warming it. 'And I'm not trying to be patronising. I'm just trying to do the decent thing.'

She lifted one shoulder, her fingers pleating the fabric of her dress. 'Well, you don't need to.'

Cassius frowned. 'Would you really have preferred me to send a palace employee out with the divorce papers, then?'

'As long as you gave me some jewellery, that would have been fine.'

Ah, yes, the jewellery. He'd once been famous for showering his lovers with expensive pieces. He'd liked giving them gifts, small tokens of his appreciation for the pleasure they'd given him in return.

He'd thought himself so generous back then, but in reality once he'd got rid of a woman he'd never thought of her again. So, yes, he'd been generous with his money, but selfish and shallow with everything else.

It wasn't something he liked to be reminded of and he didn't like it now.

'Well, since I haven't actually slept with you,' he said, 'Jewellery wouldn't be appropriate.'

Her mouth opened then shut, and she blinked. 'Uh... no. That's true.'

You shouldn't have said that.

No. It had been inappropriate. Perhaps it was the brandy. In which case he should put down his glass and not have any more.

Except he didn't put down his glass. Instead he sat back in the comfortable arm chair and extended his legs, crossing them at the ankle. He took another sip.

He was relaxed, sitting here in the quiet of the house in this little room that was starting to feel more and more cosy despite the clutter. Relaxed in a way he hadn't felt for years. He knew he shouldn't be falling back into old habits, that he had a duty to his crown and to his country, but he wasn't in the vast, cold spaces of the royal palace in Katara now. He was here with Inara and there was no one to see him but her.

'What exactly is the issue, Inara?' he asked after a moment. 'You keep telling me that nothing's wrong yet any fool can see that something is.'

She didn't respond, merely continued pleating the fabric of her dress and smoothing it out.

'You're…interrupting my research,' she said at last.

'Your research.' More amusement coiled inside him. 'And how exactly am I interrupting it?'

'Oh, just by being…' She made a vague gesture in his direction. 'Here. In the house. Hovering.'

He grinned, unable to help himself. 'Hovering?'

She wriggled her fingers. 'Yes, you know. Just by being around and being…distracting.'

That amused him too. 'I'm distracting?'

A wash of delicate pink swept through her cheeks. 'It's not funny.'

Unaccountably fascinated, Cassius stared. The pink accentuated the grey of her eyes and gave her the most pretty glow. He had a sudden vision of what she'd look like if there had been a fire in the fireplace and the warm light of it was flickering over her. If she was naked, without all that white cotton in the way, just her silvery hair flowing over her shoulders and her pale skin pink and bare. He'd pull her from that chair, lay her down on the rug before the fire, spread her thighs and kneel between them. And then he'd…

What the hell are you thinking that for?

Cassius took a sharp breath. He shouldn't be thinking such things, and especially not about Inara. She wasn't the sixteen-year-old he'd married, it was true, but he couldn't afford to start thinking of her as anything else.

She was young and innocent, and her place was in

some university somewhere, putting that genius brain of hers to work. He was going to divorce her and find another woman more suitable to be his wife. A mature, self-contained woman who comported herself with dignity and who could give Aveiras the heirs it needed.

And, apart from anything else, the whole reason he'd married her was to save her from one selfish monster, not put her in danger from another. And most especially if that monster was himself.

But Inara is here right now and she's your wife...

Unfamiliar heat wound through him, intense and raw. It had been so long since he'd been with a woman, run his fingers through her hair, touched her silky skin. So long since soft thighs had closed around his waist and tight, wet heat had brought him home. So long since he'd had kisses and hot whispers in his ear... So very, *very* long...

Cassius became aware that Inara was watching him and that her cheeks had gone an even deeper shade of pink. Something in her eyes glinted and he could feel a certain tension gathering in the space between them.

A tension that hadn't been there before and yet was familiar. He'd felt it with other women, years ago, though it had never been quite as...electric as this.

'Of course it's not funny.' His voice was thicker than he would have liked. 'You should leave. I'm not fit company for anyone tonight.'

Inara stared at him for a long moment, then slowly shook her head. 'No,' she said. 'I don't think I will.'

CHAPTER THREE

SOMETHING WAS TELLING Inara that she should do exactly what he'd said and leave, yet another part of her kept whispering that she should stay. That it had been a long time since she'd seen him like this, all stretched out, long and lean and as muscular as a panther half-asleep in the sun.

When she'd been younger, in the first couple of years after they'd married, he'd set her up in a house in Katara, with Henri and Joan to run the place and keep an eye on her. She'd been ignored by the King and Queen, Cassius's parents, because they had strongly disapproved of Cassius marrying her, but that hadn't mattered to Inara. She was used to parental disapproval, and besides, being safe from her own parents' plans had been more important than anything else.

Cassius had been a regular visitor back then. They'd have dinner together before he'd go out to a club or a party or some royal function. He'd been funny and charming and interested in what she'd had to say. His eyes hadn't glazed over when she'd talked about her mathematical studies and he hadn't scoffed at her enthusiasm or forbidden her to talk about it, the way her parents had done. He hadn't picked at how she looked, or criticised everything she did, or talked about her while she was in the room as if she weren't there.

She'd always found talking to people in social situations difficult, but nothing was difficult about being with him, and she wasn't sure why. Maybe it was simply that he was the first person who'd actually seemed to listen to her. Whatever, his visits had made her happy.

But that had been before Prince Caspian and the King and Queen had died, and Cassius had ascended to the throne.

After that, he'd changed.

He'd become distant, colder, more rigid. He didn't smile or laugh, and soon enough he didn't visit much either. It had been like watching a flesh-and-blood man turn slowly into stone and she'd been powerless to stop it.

She wasn't sure if this happened to every man when they became a king, or whether it was just him, but the one thing she was sure of was that she hated it.

Except he didn't look like stone now. He was sitting sprawled out in her favourite arm chair, the one large enough for her to curl up in and roomy enough to accommodate his broad shoulders and powerful chest with ease. The cold distance she'd always felt in him had receded and the line of his stern mouth was relaxed, as if he might at any moment give her the warm, effortlessly charming smile she'd fallen in love with.

In fact, every line of him seemed relaxed, as if he were a soldier who'd taken off his suit of armour after a hard day's battle.

She didn't want to move or even breathe in case something changed and he turned back into stone again.

He tilted his head, studying her from underneath thick, black lashes, a strange, glimmering heat in the smoky amber of his gaze.

It reminded her of him in the limo all those years ago, sprawled just like this, all coiled, muscled strength and devastating masculine charm, with his pick of the women standing at the kerb, waiting to be his chosen partner for the evening. She hadn't taken much notice of them that night—she'd been too busy being scared, yet determined to go through with her own plan—but she did remember wondering why they'd all looked so flushed and excited.

She knew the reason now, and she knew why they had been desperate, and she wished suddenly that she'd been one of them. That she'd had the chance to be his chosen lover for the evening.

Well, why can't you be?

The thought came like a light switching on in a dark room, illuminating everything, and she had to blink a couple of times to get used to the glare.

'That's probably a mistake.' His voice had deepened, the timbre of it warm, soft and velvety. 'I'm not feeling kind tonight.'

Inara barely took in what he'd said, too busy examining the new and quite frankly exciting idea that had sprung to glaring prominence in her head.

Why *couldn't* she be his lover for the night? True, he'd never shown an interest in her but, as he kept saying, that was because he still saw her as the sixteen-year-old girl who'd slipped into his limo.

She'd told him she wasn't sixteen any more, but he hadn't seemed to listen. Like everyone in her life while she'd been growing up…

Annoyance twisted inside her, along with a new determination. Perhaps she needed to be more obvious. Perhaps he needed to *see* that she wasn't a teenager any more. Perhaps she needed to prove it to him. And perhaps, if she did that, he might actually see her differently. He might… want her.

Her heart was beating very fast and her mouth had gone dry. She knew how to work out complicated algebraic equations, but she didn't have the first clue how to go about making him see her as a woman.

'I don't need you to be kind,' she said distractedly, her brain too occupied with sorting through plans and discarding them. What was the best way to go about this? Where did she start? What did other women do in this situation?

More than once she'd spent whole evenings on her computer, searching for anything she could find on him—scrolling through endless articles and gossip columns, studying the photos of him and the women he had on his arm. Sometimes they'd been drop-dead gorgeous, and sometimes they hadn't been conventionally beautiful, but they'd all seemed to have…something that had drawn him to them. She'd wondered what that something was and had concluded it wasn't something she'd ever have.

But was that actually the case? She was a mathematician, and all good equations needed to be proved. This was exactly the same. If she had conclusive proof that he didn't want her, then it would hurt, but she could accept that. She could accept the divorce too. But if he did want her…

Maybe you could make him change his mind about the divorce.

Inara swallowed. A strange tension filled the room that hadn't been there before. It prickled over her skin, made her breathing get faster.

'What are you thinking about?' Cassius asked. 'It's obviously very important.

Inara forced herself to look up from the mess she'd made of her dress. He was watching her in a very focussed, intent way, his long fingers cradling his brandy glass, swirling the liquid in it idly.

She was often guilty of over-thinking things—that came with the territory of having an anxious, over-excited brain—but maybe it was best if she didn't over-think this particular thing. Maybe she just needed to…act. Do what her instinct told her for a change.

She hadn't had any experience with that, as her instincts had always been wrong in the past—at least, that was what her parents had said—but right now she had nothing to lose. Tomorrow he'd be leaving for Katara and the palace, and her one chance to get him to see her differently, to change his mind, would be gone.

It was now or never.

So she didn't think, just pushed herself up and out of her chair, moving over to where he sat.

He arched one dark brow. 'What do you want, little one?'

'I'm not that little.' She stopped in front of his chair, considering her next move.

'No,' he murmured. 'Perhaps you're not.' His gaze travelled over her in a leisurely fashion and it felt almost as if he was looking right through the material of her dress…

Inara's skin prickled with sudden heat, her breath catching.

He *was* doing that, wasn't he? Because, come to think of it, her dress was a little see-through—not that she'd ever paid much attention, as for the past five years she hadn't had to worry about her appearance.

But now that heat was in his eyes, glowing like banked embers, and she could feel the pressure of his stare like a hand stroking slowly over her skin, she suddenly wanted more than anything in the entire world to be beautiful for him. To be sexy and desirable, to be his choice for the night. Not the scared sixteen-year-old her own parents had been willing to give to a monster.

She took a slow breath, then another, trying to control the frantic beat of her heart. Then she took a couple of steps closer until she was standing almost next to the chair. His legs were outstretched in front of him, crossed at the ankle, and she was painfully aware of how long and powerful he was. So much bigger than she was and so much stronger.

She wasn't sure why that made her so breathless, but then that was the problem with Cassius. Everything about him made her breathless.

His head rested against the back of the chair, his eyes gleaming as he looked up at her, the tension between them pulling tighter.

Say something, idiot.

'Um, I've never had brandy before,' she said, her voice scratchy. 'Can I have a taste?'

He shifted slightly and she found her attention flickering to his body once again. She noted the stretch of his trousers over his powerful thighs and the pull of the cotton over his shoulders. He'd got rid of his jacket and tie, and his shirt was unbuttoned at the throat. She could see his pulse beating beneath smooth olive skin, strong and steady…

'Never?' he asked.

There was a look in his eyes and a certain hot note in his voice that made her think he wasn't just talking about brandy. But she wasn't sure what else he could be talking about. Whatever it was, she was suddenly hotter and even more breathless than before.

'No.' She didn't know what to do with her hands except clasp them in front of her. 'Is it nice?'

Inwardly, part of her cringed. She sounded so silly. Like a little girl. But what else could she say? Social graces and small talk had never come easily to her, much to her mother's annoyance, and as for getting the attention of a man, well…

'For God's sake, Inara,' her mother had said at the first aristocratic gathering to which they'd managed to swing an invite. 'If you can't open your mouth without boring everyone to tears, then just shut it and smile. Some men like a quiet woman.'

So she'd been quiet after that, as she couldn't trust herself to say anything interesting. And clearly she shouldn't trust herself now, especially when he'd be used to all kinds of beautiful, experienced women. Women who were far more interesting than she was, and far more beautiful too. Not pale and weedy and weak-looking. Untidy and chaotic and awkward, hardly anyone's prize.

Except he's looking at you like you might be his.

And he was. Or at least she thought he was. The smoky amber of his gaze was now a hot golden-brown, like the warmed brandy in his glass, and there was something distinctly speculative in it. As if he was imagining things...

Her palms were sweaty and she couldn't breathe, and part of her wanted to turn around and leave the room, flee back to the safety of her study or her bedroom, or basically anywhere he wasn't.

'Being good at maths is useless to us, Inara,' her mother had said coldly after the last social failure. 'We need an aristocratic alliance and if you can't even manage that then what good are you?'

Good enough to turn over to an old man who had an unhealthy obsession with young girls, apparently.

But she wasn't her parents' chess piece now and she'd had five years of freedom from being criticised constantly. And, more than anything else, if she didn't follow through with this she knew she'd never find out what it would be like to be wanted by him. To be touched by him. To have a night with him...

She'd never have a chance to change his mind about divorcing her, and she'd never have something of him to keep for herself if that didn't work.

So she stayed where she was, breathless and aching, and afraid and excited all at the same time.

His mouth curved in a faint, lazy smile. 'Yes. It's very nice. Come here and you can have a taste.' He uncrossed his feet and spread his thighs, indicating that she was to come and stand between them.

The aching, breathless feeling inside her intensified.

Slowly, she moved to stand in front of his chair, between those powerful thighs, while he gazed at her, golden-brown eyes gleaming under silky black lashes.

It was strange to have him look up at her when normally she was the one looking up. Even so, she felt his power. Even when she was sitting down the impact of his presence made her want to go on her knees before him.

Cassius sat forward. 'Here,' he said softly. 'Take a sip.' And he extended his hand, holding his glass out to her.

Her heartbeat was louder now and she could feel the heat coming off him, making the fierce longing inside her tighten.

Whenever she thought about getting close to him, her fantasies were always veiled and gauzy. Kisses, certainly, though she had no idea what a kiss felt like or tasted like. She definitely imagined his arms around her, holding her, and sometimes in the dead of night she imagined his hands on her.

But those were furtive imaginings, making her restless and hot, vaguely feverish and a little afraid, so she tried not to imagine that too much.

It wasn't that she didn't know about sex. It was more that thinking about it in terms of herself and Cassius was too much. The depth of her own feeling about it was too much.

But now she was closer to him than she'd ever been in her life and it wasn't like her teenage imaginings. It was more immediate, more physical, more visceral than those gauzy fantasies had ever been.

Inara swallowed and put her hand out for the glass, only for him to pull it back slightly and out of her reach. How annoying. She took a tiny step closer, reaching out again, only for him to do the same thing.

He watched her, his mouth curving, his gaze full of what looked like challenge mixed with something hot and wicked. A tease.

He was doing this on purpose, wasn't he?

Of course he is. He's flirting with you.

What little breath she had left caught in her throat, a strange euphoria sweeping through her. Because, while she didn't know much of anything about flirting, a very female part of her told her that was what he was doing. Which could only mean one thing: he saw her not just as a woman, but as a woman he was attracted to. A woman he wanted.

'What are you doing?' she asked huskily, wanting to be sure.

'I think you know what I'm doing.' That devastatingly sexy smile deepened, his eyes gleaming. 'If you want a taste of my brandy, little one, you're going to have to come much closer than that.'

Cassius knew he was being grossly inappropriate. But the brandy had gone to his head, he was tired and it had been a long time since he'd allowed himself to enjoy the company of a pretty woman. A long time since he'd flirted with anyone. A long time since he'd felt desire at all.

Yet desire was coiling through him now, and even though she was the wrong woman to be feeling this about, the wrong woman to be using his old flirting skills on, he couldn't bring himself to stop.

She was just so…pretty. And sweet. And so very innocent, in her white dress with her mismatched underwear plainly visible underneath. She was also very slender and fragile, her eyes silvery from behind the lenses of her glasses, her hair lying loose over her shoulders like moonlight.

His child bride.

Except she wasn't a child any more. Her cheeks had gone pink and she was looking at him in a way that was intimately familiar to him. He'd seen it before in the faces of too many women to count.

She wanted him.

He hadn't expected that, though in retrospect he should have, and it was a warning sign that he needed to stop. Because nothing could happen between them. Nothing *should* happen between them, not when they were going to separate. Their marriage needed to stay unconsummated, because she was so much younger than him, and because he wasn't the man he'd once been—that reckless playboy with no purpose in life but to indulge his own selfish needs. He was trying to put distance between himself and that man, and seducing his lovely, innocent wife was definitely *not* putting distance between them.

Also, it wasn't what his parents would have wanted. They'd been appalled at his marriage, never mind that he'd done it to save Inara, and they'd certainly be appalled at what he was contemplating now. Then again, his parents had been dead for three years, and he was so tired of being good. Tired of being rigid and distant and controlled. Tired of having to set an example. Tired of being the King.

Would it be so wrong to have one night where he could indulge himself? To sip a good brandy and flirt with a pretty woman? That was all—just flirt. He wouldn't take it any further. But he could have that, couldn't he?

A crease had appeared between Inara's brows, as if she was contemplating doing what he'd said and getting closer to him, and he found himself breathless at the thought that she might.

It was not an unreasonable response. It had been years since he'd allowed a woman to get close, so it probably had more to do with her being female than it did with Inara herself.

Anyway, he wanted to know what she smelled like. Did she wear perfume? He didn't think she would. There was no artifice to her; everything about her was haphazard and untidy. But also very, very honest.

She wasn't trying to be anyone other than who she was.

Unlike you.

Ah, but he couldn't be who he was. Being a king demanded that he be more than a mere man. Something greater and more noble, more just. The ultimate in self-lessness and self-sacrifice.

Cassius's father had been the model he'd tried to emulate—compassionate yet distant. Protective yet controlled. A great king, everyone had said.

What would they all think of you now? Letting the brandy go to your head while you flirt with the wife you swore you'd never touch...

The thought came and went, and Cassius let it go. Because Inara took another step. The white cotton of her dress brushed against his trousers as she leaned down, reaching for the brandy glass in his hand.

But she wasn't looking at the glass.

She was looking at him.

He lifted the glass before she could take it and sipped some of the brandy, and then, before she had a chance to straighten, he slipped a hand around the back of her neck and brought her mouth down on his.

It was a reflex, an instinct he thought he'd long since left behind, and he knew even as he reached for her that it was wrong. But he didn't stop. And when that perfect rosebud of a mouth touched his he didn't want to stop.

Her lips were soft beneath his and he could feel the muscles in the back of her neck tense, her body going very still. Her shock was palpable, but she didn't pull away. And when he opened his mouth, letting her take a sip of the brandy directly from him, she gave a little moan.

He was right, though; she wore no perfume. Her scent was a combination of laundry powder, something flowery that must be either shampoo or soap, and a sweet, warm, musky scent that had to be intrinsic to her.

It was so unexpectedly erotic that he increased the pressure on the back of her neck, trying to draw her in closer, before he'd even thought about it. She didn't protest, the soft lips beneath his opening, her tongue shyly seeking his. Inexpert yet hungry, and clearly wanting more.

You fool. What are you doing?

He didn't know but, whatever it was, it had to stop.

Cassius sat back, releasing his hold on her, trying to draw away as he put his brandy glass on the table beside his chair. But Inara wouldn't let him. She slid her arms around his neck, leaning into him, her knees pressing against the seat of his chair. Her kiss was hungrier, her mouth hot, sweet and alcoholic, going straight to his head as surely as the brandy had.

It had been so long since he'd kissed a woman. He'd forgotten how good it felt to have a soft mouth on his and warm arms around him.

It made him hungry. So hungry.

Without thought, Cassius settled his hands on her hips and pulled her down into his lap, positioning her so she knelt on the seat astride him. She sighed, winding her arms around his neck and pressing herself delicately against him, kissing him harder, her inexperience clear, yet still so hungry for him.

It set him on fire.

The erotic scent of her skin was everywhere, the heavy silk of her hair falling like a curtain around him. He lifted his hands to it, buried his fingers in its softness and closed them into fists, holding on tight. Her arms tightened around his neck.

The heat of her mouth stole everything from him, his breath, his resistance, his common sense. It put down the King and coaxed out the man instead. The man he hadn't been in years.

Desire rushed through him like a tide, relentless, unstoppable, and before he knew what he was doing he'd unwound his fingers from her hair and was tugging at the hem of her dress, pushing it up around her hips.

She made another of those delicious, sexy, throaty sounds and, when his hands slid up her bare thighs, her skin warm and silky, she quivered. So responsive. She was everything he'd been missing and more. All the blood in his body rushed south, concentrating itself behind his fly. He was so hard, he hurt.

Her skin beneath his fingers felt hot, and when he slipped his hand between her thighs, stroking her through the lacy fabric of her knickers, she felt even hotter. She shuddered as he touched her and he could feel wetness against his fingertips.

Dear God, he couldn't think.

He curled his fingers into the material and pulled it roughly aside so he could touch her more directly. She was hot and wet, and when he found the delicate bud hidden in the slick folds of her sex she cried out against his mouth, her hips shuddering under his hand.

Beautiful, sexy little woman.

'I want you,' he said roughly. 'I want you here. Now. So if you don't want it too, you'd better tell me immediately.'

'I do.' Her voice was breathless and frayed. 'I want you, Cassius. Oh, please... *Please...*'

The need inside him was too big, too demanding. He couldn't deny it even if he'd wanted to. But he didn't want to. The world had narrowed down to the slick feel of her sex, the sweet musk of her skin and the rich, heady taste of her mouth.

For three years he'd had nothing but cold, echoing palace rooms, the sense of being constantly surrounded by people, yet always feeling alone. The iron control he had to maintain over himself all the time, and the hard edges of difficult decisions. The sharp thorns of grief and guilt.

But here in his hands was softness and warmth and pleasure. The chance to lose himself, to feel something other than those terrible, difficult emotions. The chance to feel something good.

So he took it.

He reached for the button on his trousers, undid it, then pulled down the zip. He pushed aside the fabric and freed himself, positioning her over him. Then he pulled her down onto him as he thrust up.

She cried out, her back arching, her body shuddering.

She was so tight, he could barely get a breath.

He wound his fingers into her hair and pulled back, looking up into her delicate face. Her cheeks were flushed a deep pink, the lenses of her glasses foggy, and she was looking at him in shock.

'Are you with me?' he demanded. 'I'm sorry. I can't be slow and I can't be gentle.'

She blinked a couple of times and then suddenly she was kissing him again and her body was softening around him, gripping him tight, the heat of her astonishing. Clearly, she was with him.

He couldn't hold himself back. His hands settled on her hips once more and he began to move her on him, fast and deep, because it couldn't be anything else for him, not right now. There was nothing in him but need. Nothing in the whole world he wanted right now but her.

He kissed her back, taking control, tasting her, feasting on her, his hips flexing, thrusting into the wet heat of her body. She denied him nothing, her own kisses hungry, pressing herself even closer, trying to match the movement of his hips with hers.

In some dim, forgotten part of his brain, a judgmental piece of himself was shouting at him to stop. That she was inexperienced, a virgin, the bride he'd married when she'd been sixteen and that he should not be doing this to her. That at the very least he should be gentle and careful and patient.

But there was no time to show her what to do and he had no patience left. He put a hand between her thighs once more, finding that sensitive little bundle of nerves, stroking her with firm, definite movements until she gave a soft, sobbing cry, her body convulsing around his.

Then he was moving deep and hard, single-mindedly chasing his own pleasure until it exploded like a glory around him and he was lost in the heart of it, forgetting for the first time in three years that he was a king.

CHAPTER FOUR

INARA LAY SLUMPED against Cassius's broad chest, her head resting on his shoulder, her heart feeling as if it were trying to batter its way out of her chest. The muscles of her inner thighs hurt, the delicate skin between them was burning and her mouth felt full, sensitive and a touch bruised.

She couldn't see past the foggy lenses of her glasses and the frames were askew on her face, one of the arms having come loose from her ear. Small electric shocks of pleasure continued to pulse inside her. She felt dazed, shocked, astonished and completely unable to move.

Cassius's rapidly slowing heartbeat was in her ear, his warm breath stirring her hair. His body felt hard and huge beneath her, as if she were lying on a slab of warm granite, and the familiar scent of his aftershave—sandalwood and spice—surrounded her.

She couldn't believe what had just happened. It had been…amazing. Shocking. Exciting. Incredible. Though, really, none of those words even came close to encompassing the entire experience that was sex with Cassius de Leon.

She hadn't expected that kiss, his mouth hot and firm, and then the taste of brandy on her lips. The heat of the alcohol had somehow got inside her, made her even hungrier and thirstier, and all her uncertainty and doubt had dropped away.

He'd kissed her and it had been unlike anything she'd ever experienced in her entire life. Better than those gauzy fantasies. More intense and more real, and somehow more confronting too. But so, *so* good.

And then his hands on her, touching her. Authoritative and demanding. And the pleasure that had followed in its wake…

It had been an intensely physical experience which was quite new to her. She existed so much of the time in her head, often forgetting her own bodily needs, that this had been…well…frankly overwhelming.

She'd never been so aware of physical sensation before, of her own skin and his hands on it. Of the need inside her, pleasure winding tighter and tighter, taking her out of her head and grounding her firmly in her body. She hadn't known it would feel like that, that she'd like it and that she'd want more, so much more.

He shifted, withdrawing from her and causing her to shiver helplessly in reaction. That moment he'd thrust inside her had been a shock, even though she'd been expecting it. There had been a sharp pain and a burning sensation, and the weird, suffocating feeling of having someone else inside her body.

But then that had all fallen away, leaving behind it an intense, dragging ache that had become more and more acute as he'd moved inside her.

She'd wanted to hold onto it, keep it going for as long as possible, but then his hand had slipped between her thighs, finding that exquisitely sensitive part of her and stroking her, making the pleasure fold in on itself, layering it until it had burst apart like a firework.

Inara let out a shaky breath, the memory making her shiver yet again.

But then his hands were adjusting her, smoothing down her dress, and she wasn't sure what that meant. Were they done? Was that all sex was? She didn't know much about it, but she was pretty sure there was more to it than that, surely?

'Cassius,' she began in a croaky voice.

He ignored her, holding out the brandy glass. 'Here. You might need this.' His face was expressionless, though the gold in his eyes glowed hot with the remains of desire.

She didn't want to move. She liked lying against him, but the blank look on his face chilled her. It didn't seem as if what they'd done together had been as amazing and incredible for him as it had been for her.

What did you expect? That you were special?

The chill creeping through her widened. She hadn't thought about it. She hadn't expected him to be here at all, let alone to have sex with him in a chair in the library. But now she *was* thinking about it... Yes, of course she wanted to be special, because he was special to her.

Except that clearly wasn't the case. The wicked amusement that had curved his mouth and the sensual challenge in his eyes from before had disappeared. The lines of his face were set, his gaze veiled by his long black lashes. She was still in his lap, resting against his chest, surrounded by his heat, but she had the sense that he was slipping away from her. That the warm, wicked, teasing man she'd first met in the limo, who'd visited her many times over the years, was gone again.

It was the King she was looking at now.

And maybe, for the King, she was just another in a long line of women he slept with, because she had no doubt he slept with other women. His fidelity or otherwise was something she'd never thought about, as their marriage wasn't a real marriage.

But she didn't like the thought of it now. Specifically, she didn't like the thought of being just another woman he took to his bed. The warmth and pleasure from the orgasm drained away, leaving her feeling cold and empty, so she sat up and took the glass from him, sipping the brandy in an effort to warm herself up.

He watched her, his gaze impersonal. 'Are you all right?' His voice was very deep and she could hear a slight roughness in it. 'Did I hurt you in any way?'

The questions sounded impersonal too; the only thing giving away what they'd done together was the rough note in his voice.

Inara's throat tightened despite the brandy. 'I'm fine,' she forced out. 'And, no, you didn't hurt me.'

'Good.' He studied her, frowning, then took the brandy glass away from her before she could have another sip.

She stared at him. 'I hadn't finished.'

He ignored that. 'You were a virgin, weren't you?'

'Well…yes.' It seemed a strange question to ask, especially given how young she'd been when they'd married. 'I was only sixteen when you married me.'

'But you're twenty-one now, correct?'

'Yes.'

'And you haven't been seeing anyone?'

Inara blinked, the thought so foreign to her she didn't take it in at first. The idea that she would even look at anyone else was inconceivable.

'No,' she said, astonished at the question. 'Why would I?'

He didn't answer. He glanced away, a line between his black brows making it clear he was thinking hard about something.

She didn't understand what was going on. She wasn't sure what was supposed to happen after sex, but it couldn't be questions about her virginity, with him frowning and not even looking at her? There had been romantic movies... She'd watched as the couple had held each other and kissed after sex, or had deep and meaningful conversations. It hadn't been...this.

Perhaps trying to seduce him had been a mistake. Perhaps she'd done it wrong, because she often got things wrong, or so her mother used to tell her.

You're so naive. You think you know what you're doing and you don't. You have no idea...

The need to get away, to put some distance between them, gripped her and she struggled to sit up, pushing at the hard plane of his chest.

'Don't,' he murmured, his arms tightening.

'Why?' Her heartbeat had picked up speed again, the chill winding through her intensifying. It hurt to be here in his arms, to feel as if she'd made a mistake, a terrible mistake. 'Let me go, Cassius.'

'No.' His arms held her captive and when he looked down at her she could see heat still in his eyes, glowing like embers. 'Be still.'

'Why?' She shoved at him again. 'What do you want from me? If I'm just another woman to you—'

'What do you mean just another woman?'

She took a breath, her heartbeat thudding hard in her ears. He was frowning ferociously at her as if she'd said something hugely offensive. 'Well, clearly I've done something you didn't like, because you went all cold and distant. I don't know what your other lovers—'

'I don't have any other lovers,' he interrupted flatly. 'There's just you, Inara.'

No, that couldn't be right. He was the King. He could

have any woman he wanted, and he must have wanted quite a few. His reputation as a lover had been widespread and notorious, and she'd assumed that he would have carried on in the same vein.

But…apparently not.

'What?' She stared at him in shock. 'What do you mean, just me?'

An expression she didn't understand flickered over his face. Then it vanished and the same calm mask he always wore descended once more.

'I mean exactly what I said.' His voice was very level. 'I haven't had a lover in three years.'

Inara's shock deepened. If he hadn't had a lover in three years then that meant…well…that he'd been celibate. Which for an ex-playboy was unthinkable.

His calm mask rippled—the mask of a king…she could see that now—then settled. 'Yes, you might well look at me like that. A faithful husband isn't exactly what you expected of me, is it?'

There didn't seem to be any bitterness in his tone yet she caught echoes of it all the same. She didn't understand. She hadn't asked for a faithful husband—she hadn't been thinking of sex at sixteen, and he'd been adamant he wasn't going to touch her. That he wasn't going to tell her what to do or demand things of her. It was only a legal marriage, he'd said. A signature on a piece of paper, nothing more.

And, even when she'd begun to realise that her feelings for him were not those she should have for the kindly uncle he'd told her to think of him as, she hadn't given one single thought to all the women he seduced and spent time with.

You put him on a pedestal and kept him there.

The thought was unexpected, and all the more so because as soon as it had occurred to her she knew it was true. She *had* put him on a pedestal. She hadn't thought of him as an uncle, but she hadn't thought of him as a man either. He'd been a handsome, charming playboy prince, and then a distant, almost mythical king.

Except he wasn't that prince any longer and, as she'd just found out, he wasn't solely a king either. He was a man too. A human being. A person she knew nothing about.

Something kicked hard in her brain. Curiosity.

'I never thought of you as a husband at all,' she said before she could think better of it. 'But why? Have you really been celibate for three years?'

'Yes.' This time there was no hesitation. 'I have a standard to uphold and it's a standard I believe in very much. A king has to set an example to his people, so that's what I strive to do. They expect their king to behave in a certain way, and sleeping around is not one of those behaviours.'

The chill that had crept through her just before was back, though she wasn't sure why, not when what he'd said made sense. The de Leon kings had always been exemplary in their behaviour, shining lights of compassion and justice and propriety. Certainly, Cassius's father had been a perfect example, and his twin brother Caspian a carbon copy. It made sense that Cassius would now take on that mantle.

So why did he break a three-year drought with you?

She had no idea. Desperation? Opportunity? Certainly it wasn't because she was special in any way.

'So why now?' she couldn't help asking. 'Why did you…?'

Cassius cupped her jaw gently, his touch silencing her. Glimmers of heat still shone in his eyes, but she could tell the King was very firmly in charge now. 'Because you were lovely and I forgot myself.' His gaze was very direct. 'But now we have an added difficulty. I didn't use a condom.'

Oh. She hadn't even thought of that.

Her stomach dropped away and she felt slightly dizzy at the idea that she might be expecting Cassius's child.

'It's not ideal for either of us,' he went on, his thumb absently stroking her cheek, 'but there is only one way we can solve this.'

'Solve this?' she echoed, her thoughts tumbling around in her head, her skin burning with every stroke of his thumb.

'Yes, of course. It's a problem, Inara.' His hand dropped away. 'But it's a problem that I created and therefore I will be the one to find a solution.'

Her brain felt sluggish, all her thought processes sticky as treacle. 'A solution to what?'

'To the fact that I took your virginity,' he said patiently. 'To the fact that you might be expecting my heir. Don't you see? A divorce is out of the question now.'

Inara was warm and soft and delicate against him, and her eyes had gone very wide, staring at him in shock.

Well, he could understand that. This was shocking for him too. He'd lost control. He'd forgotten himself. He'd taken her without thought, without consideration, and most important of all without a condom.

He was appalled at himself. He was supposed to be better than this. Hadn't he promised himself that? He was supposed to protect her, to be her saviour, not her ravisher. After his parents' and Caspian's deaths, he'd sworn that he'd be the kind of king they'd have been proud of. He'd never be Caspian, of course—who could?—but he'd at least be decent.

A decent king wouldn't take the virginity of a woman as innocent as Inara.

A decent king wouldn't forget a damn condom either.

Which meant that, if he wanted to be a decent king, the only answer was to keep her as his wife.

'What?' She blinked rapidly. 'You don't want a divorce? But I thought you said—'

'I know what I said,' he interrupted, ignoring the regret and bitter shame coiling in his heart. Regret over what this would mean for Inara. Shame at how easily he'd forgotten his vows to himself and his family. 'But things have changed. If you're pregnant with my heir, there will be no divorce.'

It was the only solution. No, she wouldn't be who he'd have chosen as his queen—his parents would have been horrified—but there wasn't another fix. He could divorce her, but what if she was pregnant? He couldn't have a royal bastard running around. That just wouldn't work.

And if she wasn't pregnant, he'd still taken her virginity. No one else would know, but *he* would. He'd know exactly how thin were his promises, how fragile. And, if he couldn't even keep a promise to himself, how could he keep it to anyone else? To his country?

No, he couldn't countenance it. He wouldn't.

'But I…might not be pregnant.'

'You might not,' he agreed. 'But the fact remains that I took your virginity. And, besides, you're my wife already. Seems logical that you should stay my wife.'

'But I—'

'Don't worry.' Gently, he lifted the arm of her glasses that had come off and slipped it back behind her ear. Perhaps she would be more comfortable with contacts. They might be easier to manage, given that as Queen she'd be attending functions and undertaking numerous other royal duties. 'I'll handle everything. It'll be an adjustment for you being Queen, as it was for me when I became King, but I managed well enough. And so will you.'

'Queen?' she repeated faintly. 'But I don't want... I mean, not officially...'

She'd gone very pale, looking even more ethereal than she normally did, and the shame and regret inside him sunk deeper.

If he needed another reason why this had been a mistake, then here it was. Just as he'd never expected to be King, Inara had never expected to be Queen in anything but name. He'd automatically undertaken most of the official duties on his own, because he'd sensed her discomfort with the role, leaving her safe to pursue her own interests here at the Queen's Estate.

He knew she hated the palace in Katara. She hated being looked at and talked about. Hated the social engagements that being a queen involved, the functions and parties and balls and openings she'd be expected to attend. She hated being the object of everyone's attention and, as he could do most of that himself, he'd left her to her own devices.

Choosing another woman to do that duty had seemed like a kindness, so her arguing about it earlier had made no sense. Unless of course she'd changed her mind. Now, though, it was obvious she hadn't changed her mind. She clearly regarded being queen as similar to going to her doom.

She'll have to learn how to deal with it. As you did.

Cassius wasn't a cruel man. There was no profit in it, and besides, a king should never be cruel, although sometimes justice could look like cruelty. And sometimes doing the right thing could look the same way.

It probably looked that way to her now.

'I know you don't.' He gave her what he hoped was an understanding look. 'But there are times when we don't get to choose. And this is one of those times.'

'Cassius…'

He put a gentle finger over her mouth, silencing her. 'That's my decision, little one.' Her lips were very soft, very warm, and suddenly all he could think about was how they'd felt beneath his and how she'd tasted of brandy and desire and every good thing…

If you stay here, you'll risk making the same mistake again.

It was true. He could already feel his body begin to harden once more, responding to her soft weight in his arms and her sweet scent, the delicate curves of her body pressing against him.

He could have her again. He could take her upstairs and spend the night with her. It wouldn't make any difference to his decision and, if he was going to keep her as his wife, then it would be a marriage in all senses of the word. There would be no celibacy for him any more.

But, although it was tempting, he needed to get some distance between himself and the appalling mistake he'd made. Some time to recall his own promises and put in place safeguards to make sure he wouldn't lose himself so completely again.

She'd need some time to come to terms with what he'd told her too, and what it would mean. And there'd definitely have to be a period of adjustment. Which meant that sitting here with her in his lap was probably not a good idea.

Carefully, Cassius shifted her off him, getting up from the chair then settling her back into it. She looked up at him, small and, fragile and wide-eyed, curled up on the big leather seat.

'So…that's it?' Inara said. 'I don't get a say in this?'

'As I said, sometimes we don't get to choose our path in life, and this is one of those times.' He checked his watch, impatience gathering in him. Normally he'd ignore it, as impatience was not an admirable quality in a ruler, but right now he had a few things to do. There were arrangements to be made and certain things to be put in place if he was going to bring Inara back to the palace, which he would. As soon as possible.

'But you didn't want me to be your queen. You wanted someone else. You said I wasn't a suitable choice.'

There was a desperate note in her voice that made his chest tighten, though he wasn't sure why she was trying to argue with him now, when she had seemed so opposed to the divorce only a few hours ago.

'You're not. But I don't have a choice about this either.' He tried not to let his own regret and impatience show, given it was clear she needed some reassurance, and him getting angry wouldn't help. Especially as it wasn't her fault. The blame lay entirely with him. 'Don't worry, Inara,' he went on in softer tones. 'I'll do all I can to ensure that you'll be the best queen Aveiras can hope for.'

She said nothing, her face white, her eyes going dark behind the lenses of her glasses. She was looking at him as if he'd dealt her a mortal blow.

Perhaps he shouldn't have told her that he'd been celibate for so long. Certainly, that hadn't helped matters, as she'd appeared genuinely shocked when he'd mentioned it, even upset. He wasn't sure why that was, but no wonder she was shocked. She probably still thought he was the feckless prince he'd once been, indulging himself at every opportunity.

The one who'd begged his brother to swap places with him on the trip his father had insisted they take to the cemetery in the mountains, where all the de Leon kings were buried, in a last-ditch effort to try and instil in Cassius a sense of history and propriety. An understanding of the weight of the name he carried and what it meant, especially after the scandal of his disastrous marriage.

But he'd spent the night before the trip drinking, and had woken up late in the bed of some socialite. He'd called Caspian and bribed him to take his place—a habit they'd got into as boys, as their parents couldn't tell them apart. He had then had gone back to sleep…only to wake a few hours later to the news that the King, Queen and Prince Caspian had been killed in a helicopter crash.

It was his responsibility, no one else's. He might not have caused the crash, but he'd sent his brother to his death all the same, and deprived Aveiras not only of its current king, but of its heir too. There was no coming back from that. There was no fixing it either. All he could do was try his best to make up for what his country had lost.

Inara's pretty mouth opened, and then she shut it again and looked away. He didn't like feeling that he'd hurt her somehow, and it was clear to him that he had.

Of course you have. And telling her she'll simply have to make the best of it isn't helpful.

Perhaps it wasn't. He'd had to deal with his own personal version of hell, because he didn't have another choice. Aveiras had needed a ruler and he had been next in line to the throne. Renouncing the throne at a time of intense public grief would have been unforgivable, so he'd forced down his own personal grief, and the iron weight of his guilt, and he'd done what he had to do. He'd become King, even though it had been the very last thing on earth he'd wanted to do.

Those first few months had been the worst. It hadn't been easy stepping into his brother's shoes, especially considering the public's adoration of Caspian and their low opinion of him, and he hadn't had anyone to help him through it. He'd done it all on his own. But in the end the people had accepted him and, if he hadn't been exactly what they'd wanted, he'd at least managed to get to a point where he wasn't exactly what they *didn't* want.

Still, Inara was young, and if he could spare her having to go through the same fire he had then he would.

'What's upsetting you?' he asked. 'You didn't want a divorce just before and yet now you don't like the idea of staying married. Care to explain?'

She bit her lip, white teeth sinking into all that plush softness, and the simmering desire inside him grew hotter.

He ignored it.

'I just…want things to be the same,' she said hesitantly. 'I don't want to leave the Queen's Estate.'

'I know you don't. But the estate will still be here for you whenever you want to have a holiday.'

'That's not the point. I'm… I'm….' She broke off all of a sudden, her misty grey eyes gone dark and stormy. 'I suppose what I want doesn't matter at all, does it?'

A part of him understood the note of anger in her voice, because he'd felt the same way at having to take the crown. But some things wouldn't be helped by understanding and sympathy. The only way through was acceptance, regardless of one's feelings.

'No,' he said firmly. 'It doesn't. You can't put yourself and what you want before your country, little one.'

She paled even further at that. 'No. That's…that's not what I meant.'

'Then what did you mean? Aveiras needs a queen and, whether you like it or not, that queen is you. Your feelings or otherwise are irrelevant.'

Something passed over her delicate features and then was gone. She looked away, obviously upset.

The tight feeling in his chest constricted further, and he opened his mouth to issue another empty reassurance when she said woodenly, 'I suppose I'll have to pack some clothes, then.'

The urge to touch her cheek or take her hand in comfort gripped him, but he restrained himself. Touching her was a bad idea right now. Perhaps later, when they returned to the palace, he'd take some time to allay any fears she had.

So all he said was, 'Yes, that would be wise. We'll leave for Katara tomorrow morning.'

'So soon?'

'There's no need to wait. The quicker you're installed in the palace, the better.'

Her mouth had a vulnerable look to it, and there was a lost expression on her face, but even as the urge to comfort her intensified her mouth firmed and the lost expression vanished. She drew herself up, small and straight-backed, and when her gaze met his there was nothing misty about it. It was all stone and steel.

'Fine.' Her voice was hard. 'I'll see you in the morning, then.'

Then she turned and went out.

CHAPTER FIVE

INARA DIDN'T SLEEP much that night and woke the next morning with a head full of cotton wool and scratchy eyes. She felt tender between her legs, her inner thigh muscles were sore and there was a certain electricity humming in her blood.

She didn't want to think about Cassius, not when she'd spent most of the night going over and over what had happened between them in the library, but there was no avoiding it this morning.

He'd taken her virginity. He'd decided against a divorce.

He wanted to stay married to her.

She'd be his wife and his queen, not just in name only this time, but for real.

Inara rolled over and tried to burrow her way back underneath the blankets as if she could escape the reality of her situation. But there was no escaping it. What she'd secretly always wanted, had secretly always longed for, was happening, yet in the most nightmarish way possible.

Once again she was being shunted around, at the mercy of other people's decisions, her own thoughts, feelings and opinions not mattering one iota. Her parents had never made any secret of the fact that she was only a tool to them, a disappointment, not the son they'd been counting on, and so it had been her responsibility to make up for it by being useful to them.

It had been bad enough knowing she wasn't what her parents had wanted, but it was a million times worse knowing she wasn't what Cassius wanted. She loved him. She cared about his opinion. And, as he'd pointed out so clearly the night before, she wasn't his choice. He was stuck with her and that hurt.

But of course he wouldn't want a small, stringy, awkward and chaotic maths genius as a queen. He'd want someone tall, beautiful and charming. Someone with perfect manners and all the social graces. Someone with natural authority and dignity, someone who looked the part.

Five years ago when her parents had told her that she was to be promised to Stefano Castelli—after she'd failed to make an impression on the duke's son they'd been eyeing for her—she'd taken matters into her own hands and run away, going straight to the only man in the world she'd thought could help her.

But the man who'd helped her then was the same man who was forcing her into an impossible situation now, and there was nowhere to run to this time.

He was the King. If he wanted to keep her as his wife, as his queen, then he would and there was nothing she could do to stop him.

You'll disappoint him in the end, just as you disappointed your parents. And not just him, but the entire country.

The thought made her feel ill, so she dragged herself out of bed at last and into the shower, hoping that the warm water would help her feel better. But when at last she stepped out, wrapping a towel around her as she wandered back into the bedroom, she still felt as ill as she had when she'd woken up.

The urge to lose herself in the research paper she was currently writing with a colleague in Helsinki gripped her. Numbers were simple. They were clear, logical and had absolutely nothing to do with the confusing mass of emotion currently tangling inside her. But there was no time for that. So she pulled on whatever clothes came to hand, then spent ten minutes packing the rest in a small suitcase.

It wasn't much. After years of having her appearance checked over constantly by her mother, she'd let everything slide while living in the Queen's Estate. It had been a relief not to worry about her hair, or make-up, or her posture, or her dress. Living here meant she was essentially forgotten—which was fine by her. The Queen's Estate was her haven, her refuge.

A cage.

The thought came out of nowhere and for a second was so alien that she looked around to see if someone had spoken it aloud. But, no, apparently that thought had come from her own head, from a deep part of her subconscious even she hadn't known existed.

It was wrong, though. Very, *very* wrong. The Queen's Estate wasn't a cage. How ridiculous. It was her place of safety and she was sad to leave it.

She stuffed a dress into her case, suddenly annoyed. At Cassius and his insistence on his kingly duty. At herself and her decision to seduce him. At the stupid crush she had on him and how that had led her to this moment, forcing her to leave her place of safety for the cold halls of the palace in Katara where her failings would soon become obvious to everyone who looked at her.

Then you have a choice, don't you?

Inara forced the top of the case down and zipped it up, then stood there a second looking down at it.

Cassius had told her the night before that she couldn't put her feelings before her country, and that was very true. It was also very true that she had a choice before her: she could choose to spend her future being miserable and, reluctant and negative about being Queen or, as she couldn't change what would happen, she could choose to accept it. She could choose to try being the kind of queen Cassius wanted. And just because she'd failed her parents, it didn't mean she'd fail him.

After all, hadn't she wanted to be his wife? A real wife, sharing his bed, sharing his life. Having his children, living with him, being with him.

She'd always hoped that being his wife for real would include him being in love with her, but perhaps that would come in time. And if love wasn't on the cards, then she'd settle at least for some respect. That would make being Queen easier, hopefully, and if not it would surely be some consolation?

At that moment there was a knock on her bedroom door that turned out to be Henri, advising her that the helicopter was here to take her to Katara. The King, as it turned out, had left hours earlier to prepare for her arrival, which meant they wouldn't be travelling together.

Inara was relieved. Right now the thought of having to share the tiny space of a helicopter with Cassius was too much for her. She wanted some time alone before she was confronted with him again. Some time to think about how she was going to approach this, because if she decided to accept his decision and take her place as his queen—and really, she had to accept it, because she didn't particularly want to be miserable for the rest of her life—then she needed to figure out how.

Ten minutes later, safely ensconced in the helicopter and flying over the mountains and down towards the coast where the palace was located, Inara decided to put her anxiety about being Queen to one side for now and concentrate instead on being Cassius's actual wife.

And it required some thought, because what did a wife do, exactly?

She only had her own parents' experience to go on, which wasn't encouraging. Their marriage, like their parenting, had been cold, her father interested in nothing but his political machinations, her mother in her social ones. Neither had seemed to like the other much yet they didn't argue. They treated each other with the same chilly politeness with which they treated her.

Would it be like that with Cassius? She knew he wasn't a cold man, or at least he hadn't been the previous night, so maybe it would be different between them.

Except she didn't much like the gentle condescension he'd been affecting with her the past couple of years. Perhaps once they started living together as husband and wife that might change.

Although...would they be living together as husband and wife? All Cassius had said was that she would remain his wife and take her place as queen. Did that involve living together? Sharing a bed? Or would they have separate rooms at the palace? Would they only meet for formal occasions and official functions, continuing on with their separate lives? Or would they spend time together outside of those times? Alone with each other. The way they used to...

Longing curled in Inara's heart.

Yes, that was what she wanted. A marriage like that— talking together, easy and friendly. Laughing and discussing things of interest, with the occasional argument that didn't get too serious. Not her parents' icy formality, but something warmer and more real. Friendlier.

And sex. You want that too.

Inara shifted on the seat cushions, remembering the night before—Cassius beneath her, all long, lean muscle and power, looking at her with fire in his eyes. Looking at her the way she'd desperately wanted him to for so long. Him moving inside her, giving her the most intense pleasure…

Heat prickled over her skin. Yes, okay, maybe she wanted that as well. But…would he? Would a marriage to him include that? Or was what they'd shared together in the library a one-off thing that wouldn't happen again?

He'd said that he hadn't had a lover in three years, that she was the first one he'd taken in all that time, so surely…? But then again, if he'd managed to go without sex for so long then perhaps he didn't need it…

No, there were too many variables, that was the problem, and too much she didn't know. The answers to those questions could only be solved by more research, and that meant talking to him, which she would have to do when they landed.

Feeling somewhat better now that she'd thought a few things through, Inara watched as they flew over Katara, the capital city of Aveiras.

It was famously beautiful, with a historic walled town located near the central business district and by the sea. The old palace was the centrepiece of the old town, built out of weathered white stone with beautifully laid-out formal gardens. It was the seat of the royal family of Aveiras and had been for centuries. Inara had always disliked it.

Despite how picturesque it looked, the palace had felt cold and echoing and unfriendly whenever she'd visited and, as the helicopter descended to the helipad located in the palace grounds, creeping doubt wound through her.

Regardless of what kind of wife she would be, she would also be Queen. What would the palace staff think of the King's decision? What would the people of Aveiras think? Cassius's mother had been revered and deeply loved, and her death had been bitterly mourned. No one would want Inara stepping into her shoes, surely?

A phalanx of palace staff waited as the helicopter landed, and as soon as she stepped out they surrounded her, taking her one pathetic suitcase and shepherding her towards the doors that led into the palace. All of them looked business-like and not one smiled at her. It made her homesick for the Queen's Estate, where there was no one to look at her and judge her. No one to disappoint. Only Henri and Joan, who cared about her.

And now you have no one...

The thought threw dark shadows everywhere so she pushed it away, hoping that Cassius might come to meet her. But it was soon clear that he wouldn't, so she told herself it was fine and she didn't mind. He was the King. He probably had better things to do, and anyway, though it would have been nice to see a friendly face in amongst the crowd of grim-looking palace employees, she didn't need it. She would manage. Of course she would. She would have to.

Inara was ushered down the long, echoing stone hallways of the palace with high-vaulted ceilings and long lines of dark, formal portraits of the de Leon royal line. The chill of the palace crept into her bones as she walked, though she tried not to let it, and the disapproving gazes of the people in the portraits followed her.

The palace had always felt oppressive, and it wasn't any different now, the heavy weight of history and its judgment pressing down on her. It reminded her of being in her parents' house and the constant critical attention they had subjected her to—always measuring her, always judging her.

And this is now your home.

Inara did her best not to think of that.

Eventually she was led to the royal apartments and ushered into what turned out to be a rather pleasant sitting room located in a part of the large, sprawling palace that overlooked the famous Aveiran white cliffs and the deep blue of the sea that lay below them.

Inara had never visited the royal apartments and had always assumed they would be just as cold and empty and echoing as the rest of the palace. But this room was neither cold nor empty nor echoing.

It had large windows that looked out over a small but beautiful and slightly overgrown garden full of flowers, with the jewel-blue sea beyond it. There were rugs on the floor that echoed the colour of the flowers outside, and a couple of deep, comfortable-looking chairs upholstered in dark-blue velvet, with a matching sofa. Cushions had been scattered artfully everywhere and bookcases full of books stood against the bare stone walls. And most surprising of all, on the side tables, sideboard and numerous shelves, there was a plethora of small shrubs in decorative pots. The plants softened the atmosphere, making it seem lived-in and inviting, even though the whole room reeked of a tidiness that was foreign to Inara.

She took a few steps over to the windows and glanced out at the early afternoon steadily advancing.

Nerves coiled tightly inside her. Presumably she'd been brought here to…what? Wait? For whom—Cassius? Or would someone else come for her? And what was she supposed to do, exactly?

Inara swallowed, her hands closing into fists. She hated

not knowing things and there was nothing worse than questions she didn't know the answers to. Especially when the answers were dependent on someone else who wasn't around. It meant there was nothing to stop her brain from throwing up yet more questions until her thought processes were going round and round like mice running on a wheel.

It didn't help that, along with her nerves, there was also a strange, prickling sense of anticipation, the same feeling she got whenever she knew Cassius was coming to visit, except not quite.

Before, she'd been full of a simple joy. Now, the joy was tempered with other things, more complicated things. Nerves and a little rush of fear, along with heat and a strange sort of excitement. Normally when she felt this way she retreated into her research, but she couldn't do that now, so to relieve the tension Inara walked slowly over to one of the tables to examine a tiny, gnarled bonsai in a blue glazed pot that sat on it.

Too busy looking at the bonsai, she didn't hear the door click softly behind her.

'Inara,' Cassius's deep, authoritative voice said from behind her. 'Welcome to the palace.'

She hadn't dressed for the occasion, Cassius observed with some disapproval as Inara straightened from looking at the bonsai juniper that sat on the table near the couch.

She looked as if she'd pulled on any old thing that had come to hand, which in this instance was a pair of worn jeans and pale pink T-shirt with a coffee stain on the front of it. Her silvery hair was caught in a simple ponytail at the nape of her neck and she wore no make-up whatsoever.

Yet still desire gripped him by the throat, refusing to let go as a deeply possessive, very male part of him noted how closely the T-shirt moulded to her figure, highlighting the soft roundness of her breasts and the elegant curve of her waist. The jeans, though they were entirely unsuitable for a queen, certainly made him want to put a hand on her pretty rear and squeeze her gently.

Unacceptable.

He hadn't slept much the night before, having left the Queen's Estate at dawn so he could get back to the palace as quickly as possible in order to prepare for Inara's arrival. Also, if he was honest with himself, to get rid of the heat that lingered in his blood whenever he thought of her.

He'd thought having the entire morning to prepare and then attend to his other duties would have dealt with any remaining lustful thoughts, but apparently that had just been a convenient lie he'd told himself.

Apparently all that was needed for those thoughts to roar back into life was her physical presence, in simple jeans and a T-shirt no less.

It was unseemly. He needed to control himself, to discourage his baser instincts, not look at her hungrily, thinking about what he'd like to do to her. He should remember that he was the leader of a nation and not a teenage boy with more hormones than sense.

It was a good thing he'd spent some time this morning deciding on an appropriate code of conduct between them, which was why he'd brought her here, to one of his favourite rooms in the palace. He hoped she'd find it a relaxing environment in which to be informed of her duties as Queen and what the shape of her future at the palace would look like. Also his expectations of her as his wife, a subject he'd given much thought.

Since returning from the Queen's Estate, he'd immediately informed his council and parliament of his intention to remain married and for Inara to stay on as Aveiras's queen. This had prompted some disapproval, which he'd expected, and he'd had to put his foot down about the decision. However, he was hoping that a strict regimen of stylists and lessons in protocol and etiquette would soon sand the sharp edges off and make Inara more palatable to both his parliament and his people.

It was important to him that they accept her, especially when they'd already had to accept him, the black sheep of his illustrious family. He'd been hoping to give them a queen they could love, like they'd loved his mother, but as that was now out of the question he hoped to give them a queen that they could tolerate at the very least.

Being patient was key. Inara needed some time to come to terms with her new position and to learn her official duties, and that couldn't be rushed. In the meantime, he'd organised a small function to present her to his court and his parliament. Nothing too formal or too large, but enough to remind people that Inara was their queen and would remain so.

Already, gossip about her was rife, and he'd decided that wasn't a bad thing. The more people talked about her, the more she'd be in the public consciousness. She'd be a novelty at first, but then she'd become ubiquitous, as he had.

She turned from the bonsai, her eyes wide behind the lenses of her glasses. Then she straightened and her shoulders went back, as if bracing herself. 'Hello, Cassius,' she said, her sweet voice very formal.

He frowned. Something was missing. And it took him a moment or two to realise that what was missing was the smile she always gave him whenever she saw him—the warm, joyful one. The one that made him feel as if he was a bright spot in her particular world. The one that made him feel like a friend. Like a person instead of a figurehead.

Why would you want to be a person? Especially the person who caused his brother's death...

Cassius shoved that thought away.

'The palace staff will bring us a late lunch shortly,' he said. 'I thought it might be easier for you to have an informal meal for your first day in the palace. It will also give us some time to discuss what happens now.'

'Oh. Uh…yes, that would be very…pleasant.' She shifted on her feet, a pink flush staining her cheeks. 'I don't know where my suitcase is.'

The suitcase in question had been taken to the Queen's apartments, though if she'd only brought one case then there hadn't been much point in bringing anything. Not when he'd provide her with everything she needed.

'It's in the Queen's rooms,' he said. 'Which will be exclusively for your use, of course. At night, however, you will share mine.'

She blinked rapidly. 'Yours?'

'Yes. Not right away, of course,' he allowed. 'You will need some time to feel comfortable with me, and I understand that. But you will be my wife, Inara. And that does not mean separate beds.'

It was something he'd thought long and hard about, especially after his lapse in the library with her. Grief and shock had killed his desire, and three years of abstinence hadn't helped. But now it had returned and with such a vengeance that it was clear he needed an outlet for it. He needed someone in his bed and, logically, that someone should be his wife.

It was convenient that she was the one he wanted, too. Perhaps if he had her in his bed every night he'd be better able to control himself, not let himself become so desperate that he'd fall back into old habits.

'Oh,' she said again. 'I suppose so.'

It shouldn't have been a source of irritation that she didn't look entirely happy with the suggestion, but he was irritated all the same. It was an emotion he had no right to, of course. He'd been the one to take her innocence the night before, to lose control. He'd thought of no one but himself and his own pleasure and, if he needed yet another lesson in what a mistake that was, he was looking at it right now.

It's no less than what you deserve.

Oh, he was well aware. Being King was his penance and one he undertook willingly.

Cassius ignored his irritation. 'If you're not comfortable with that tonight, you may sleep in the Queen's rooms,' he said levelly. 'But I should warn you that this will not be a union of convenience only, not now.'

'I see. Well, I understand. And no need for me to go to the Queen's rooms tonight.' Something hot gleamed in her eyes, a little spark.

So it seemed she was happy being in his bed after all.

Careful.

Yes, he needed the reminder, because already the smouldering embers of his desire were beginning to ignite in response to that spark. It wouldn't take much for them to burst into flame...a kiss, a touch...

The thread of unease he'd felt when he'd walked in wound tighter.

His desire for her was more...consuming than he'd expected it to be and he didn't like that one bit. This wasn't the library at the Queen's Estate. This was the palace where he was king, and a king shouldn't be so desperate to sleep with his wife that he literally couldn't think of anything else.

That was the man talking and the man couldn't be trusted. He knew that already.

Perhaps he shouldn't have her in his bed tonight after all. Perhaps he should use tonight to remind the man of how a king should act so that, when she finally joined him, it would be the king who'd be in control.

Besides, she could probably use a night to adjust to her new position too, no matter that little spark in her eyes.

He strolled over to the windows, paused to glance out at the blue sea, then carried on over to the fireplace, Inara watching him all the while.

It made him uncomfortable. Made him feel oddly transparent, as if she could see the exact nature of his restlessness. As if she knew that the title of king was just a mask he wore, and a badly fitting mask at that. As if she could see beneath that mask to the same careless prince he'd once been. A man driven by his own selfish desires and desperately unsuited to be the ruler he now was. A man who hadn't respected the throne or the role he'd been given to play.

A man whose own brother was dead because of him.

It was a good thing *that* man was now as dead as Caspian.

Cassius met her gaze, his mask firmly in place. 'Good. I have drawn up a schedule for you this week, which will involve a stylist and wardrobe consultation, meetings with the palace PR people, media training plus protocol and etiquette instruction. That won't be enough time to prepare you for a formal royal ball, but it should allow you to feel more comfortable at the small gathering I've organised to reintroduce you to my court.'

A flicker of unhappy surprise crossed her face. 'A… small gathering? How small?'

'It's nothing,' he said dismissively. 'A couple of hundred people. Not many.'

'A couple of hundred…' She looked abruptly down at the floor. 'No,' she said as if to herself. 'No, I can do that.'

Cassius, expecting an argument, was thrown off balance. 'I know it's not what you particularly enjoy but—'

'It's part of being a queen,' she interrupted, brisker this time. 'I understand.' She lifted her gaze back to his, somehow standing even straighter. 'I'll do it. I can manage. And I… I'm sorry about my behaviour yesterday in the library. When you suggested I take on royal duties, I was…shocked. And a bit scared. I've been living at the Queen's Estate for five years and…well…change is always difficult. But, as you said, neither of us has a choice about this, so I'm going to try.' Her chin lifted. 'I want to be a good queen for Aveiras and I'm going to work hard not to let you down.'

Surprise rippled through him. He'd expected her to give in at some point, because he wouldn't be moved on this, but he'd thought he'd have to insist or perhaps argue with her.

He studied her, aware of something shifting inside him. A curiosity he hadn't been conscious of before. She'd always been an open book to him, but this was…different. 'What brought this on? You weren't at all happy about it yesterday.'

'I know.' She shoved her hands into the back pockets of her jeans, her feet moving about as if she couldn't figure out how to stand. His mother would have found that appalling. She had been a stickler for correct behaviour, and fidgeting was not correct behaviour, especially not for a queen.

'I've had some time to think about it,' Inara went on, oblivious to her bad posture. 'And you were right about having to accept things. About putting my feelings before my country, too. Aveiras needs a queen, and I'm that queen whether I like it or not.'

Cassius knew he should have been happy that she'd made peace with his decision, that she was willing to try being the queen Aveiras needed. Yet her little speech irritated him. Had he been expecting something more, something he could fight her on? Did he *want* to fight her?

Ridiculous. He didn't want a fight. The last few years his parents had been alive had been a constant battle against his father's repeated calls for him to display some kind of restraint—especially after his 'ill-conceived marriage', as his father had termed it. He'd accused Cassius of disrespecting the crown, accused him of loving himself more than he loved his country.

His father hadn't been wrong. Cassius had taken great pleasure in disobeying his father's rules and strictures, even making a game out of it with mocking statements, snide observations, sarcastic sound bites and compromising press photos. And the worst part about it was that now he barely even remembered why he'd done all those things.

One thing he was sure of was that he didn't do them any longer, and neither did he fight. He didn't lose himself to anger—or indeed any emotion inappropriate to his position—so he shouldn't be regretting his wife's capitulation, not at all. He wanted this to go smoothly and easily, and the fewer challenges from her the better.

Yet, despite what he wanted, he still felt restless and irritable, moving from the fireplace and pacing over to one of the tables where he kept another bonsai, a cherry blossom. Reflexively, he looked the miniature tree over, taking note of the soil conditions and the tree itself. Tending plants was useful for all kinds of emotional disturbances. Sometimes he preferred more physical outlets, such as swimming endless laps of the palace pool, or running for miles on the treadmill in the gym, but when that was impossible he liked to come into this room and check over the pots. It focused his mind and helped him concentrate. Helped him stay in control.

He'd done that even as a boy, when the interminable school-room lessons that Caspian had seemed to handle with no problem had become too much for him. He'd never been able to sit still and concentrate for long before the need to move would take him, so he'd disappear into the gardens, hiding out with the head gardener, who used to take him on a tour of all the plants.

It had calmed him then and it calmed him now.

He picked up a tiny pair of scissors and trimmed part of the tree carefully.

Inara wandered over and watched him. 'What are you doing?'

He snipped off a tiny branch. 'Trimming the bonsai so it retains its shape.'

'Oh. Do you do that yourself then?'

'Yes.'

She peered at the tree. 'Why? Don't you have staff to do everything for you?'

He'd never had to explain his interest in plants to anyone. No one had ever asked. Not many people—apart from the staff who tended to the King's private rooms—even knew about his hobby. He didn't like to talk about it, not when it revealed certain things about him, and still less to someone as sharp and intelligent as Inara.

Still, not answering was also revealing, so he said, trying not to sound reluctant, 'I make a lot of decisions that impact a lot of people and I have to do that every day. Tending to a few plants that don't require much beyond watering and some nutrients is a nice change.'

'I see.' She glanced around at the pots scattered everywhere. 'Are all these yours?'

'Yes.' She was standing quite close and he caught a faint hint of delicate musk in the air, along with the flowery scent of her shampoo. It sent a thread of heat through him.

'Wow. They look amazing.'

She sounded genuine, and when he glanced at her the expression on her face made it clear that her admiration was, in fact, genuine. And he was shocked by the warmth that bloomed abruptly behind his breastbone, as if part of him enjoyed her praise. As if he almost…needed it.

And why not, when you never had any as a boy? Only relentless, constant criticism.

That was true. He hadn't had much praise in his life, not as a boy and not as a man. He'd more often been told of the many ways he didn't measure up, never about the things he did that were right, and in the end he'd stopped caring. What was the point in trying to measure up to a standard you'd never achieve? Or constantly trying to be something you weren't? Better to embrace who you actually were instead. Accept yourself, as no one else would.

He'd told himself he didn't need to be praised, that he didn't care what anyone thought of him, and he believed that. So he had no idea why this one woman's obvious delight in his house plants should please him so much. It was ridiculous.

No, you know why. Her opinion has always *been important. Right from the very first moment she climbed into your limo and looked at you like you were her own personal saviour.*

'It's just water and the right fertiliser,' he said dismissively, ignoring the voice in his head.

'No, it's not.' Inara shook her head, staring down at the cherry blossom he'd been pruning. 'If it was that simple, all my plants wouldn't die. I have a black thumb.' Gently she reached out and touched one of the blossoms on the tree. 'Numbers I can figure out. But taking care of a plant, not so much.'

'Numbers are slightly more important than keeping a few house plants alive.'

She lifted a shoulder. 'I guess. Sometimes. But they're not exactly practical, are they?'

He remembered suddenly a similar discussion they'd had years ago, about her university studies. She'd been having a small crisis of confidence about her master's thesis and he'd tried to encourage her, even though he'd had no idea how he, a man who was more interested in parties and women, could possibly make her feel better about her own phenomenal intellectual abilities.

He'd made a joke out of it, made her laugh, though he'd known even back then it was simply to cover up his own inadequacies.

Now, he didn't feel so inadequate, yet it was clear she still had the same doubts. Where had those come from?

Ah, but he knew. Her family. They'd been so obsequious when he'd married her, both parents bowing and scraping, and making much of the fact that they'd never expected their daughter to do so well for herself as to marry a prince. They hadn't cared that he was over ten years her senior. They hadn't seemed to care much about their fiercely intelligent daughter at all, or know what to do with her beyond marrying her off for social gain.

You didn't really know what to do with her either.

He did now. He was going to turn her into his queen.

'I'm sure we can find some practical applications,' he said. 'And in the meantime, with a bit of polish and some deportment lessons, you'll do a very fine and practical job of being a queen.'

Inara glanced up at him, her expression solemn. 'I'm going to try, Cassius. I promise.'

He could feel the warmth of her body. See the pulse beating at the base of her pale throat. She stood so close to him that the curve of her breast nearly pressed against his arm.

Heat licked through him, and just like that his control was hanging by a thread. And he knew that all the concentration in the world on his damn plants wasn't going to make a difference. That he wanted her right here, right now. On the floor before the empty fireplace. Her clothes ripped away, those delicate limbs wrapped around him, her body welcoming his, clutching him tightly as he drove himself inside her. Giving him pleasure for just a little while…

But no. That was the man talking. The flawed, selfish man, motivated by his own crude appetites and base emotions. He couldn't allow the man to gain control again.

A king was above that. A king was better than that. He had to be. And so must Cassius.

He put down the scissors carefully and straightened. 'I think tonight I'll allow you some time to get comfortable in the Queen's private apartments.' His voice was cold, but he couldn't help that. 'If you need anything, please don't hesitate to let the palace staff know.'

Then he strode from the room before the thread on his control snapped completely.

CHAPTER SIX

INARA DID NOT enjoy the following week. The lessons in protocol and etiquette were boring and, no matter how hard she tried, she couldn't remember the names and lineages of all the people she'd be introduced to, still less their potted family histories.

She kept curtseying when she shouldn't curtsey at all, or bowing when she should have extended a hand. She walked too fast, walked too slowly, laughed when she shouldn't and so on.

It was all far too similar to the lessons her mother had drilled into her, complaining that, for a mathematical genius, she was very stupid. How could she remember formulae when she couldn't remember one person's name?

Inara hadn't known the answer then and she didn't now. All she could do was try, but it felt as if her brain was made of Swiss cheese and all the important things kept leaking out through the holes.

The meetings with the PR people were as bad—lots of advice on what to say and what to do, most of which she couldn't remember. She'd hoped the time she'd spend with the stylist would be better, but no. Her opinion on different outfits was needed, plus she had to keep still as she was measured and pinned to within an inch of her life.

She had no time to herself. No time for her research, to

rest her brain in the cold, clean air of numbers where she could lose herself.

It was awful and she hated it.

Of course, it would also have been a million times more bearable if she could have spoken to Cassius—however briefly—but he was absent the entire week.

He seemed to have retreated from her like a mirage, vanishing into offices and receiving rooms, constantly surrounded by advisors and courtiers. Forever meeting dignitaries and heads of state. Always in some kind of meeting or other.

She barely caught a glimpse of him.

She'd tried asking one of his aides if she could speak with him, but was told his schedule was full for the week, and that he would see her the night of her official presentation.

Inara couldn't shake the sense that he was avoiding her. The night she'd arrived he'd been very clear about what he wanted, going on about lessons and etiquette, and something about a formal presentation. But the only thing that had caught her full attention was that he expected them to share a bed.

She'd wanted that too, very much, and then quite suddenly, just as they were having a perfectly lovely conversation, he'd changed his mind. Without explanation. A staff member had come in within seconds of Cassius's departure, ushering her through to the Queen's private apartments and leaving her there.

Inara hadn't minded that night. Instead she'd explored her new home, confident that the next day he'd come and find her and then perhaps they'd start their married life together.

But he hadn't. It had been an aide instead, armed with a schedule, who'd chivvied her from one lesson to another, pleading ignorance whenever she attempted to ask about Cassius.

And he hadn't come that night either. Or the one after that. Or the one after that. And, as the days had gone by, she'd gradually realised that he wasn't going to come for her at all.

Inara ignored her disappointment, told herself he'd come for her when he was ready and, in the meantime, she'd do her best to be what he wanted. But as time had gone on and no word had come, she'd become less and less sure that he'd ever send for her. Less and less sure that he'd ever wanted her.

Less and less sure that he wanted a wife at all.

Perhaps he didn't. He'd said that it wouldn't be a union of convenience, and yet nearly a week later she was still on her own. Still in the Queen's apartments, with its delicate, spindly furniture and hard floors of polished marble. With its echoing, vaulted spaces and views over the regimented lines of the formal gardens.

Still alone.

He'd forgotten about her. The way he always did.

Inara didn't want that to ache like a thorn in her heart. But it did. He'd made such a big deal out of their marriage, about her coming to Katara to live at the palace, about her being Queen, and she'd accepted it. She'd put aside her own wishes, swallowed her fear, held on to her courage and left her home of nearly five years to come to the palace she hated.

And he'd ignored her almost completely.

She knew she had no claim on him, that their marriage had never been one of the heart, yet she'd thought he was her friend at least. Certainly after that night in the library, when he'd taken her virginity, she'd expected there to be…some kind of bond. That he'd at least think of her at some point.

But, no. Apparently not.

If she'd needed further proof that he felt nothing for her, then his silence and his absence confirmed it. She even started to doubt she'd see him the night of her first appearance as Queen.

Sure enough, when the night itself arrived, she was scrubbed and plucked and made up, then zipped into her gown without any mention of him. Then she was ushered down more long, echoing palace hallways and into a small, cold room off the main ballroom, where her aide told her to wait before disappearing, leaving Inara none the wiser as to why she had to wait here or what was going to happen next.

The room was empty of anything save some gloomy formal paintings and an icy-looking marble fireplace covered in too much gilt. Through the closed double doors that led to the ballroom, she could hear people laughing and talking and the delicate sounds of music.

It made her feel sick, made everything she'd been taught during the whole vile week go straight out of her head—not that it had ever been in her head to start with. Her palms were sweaty and she felt as though she were encased in armour instead of a glittering confection of a gown, all silvery tulle with silver embroidery and crystals sewn into the frothy skirts. Her hair had been piled on top of her head, a delicate diamond tiara set among her curls, and she didn't want to move too quickly or tip her head in case the whole thing came tumbling down. The pins hurt and her eyes felt dry and sore with the new contact lenses.

She felt like a little girl dressing up in her mother's clothes, the way she always had back when she'd been trotted out to all the parties her mother had insisted she attend.

Her mother had said that everything—even her—could

be improved with a pretty dress, yet for some reason there had never been a dress that could magically improve Inara, and it was likely this dress wouldn't either.

What would they all think when she walked into the ballroom? What would they be expecting? Probably the child bride their prince had married so foolishly all those years ago and had since forgotten.

Inara had begun to tremble with nerves when the door that led to the corridor opened and Cassius walked in. He was, as usual, surrounded by people, but he lifted a hand and they all withdrew, leaving her alone with him at last.

It had been a full week since she'd seen him in that lovely room with all the plants, and the impact of his presence was almost a physical force.

He was dressed formally, in tailored black evening clothes with no adornments bar the royal crest of the de Leon family—a set of scales signifying justice set in a jewelled pin on his lapel.

The ascetic lines of his clothing only emphasised the sheer masculine beauty of the man who wore them—his height, the width and breadth of his shoulders and chest, the lean span of his waist and the powerful length of his long legs.

His charisma was a palpable thing, regal, commanding and utterly authoritative. It made Inara's knees weak, and her heart beat far too fast. And, when his smoky amber gaze met hers, something inside her burst into flame.

She forgot her nerves. Forgot the ball in her honour happening just outside the doors. Forgot the entire week of hell she'd endured and how he'd ignored her. She forgot everything except that at last they were in the same room.

'C-Cassius,' she stuttered, taking a helpless step towards him. 'You're here.'

'Of course.' His deep voice was as cool and measured

as ever, the perfect lines of his face revealing nothing but calm. 'Where else would I be?'

He was the only familiar thing she'd seen all week, and she wanted very badly to get close to him, to put a hand on his broad, hard chest and take some of his strength, some of his control and authority, for herself.

Except there was something about him that held her rooted to the spot, an icy distance that made her certain he wouldn't like her touching him one bit.

Inara swallowed, closing her hands into fists to stop herself from wiping them on her glittering gown. 'I…wasn't sure. I've been trying to see you all week, but everyone kept saying you were busy.'

'I was busy. Didn't they tell you that I'd see you tonight?'

'Yes, but—'

'But what?' One imperious black brow rose.

'But…' She stopped.

He looked so unapproachable, so untouchable. Would he really want to hear about how homesick she felt, about and how nervous she'd been and still was? How hard she'd found this week, trying to remember all the things she had to do and say and in what order?

A few years ago she wouldn't have thought twice about confiding in him. Maybe even a few months ago. But now…it felt different. They were in the palace, in his territory, and he was the King. The heavy gold ring of state was on his right hand, and he was looking at her as if she was merely a poor petitioner come before his throne rather than his queen…

'Nothing,' she said at last, her mouth dry. 'It's fine.'

Cassius surveyed her for a second, his gaze inscrutable as it drifted from her elaborately curled hair and tiara, down over the strapless, embroidered silver bodice of her gown to the layers of tulle and crystal of its skirts.

She had no idea what he thought of it, or whether he approved, but she wanted him to be impressed with her. To think she looked like a queen at least. To think that she was beautiful…

Are you crazy? Why would he ever think that, when even your own mother thought you were at best only acceptable?

She shoved the thought out of her head, trying to force down how intimidated she felt in his presence and how the apprehension about the moment they would step out into the ballroom was getting to her. How ill it was making her.

She'd do this because that was what she'd promised him. To be his queen, one who hopefully would shame neither him nor Aveiras. Because this was important to him and she didn't want to disappoint him.

Not like she'd disappointed everyone else.

So she didn't speak about any of her fears, trying not to let his lack of reaction get to her. When he presented his arm, she took it, resisting clutching at it like an over-anxious child. Then they turned towards the double doors, which were then thrown open, the glittering lights and noise of the ball crashing over her like a wave.

'His Royal Majesty, King Cassius,' the usher announced loudly as the noise of the crowd quietened. 'And Her Royal Majesty, Queen Inara.'

And, whether she wanted to or not, Inara found herself being drawn relentlessly into the ballroom.

Inara was so bright he couldn't even look at her. He didn't dare. She was small and delicate and exquisite in a silver confection of a gown that looked as though it had been scattered with stardust. And she, alabaster-pale, her grey eyes luminous, was the star.

He'd thought a week of avoiding her would put some distance between him and his unnervingly powerful desire, but it hadn't. The moment he'd stepped into that room and set eyes on her, watched the bright, joyful thing ignite in her eyes when he looked at her, everything possessive, hungry and desperate had roared up inside him and demanded its due.

It should have been enough, burying himself in all those impossible, endless meetings that he loathed with a passion, the never-ending round of requests made, answers he must give, decisions he must make. The constant procession of audiences and petitions and grievances and complaints...

All those duties, the duties of a king, should have reminded him how petty were his own passions and appetites. How unimportant next to the needs of his country. Yet all he'd been able to think about was how he wanted to cancel every meeting he had to go looking for her. To go hunting for her, to catch her and drag her from the Queen's apartments and into his bed.

But he knew himself too well and how those base desires and primitive emotions could take hold. They were all-consuming. They'd once made him put the pursuit of them before his family, before his country. They were flaws.

And a king had to be flawless.

So he tried to ignore the woman on his arm, so bright and glittering, delicate and beautiful, as he guided her around the ballroom and introduced her to the important people of his court. And, because he couldn't look at her, he didn't see how pale she'd become under the glittering crystals of the chandelier, or notice how she kept looking at him whenever he spoke someone's name. He told himself that he didn't need to pay attention, because all those etiquette and protocol lessons and PR consultations would have given her everything she needed to handle this little soirée.

Nerves were expected, so he didn't worry when she stammered, curtseyed to someone instead of shaking their hand or looked bewildered when she called the Prime Minister by someone else's name, then appeared to forget that Aveiras even had a prime minister.

As the evening wore on, he could hear people whispering, and caught the looks of disapproval sent their way as Inara forgot yet another name, and then used the wrong title, and then stopped speaking altogether.

He told himself that it would get better for her, that this was a rite of passage she had to bear and that, once it was done, she'd find things easier, but for some reason all those things sounded like hollow justifications.

It never got easier for you.

No, but he'd been thrown in at the deep end after the accident and, faced with drowning, he'd simply learned how to swim. Inara wasn't in the deep end and she'd had a whole week's preparation. And she had him at her side. It wasn't the same at all.

Except it was becoming apparent that, despite what he'd told himself, Inara was a long way from learning to swim in these particular waters.

After she made yet another mistake with a name, he finally forced himself to look at her. She was so pale and her eyes looked red and irritated. Her shoulders were tense and she held herself awkwardly, her movements stiff and unsure.

She seemed to jolt suddenly as his gaze rested on her, as if she'd just become aware of his attention, making a sharp, involuntary movement that looked almost like a flinch, and knocking some woman's elbow and the wine glass she was holding out of her hand. The glass smashed on the marble floor, red wine splashing everywhere like blood.

The music stopped, people pausing in their conversations to look in Inara's direction.

A terrible, awful silence fell.

She stood there in her beautiful gown, red wine staining her skirts, an expression of utter horror on her face. 'I—I'm so sorry,' she stammered, white as a sheet and trembling.

Cassius put out a hand to her, but she ignored him, turning without a word and running straight through the massive double doors that led to the terrace and the formal gardens beyond.

Whispers began, the wind of disapproval blowing through the ballroom, heads turning, attention focusing. Everyone looked at him and he knew they'd be gauging his response, wondering how he'd handle this unseemly display.

This is your fault. You ignored her all week, because you couldn't handle yourself in her presence, and now look what's happened. She wasn't ready and you threw her to the wolves.

Yes, he'd done that. This mess *was* his fault. He'd ignored her because he didn't like the way she'd made him want her, leaving her in the hands of palace employees who clearly hadn't done a good enough job of preparing her. He should have overseen her lessons or at least checked in on her.

Well, if the court wanted to see his response to the Queen's chaotic and abrupt departure, then he would show them.

Allowing no emotion to be displayed on his face, Cassius murmured to the aide at his elbow, then proceeded to soothe the ruffled feathers of the woman whose arm had been knocked. Palace employees rushed in to sweep up the glass, and within moments the music had resumed, conversation buzzed again and the ball went on as if nothing had happened.

Five minutes later, once attention on him had shifted, Cassius told his aide curtly that he'd be seeing to the Queen, before striding from the ballroom after her. The ball could go on without him for a while, especially as the whole reason for the ball in the first place had disappeared.

Outside, even though it was night, the discreet lighting of the formal gardens ensured that it wasn't completely dark. Fountains played, and beneath their delicate music he could hear the sound of the sea crashing against the white cliffs below the palace.

He couldn't see Inara anywhere, though he searched all the places in the gardens where she might have gone, the stone benches near the fountains and beside the rose beds. The pretty archway of bougainvillea. The magnolia copse.

At last he came to a pavilion of white stone that stood on the cliffs, looking out over the ocean. He gave it a cursory glance, because it didn't look as if anyone was inside, then stopped, his gaze caught by a slight glitter.

In the shadow of one of the pillars, sitting on the stone bench with her skirts caught around her, was Inara. Her head was turned away, her gaze on the ocean throwing itself against the cliffs.

Despite it being late summer, the sea breeze was cool, so he moved over to where she sat, shrugging out of his jacket as he went so he could drape it around her pale shoulders.

She turned her head as he approached, obviously hearing his step. Even though she hurriedly wiped her face, he could see the tears there.

You hurt her. Like you hurt everyone close to you.

His heart twisted hard with a familiar pain. Well, that

was nothing new, but at least with Inara he could do something about it.

He came closer, holding his jacket out, but she shook her head, her tiara slipping to one side. 'No. Stay where you are.' Her voice sounded thick. 'Just…give me five minutes.'

Cassius stopped. 'Inara.'

'I'll come back, I promise.' She surreptitiously wiped at her face. 'I hope that lady was okay. I didn't mean to knock her elbow, I just… I don't know what happened.'

'Inara,' he said again.

'I'm sorry. I tried, I really did, but when I told you I wasn't good in social situations, well, I meant it.'

He stood there stiffly, holding his jacket in one hand, staring at her small figure curled up on the stone bench. Remembering her white face and her red eyes. The feel of her fingers on his arm, clutching at him.

Remembering joining her in that little room before the ball, reeling from the gut punch of her beauty and trying not to show it. Trying not to see the way she looked at him, as if for reassurance. Trying not to hear the hurt in her voice as she told him that she'd asked for him…

She's always looked at you as if you were her hero. And you let her down.

His stomach dropped away, the truth of it settling in his heart. Denying the man had worked very well for three years. He'd controlled his appetites, excised the selfishness from his heart and, following his brother's example, he'd done everything he could to become a perfect king. But that didn't allow for much else. It certainly didn't allow for a woman who was new to royal duties, who hadn't been brought up with them the way he had.

A woman who was only here because of him and the mistake he'd made. He couldn't fix what had happened with Caspian, but he could fix what happened with Inara.

He'd lost control with her when he shouldn't have and, while nothing could change that fact, he could admit that the decision to keep her at arm's length had clearly been a foolish one.

He'd decided she would be his queen, but Inara wasn't a princess brought up in the palace spotlight. She was a girl he'd married at sixteen and left to her own devices in an isolated manor house in the countryside for the best part of five years. Throwing her into court on her own after a mere week's training, and expecting her to behave like a woman born to it, was ludicrous.

Worse, it was selfish, because it was about his own discomfort rather than anything to do with her. And it had hurt her. His control was usually excellent these days. Yes, he'd lost it with her once, but that didn't mean he'd lose it every single time. And, anyway, he wanted heirs. How could he get those heirs if he avoided taking her to his bed?

She was his wife. His bed was where she belonged and it was high time he showed her that. Without a word, Cassius strode over to her and draped his jacket around her shoulders.

She looked up, her eyes wide. 'What are you doing? Just give me another minute and I'll come—'

'You're not going anywhere except back to my rooms,' he said coolly. Then he bent and picked her up in his arms.

Inara stiffened, twisting in his grip. 'Put me down. I don't want…'

'Hush.' He tightened his hold, keeping her safe against his chest. 'We won't be returning to the ball. We're going to my apartments where we can talk in peace.'

She took a breath and he could feel the resistance bleed out of her, her small, delicate frame going limp against him. 'I'll get wine on your clothes.'

'I don't care.'

He stepped out of the pavilion, making his way through the dimly lit gardens, conscious of how warm she was, and how beneath the acrid smell of spilled red wine he detected the faint musky scent that was Inara.

It made him feel hungry and possessive, like a leopard with its kill. Ordinarily he would have ignored that kind of feeling. He would have pushed it away. But not tonight.

Avoiding the ballroom, Cassius entered the palace through a side door. He nodded to the guards stationed on either side and strode on down the corridors, heading towards his private apartments.

'I'm sorry,' Inara said, a bitter note in her voice. 'I failed.'

He glanced down. Her head rested against his shoulder, silvery hair caught in the black fabric, and she was staring at nothing in particular. Her pretty mouth was soft and vulnerable, her cheeks still very pale. He remembered the bright smiles she always had for him, the joy that had lit her expression whenever he'd visited, and now…

Now she looked defeated, all the brightness, all the joy, gone.

You did that to her.

He had. And so he'd fix it.

'You didn't fail,' he said flatly. 'What happened in the ballroom was my fault and mine alone.'

She looked up at him, frowning. 'What do you mean, it's your fault? You're not the one who forgot everyone's name or knocked a glass out of—'

'No, but I'm the one who ignored you the entire week, giving your preparation over to someone else who clearly had no idea what they were doing. I'm the one who didn't check on you to make sure things were running smoothly. And I'm the one who didn't ask you tonight if you felt prepared or take any notice of how pale you were or how frightened you looked.' He stared into her reddened eyes, wanting her to be absolutely certain. 'It won't happen again. Do you understand?'

Her cheeks had gained a little colour, which was good. 'Did I really look that frightened?'

'Yes. You looked terrified.'

Her silvery lashes descended, veiling her gaze. 'I didn't mean to. I'm…not very good at hiding my emotions.'

'You'll learn. But not in a week.' He came to the doors of his private apartments, the guards rushing to open them so he could walk through. 'And, given that for the last five years you've been living in the country with no court experience at all, it was unconscionable for me to expect this of you so quickly.'

'You don't need to blame yourself,' she said quietly. 'Some of this was my fault too. It reminded me too much of all those parties my mother kept dragging me to and I suppose I…panicked.'

He knew what her mother had put her through. She'd told him, in the months after their wedding, when he'd visited her, how her parents had never been happy with her and how she'd always disappointed them.

He hadn't realised, though, that balls and social engagements would still be an issue, even all these years later.

You should have.

Yes, damn right he should have.

'No, it was not.' He couldn't bear for her to take the blame, not even a small part of it. 'I'm the King, and you're my queen, therefore it's my responsibility to prepare you for your role. And I should have remembered that about your mother.'

His footsteps echoed on the marble floor as he passed by the door of his study, carrying on down towards his bedroom.

Because that was where this had to end.

It was his own desires that had got Inara tangled up in this, so it would be his own desires that he'd deal with first. And perhaps, once he had, he could then focus on the important work of preparing her to undertake her queenly duties properly.

He was conscious of Inara's gaze on him as he walked, of her warm body in his arms and how it seemed to fit there perfectly. Of how his hunger seemed to grow with each step and how his anticipation gathered tighter and tighter.

'I didn't think it would be such an issue for me, so why you should have been able to anticipate it I have no idea,' she murmured. 'You don't have to take responsibility for everything, you know.'

He didn't deign to respond. Of course he had to take responsibility for everything. He was the King. What else did a king do?

But it was becoming difficult to think of anything beyond the feel of her in his arms, and how he hadn't been able to look at her all evening. Yet now, in the privacy of his bedroom, he'd strip that gown from her body and look his fill.

No one will be watching you. No one will be judging you.

His breath caught as realisation gripped him tight.

In his bedroom he could be anyone he wanted. There'd be no one to see him. No one to know if his crown slipped a little, or even a lot.

No one but Inara. And she already knew who he truly was inside. She always had.

'Where are we going, Cassius?' She sounded as if she already knew.

He glanced down once more, meeting her gaze. 'Where we should have gone the night you arrived. To my bedroom.'

CHAPTER SEVEN

INARA'S HEART WAS beating very fast. The awful, sick feeling in her stomach and the tightness in her chest that she'd felt in the ballroom had vanished, both feelings melting away as soon as Cassius's arms came around her, holding her tight.

The evening had started awfully the moment Cassius had led her into the ballroom, and from there it had gone from awful to terrible, then to even worse. She hadn't been able to remember anyone's names, and her attempts at conversation had only prompted frowns, strange looks and judgmental stares. No one had been friendly. No one had smiled. Everything the etiquette people had taught her had gone completely out of her head and she'd felt paralyzed, certain that the moment she opened her mouth she'd only make it worse.

She hadn't wanted to move, in case she'd tried to curtsey instead of shaking hands or stood accidentally on someone's foot. Her eyes had been sore because the contact lenses were irritating, and her head had hurt because the pins in her hair were digging into her scalp. She wasn't used to wearing the tall silver heels they'd given her to wear, either—they'd made her feel as if she were wearing a pair of stilts.

And through it all, his arm like iron beneath her fingertips, had moved Cassius. Tall and broad, as unreachable and untouchable as Mount Everest. She'd wanted to impress him so badly, yet every time she'd opened her mouth or taken a step she'd made some mistake. And he'd seen. He'd watched her fail, fail and fail.

Failing her parents was one thing, but failing him was quite another.

It cut her to the bone.

He'd lost his family, had had to pick up a duty he'd never asked for, and the least she could do for him was to give him a queen he could be proud of.

But then she'd knocked that woman's elbow and wine had gone everywhere, splashing her beautiful dress and causing a scene. Reminding her of that garden party years ago, when she'd tried her best to catch the eye of the duke's son, only to stammer and forget every rule of conversation the instant he'd spoken to her. She'd been so embarrassed that she'd run away.

Back then she'd been young, only sixteen, yet tonight she'd had no such excuse. She was now an adult and a queen, and she should have stayed in the ballroom and dealt with the mess she'd made, not bolted like a frightened rabbit.

In fact, she'd been on the point of mustering her courage to go back when Cassius had appeared. Everything in her had tightened as she'd braced herself for his judgment and then…it hadn't come.

He'd seemed angry, coming over to where she'd sat on the cold stone bench, his gaze full of fire. But he hadn't given her a tirade. Instead, he'd shocked her by draping his jacket around her shoulders then picking her straight up in his arms.

And it had come as another shock to realise that he was

only angry with himself. He'd taken responsibility for the entire evening.

That shouldn't have surprised her. He'd assumed a duty he'd never wanted, becoming king because of a tragic accident. It had always puzzled her that he'd done that because, although he had been next in line to the throne, he hadn't had to take it. There were others he could have handed the responsibility on to, yet he hadn't. Some would have said it was power he was after, but Inara knew he wasn't that kind of man. He never had been.

So why did he take it?

But she didn't have an answer to that and, with his sharp, intense gaze on her, the question began to fray and break apart.

She was in his arms in her glittering, wine-soaked dress, after having made a fool of herself in front of his entire court, and yet instead of yelling at her he'd told her it was his fault and now he was carrying her into his bedroom…

'Why?' The question came out breathily as he strode into the room, kicking the door shut behind him. 'You changed your mind when I first arrived, so why now?'

He moved over to the tall stone fireplace, a blaze leaping in the grate. It looked as though it had been freshly lit, and she was aware all of a sudden that she'd been cold sitting in the pavilion. Yet she wasn't cold now. His arms were strong, his hard chest like hot stone. His jacket around her shoulders was warm too, and it smelled of him, a masculine spice with an earthier scent that was all Cassius.

Her mouth went dry, a bone-deep, physical longing curling through her. It was very hard to think about what had happened earlier and her own conflicted feelings when he was here, he was holding her and it was very apparent what he intended to do.

Gently, he put her down in front of the fire, which quite

frankly felt like a crime when she wanted to stay in his arms and never leave.

'Because I thought it best to give you some time to become accustomed to palace life.' He moved behind her, easing his jacket from her shoulders.

Inara shivered as his fingertips brushed her bare skin, the physical longing becoming deeper and more insistent. It was getting difficult to think, and part of her just wanted to surrender, to let the desire overtake her, because she'd done nothing but think all night and she was tired of it. She wanted to escape. Numbers had always been that escape, but it wasn't the stark purity of numbers she wanted now. She only wanted him.

Except...he wasn't giving her the entire truth, was he? He'd changed his mind so abruptly that day in his study after making all those grand proclamations. Why? It wasn't simply because he wanted to give her some time to adjust, she was sure. He'd walked away from her so quickly after she'd got close to him...

'No,' she said huskily, staring at the flames leaping high in the fireplace, every sense concentrated on the man standing behind her, on the heat of his body and the scent of him that wrapped around her, making her feel so safe, the way it always had. 'That's not the reason.'

His fingers moved in her hair, carefully extracting each painful pin. 'The reason doesn't matter.'

Her hair began to come down, slipping over her shoulders, her scalp aching in relief as he pulled away the tiara, dropping it onto a nearby armchair.

'Yes, it does.' She shivered as his fingers wound into her hair, combing through it. 'At least, it matters to me. You could have come for me any time this week and you didn't.'

'The time wasn't right.'

Inara turned, looking up into his familiar, achingly

beautiful face. He was so very tall, built so broad, so muscular. A warrior who could crush her without even thinking. But he wouldn't. All that magnificent male strength was tightly leashed, so painstakingly controlled.

Everything about him was so painstakingly controlled.

He didn't used to be, remember? He used to be much more relaxed, so much...happier.

Yet there was nothing of the man he'd once been in his face. The duties of kingship had stripped it all away, taking that happiness with it.

Her heart ached with a sudden, painful realisation. She'd never thought much about him as a man. He'd always been a fantasy figure, a template on which she could hang her own longings and desires.

But he wasn't a template. He wasn't even a king—that was only a title. First and foremost, he was a man, and a complicated one at that.

She stared up into his level amber gaze. 'It's not about timing. You changed your mind very suddenly that night and then you left me alone for an entire week. You didn't even respond to the messages I sent you.'

The expression on his face was set, and he radiated tension like the fire behind him radiated warmth, yet in his eyes were flames hotter than those in the grate.

She could feel herself begin to catch fire too, though she resisted the pull. This was too important, like the key to solving an equation she'd been studying and hadn't found a solution to yet.

'Turn around, little one,' Cassius ordered, his voice very deep, his gaze turning from smoky amber into brilliant, burning gold. 'The time for talking is over.'

Her whole body tightened with the need to obey him but she knew, if she did, if she let this moment pass, it would set a precedent for their marriage that would be difficult to depart from.

He'd told her he didn't see her as a child any more, but even so he was still treating her like one. He was the one in charge, telling her what to do, where to go, that this was how it should be, and she'd accepted it. And not simply because he was her king, but because she'd so badly wanted his approval.

He'd taken control, but only because she'd let him.

And you'll always be a child to him as long as you keep doing so.

Determination hardened inside her. If she continued to fall in with his wishes, to accept it every time he said no, then things would never change between them. He would continue to view her as his child bride, and their marriage would simply be an endless set of orders she obeyed, while he got to dictate everything.

Well, that ended tonight.

'The time for talking is not over.' Inara lifted her chin. 'If you want me, Cassius, you need to tell me the truth.'

The flames in his eyes glowed brighter. 'Are you trying to bargain with your king?'

His voice was calm, yet there was an edge to it, a note of warning that sent a small electric thrill through her, excitement gathering in her throat.

The growing intensity in him was making it harder to resist, but this mattered. She couldn't let it go.

'Maybe,' she said, her breathing getting faster.

'You can't bargain with me, little one.' His hands settled on her shoulders and gripped her gently but firmly, the heat of his touch stealing all the breath from her lungs. Then he turned her round so she faced the fire once more, with him at her back. 'Kings take what they want. And they don't accept bargains.'

Anticipation coiled low inside her, bringing with it a nagging, insistent ache. Tension crackled in the air around them, not the same tension that seemed to be holding him back, but something else. Something hot and electric. She'd felt it that night in the study, when he'd teased her, flirted with her, and she'd challenged him. He'd liked that then and she was sure he liked it now.

Maybe that was the key to unlocking him. Maybe she should take this further, play this game and see where it led. Maybe she'd get the truth out of him, and some power and respect for herself.

'They don't?' She hoped she sounded more in control than she felt. 'Surely if it was in this king's interest he might?'

'In my interest, hmm?' His thumbs stroked over her bare shoulders, searing her skin, sending delicious chills through her. 'And what have you got to bargain with?'

Inara closed her eyes, every sense focused on the man at her back and, despite the fact that he towered over her, all hard, masculine strength and power, she'd never felt so safe.

Yet at the same time she knew she was also in danger. Danger of the most exciting kind.

'Tell me why you sent me away,' she said huskily, 'and I'll let you do anything you want to me. Anything at all. You won't need to ask. You can just take.'

Cassius stilled. Her skin beneath his fingers was soft, and very, very warm, and he felt like a starving beast he was so hungry.

He took a breath, then another, trying to focus on what she'd just said, because she couldn't mean it. She couldn't. She was small and delicate and very innocent. Too innocent. She couldn't mean what he thought she meant.

'You don't want that,' he said roughly. 'You don't know what you're—'

'I know exactly what I'm offering.' She sounded almost…cool. As if she was the one with the control here, not him. 'And I mean it, too. You can have me, all of me, for as long as you want, doing anything you want. I give you permission right now. All I want in return is for you to be honest with me.'

Her shoulders beneath his hand felt narrow and fragile, and yet the heat coming off her… She was hotter than the fire in front of them. And she smelled of sex and sin and all the things he'd denied himself. All the things he could have right now in the privacy of his own bedroom. No one to watch him. No one to see if he let himself be just a man for a few hours. Just for tonight. Just with her. She was his wife, after all. It was allowed.

Except she wouldn't allow it unless he gave her the truth. He hadn't expected her to want to know. He hadn't expected her to be interested. What he'd expected was her complete surrender, the way she'd surrendered to him in the library that night. The way she'd surrendered out in the pavilion overlooking the sea, letting him scoop her into his arms.

He hadn't expected her to question him or to hold out when he'd told her not to. He hadn't expected her to push him.

The predator he'd once been growled low and hungry, liking this challenge to his authority. Liking her determination too, because he'd never been a fan of a pushover. He preferred women who knew what they wanted and weren't afraid to say it. And it had been a long time since anyone had challenged him like this, because no one challenged the King.

Except, clearly, his queen.

'Why are you so interested?' He brushed aside the silvery mass of her hair, baring her nape before bending and pressing a kiss there. 'I've given you the answer to your question.'

She shivered. 'What you gave me was an excuse. And now you're making this into a big deal.'

She's not wrong.

He pressed another kiss to the top of her spine, inhaling the sweet scent of her body. His hunger was becoming more and more difficult to contain. The restraints he'd put on himself were starting to fray. If he hadn't already given himself permission, it might have worried him, but he had given himself permission, and now all he felt was impatience.

Yes, he was making this into a big deal. What did it matter if she knew that she was the reason he'd kept his distance this week? It gave her a certain power over him that he was reluctant to let her have but, whether she knew it yet or not, she was already using that power over him right now, right here, in this room. And it was working.

Cassius had never taken a woman without permission, even when he'd been at his worst, and he certainly wasn't about to start now, so he murmured in her ear, 'Why did I change my mind that night? Why did I keep my distance all week? I think you know why already, little one.'

He took hold of the zip of her gown. 'It was you. I changed my mind because of you. Because I want you. Because a good king is controlled and measured in all things and you make me forget that. You make me remember who I used to be and I cannot have that.'

Slowly he began to draw down the zip, the silvery fabric parting to reveal silky pale skin and the elegant curve of her back. She made no move to stop him, but he could feel her tremble. 'But…why? Why can't you remember who you used to be? What's so bad about that?'

He didn't want to get into that. Didn't want to tell her the bitter truth about himself and how flawed he was. How he'd sent his own brother, his twin, to his death.

He never wanted to tell *anyone* about that.

So he unzipped her gown all the way and pushed it from her body, letting it fall at her feet in a pool of glittering wine-soaked fabric, leaving her wearing nothing but lacy underwear and silver high heels.

'Cassius,' she murmured, her voice sounding slightly uncertain.

He put his hands on her hips, drawing her back against his body and holding her there. 'Not now,' he said quietly in her ear. 'I gave you what you wanted. It's my turn now.' Then he turned his head, brushing his mouth over the sensitive place between her shoulder and neck before biting her there lightly.

She gasped, so he bit her again, sliding his hands slowly and with care up her sides and then back down again, tracing the glorious feminine shape of her.

Delicate and finely made, his queen. She hadn't yet become sharp and rigid and unbending, as he had. She was still hot and soft, like candle wax melting so beautifully under his touch. There was passion in his bride, so much of it, and she was going to give it all to him.

It was a gift, and he knew it. And not just her passion, but her trust too. Anything, she'd told him. He could do anything to her and she'd let him....

He nipped her again, gently, then dropped to his knees behind her, pressing kisses down her spine as his hands went to her hips, his fingers slipping under the waistband of her knickers. She gave a trembling sigh as he eased them down her legs to her ankles, helping her to step out of them and the miles of tulle of her gown. Then he swept the clothing aside so she stood free and unencumbered, naked but for the sexy silver heels.

She began to turn, but he gripped her, keeping her right where she was. 'No. Stay still.'

Then he ran his palms down the outsides of her thighs to her knees, and then down further, tracing her calves and then her ankles. He could hear her breathing, fast and erratic, and she kept shifting on her feet. He stroked her again, from her ankles up to her hips then back down again, glorying in the feel of her skin. It had been so long since he'd touched a woman...

He frowned at her feet and the backs of her heels where the leather of her shoes had obviously rubbed, turning the skin red. 'Are your feet sore?'

'Only a little,' she said breathlessly. 'I'm not...used to heels.'

Another reminder if he needed one that tonight must have been a nightmare for her, and that he'd let it happen.

But he'd fix it. Right now, right here, he'd make it better, the way he used to, by giving her the only good thing he was capable of: pleasure.

'You're unbelievably sexy in those heels,' he murmured, running his hands up her legs once more, pressing kisses to the small of her back. 'But I can't have them hurting you.'

'Oh, it's okay. I don't mind. Not if you like them.'

'I do like them. But I also mind that they're hurting you.' Sitting back on his heels, he closed his hand around one delicate ankle and lifted it, easing the shoe off, before doing the same to her other foot. Then he knelt there and began to touch her body, outlining every dip and curve with his fingertips. The narrow indentation of her waist and the soft roundness of her bottom. The sweet swell of hips and thighs. The delicate arcs of her shoulder blades and the graceful curve of her neck.

She shook as he traced her, but he didn't rush it. He wanted to take his time, because if he was going to allow himself a whole night to indulge in her...with permission to do whatever he wanted...then he was going to make the most of it.

His hunger simmered as he fed it small bites. The velvet of the back of her neck. The petal softness in the crook of her elbow. The creamy taste of the small of her back as he pressed his tongue there.

Her breathing became louder and more erratic as he went on, and she leaned against him, as if she couldn't hold herself upright any longer. But he'd only just started, and he wasn't done with her yet, not even close.

When he'd explored every inch of her from behind, he turned her round to face him at last, staying on his knees because he wanted to savour her up close.

And what a sight she was, her pretty face flushed with heat, her silvery-grey eyes darkening into charcoal. She had the most perfect round, pink-tipped breasts, and the soft curls between her thighs were as silvery as the hair on her head.

His breath caught at the sight of her, the simmering hunger beginning to boil. He was so hard and so ready, but his long years of self-control had taught him well so, instead of picking her up and throwing her on the bed the way his sex was demanding, he stayed where he was, put his hands on her hips and drew her closer.

She reached for him, swaying on her feet, clutching at his shoulders, her gaze open and so full of longing and heat that for a second every thought went straight out of his head.

He'd seen an echo of that look before, every time he'd visited her. When she'd come rushing into the room to greet him, her face lit up, eyes shining. And it hit him all of a sudden that she'd been the brightest part of those years before his family had died.

He'd thought he was happy then, rebelling against his rigid upbringing and all the palace rules. Throwing them in his father's face and indulging himself whenever and wherever he could.

But he hadn't been happy. He'd been at war with his family…at war with the ideals that he felt had been forced on him…at war with his place in the world. He'd been living selfishly and a part of him knew it.

Really, the only time he'd ever felt true happiness was when he'd come to visit her. When she'd smiled at him, taking him out of his own petty grievances and pain. Distracting him, teaching him what it was to be interested in another person, not just himself.

He'd married her because of the way she'd looked at him that night in his limo, seeing in him something better, something worthy. A hero. A saviour. And that was how she'd continued to see him, no matter how awful or selfish he'd been. No matter how imperfect. No matter how flawed.

She saw the good in him and it gave him hope.

She wasn't smiling now, but that same look was glowing in her eyes, only this time it was hotter and tinged with passion. And suddenly he was almost beside himself with desperation. To touch her, taste her, explore every part of her. Take her out of herself, the way she'd done to him.

To feel like he was worthy.

He pulled her closer, pressing his mouth to her stomach, licking her and then moving higher to take one of those little pink nipples into his mouth. She tasted so sweet, like strawberries and champagne from a long-lost summer, and when she groaned, arching into him, offering herself, she sounded even sweeter.

He was starving, desperate for her. Releasing her breast, he licked his way down her over her stomach to the soft, sensitive place between her thighs. She gasped as he nuzzled against her damp curls and then, when he slid his hands over the curves of her bottom to hold her steady, sliding his tongue through her slick folds, she cried out.

She was delicious, the best thing he'd tasted in his entire life, and he couldn't get enough. She sagged against him, folding herself over him, panting out her pleasure, saying his name like a prayer as he explored all the delicate textures of her, silken, slick and hot.

And, as he lost himself in her, he had the oddest feeling that it was her sheltering him, her holding him up, rather than the other way around.

He wanted to hold her there for ever, forgetting everything but the sound of her cries and the taste of her on his tongue. But her pleasure was a double-edged sword, because her every cry sharpened his own hunger until he couldn't stand it any more. He pushed his tongue deep inside her, gripping her hard as she cried out his name and convulsed in his arms.

He stayed where he was through sheer will power alone, holding her as she quietened. Only then did he rise to his feet, sweeping her into his arms and carrying her over to the bed.

Then he laid her on it and followed her down, putting one hand on either side of her head, stretching himself over her.

He looked down into her darkened eyes, tendrils of silver hair clinging to her damp forehead.

'Time to make good on your bargain, little one,' he growled.

CHAPTER EIGHT

INARA COULDN'T THINK of anywhere she'd rather be than right here, in Cassius's bed, beneath him, his gaze gone brilliant with hunger and desire, and all for her.

Yes, *her*.

She'd wondered why he'd kept his distance and, even though she'd shied away from thinking about it, some deep part of her had doubted. Doubted that, despite his lapse in the library at the Queen's Estate, it hadn't been about *her*. That it was just because he hadn't had a woman in years. That he didn't really want her after all.

It hadn't been something she'd wanted to admit even to herself, though, so she'd deliberately pushed it away. The way he'd carried her into his bedroom had relieved her somewhat, but the deeper doubt had remained.

Until he'd given her the truth. She *was* the reason he'd kept his distance. Not because he didn't want her, but because he did. Too much.

You make me remember how I used to be.

That admission troubled her, caught at her, made her want to know more. Because there had been something conflicted in his voice, as if remembering who he used to be was a bad thing. As if he *wasn't* that person any more and was now someone different.

He is different. He changed when he became king.

He had. He'd become so distant, so…not cold, precisely, but chilly. As if there were oceans between him and everyone else. She'd assumed that was just part of being a king, but maybe it wasn't. Maybe there was something more to it.

Except it was difficult to think of that now, with him crouched over her like a beast, his brilliant, hungry gaze on hers.

Aftershocks of pleasure still jolted through her. After the intense climax he'd given her with his mouth right there in front of the fire, she'd thought it wasn't possible to be ready for another so soon. How wrong she was. The way he looked at her, as if he wanted to eat her alive, made her whole body tighten with need and desire.

'Anything,' she said thickly, staring up at him, meeting his fierce stare with her own. 'You can have anything. I promised and I meant it.'

She *did* mean it. She'd never been so sure of anything in her life. She had no experience whatsoever, not like he did, but that didn't matter. He'd keep her safe. She knew that on an almost cellular level. There was nothing he could do to her that she wouldn't want, nothing that she wouldn't enjoy.

She wasn't afraid of him or what he might to do her in the slightest.

It's not your body you should be worried about. It's your heart.

The thought was a cold thread cutting through the heat, and she didn't want it there, so she ignored it.

That didn't matter—not here, not right now.

Slowly Cassius straightened, still watching her with that hungry amber gaze. He lifted his hands to the buttons of his shirt and began to undo them, slowly, teasing her, and she loved it—the slow reveal of his bare chest as the cotton parted, letting her see at last the hard, ridged lines of his chest and abdomen, sharply defined, as though he'd been chiselled from rock by a master sculptor.

She pushed herself up, hungry to touch him, but almost as soon as she put her hands on his hot, smooth skin he grabbed her wrists and pushed her back down against the mattress.

'No.' His voice was rough and guttural. 'Not yet.'

'Oh, but I—'

'You'll get your turn, I promise. But I'm too hungry for you to do that right now. My self-control isn't limitless where you're concerned.'

She loved that too. That she really *could* test him. That his desire for her was apparently just as hungry as hers was for him. It made her feel strong, a current of unexpected power running through her. That she, the failure, the girl her parents had never particularly wanted, could tempt a king.

She wanted to tease him the way he was teasing her, so she gave him what she hoped was a flirtatious look from beneath her lashes. 'Hurry up then, Your Majesty. I'm getting impatient.'

Then she wondered if she'd done something wrong, because he stared at her for a few seconds with that blank expression she was beginning to think was his default when he was shocked. But, just as a flush of embarrassment threatened, his beautiful, sensual mouth curled in the most devastating smile she'd ever seen.

He'd never smiled like that at her. In fact, it had been three years since she'd seen him smile, full-stop.

Her heart twisted, giving one hard, desperate beat, and she swore in that moment that, if nothing else, she'd spend the rest of their marriage trying to make him smile like that again. No—she'd dedicate her entire life to it. He was so beautiful when he smiled. Warm and wicked and unbelievably sexy. No wonder he'd had a never-ending stream of women all queuing for a night in his bed.

'Are you perhaps teasing me, little one?' His voice was low and rough, a velvet growl.

'Maybe.' She felt triumphant, as if she'd won a Nobel prize. 'Though it's not the done thing, is it? To tease a king?'

Cassius shrugged out of his shirt and let it fall, his hands dropping to the belt on his trousers. 'No, it's not. Kings are very serious and hate being teased.' He began to unfasten his belt. 'There are laws, you know. And consequences.'

Inara was thrilled. Who'd have thought that she'd love flirting? Because that was what they were doing, wasn't it? They were flirting. And, unlike that night in the library when she'd been so uncertain, she wasn't uncertain now. Not when it was clear he was enjoying this as much as she was.

'Consequences?' She took in his hard-muscled torso before focusing on what his hands were doing with his belt— undoing it, pulling it from the belt loops and discarding it. 'What kind of consequences are there for teasing a king?'

He pulled down the zip of his fly. 'Give me five minutes and I'll show you.'

'Five minutes?' Inara's mouth went dry as he shifted on the bed, pushing his trousers down and taking his underwear with them. 'Is that all?'

Cassius laughed, roughly, deeply and unbelievably sexily. 'Not a response I'm familiar with, I have to say.'

Inara blinked, staring at that most male part of him, all flirtatious banter instantly going out of her head. Back in the library she hadn't had a chance to see him properly, hadn't even had a chance to touch him, but now... Oh, now...

'I didn't mean th-that,' she stuttered, sitting up as he

got off the bed to get rid of the rest of his clothes, then reaching for him as he came back, stretching himself out over her. 'I meant…'

'I know.' He caught her wrists once again and put them down on either side of her head as he eased his big, muscled body between her thighs. 'Time to stop talking now.'

And, before she could say another word, his mouth was on hers, hot and demanding, ravaging her mouth. She tried to kiss him back, but he gave her no quarter, conquering her so completely that she simply surrendered, letting him take whatever he wanted.

Then his hands were sliding beneath her, lifting her hips, and she felt him thrust into her, a long, deep slide that made her cry out in pleasure.

It was different from before. Then, she'd been on top of him, his hands on her hips gripping her so that, even though they had been joined, there had been a distance between them.

Now, there was no distance. She was surrounded by him, by his heat and his scent, by the rough sounds of his ragged breathing and the exquisite friction of him moving inside her. There was no pain now and no awkwardness or uncertainty. Only a growing intensity, a longing that gripped her as tightly as he did.

She put her hands on his powerful shoulders, feeling the flex and release of hard muscle, the strength in him a wild thrill she'd never imagined. And she hung on, wanting to get closer, even closer than they were already, because it wasn't enough.

'C-Cassius.' His name was both a hoarse prayer and a plea, though for what she had no idea.

But it was clear that he knew, because his mouth was on hers again, kissing her as he moved, driving her relentlessly towards the edge a second time.

Then everything began to fray around the edges, pleasure blooming inside her like the most intricate and elegant of equations, the solution to it so, so close. So very, very close…

It was him, wasn't it? *He* was the solution. *He* was the answer to every question, every problem, every difficulty she'd ever had. It was him.

It had always been him.

Inara wrapped her arms around his neck, desperate to hold onto him, unable to escape the feeling that, once this was over, she'd lose him. That this sexy, wicked man would slip away, turning once more into a king.

But nothing was going to stop the climax from happening and, when he slipped his hand between her thighs, stroking her gently, she could feel herself break, shattering like a fragile piece of glass thrown onto a tiled floor.

She sobbed as the pleasure overwhelmed her and she broke apart. She was only dimly aware of him letting go of the leash on himself, slamming into her hard, fast and out of rhythm, until she felt his teeth against her shoulder, a growl of pleasure escaping him as the climax came for him too.

For a while after that, time drifted and Inara let herself simply lie in his arms, enjoying having him so close, holding her, his body pressed the length of hers, his breath ghosting over her skin. She lay underneath him, safe and protected by his strength, and there was nowhere else she wanted to be.

Right now, he wasn't distant or chilly. He wasn't the King. He wasn't even wicked Prince Cassius, scourge of the bedrooms of Europe. He was just Cassius, her lover, another side of him that she'd newly discovered. Another part of him that she'd fallen in love with.

She let out a soft breath.

Perhaps this marriage would work. Perhaps it would be okay. During the day he might be a distant king, and she'd have to concentrate hard on learning how to be his queen. But all that would be bearable if she could have Cassius, her lover, at night.

If they had this, then surely she didn't need anything else?

Finally, he stirred, lifting his head and looking down at her, examining her critically. Then he smiled that devastating smile again, the one that set her heart racing and her pulse sky-rocketing.

'You said I could do anything to you, didn't you?' Desire burned in his gaze.

Inara swallowed, feeling that longing for him begin all over again. 'Yes.'

'Good.' Then he flipped her over onto her stomach and covered her with his body.

Cassius kept Inara up most of the night, sating his pleasure and hers in as many ways as he could think of which, considering the wide breadth of his experience, was quite a few. Eventually she fell into an exhausted sleep and he let her, though he didn't sleep himself.

He was content to hold her, aware of nothing but how good her warm, silky body felt against his, and how calming he found the soft, regular sound of her breathing. It was good, too, to think of nothing. To be nothing more in this bed than a man holding a woman.

But as dawn came he knew he couldn't afford to stay being a mere man, that he would have to be King again in a few short hours, and he couldn't prepare himself adequately for that while she was in his arms.

So he shifted without waking her, slipping from the

bed and pulling on his trousers, moving out of the bedroom and walking down the stone corridors to his study.

The first rays of morning light were shining through the windows, the sound of the sea wild outside.

It was his morning ritual to tend to his plants. It calmed his mind and settled him for the day ahead, allowing him to put aside his own petty concerns and feelings and to become the king he needed to be.

It usually worked.

But this morning he couldn't concentrate. His mind was too full of Inara and the memories of the night before. Of her skin beneath his hands and the delicate scent of her arousal. Of her cries and sobs of pleasure and the husky way she'd said his name. The way she had made good on her promise, letting him do whatever he wanted to her, and clearly loving every moment of it. There had been no fear in her, only absolute trust. It had shone in her eyes so brightly, it made something in his chest ache.

He didn't deserve it. He'd married her because it had made him feel good that she'd looked at him as if he was her saviour, not out of any real concern for her, and then, apart from a few visits, he'd forgotten about her. For years. Then he'd tried to get rid of her with a divorce, only reluctantly agreeing to stay married when circumstances had forced him to...

But that's you all over, isn't it? You only take responsibility when you're forced to.

Cassius gritted his teeth, trying to get his thoughts under control as he examined the small azalea he was in the process of sculpting.

He shouldn't be thinking about this. He should be thinking about the day ahead and the things he had to do, not his own personal failings—of which there were many, naturally, but he didn't let them get in the way of his job.

He'd dedicated the last three years of his life to *not* doing that.

But aren't you doing it again? Letting her get to you?

Cassius snipped off a small branch. No, a delay in settling his thoughts was *not* letting her get to him. Another half an hour and he'd be fine. He wouldn't think of her again for the rest of the day.

She needs more guidance. What are you going to do? Ignore her for another week? Sabotage her chances of being the kind of queen you wanted?

Without thinking, Cassius snipped off another branch, realising only at the last minute that it wasn't one he'd meant to cut. Muttering a filthy curse, he tried to haul his mind back to the task at hand and not let it get distracted by Inara, but then he heard the sound of the door opening then closing behind him.

He didn't turn. He knew who'd come in. He could smell her warm scent getting closer, making his body harden instantly.

'What are you doing in here?' Inara asked.

He wanted very much to drop his scissors, turn round and take her back to bed to replay some of his favourite memories from the night before, but it was morning. A new day. And in an hour or two his presence would be required and he would need to act like a king instead of a hormonal teenage boy. He'd have to explain his abrupt absence from the ball the night before, for a start.

'I'm preparing myself for the day,' he said, without looking around. 'Go back to bed, little one.'

Inara ignored him, coming closer, and then a small, warm hand rested lightly on the bare skin of his back.

'What kind of tree is that?' she asked curiously, peering at the azalea on the shelf in front of him. 'It's very pretty.'

Every thought went straight out of his head. All he could

think about was her hand on his skin and how it made him burn. How it made him want. As if all the desires he'd successfully managed to contain for years were in danger of bursting out.

She's put a crack in your control.

No, that wasn't true. He hadn't been at all controlled the night before, admittedly, but that had been purposeful. He'd consciously put being a king aside and let himself be a man for once.

He could put the man aside at any time. It wasn't a problem. Still, he shifted minutely, causing her hand to drop away. His attention was on the tree, but he could feel the surprise radiating from her. He told himself he didn't feel the warmth lingering on his skin from her casual touch.

A silence fell.

Cassius made another precise snip with the scissors.

'You're him again, aren't you?' Inara's voice was very quiet.

He examined the cut he'd made. 'Him? What do you mean?'

'You're the King again.'

'I'm always the King.' He ignored the thread of what sounded like disappointment in her voice. 'I don't stop being him.'

'But you never wanted to be. You told me your brother was welcome to the job. That you'd rather die than have it.'

He remembered that conversation, over a long and leisurely lunch at the townhouse she'd lived in before he'd ascended the throne. She'd asked him in her usual blunt, curious way about whether he was disappointed at being younger than his brother by a few minutes and whether he'd ever want to be King.

'Caspian is welcome to it. Personally, I'd rather die than have the job.'

A throwaway comment. Such a careless remark, when a year later...

It should have been you. You're the one who should have died. But you didn't. It was your brother who took your place, the way he always did.

Everything in him went tight and sharp and hot, and before he could stop himself he said, 'Yes, well, as it turned out it wasn't me who died. Caspian took that honour and I got the job anyway.'

He hadn't meant to sound so bitter and as soon as the words were out he wished he hadn't said them. They revealed too much. But it was too late and he knew it.

In the echoing silence he could feel her looking at him. He didn't look back, concentrating on the tree instead.

'Why did you take it, Cassius?'

He didn't want to talk about this, not when he had less than an hour before he had to be in his office. So he couldn't understand why he answered her. 'Because there was no one else.'

'But didn't you have a cousin somewhere? Couldn't she have taken the throne?'

This had to stop.

He dropped the scissors and turned.

Inara was standing right next to him, her silvery hair loose down her back, and she was wearing his shirt from the night before. It was far too big for her, the sleeves rolled up hugely, the hem almost reaching her knees.

It should have looked ridiculous. Instead, she was so indescribably beautiful it made his chest hurt and that primitive, possessive thing inside him growl with satisfaction.

She wore his shirt and she smelled like him.

Yours.

Oh, yes, she was. Which made this battle with himself and his desires pointless, an old pattern of behaviour he didn't need, not now. She was his wife; she was living with him; she'd be in his bed every night. Which meant that, while during the day he had to be the King, at night he didn't. He could be himself. And it wasn't losing self-control. It was only sex, only relaxing after a hard day's work. After all, every other person on the planet did it; why couldn't a king?

'No,' he said. 'My cousin couldn't take the throne because it was my responsibility.' He put the scissors back on the shelf. 'A throne isn't like any other job, Inara. It's a duty. You can't just decide not to do it because it's too hard or you don't like the work. It's not about *you* at all. It's about the role, the responsibility you have to your subjects.'

Her brow wrinkled. She had her glasses on again and her luminous grey eyes seemed less red. Clearly the contacts she'd been wearing had irritated her eyes. He made a mental note to let the stylist know that the Queen preferred glasses. He should never have made her wear contacts.

'But Aveiras didn't want you,' she pointed out bluntly. 'You could have passed it on to someone else and they would have been fine with it.'

A formless anger simmered inside him, an anger he hadn't been aware of before, and yet it tasted familiar. As if it had been there all this time.

'Careful,' he said. 'Be very careful what you say.'

'Why?' She looked stubborn, determination glittering in her eyes. 'Does no one ever talk to you about these things? Does no one ever question you?'

'No, they don't.' The anger twined with the embers of his desire, creating something hotter, more demanding. 'I'm the King.'

'Actually,' Inara said, 'I'm beginning to wonder if you're not so much a king as a world-class martyr.'

Something jolted hard inside him, as if she'd struck him, and the simmering anger and desire began to boil over.

Cassius reached for her, pulling her hard up against him. 'Don't push it, Inara,' he growled. 'I'm not the Prince any more. You can't—'

'Well, you should be.' She stared at him as if he was no threat to her whatsoever. As if his anger was nothing. As if he was just a normal man she was arguing with and not the leader of an entire nation. 'At least that prince was honest with himself. He didn't nail himself to the cross of duty like you're doing right now.'

'Of course he didn't,' Cassius ground out before he could stop himself. 'Because that prince hadn't yet killed his brother.'

Inara's pretty mouth opened in a soft O of surprise, her eyes going wide. Her hands were on his chest, her palms like hot coals on his bare skin. 'What? What do you mean, he hadn't killed his brother?'

Let her go. Walk away.

He should. But the anger needed to do that had gone, leaving in its place only a burning desire to tell someone. He'd kept it a secret for so long, a heavy weight he'd been dragging around for years, and he was tired of it. So very tired. And he had no one else to tell. A king didn't have friends or confidantes; a king had no one but himself and his own secrets. But his secrets were eating him alive.

So who better to tell than the person who knew him better than anyone else? The person he'd always been honest with, always himself?

'Caspian wasn't supposed to be on the helicopter that day,' he said roughly. 'I was. But I made him swap places with me because I had a hangover and I didn't want to go.'

Shock rippled over Inara's lovely face. 'Oh, Cassius.'

He didn't know what kind of response he wanted

from her, but it wasn't the pity he heard in her voice. She shouldn't pity him. She should be horrified. Not only because of how he'd sent his brother to his death, but his parents as well.

He let her go. Suddenly, he didn't want her warmth near him, touching him. Reminding him of all the things he couldn't allow himself to have. Because he didn't deserve it, not any of it.

'The trip to the mountains that day was my fault too.' He stripped the emotion completely from his voice so all that was left was the truth. 'My father was displeased with my behaviour and wanted me to see the tombs of the de Leon kings so I was aware of the legacy I was supposed to uphold. I hated all the rules I was supposed to obey. All the limitations on what I could say, on what I could do. I wasn't the heir so I didn't see why I should have to follow them.'

Inara opened her mouth, but he held up a hand, silencing her. She might as well know everything now.

'My father told me I had to come on the trip, that I wasn't allowed to say no. But I was angry with him, so I made Caspian go in my stead. My brother wouldn't have been on that helicopter if it hadn't been for me. In fact, there would have been no trip at all if it hadn't been for me and my terrible behaviour. My entire family would still be alive.'

Her mouth had gone so soft, her eyes liquid. 'Cassius...'

'So you can call me a martyr all you like,' he went on, as if she hadn't spoken. 'But my father and my brother left me a legacy, and I will continue that legacy, to the best of my ability, for as long as I can. I will be the king my brother never got a chance to be and I will continue to do that until the day I die. It will be my memorial to them.'

Her expression twisted and she reached out a hand to

him, but he was done. He'd got rid of his secret, he'd told her, and now that was over he had a job to do.

'I will see you tonight, little one.' He found a thread of his usual calm and held on tightly to it. 'In the meantime, I have a job to do.'

And, ignoring her hand, he turned on his heel and went out.

CHAPTER NINE

INARA SAT IN one of the formal sitting rooms in the palace, her head aching. One of the palace historians had been giving her a lecture on the history of the de Leon royal family for the past couple of hours but she had a horrible feeling that, no matter how hard she tried, she was going to remember precisely none of it.

Not that she hadn't tried. She really had because, after Cassius had told her about his family and the legacy he was trying to carry on, she'd decided she had to make this work. Because, like it or not, she was part of that legacy. And she couldn't let her part be a chaotic queen smashing glasses, forgetting names and dashing out of the palace when things went wrong.

That morning, when she'd found him in his study, she'd automatically treated him the way she had when he'd used to visit her, putting a casual hand on his back and wanting to know what he was doing. But he'd stiffened and then gone distant, shrugging her hand away. Becoming the King.

Perhaps she shouldn't have got angry, but the way he'd shrugged off her touch, after being so hungry for it the night before, had hurt. He was a different man when he was the King, and she didn't like it. And, what was more, she was tired of it.

She shouldn't have called him a martyr, though; that had been far too blunt. Especially given what he'd told her about his brother, about his parents. About how he was to blame for it. She'd wanted to know more, to talk to him about it, but he'd turned and walked out before she could.

She'd thought he might say more that night, when she'd been summoned to his rooms, but conversation clearly had not been on his mind. She'd stepped into his bedroom to find him pacing before the fire and she'd barely greeted him before he'd crossed the room, taken her in his arms and then taken her to bed.

And he'd kept her there all night.

That had set the pattern for the past week. Her days were full of 'queen training', as she liked to think of it, while her nights were full of him and 'wife training'. The wife training she liked. She took to those lessons enthusiastically, and she never forgot them either, because learning how to please him pleased her too.

But he didn't talk more about his family or about himself and, even though he'd check in with her during whatever lesson she was having at the time, the only conversation they had was about how she was getting on and whether she was finding it difficult. He was always pleasant and calm and, though he was less condescending, he was no less distant.

That part she didn't like. That part she wanted to change. It wasn't the King she wanted, it was the man he was when he was with her in the depths of the night, warm and vital and hungry. Except she didn't know how to reach that man.

Inara bent over her notepad, hoping the historian wouldn't see as she closed her eyes and rubbed at her temples, trying to get rid of the headache.

'The Queen is tired,' a deep voice said. 'I think that's enough for one day.'

Inara looked up sharply.

Cassius stood in the doorway, dressed in an immaculate dark suit, white shirt and a tie the same smoky gold as his eyes. He glanced briefly at her, his expression impenetrable, then strode over to the historian and had a brief murmured conversation before the man nodded and went out, leaving Inara and Cassius alone.

'I'm all right,' Inara said, annoyed by her headache and the peremptory way Cassius had dismissed the man. 'I was just tired.'

Cassius came over to the uncomfortable couch she was sitting on, giving her a critical once-over. 'You're not all right. You're wearing those contacts again and I can see the circles under your eyes.'

'And who's fault is that?' she said crossly. 'And as for the contacts—'

'They're not needed,' he finished for her, still infuriatingly calm. 'I told you that you could wear your glasses. Why aren't you?'

'I was trying to get used to the contacts.' She rubbed at her eyes. 'Give me a few days and it'll get better.'

'Inara.'

'What?' She glared at him.

He stared back, his gaze very direct. 'I've been talking with people and they all say the same thing. That you have difficulty concentrating, that you don't retain the information you're given and that you're finding it difficult.'

Anger wound through her, along with a certain defensiveness. She'd hoped to have improved since last week, especially as she was now trying even harder, and him finding out that she hadn't was galling.

'I'm trying,' she said flatly. 'But all this protocol and

etiquette and other royal stuff…' She stared down at the notepad on which she'd written no notes whatsoever, flashing back to the endless social etiquette drills her mother had put her through. 'Or maybe it's just me.'

There was a moment's silence and then, unexpectedly, Cassius said, 'It's not just you.'

She glanced up at him, surprised. 'Oh?'

'It was…difficult for me too.'

His expression gave nothing away, and yet she heard something almost reluctant in his voice, as if he hadn't meant to say it.

Interesting. That was not what she'd thought he'd say. A memory came back to her, of him in his study and how he'd mentioned that he'd hated all the rules and restrictions placed on him. Was that part of it?

'Why?' she asked, curious now. 'I'd have thought it would have been easy for you, when you were brought up with all of this.'

'Just because I was brought up with it, doesn't mean it was easy.' He sat down beside her, sadly not close enough to touch; during the day it was obvious he preferred some separation between them, which she found annoying, yet she wasn't quite brave enough to push it. Not yet.

'My father always insisted on stillness and absolute attention,' he went on. 'He said it was rude to fidget and to look bored, and that one of the first rules of being a good ruler was to be patient and attentive to whomever was speaking.'

Cassius let out a breath. 'But I could never sit still or concentrate, and I found all the protocol and royal etiquette we had to learn boring. Caspian never had a problem with it, only me.' He glanced at her, an unexpected glint in his eyes. 'I used to escape into the gardens to hide with the head gardener. He'd tell me all about the plants he was putting in the ground, and how they grew and what they needed, and I found that far more interesting.'

Inara didn't want to move. She didn't even want to breathe. He wasn't the King now. She could tell. He was Cassius, sitting beside her, talking to her the way he used to. She wasn't sure what had prompted the change, but one thing she did know: she wanted to keep him like this for as long as possible.

'So is that why you have all those plants in your study?' She kept the question neutral. 'You said they helped your mind settle.'

'Yes, they do. I still remember telling my father that I wanted to be a gardener, not a prince.' There was a note of dry humour in his voice. 'He wasn't impressed.'

Inara smiled, thinking of Cassius as a little boy, digging earnestly in the dirt. 'I'd imagine not.'

'You need something similar, I think.' There was a shrewd look in his eyes. 'And you already have it, don't you? Numbers are your escape.'

A little jolt went through her. She hadn't expected him to know what mathematics meant to her, let alone to have thought about it. They'd discussed it, of course, but she just hadn't expected him to remember.

'Yes,' she said, her cheeks heating with a ridiculous blush. 'I suppose they are. Numbers feel easier than dealing with people.'

'Easier than etiquette and protocol, yes?'

She nodded. 'And talking to people and all that…social stuff.'

'Yes, I remember. You found that difficult.'

A warm feeling blossomed in her heart. He'd remembered their conversations, when she'd chattered artlessly about how painful her upbringing had been.

'It still is, to be honest.' Inara picked up her pen and

fiddled with it. 'And Mama didn't help. She watched everything I did and always had a criticism. It was always, "Stand up straight, Inara. Smile. Be more graceful. If you can't be beautiful, then for God's sake at least be interesting."' She stopped, her throat tight and, though she could feel Cassius's gaze on her, she didn't want to look at him. She couldn't bear the thought of him measuring her against the same impossible standard her mother had once used.

Firstly, would he really do that? And secondly, do you care?

Perhaps he wouldn't. His standards for himself were high, but he didn't put those onto other people. And, as for whether she cared or not, sadly, she did.

Be brave. You're stronger than that.

It was true. She brought a king to his knees every night. Surely she could look that same king in the eye during the day, unafraid of his judgment?

Inara lifted her chin and looked at him. 'I couldn't do any of those things. I couldn't stand up straight or smile or be graceful. I couldn't be beautiful, and I could certainly never be interesting. That's why they lost patience with me. That's why they gave me to Stefano Castelli.'

Cassius's gaze was steady and direct, a familiar heat burning in it. 'If you're expecting me to agree with your mother's opinions, then you're going to be disappointed,' he said levelly. 'Because I'm glad you couldn't do all those things. I'm glad you failed. And I'm glad that you were given to Stefano Castelli, because otherwise you wouldn't have come to my limo that night. And you wouldn't now be my wife.'

The warmth in her chest blossomed further.

'Not that I would call any of that a failure,' he went on. 'I've always thought you were interesting, and indeed beautiful, though I shouldn't have thought that when you were sixteen.' He paused, holding her gaze. 'You're even more beautiful now.'

Her eyes prickled, the warmth flowing through her. How strange that being told such lovely things should make her feel like crying.

She wanted to say something—maybe that he was wrong, that only at night in his arms she felt it might be true—but her voice had somehow become stuck in her throat.

Not that she needed to speak, because he continued, 'I've been going about this wrong. I've been forcing you into all the same things as your mother.'

'You're not forcing me,' she managed thickly. 'I'm doing all of this because I want to.'

'Why?'

It was on the tip of her tongue to tell him that he hadn't exactly given her a choice, but then that wasn't quite true, was it? She could have said no. She wasn't sixteen any more, with all her choices made by her parents. She was a grown woman and her choices were her own, and being here in this palace, with him, was a choice she'd made.

Inara swallowed and gave him the truth. 'Why do you think? Because it's important to you, and what's important to you is important to me.'

He said nothing. He just stared at her, his expression utterly impenetrable.

'You said your reign was your memorial to your family, your legacy,' Inara went on, needing to say it. 'And I don't want to be the weak link in that legacy. I want you to have a queen you can be proud of, because let's face it... You didn't exactly choose me. You got stuck with me.'

Some intense emotion flickered over his face, but it was gone before she could name it. He looked away, then abruptly pushed himself off the couch and walked over to one of the long windows that looked out over the formal gardens. He stood there tensely a moment, then said, 'That's true. I didn't choose you. But I wouldn't say I was "stuck" with you.' He turned around, his gaze suddenly fierce. 'You're not a weak link either. I'm already proud of you.'

The warmth in her chest felt like the first touch of sun after a long, cold winter.

'But I haven't done anything except forget people's names, smash glasses and run away.'

'You've done something.' His gaze intensified. 'You're here. You did your best to learn and, even when it doesn't quite work, you're still here and you're still trying. That's tenacity, Inara. And resilience and courage. And queens need all of those things.'

The sun rose higher inside her, warming her straight through, thawing something that had been frozen in the centre of her soul.

He meant it. He *was* proud of what she was doing.

She opened her mouth to thank him, but then he said suddenly, 'This protocol and etiquette you're learning is nonsense. And we're wasting your talents. Numbers are your strength and Aveiras can benefit from it.' He gave her a narrow look then strode back over to the couch again. 'I should be introducing you to our finance minister and you and he can talk economics.'

Inara hadn't done much with economics but it couldn't be worse than what she was doing now. 'I thought you needed someone to do all the social engagements and be gracious and talk to people.'

'Yes, but I can do that. The people stuff is my strength.' He gave her a sudden brief smile, like a shaft of sunlight glinting through cloud. 'This is a partnership. We share the load.'

Her heart throbbed in her chest and impulsively she reached out to him. 'You really mean that?'

He glanced down at her hand then took it in his, threading his fingers through hers. Warmth travelled up her arm and into her heart, making a home for itself. 'Yes, I mean that.' He looked at her. 'You have many skills, Inara. We were just focusing on the wrong ones.'

Her heart warmed. Everything inside her warmed.

'Maybe that's what happened with you too,' she said unthinkingly. 'Your father should have concentrated on the things you did well, not the things you didn't.'

He stilled, like a man carved from stone. 'And what things do I do well?' The words were so determinedly neutral that she could tell this was important to him. Strange. She hadn't thought her opinion would matter too much to him.

'Well, you *are* good with people. And you're very protective. You notice things. You're observant. And you're very patient. You care about your subjects and your country, all the people you're responsible for. Their well-being matters to you.' She took a breath and smiled. 'You have serious green fingers. You're also extremely good at kissing—which not many people know about you, I don't think. Or at least, they'd better not.' Another pause. 'You also have a wicked sense of humour and when you smile the whole world stops.'

He stared at her, and it seemed as if he might say something, but he didn't.

Instead, after a moment, he gently removed his fingers from hers and walked away without a word. Leaving Inara sitting there with the warmth of his touch lingering on her skin, while a cold thread wound through the warmth in her heart.

Cassius dealt with a few last pressing issues then turned his attention to the grand ball he was in the process of organising in order to formally introduce and welcome Inara as Queen. This one was to be even more formal than the one he'd held a couple of weeks earlier, as this one would not only include heads of state from other countries, but an appearance on the balcony of the palace where the people could welcome her.

The balcony appearance was a grand tradition in Aveiras; it had to be done and possibly was both the easiest and the hardest of the formal occasions. Easy because it required nothing but standing there and waving, hard because the Aveiran people weren't shy when it came to voicing their displeasure if they didn't like something.

And Cassius wanted them to like Inara. He wanted them to welcome her. She wasn't the kind of queen his mother had been. She was…different. But over the past week he'd begun to think that different might be a good thing. Since he'd stopped the etiquette and protocol lessons, and all the other nonsense, replacing it instead with meetings with his finance ministry and the various economic branches of his parliament, she'd blossomed.

Money and numbers bored him to tears, but not her. She'd taken to it like a duck to water, involving herself in all aspects of Aveiras's economy, using her clear, logical brain to work on some of the country's thorny financial difficulties, and then pointing out several new ways they could fill the treasury. She had a gift not only for numbers, but for money and the financial markets, which would benefit Aveiras considerably.

He'd continued to oversee her progress, and for the past week the only feedback he'd had about her was glowing praise of what a brilliant thinker she was, how perceptive she was when it came to economics and how she had the potential to revolutionise the country's fiscal policy.

His finance ministers loved her, and he knew he shouldn't take pride in seeing her walk by him, sometimes deep in conversation with a small group of ministers and advisors, but he did. Especially when it was clear her stylists hadn't caught her in time and she was dressed in one of her floaty dresses with her hair loose over her shoulders.

Sometimes he'd even stand in the corridor, waiting to see if she'd notice him as she swept by, but most of the time she didn't. And neither did his ministers. It amused him that they'd be so deep in conversation they didn't even notice their king. However, he was less than amused when Inara didn't notice him. Which was new. Most of the time he found the constant attention from people tiring, but apparently that didn't extend to her.

Cassius frowned as he went over the plans for the ball, not seeing them as his mind drifted once more to his wife. His pretty little fairy of a wife who couldn't care less about clothes or balls or appearances, who could balance a budget in seconds and who was as hungry for him as he was for her when she came to him every night.

He'd told her a week ago, when he'd found her red-eyed and miserable in one of the formal sitting rooms, that they were a match, and even though he hadn't thought so initially, he was beginning to see the truth of that now.

When he'd looked at her that day, the feedback about her from his consultants filling his head, he'd seen himself all those years ago trying to sit through endless lessons about things that hadn't interested him, cudgelling his reluctant brain into retaining dates and names and arcane, pointless protocol. Trying and always failing.

At the time he'd thought there was something wrong with him, as he'd never had any issues concentrating or remembering things when it came to scientific plant names and what specific conditions each plant needed to grow. But there hadn't been anything wrong with him.

Because look at him now, doing everything his father

had, everything Caspian had, and doing it successfully. He'd overcome his failings, his flaws, but he wouldn't put Inara through the same mill by insisting. Because, if there was one thing he'd learned during the last three years, it was that people performed better when you focused on and utilised their strengths, rather than fixing their failings. If people were happy and enjoying themselves, then the resulting confidence boost tended to minimise those failings anyway.

And you? What about you?

He was irrelevant. He was the King and his enjoyment, his happiness, didn't matter.

Not that you deserve any.

Cassius abruptly pushed away the plans he'd been staring at. This train of thought was pointless. Perhaps some time in the garden was needed to settle himself. He hadn't yet told Inara about the ball, which he should have done, but she'd seemed happy and much more settled recently and he didn't want to upset her.

Since when have her feelings become important to you? If yours aren't relevant, then hers aren't either.

Cassius shoved his chair back and got to his feet, trying to ignore that thought. Because it was wrong. Of course her feelings mattered, as did everyone's. The King's didn't because he was the leader, the figurehead. He was the example everyone looked to, the example everyone followed. You couldn't have feelings as a king. You couldn't be a person, not in the same way as everyone else. Inara had accused him of being a martyr, but she was wrong. He hadn't nailed himself to a cross when he'd taken his crown. He'd taken it willingly. And he was at peace with his role.

So at peace you walked out of a ball you should have remained at to follow a woman because you were angry. And then you took her to bed because you wanted her.

And then you stopped important, vital protocol lessons to make her happy. And now you can't concentrate on the ball you're supposed to be organising because all you can think about is her...

Cassius gritted his teeth as he strode down the echoing marble hallways of the palace, not wanting to acknowledge the truth of all of that, yet not able to ignore it either. Because it *was* true. There had been minimal fallout from the ball, but only because of the stellar work of his PR team.

And, with another formal ball coming up, halting Inara's protocol lessons had possibly been a mistake. He should insist she continue with them. He should get stricter with her, not relax the rules. Necessity had finally made all his father's lessons stick; perhaps he should try the same tactics with her.

No, this isn't about her. It's about you. You taking her to bed every night. You indulging your own appetites, your weaknesses, your flaws...

Tension gripped him as he approached his private apartments, giving a curt nod to his guards as they opened the doors for him and he stepped through. He'd thought he could keep what happened at night in his bed separate from his duties during the day, that he could keep the man separate from the King, but it was becoming very clear that was impossible. Yet he'd already tried denying himself, and that hadn't worked, so what else could he do?

Perhaps it was his need to hold her after they'd made love that was the issue. His need to drown in her scent and listen to the sound of her breathing. The strange desperation he had to get closer, even when he knew what he should do was keep his distance. He could allow himself a physical release, but anything more, anything emotional, was...wrong.

It was his emotions that had led him astray, after all,

his frustration as child and then his impatience with the restrictions imposed on him as a young man. His anger at his father's continual disapproval.

Perhaps he needed to limit Inara's visits. Perhaps he needed to turn her away or not send for her. At least for a little while, or maybe just not every night, enough to remind himself that his own desires were not paramount. And maybe that would help him be stricter with her during the day. He couldn't compromise the legacy he was trying to build. Not again.

He came to the door of his study, noting with displeasure that it was open, which meant that one of the cleaning staff hadn't closed it properly. Annoying. He kept the room at a specific temperature optimal for his plants, as several didn't like the cool of the rest of the palace, which meant he preferred to keep the doors closed.

Irritated, he made a mental note to remind staff to always close the door, then he stepped inside himself, closing it firmly behind him.

Only to discover that the room wasn't empty.

Inara sat in one of the blue velvet arm chairs. She had a stack of papers on her knees, some of them overflowing onto the floor, and various pens scattered on the cushions next to her. On a small side table beside the arm chair stood three teacups, all with different liquids in them; the small orchid he kept there had been shoved unceremoniously to one side.

Today she wore a pencil skirt and a plain white blouse, but the pencil skirt was creased, the blouse crumpled and coming unbuttoned. Her hair was in what had probably once been a neat chignon, but was now half-coming down, silvery wisps haloing her face and one long lock draping over her shoulder. A pair of high-heeled pumps was scattered on the carpet in front of the arm chair, as if she'd just kicked them off and left them where they lay.

She should have looked like a disaster, the very antithesis of a queen, and yet... All he could think about was what one of his financial team had told him the day before, raving about how approachable the Queen was, how accessible. Making it obvious that Cassius's parents suffered in comparison.

It had shocked him. His father had always been held up as the ideal, and Caspian had followed in his footsteps. But it could never be said that Cassius's father had been either accessible or approachable. *Be respectful*, his father had always said, *but maintain your distance.* Allowing people to get too familiar undermined your authority, and above all a king had to maintain his authority.

People had respected his father, yet he hadn't been an easy man to get to know. He had been reserved, never demonstrative. He had been gracious and perfectly pleasant to his subjects, but distant, remaining a cipher, an enigma, even to his sons.

There was nothing enigmatic about Inara. She sat in his study, in his armchair, with her shoes off, papers everywhere, half-drunk cups of tea crowding out his plant, her hair coming down. And yet... She wasn't distant. She wasn't chilly. She was approachable. Accessible.

She was human.

His heart clenched tightly for no apparent reason. And then she looked up from her papers, seeing him, her beautiful mouth curving in a smile like the sun rising. And the tightness in his heart constricted further, his whole body tensing in a kind of shock. As if her smile was something that hurt him.

'Oh, hi,' she said. 'I hope you don't mind. I couldn't concentrate in the Queen's office, so I thought I'd come in here. It's such a relaxing space...' She trailed off. Whatever expression was on his face, it couldn't be anything good, as her smile faded. 'I'm sorry,' she went on quickly. 'I'll go. It was probably a bit forward of me to—'

'Stay.' His voice came out far rougher than he'd intended. 'I'll come back later.'

But Inara's brow creased. 'I don't want to intrude on your space. I'll stay very quiet, I promise. I always do when I'm working.'

Part of him wanted to leave, to put some distance between her and the tight feeling in his chest, but he also didn't want to let that feeling win.

'All right,' he allowed. 'But stay quiet.'

She nodded, giving him another quick smile then returning her attention to her stack of papers.

Cassius moved over to begin his inventory of the bonsai and the other plants. And it was with some surprise that he found himself not quite forgetting she was there, but finding her presence...restful. It was strange, given her general level of untidiness, but she was silent while she worked, the only sound the faint rustling of paper and the scratching of her pen.

A companionable silence settled over the room and some time passed...he wasn't sure how long. The tight feeling in his chest had faded, the snide voice in his head quietening. He watered the last of his plants and then turned, moving over to the arm chair opposite hers and sitting in it.

She didn't look up, still furiously writing something. Not wanting to interrupt, he relaxed, letting the silence and peace of the room seep into him. After a moment, Inara looked up from her work and gave him another of those heartbreakingly beautiful smiles.

'You like working with a pen and paper?' he asked, idly curious. 'Not a computer?'

'No. Writing it down myself helps me feel more…connected to whatever problem I'm working on. Which probably sounds weird.'

'No weirder than a king who likes pottering with his houseplants.'

She laughed, the sound delighting him, as it had been a long time since he'd made a woman laugh.

'It's clearly good for you, though.' She tilted her head, giving him a speculative look. Then she put aside her papers and pen, got out of her chair and came over to him.

He stayed where he was, curious to see what she intended. Probably a mistake, given his earlier thoughts on the subject, but he found he couldn't bring himself to move.

He liked her being here. He liked being in the same room, both of them doing separate things, yet together. It made him realise that he hadn't had the company of another person in quite this way for three years… No, longer. In fact, had he ever had this quiet, companionable feeling with another person? Even back when he'd been a prince, the company he'd kept had been of the loud, drunken variety, or soft, welcoming and female. And working quietly had been the last thing on his mind.

Inara reached for his tie and loosened it.

'What are you doing, little one?'

'Helping you relax.' She pulled the tie away from his neck, bending over him to undo the buttons on his shirt.

He should stop her, he really should, because her scent was surrounding him, along with the warmth of her body, and it made him think of the previous night when he'd had her beneath him, panting in his ear…

'I'm not sure taking my tie off will help me relax.' He looked up at her. 'In fact, I can safely say that relaxed is the last thing I feel with your hands on me.'

She wrinkled her nose, going the most adorable shade

of pink as she fussed with his buttons. 'I'm not talking about *that*. You're always so…uptight. You could stand to be a little…looser.'

He wanted to pull her down into his lap, cover that gorgeous mouth with his own, and it was difficult to remember why that was a bad idea. Certainly, his brain had told him something of the sort earlier, but with her bending over him, so pretty and warm and human, he couldn't seem to remember why that was such a bad idea. He couldn't seem to remember why any of the things he'd been telling himself about following his father's example and leaving a legacy was such a good thing. Not when she was here.

You know it's not about leaving a legacy. Or even following an example. You're punishing yourself, because it's what you deserve.

Inara's fingers were warm at his throat, brushing his skin as she pulled open the buttons of his shirt, but he felt suddenly cold, as if all the blood in his veins were icing over. He'd reached up to brush her hands away before he could stop himself.

Instantly Inara straightened, her expressive features tightening. 'I'm sorry, I didn't mean…'

'It's fine.' He pushed himself out of the chair, all his good feelings draining away.

No, this had been a mistake. He should be back in his office, preparing for this ball, not here in his study, indulging himself.

Indulging himself. That had always been his problem.

'It's not fine,' Inara said. 'What did I do?' She was standing in front of him, blocking his path to the door, her grey eyes full of concern.

'Nothing,' he said curtly. 'Move, please, Inara. I have to get back to work.'

Something flickered in her gaze, that spark of challenge, the sign of a will that was becoming more and more formidable.

'I did do something.' She stayed exactly where she was. 'You were fine until I undid your tie.'

'Because it reminded me that now isn't the time to relax,' he snapped. 'It's the middle of the day and I should—'

'If it was only that, you wouldn't be so angry. And you're angry, Cassius, I can see it in your eyes.'

He took a breath, fighting down the heat gathering inside him. 'It's nothing you did,' he forced out calmly. 'Please, Inara, I have to—'

'Why?' There was something fierce in her gaze now, a silver flame, burning brightly. 'You're angry at something. Is it me? Because this is the second time you've walked away from me without a word.'

He tried to find the calmness inside him, the patience he needed to control his emotions.

'I'm not angry,' he said, knowing even as he said it that it was a lie. Because he could feel that heat inside him growing ever hotter, burning more furiously, and all the denying in the world wasn't going to make it go away.

Inara's mouth softened, the crease between her brows deepening. 'You'd forgotten, hadn't you? You'd forgotten for a moment that you were a king and something made you remember.'

She was right. He wasn't sure how she knew, how she could see that in him, but it was true.

Before he could say a word, she stepped forward, raising a hand to his cheek, her palm warm against his skin. 'It's okay, Cassius. You can have a few moments of forgetfulness. Surely that's allowed?'

His hand came up before he could stop it, circling her wrist and pulling that comforting palm away. 'No,' he said woodenly. 'It isn't allowed. I can't forget, Inara. I can't ever forget. Self-indulgence and selfishness got my family killed and it will taint my reign if I let it. Remembering what happened and who I was is the only way I can make sure that my father's legacy remains intact.'

'I understand why that's important to you. But your father is gone... And so is your brother. *You* are the King. So shouldn't your reign be *your* legacy rather than theirs?'

Something echoed inside him, like a bell tolling, but he ignored it, the flames of his deep, formless anger burning too high.

'Yes, why not?' He released her wrist, bitterness tingeing the words. 'A legacy of parties and drunkenness and sex. Of a petty prince indulging his own petulant resentment. A legacy of selfishness. Yes, that's exactly what Aveiras needs, a king who puts his own emotions before the needs of his subjects.'

She stared at him as if he were a stranger. 'Is that really how you see yourself? How you saw yourself back then?'

'It's not how I see myself,' he spat. 'It's how I *was*.'

Her chin came up, the silver flame flickering in her eyes, as if she was preparing to challenge him. 'No, that's *not* what you were. What you were was a man who helped a lost and desperate teenager. Who protected her. Who visited her and showed an interest in her that no one ever had. A man who discussed things with her, laughed with her, made her feel good about herself for the first time in her life. A man who, when his family died, stepped up and took responsibility even though he didn't need to.'

The ferocity in her gaze gripped him, held him still. 'That's the kind of man you were, Cassius. Yes, you had failings, didn't we all? But punishing yourself for yours isn't going to give you the legacy you're trying to build. It'll only end up tearing you apart.'

Her words felt like arrows, striking him in unprotected parts of his body, causing pain wherever they landed.

'You're wrong.' His voice was finally stripped of all emotion. 'I was never that man. That man was a lie.'

Her gaze flickered then, as if the flame in it had finally burned out. 'Fine,' she said. 'Tell me I'm wrong. Tell me I was too young, too innocent. That I didn't know my own feelings. But nothing will change the way I saw you then, Cassius, and nothing is going to change the way I feel now. You're still that man underneath. I know you are. And, whether you like it or not, that man was a good person.'

She took a little breath. 'I…loved that man.'

It felt as though she'd struck him with a punch direct to the gut, stealing all his air.

'What?' His voice echoed strangely in his head.

She just looked at him, the truth laid bare in her face, in her eyes. A truth that had probably been there all this time. He'd just never seen it.

You never wanted to see it, either.

She stared at him a second longer, then lifted her hand once more and touched his cheek briefly.

Then she turned and, not stopping even to grab her shoes, went out of the room. This time leaving him to be the one who was alone.

CHAPTER TEN

INARA FOUND IT difficult to work the rest of the day. It was even harder when Cassius didn't send for her that night, leaving her to pace about the Queen's cold and echoing apartments by herself.

It wasn't any mystery why he didn't send for her, though. She'd confronted him, pushed him. Then she'd thrown that confession at him and he'd looked…stunned. As if she'd slapped him or hit him over the head.

Perhaps she shouldn't have said it. Then again, she didn't regret telling him, because she hadn't been able to stand the self-loathing in his voice. He hated the prince he'd once been and she could understand it. He believed he'd sent his entire family to their deaths, and it was obvious he was trying to put as much distance between himself and that person as he could. She understood. She really did.

But she'd fallen in love with that man and she loved him still. And she hated the way he viewed himself. She didn't see someone who'd killed his family. She saw a warm, empathetic prince who'd protected her, talked to her, been interested in her. Who'd made her feel good about herself for the first time in her life.

Yes, he had his failings. He was angry, and even back then she'd been able to see that anger. It had been evident in the edge to his voice whenever he spoke about his father, and it had been clear that he was unhappy. She'd often wished she knew why, but she hadn't been brave enough to ask, and he'd never said.

But she thought she knew now. It had something to do with what he'd told her that day in the sitting room, about how he'd never been able to sit through those lessons in royal etiquette. How he'd had to escape into the gardens and how his parents had been so disapproving of him.

She ached for that little boy. She wanted to gather him into her arms and hold him, tell him it was okay to be the way he was. That he had his strengths, and they were just different from his brother's and his father's, just as hers were different. That he was just as worthy, just as admirable, as they were.

But she suspected the helicopter crash had only turned the scratches his family had inflicted into mortal wounds.

He couldn't accept himself as he was, and she knew deep in her heart that if he continued trying to be the king his father had wanted, the king his brother should have been, then it would eventually tear him apart. And as his queen she'd have to stand by and watch him disintegrate, unable to do anything for him. Unable to help.

She *hated* the thought of it.

Days went by and the only communication she had from him was notification of the formal ball that would take place to introduce her to the nation. She was in a meeting with one of her favourite financial ministers when she heard, and for a second she just looked at the note that had been passed to her, her heart beating very fast.

But not because she was afraid, though a couple of weeks ago this would have been her worst nightmare. Now, it gave her an idea. She kept that idea in her head the whole day, letting it sit there, shining brightly, and only once she was alone in the Queen's apartments did she examine it closely from all angles.

If she wanted to save her king, there was only one thing she could do. She had to show him there was a different way. A better way. That he didn't need to base his entire life on examples that trapped him, that hurt him, that denied who he was deep down. That instead he should be true to himself, trust that he could be the king he was meant to be, not the king he thought he *should* be.

It might not work, but it was all she could think of. Especially given his tendency to distance her whenever she got too close. That last time she'd been the one to walk away, but only because she'd known that if she stayed the rest of what was in her heart would come tumbling out. How it wasn't only the Prince she cared about, but the King as well. They were both part of the man. And it was the man she loved, every difficult, sharp and complicated part of him.

But she couldn't tell him that. He'd only distance her even more.

He stayed away the entire week, closing himself off, and she let him. She didn't want to give away any part of what she intended for the upcoming ball, because she was certain that if he knew he'd try and stop her.

More lessons in protocol appeared on her schedule, and this time at the King's insistence. She didn't protest. She sat through them, giving all the appearance of listening avidly while her mind took note of all the things she *wasn't* going to do.

Because he was wrong. And his father had been wrong too. It wasn't protocol and etiquette that made a good king, it was connecting with people. And that wasn't something she'd thought of two weeks ago and, even though he didn't realise it, it was Cassius who'd showed her that.

He'd told her that Aveiras should use her strengths and,

since being involved with Aveiras's finances, which she'd discovered she loved, she'd realised how powerful that was. That it wasn't people as a whole she had difficulty interacting with—she had no problem talking to the ministers and staff in the finance ministry—just some people.

And that was okay. Not remembering names was okay. It was the connection that mattered, being interested in someone and demonstrating that. She still needed practice in that area, but for Cassius it was instinctive.

If only he could see that.

The week passed far too quickly.

She made no effort to contact him. Sometimes she heard his deep voice echoing in the cold halls of the palace and had to stop herself from running after him. That would undermine the point she wanted to make, so she didn't. Instead, she made sure every report the etiquette people took back to him was glowing—that the Queen was making progress and they were happy with her efforts.

A schedule of events, seating plans, names and potted histories of VIPs arrived. She was advised who to talk to, whose hand to shake, who to merely nod at and who actively not to show favour to. Times were given and she was told very sternly that they must be adhered to. She nodded and smiled and forgot everything. Purposely.

A gown arrived, formal and decidedly neutral, stiff with embroidery. She allowed herself to be fitted for it without complaint, while in secret she talked to one of the royal dressmaker's assistants. She didn't want the King to know what she was planning, so everything had to be kept hidden.

The night of the ball soon arrived and Inara was led away hours beforehand to be scrubbed and plucked and primped to within an inch of her life, zipped up into the armour of a dress, painful contacts in her eyes. Her hair was smooth, sleek and shining, coiled up into intricate twists on her head, held in place by diamond pins. Careful contouring of her face was done, with a metric ton of make-up designed to look as if she was wearing no make-up at all.

And, last of all, the crown of Aveiras—thick and ancient gold set with antique diamonds, and brilliantly blue sapphires to represent the sea. It was heavy and made her head hurt, and she could only think of poor Cassius and the crown he had to wear, which was even thicker and heavier.

She would free him from that if she could.

With an hour to go, she dismissed her aides and attendants. She wasn't used to giving orders, and had secretly worried that they wouldn't obey her, but when she added that she needed some time to go through the schedules by herself they all agreed.

As soon as the door closed behind them, Inara sprang into action.

It didn't take long. Everything she needed had been delivered to her apartments earlier that day, so it was all to hand. She was ready in half an hour, which was half an hour before the King and Queen were to appear at the ball.

Perfect timing.

Inara didn't wait to be summoned. Didn't wait to call her attendants back. She simply strode along the cold, marble hallways of the palace, past the judgmental eyes of the de Leon rulers.

She ignored them.

The double doors of the ballroom were closed, the guards stationed outside staring at her in some surprise as she approached. She gestured at them and, after a glance at each other, they pulled the doors open for her.

Inara didn't hesitate. She strode through into the glittering light of the ballroom, surrounded by the buzz of conversation and music, the loud noise of hundreds of people all gathered in one place.

The usher by the stairs looked at her in consternation, but she only smiled. 'I know,' she said. 'I'm early. Announce me anyway.'

The usher glanced behind her, as if he hoped to see the King, or anyone who might countenance this complete break with tradition, but there was only Inara. And she was the Queen.

He took a breath, then nodded and turned to the crowded ballroom.

'Her Royal Majesty, Queen Inara of Aveiras,' he announced loudly.

Everyone stopped talking and turned in her direction.

Inara braced herself, then started down the stairs.

'Your Majesty, the Queen is already there.'

Cassius, in the middle of inspecting the crown he wore for official occasions, looked up. 'What? What you do you mean, she's already there?'

The aide looked apologetic. 'I mean, Her Majesty arrived at the ball twenty minutes ago.'

Shock and anger twisted in Cassius's stomach.

He and Inara were supposed to enter the ballroom together, the way they had the week before, properly announced and properly greeted. She should know that; he'd sent her the schedule days ago. Had she forgotten? She'd had difficulty with the schedules and protocols and etiquette…he knew that. But his people had assured him that the Queen had been attending their sessions and knew exactly what was expected of her.

He hadn't monitored her personally. He'd simply let her know that these things would be required and had expected her to comply.

It was the only way. He couldn't allow what she'd told him that day in his study to matter. He couldn't allow it to affect him. She'd said she loved the man he'd once been and the truth of it had been there in her eyes.

But she'd been blind. That was her problem. How could she love a man that selfish, that self-centred? That flawed? A man so consumed with his own petty annoyances and ridiculous grievances that he hadn't seen the damage he was causing.

That's not the way she sees you and she told you that.

No. She'd told him that he'd made her feel good about herself, made her laugh. Protected her.

Punishing yourself...isn't going to give you the legacy you're trying to build. It'll only end up tearing you apart.

He could still hear those words in his head, and they made even less sense now than they had at the time. He wasn't punishing himself. He was simply doing what needed to be done.

Regardless, he couldn't afford to think about this now. Inara was somehow going off script and he needed to get her back onto it. This was an important ball and she had to get things right if she wanted to be accepted by the people of Aveiras.

'I'll be there directly,' he said in curt tones, dismissing the aide.

He didn't bother with the crown, leaving his rooms and striding straight to the ballroom. The guards spotted him and instantly threw the doors wide.

He went on through then paused at the top of the stairs that led down into the ballroom proper, searching for Inara.

He saw her immediately and all the breath left his body. She wasn't wearing the gown he'd commissioned or the crown of the queens of Aveiras. The gown she wore was simple and unadorned, a bias-cut slip dress in sapphire-blue satin with a very small, flowing train that fluttered behind her as she walked. Her hair was in loose silver curls down her back and, instead of the crown, there was a simple circlet of twisted silver strands studded with sapphires. On her feet she wore blue satin slippers, no heels, and on her nose were perched her glasses.

She was surrounded by the finance ministers she knew, plus a couple from other countries, all deep in conversation about something. The people in the ballroom swirled around her, some of them openly disapproving, but more than a few clearly intrigued.

Then, as he watched, Inara broke away from her little coterie and moved over to another group of people—ambassadors from France, from the looks of things. She shook their hands, not bothering to wait for her aide to introduce her, and smiled, exchanging a few words then moving on. She did this a number of times, and then stopped as someone else joined her group and another deep, intense conversation ensued.

His heart felt so tight he couldn't breathe.

She wasn't in the crown or the gown, and she'd arrived early and hadn't waited for him. She was clearly without an aide to introduce her, and as for the schedules…they were apparently long gone.

She wasn't at all the queen he'd wanted or the queen he'd expected. She was…better. She was warm and human and approachable. The gown she wore was simple and yet elegant, flowing around her like water. She looked young and carefree and so heartbreakingly beautiful that the entire world stood still.

The usher saw him standing there transfixed and announced him immediately. It took him a couple of moments to realise that everyone was staring at him and that he hadn't moved because he was too busy staring at Inara.

She turned with everyone else and her lovely face broke into the most incredible smile. Without waiting for him to come to her or for an aide to approach, she marched straight through the crowd and up the stairs. Then she took his hand as if he was merely her lover and not the King, her warm fingers threading through his, and led him down into the crowds.

He knew he should stop her. He should pull her hand from his and insist on the proper protocols, insist that they needed to adhere to the schedule and the timing, because this was a formal event. There were heads of state here and he needed to set an example. But he couldn't bring himself to do it. A part of him was captivated by his lovely wife, and curious to see what she would do and what would happen next.

So he let Inara set the example.

He'd always found royal duties interminable and difficult, something to endure instead of enjoy, but tonight it felt different. It was Inara who led him round instead of his aide, approaching people and asking their names without caring that a queen should already know.

And what was even more surprising was that people didn't seem to mind. She was artless, utterly without guile, completely open and honest. Sometimes awkward, but laughing at herself too, and he could see how that put people at their ease. He had no idea why she'd ever thought she wasn't good at the social stuff, because if anything it was the opposite.

She put something inside him at ease too, a tightly leashed part of himself he never let out. And before he knew what was happening, he was smiling and talking to people as if he was still that prince, the charming one who'd always known what to say to make himself the life of the party.

People responded. He could see it in their faces. And

soon he and Inara were surrounded, with more people coming over to talk with them, schedules out of the window, no distance, no formality.

His father would have been appalled.

But as the evening went on Cassius couldn't bring himself to care. Inara's hand was warm inside his, her presence beside him bright and beautiful, and he didn't want to let that hand go. He didn't want her to leave his side. Once or twice he glanced at her to find her looking back, her eyes shining with an emotion that made his heart ache.

Much later, an aide approached them, informing them that they were due to make their appearance on the balcony. As that was one formality they couldn't ignore, he found himself leading Inara from the ballroom and through the corridors to the formal reception room that opened out onto the balcony.

'Why?' he asked quietly as several palace employees began to prepare the room. 'Why did you do all of this?' He didn't elaborate; she'd know what he meant.

Her fingers tightened around his. 'I wanted you to see that you could do something differently. That you didn't have to follow your father's example. That you could do things your way.' She shifted closer, looking up at him, a fierce light in her eyes. 'That you could create a legacy that's yours, that isn't bound by anyone else's protocols or idea of what's right and proper. A legacy that's about you and the kind of king *you* want to be.'

He'd never thought about it in that way before, and it struck him all of a sudden that it was because he'd never really viewed the role of king as his before. It had always been about his father or his brother. A position he'd taken almost as a caretaker of their memory, not something he could put his own stamp on.

But…he could, couldn't he?

Just as Inara had put her own stamp on being a queen.

They're dead because of you, though. Can you really dishonour their legacy like that?

It was true they were dead and, yes, because of him. But was it really such a dishonour to do things differently? To be the kind of king *he* wanted to be, not what his father had been or his brother would have been?

Cassius lifted her hand and pressed his mouth against the back of it, then they were stepping forward to the balcony that overlooked the central city square, the sound of the crowd rolling over them.

He felt Inara tremble beside him, but he lifted her hand and held it out, showing her to his people, and smiled. Cameras everywhere beamed that smile to screens set up around the square and to TVs all over the nation, just as they beamed the approving roar of the crowd.

Adrenalin filled him, a surge of hope he hadn't felt in far too long. Hope that soon turned into something hotter and more joyful, centred on the woman who'd brought him to this point.

His queen. His Inara.

They stepped back from the balcony, and as soon as the doors were closed, and the shutters across the windows pulled tight, Cassius dismissed everyone from the room.

Then he turned to her, glowing and beautiful in her blue gown, and gently but surely pushed her up against the balcony doors.

She didn't protest. Her lovely face was flushed, her eyes still shining, looking at him as if he was the only thing worth looking at in the entire world.

'They loved you,' he said softly. 'I knew they would.'

But this time she didn't smile.

'What about you?' Her voice sounded hoarse. 'Do you love me too?'

CHAPTER ELEVEN

SHE HADN'T MEANT to just come out with it. She hadn't meant to say it at all but, looking out over the crowds, watching them shout for him, cheer for him, gaze at him as if he was the centre of their world, she felt that very same adoration burning like a coal at the centre of her chest.

In that moment, as he'd taken her hand and smiled at the crowd, she hadn't cared if they accepted her or not. She hadn't cared about them at all.

The only thing that mattered to her was him.

And she wanted him.

She wanted to mean something to him too.

Tonight she'd watched him become the kind of king he should be, not bound by his father's legacy or trying to fit his brother's shoes. A less formal, more accessible kind of king. A king who wasn't only respected but who was loved too.

A king she could love. A king she already loved. It should have been enough to be his wife, to know that she'd helped him be all he could be, the way he'd helped her. To be his queen. To be his lover.

It was more than she'd ever thought she'd have and yet...

It wasn't enough.

And she was scared. While it was clear he was ready to take her to bed again, she wasn't sure how long that would continue. This whole week, he'd shut her out, and he'd done the same the week before. He distanced himself whenever she challenged him, making her feel as if she was walking on egg shells around him, and that felt... precarious.

This situation—their marriage and thus her future—felt precarious. Was this what it would be like between them from now on? Would it be her, loving him from afar, surviving on whatever attention he chose to give her? Never knowing whether she'd say the wrong thing and end up being shut out again?

She'd never had anyone accept her for who she was, not the way he'd accepted her. She'd never had anyone who thought she was beautiful or interesting, or even worth knowing, the way he did. And though that was wonderful, there was still one thing she'd never had, not from anyone.

Love.

Was it so wrong to want that? So wrong to ask for it?

Cassius lifted his head, staring down at her, a hot amber glow burning in his eyes. 'Let's talk about this later.'

'When later?' The words came out before she could stop them. 'Before or after you refuse to speak to me for another week? Or refuse to take me to your bed?'

'Inara, I—'

'It's a simple question, Cassius. Yes or no?' She was trembling all of a sudden, her chest gone tight and sore. 'And I'm guessing that, since you can't answer it, you don't.'

He stared at her for a long moment then took a step back, lifting a hand and shoving it distractedly through his black hair. 'You surprised me. I wasn't expecting you to ask a question like that.'

She swallowed, her heart a piece of broken glass embedded in her chest, jagged and sharp. 'I told you I loved you, Cassius. And then you ignored me for an entire week. You wouldn't even let me come to your bed.'

His hand dropped. 'You told me that you loved the prince.'

'Yes. And I love the King too. I love *you*. I've loved you for years.' There wasn't any point hiding it. He'd told her his secret and now it was her turn to share hers, and there was a kind of freedom in that.

Emotions flickered over his face, gone too fast for her to see what they were, before his features finally settled into the expression she hated so much. The calm one, the condescending one. The mask he used when he wanted to distance people. When he wanted to hide.

'I know I've treated your poorly,' he said levelly. 'I'm sorry. I shouldn't have done that but—'

'Is this what our marriage will be like from now on?' She took a step forward, anger igniting inside her. A cleansing, freeing anger. 'I only get whatever crumbs of attention you give me? Ignored whenever I challenge you, barred from your bed whenever I offend you?'

'No, that's not—'

'Will it be like it was before, Cassius? Will I be banished to the Queen's rooms, like I was banished to the Queen's Estate? Existing only when you choose to recognise my existence? Wheeled out for state functions or whenever you need a queen on your arm? Summoned only when you need a woman in your bed.'

The calm mask cracked, a fierce glow beginning to burn in his eyes. 'I never banished you. No, I didn't summon you last week, but you never tried to contact me either. You didn't come to my door. You told me you loved the prince I once was and then you walked out.'

It was true. That was exactly what she'd done. 'Because I thought you needed some time to think about it and I didn't want to crowd you. Plus, tonight required a bit of planning, and I didn't want you to know about it. And even if I hadn't been doing all of that, would you have let me in if I'd come to you? Or would you have sent an aide to tell me you were "too busy"?' She took another step towards him, her anger burning hotter. 'And why should I be the one who always has to come to you, anyway? Why should I be the one who has to wait for you to be ready to receive me?'

A muscle flicked in his jaw. 'What is it exactly that you want from me, Inara? You want the freedom to come to my bed whenever it suits you? Is that it?'

'No, you idiot man.' She was now only inches away. 'What I want is a real marriage. I want to be your wife in reality, all the time, not only when it suits you. And I want you to love me the way I love you—because no one ever has, Cassius. Not even my parents.'

His gaze flickered, but there was no softening in his expression. 'You want the truth? You really want an answer? Fine. I don't love you, Inara, and I never will. I'll never love anyone. It's all I can do to carry the weight of the crown, to love my country and my people.'

Inara felt something die a little inside her, the fragile tendril of her hope crushed utterly. Because looking at the hard, set lines of his face and the anger burning in his eyes, it was worse than she'd thought.

Love was a burden to him, an extra weight he didn't need, not with all the expectations he'd heaped on himself already. And why would he expect love to be anything else? After the way he'd been brought up and the standards he'd been measured against by his own family?

Her own had been no different. It was just…her love for him had brought her confidence and freedom. But it was clear that lesson hadn't gone both ways.

You failed. Again.

Inara swallowed past the lump in her throat, trying to find the right words, the right thing, that would help him see. 'Love isn't a weight,' she said thickly. 'It's not a burden to bear. It sets you free. How can you not see that?'

He gave a harsh laugh. 'Free? I loved my parents and my brother, but do I look free to you? Do I look unburdened?'

Tears pricked at her eyes. 'No. You look like a man beating himself to death over something that wasn't his fault in the first place.'

His expression twisted, anger flaring across it. 'Of course it was my fault. I was expected to at least act like a prince of the realm and I couldn't even do that much. I was too selfish, too angry. Too caught up in—'

'You were a boy who'd been measured all his life against standards he could never possibly live up to,' she interrupted, suddenly and completely furious. 'You're just like me. *Exactly* like me. We both had parents who wanted us to be something different, who couldn't accept us for who we were, and I understand how that hurts. But there comes a point where you have to decide whether to let that be a stick you keep beating yourself with. Or you choose to let it go and accept who you are. Like I did. Like *you* taught me to.'

A light flared in his eyes and for a second she thought she might have got through to him. But then it vanished, forced away beneath that blank mask once again as he took a step back from her, putting distance between them.

'I'm sorry, Inara,' he said, hard and cold. 'But, whether you like it or not, those standards are part of my world now. And I *have* met them. And I'll continue to meet them for the good of my country and my people.'

Her anger drained away just as quickly as it had come, leaving her empty and hollow. It was becoming more and more obvious with every passing moment that there was nothing she could say that would help him.

Nothing she could do.

He was committed to his own punishment and eventually it would crush him.

Her heart broke, that piece of jagged glass splintering, knowing that there was only one choice left for her.

She could stay in this precarious marriage, suffering quietly every day, in the hope that one day his feelings would change, that one day he'd turn around and tell her that he loved her. Or she could leave him, leave this marriage, accepting that change wasn't possible and would never be possible for him.

Everything she'd done since she'd got here had been for him, but she couldn't keep on doing it. She couldn't keep on giving pieces of herself away, getting smaller and smaller, weaker and weaker, every day.

She had to keep something for herself.

'Okay,' Inara said thickly 'If that's the way it has to be, then that's what it has to be. But I'm afraid I'm not going to stay being your wife, Cassius. I can't. I don't want to be banished to the Queen's apartments, or wherever you think I need to be, summoned whenever you need me then forgotten about when you don't. I don't want to be that child bride you visit whenever you're bored. And I can't stay here and watch you tear yourself apart.'

'Inara—'

'Cassius, I want a divorce.'

He couldn't believe it. His beautiful wife, his lovely queen, the woman who'd showed him that there was a different way, a better way, was asking him for a divorce.

And all because he wouldn't tell her he loved her when she demanded it.

That was love, though, wasn't it? A demand. An expectation. Something that was only given when certain conditions were met. You were worthy only if you acted in a certain way, behaved with dignity and propriety. When you were perfect.

Like Caspian. He was worthy, but you never were.

His father's chilly distance had always made that very clear. The opportunity to earn that love was gone now, along with his father, but that didn't mean he should stop trying. That was what he'd dedicated his life to. Trying to be worthy of the title he'd inherited.

He'd fashioned himself into a king his country would be proud of, and that had taken nearly everything he had. How could he also fashion himself into a good husband? A man worthy of Inara's love? Being a king was a heavy enough burden. He didn't need to add to it.

He stared at her, a possessive, hungry anger boiling inside him, demanding to be let out. Demanding that he close the distance between them and take her in his arms, kiss that beautiful mouth, tell her that there would be no divorce—not now, not ever.

But he forced it aside. If he couldn't be what she wanted him to be, then he could hardly demand the same of her. Insisting that there would be no divorce would be the height of hypocrisy and he couldn't do that.

She's yours...

No, she wasn't. She'd proved herself a worthy queen, far more worthy than he deserved. It would be better to let her go.

Something in him felt as though it was being torn in two, but he ignored it, shoved the lid on his anger and his pain and let it boil dry until there was nothing left but the hard shell of a king.

He drew himself up. 'Very well,' he said. 'I won't insist. If a divorce is what you want, then that's what you'll have.'

Shock crossed her face, followed by a brief flare of agony that drew an echo of pain from him too.

'Just like that, Cassius?' Her voice was hoarse and it was clear she hadn't expected him to agree. 'You give in just like that?'

He ignored the part of him that wanted to take her in his arms, soothe her hurts and tell her that he wanted to keep her for ever. But he couldn't do it. He couldn't bear the weight. The expectations of a king were crushing him already; the expectations of a husband would kill him.

'There's no point fighting about it.' He could hear his own voice, cool and calm, as if it were someone else's. 'I'll admit it's not what I want, but I won't stand in your way if you want to leave.'

She blinked again furiously and he could see tears behind the lenses of her glasses. They felt like knives to his soul. Yet another sign that he was doing the right thing, of course.

'What about us having no choice? If I'm pregnant then—'

'If you're pregnant then we'll cross that bridge when we come to it.' Something in him settled, hardened, became rigid. And he let it. 'In the meantime, I'll get the papers drawn up. If you require anything, anything at all, it's yours.'

Her mouth was soft and vulnerable, and tears trailed down her cheeks. 'Anything but your heart, right?'

'You don't want my heart, Inara,' he said. 'There's not much of it left. You deserve more than what I have to give you.'

She looked unbearably regal standing there in her blue gown with her hair loose, the crown glittering on her head, her chin lifted. Vulnerable, yes, but there was also a strength to her.

His people had accepted her, but she'd never be his queen. He'd find someone else, someone who wouldn't demand things from him. Expect things from him. Someone who'd accept what he had to give and never ask for more.

'You're right,' she said. 'I do deserve more. I deserve to be loved, and by you.'

Something in his heart tore, but he ignored that along with everything else. 'Find someone else, Inara. Someone better. Someone who doesn't have a crown to bear as well. I can only carry one thing, and I'm sorry, but that's my country. I can't carry you as well.'

She took a heaving breath, opened her mouth to say something and then, clearly thinking better of it, pressed her lips together and looked away. She nodded, her pretty crown glittering in the light. 'Very well,' she said at last. 'If that's how it's going to be, then I'll require a flight to the Queen's Estate, please. Tonight.'

She didn't wait for him to respond. She simply walked to the door.

'I thought you were better than that,' he heard himself say, even though he hadn't meant to…even though he thought he felt nothing. 'I thought you at least would accept me for who I am.'

She paused, her hand on the door. 'This is not who you are, Cassius.'

'You're wrong. This *is* who I am. And if you can't accept that, then you're better off leaving.'

A tear trickled down her cheek. 'Perhaps you're right,' she said softly. 'Perhaps I am.'

Then she quietly opened the door and went out.

CHAPTER TWELVE

INARA PACKED A bag that night. She didn't take much—she'd come with nothing, so that was how she would leave. With nothing. There was nothing she wanted to take with her anyway. If she couldn't have him, she didn't want anything else.

Grief tore at her heart. Not so much grief for herself, though that was there too, but grief for him. For how he'd become so stiff and rigid before her eyes, the Prince she'd loved vanishing, becoming the King.

She hated the King.

Is that fair?

She grabbed some dresses at random and flung them into her suitcase. Her glasses were fogging up so she had to pause and take them off, rubbing at the lenses, tears still pouring down her cheeks.

Her heart wasn't just broken glass in her chest in any more; it felt like barbed wire, cutting at her soul.

Whether it was fair or not, he was right about one thing. She deserved more than he could give her. She did. No one had loved her for her entire life and, now she knew what it felt like to have someone, she didn't want to do without it. And if it couldn't be him, then it would be someone else.

You don't want anyone else.

She ignored that voice as she tossed a T-shirt into her

case. Somewhere out there would be someone who'd want her. Someone who wouldn't shut her out, who wouldn't blow hot and cold, who'd tell her unequivocally where she stood. Someone who'd love her the way she so desperately wanted to be loved.

It just wouldn't be him.

You're being as unfair to him as he is to you, demanding things of him that he doesn't know how to give. No wonder he thinks love is a burden. You're demanding he be the person he was back then, but he'll never be that man again.

'I thought you were better than that,' he'd said to her. 'I thought you'd accept me for who I am.'

Inara's throat felt tight and sore, the barbed wire in her heart twisting.

Maybe there was some truth in that. But what else could she do? Stand by and accept whatever he had to give her? Try and love the hard, distant man who wouldn't let himself be loved? Who viewed it as a burden?

Who viewed himself as a burden.

Tears slipped down her cheeks as it slowly became clear to her what she must do. She didn't want anyone else. She'd *never* want anyone else.

And she couldn't leave him. She couldn't reject the man he was now simply because he wouldn't give her what she wanted. Would she be any different from his father? From his parents, who'd made him feel that he was unworthy somehow?

And how would he ever learn that love wasn't a burden, wasn't a weight, wasn't an expectation he had to meet, unless she showed him?

Love wasn't conditional, but sometimes it required sacrifices. Sometimes it required compromises. So if she wanted him, she'd have to be the one to take that first step, because it was clear he couldn't. Not yet. In fact, he might never be able to take that step. But love wasn't just sacrifice, it was faith as well, and if you didn't have faith in love what else could you have faith in?

She had to be the one to set the example this time. And one day, he'd learn. Perhaps not right now, but some day.

She just had to hope that he would.

Cassius organised a helicopter to take Inara to the Queen's Estate, then stayed in his office to organize having the divorce papers drawn up. He didn't want her to wait a second longer, as staying married to him was obviously such a trial.

He told himself he felt nothing, that the shell he'd developed after his family had been killed had hardened. That it was part of him now. And he ignored the anger and pain and betrayal at how she'd walked out. Ignored, too, the deeper emotion that went with it. It was a hot, powerful current that couldn't be allowed to roam free.

Instead, he liaised with his legal team then drew himself up a schedule of what he had to do in the morning. Number one of which would be finding himself a new queen.

But what if Inara is pregnant? What will you do? How can you let her go?

He shoved back his chair, trying to ignore the questions tumbling round in his head. Trying to ignore the strength of the emotion inside him, desperate for release.

He *had* to let her go. He couldn't give her what she wanted. She deserved better.

There comes a point where you have to decide whether to let that be a stick you keep beating yourself with. Or you choose to let it go and accept who you are. Like I did. Like you taught me.

Her voice drifted through his head and he tried to shove it away.

She was wrong. He couldn't let those standards slip and he *had* accepted who he was. It was she who hadn't accepted it.

And if she did…if she just loved you…if she accepted you for who you were without you having to do a thing… why didn't anyone else?

But he couldn't go there, couldn't think about that.

Sleep was too far off, his mind far too active, so he left his office, heading through the quiet halls to his private study.

He opened the door and walked straight in.

Only to find Inara standing in front of the fireplace, still in her blue gown, her hands clasped tightly in front of her, her cheeks still wet.

Not gone to the Queen's Estate after all.

Shock rooted him to the spot, swiftly followed by a wild joy he couldn't quite shake.

'What are you doing here?' His voice was rough.

The expression on her face was raw with pain, open with longing. 'I can't leave you, love. I tried and I can't. Because you're right. I wanted the Prince, not the King. But that isn't love and I…wanted to show you that love isn't about expectations, and it isn't a weight. It's not a burden. Love is acceptance and…'

She swallowed. 'I love you, Cassius. I love you as the King as well as the Prince. I love the man you were and I love the man you are now. And so I'll stay here with you, for as long as you want me. You don't have to do anything. You don't have to be anyone. Just be you. You as you are, right now, is all I want.'

There was a roaring in his ears, as if someone had let off a bomb somewhere nearby and the sound of the explosion was still echoing.

You as you are, right now, is all I want.

That couldn't be true. It couldn't.

'You don't want that,' he said hoarsely. 'You can't want that. I'm…flawed, Inara. Don't you see? Don't you understand? If I don't have to do anything…if I don't have to be anyone…' He stopped, pain twisting in his heart at a truth he didn't want to face. 'Then why couldn't my father…?'

She crossed the room to him, coming to stand in front of him, her small hands lifting to take his face between them. The heat of her palms seared him all the way through.

'Didn't you ever think, love, that the problem wasn't you?' Her voice was soft and there was no hiding from the bright flame in her eyes. 'That the problem was him?'

How she understood what he was talking about, he didn't know, but she did. And he found he'd lifted his own hands, his fingers circling her wrists, pressing against the fragile bones, feeling her heat and her strength. 'How could it be him? He loved Caspian. He never had any issue—'

'It was never you, Cassius,' Inara said thickly. 'And if he couldn't see the kind, generous, wonderful man you actually are, the selfless, compassionate King you've become, then he was blind. And he was stupid. And he was wrong.'

He wanted to tell her that that couldn't be the truth, that it couldn't be as simple as that, but her grey eyes had gone luminous and everything he'd been going to say had gone clean out of his head.

'It's time to stop punishing yourself, my love,' she said quietly. 'Let your family go. You don't need to keep them here any longer. You have me now, and I'll keep you safe.'

Something inside him suddenly cracked apart, the hard shell he'd drawn around him shattering, letting out all the flawed emotions he'd been so desperate to keep inside. The grief and the guilt and the pain and the anger.

And, most of all, the love.

Because she'd stayed. She'd stayed. She'd stayed for

him. She didn't want him to be anything else. She didn't demand it.

Love was sacrifice and duty, but love was also Inara—here, after he thought she'd left him. Inara, who'd accepted herself and who'd accepted him too. Who'd taught him that he could be himself, that he could be both king and prince. But, above all, a man.

A man who loved her.

Cassius let go of her wrists, sliding his hands down her arms, down her sides to her hips. Then he pulled her hard against him, every cell in his body craving her presence. Craving everything she had to give and more.

'Inara,' he whispered. 'Inara…' He had no other words.

But then she solved the problem by going up on her toes and kissing him. Making it clear that he didn't need to say a thing.

So he didn't try. Instead, he tore her gown away and took her down onto the floor of his study, telling her with his hands on her body and the kisses following in their wake, and with his sex as he eventually pushed inside her, what she meant to him.

He couldn't say the whole of what he felt; he didn't know how. But he could learn. He was willing.

So she taught him all she knew, a lesson that began that night in his study and continued on through all the years of their marriage—lessons in joy, in happiness. In comfort, and pleasure, and most important of all in love.

And eventually Cassius found the words to tell her what he felt for her, how she'd freed him, how she'd changed him. How she made him more himself every day.

But by then he didn't need to.

She already knew.

EPILOGUE

Inara wandered over to the windows of her and Cassius's private study and peered out into the garden. Roman, their son, had disappeared yet again and his tutor was getting tetchy. Inara had an important meeting with one of her ministers that afternoon, but she wanted to find Roman first, plus she had something to tell Cassius.

Sure enough, the pair of them were outside, staring critically at one of the rose bushes. Cassius pointed at something and Roman, who was getting tall even at only eleven, frowned and nodded.

Inara smiled. Her son loved these moments with Cassius, both of them focused on soil conditions and pest control, and whether the flowers needed more fertiliser. It didn't happen often, as Cassius was very busy, but he always made time for his son, especially as the boy hated sitting still as much as his parents did.

In the corridor outside came the sound of girlish voices arguing. The twins were shouting about whose turn it was to be the prince in the game they were playing. Neither of them wanted to be the princess, to Inara's eternal amusement.

She turned from the window, thinking she might have to adjudicate before the hair pulling began, but then she heard the door to the garden open behind her. Roman dashed past to join his sisters in the corridor, and then a strong arm wrapped around her waist, a warm mouth pressing a kiss to the nape of her neck.

'Have I told you today that I love you?' Cassius murmured. 'I feel I haven't.'

Inara sighed, the warm contentment and joy she always felt in her husband's presence filling her as she leaned back against him. 'You have. Only an hour ago, in fact. But feel free to tell me again.'

'I love you, little one.' His mouth moved to the side of her neck, his hands beginning to roam. 'I love you for ever.'

'I'm glad.' A little bolt of excited happiness sparked inside her. 'Because I have something to tell you.'

'If it's about the twins and the frog they put in the nanny's—'

'No, it's not about the twins and the frog.' Inara turned in his arms and stared up into his beloved face.

His eyes were glowing the way they did when he wanted her, all smoky amber and heat, and his mouth was curving in that warm, wicked way. 'Then what is it? Be quick. I feel I might be about to ravish you in the garden if you're not careful.'

'I'm never careful; you should know that about me by now.' Inara smoothed the lapels of his jacket. 'How would you feel about being a father again?'

His smile was slow and devastating and full of joy, and even all these years later it still had the power to set her on fire. He bent his head and kissed her hard, then murmured against her mouth.

'I feel that nothing else would give me greater pleasure.'

It had been a long road, a difficult road, but they'd journeyed it together.

One by one he'd let go of his guilt and his grief, allowing his family finally to be free. Allowing himself to be free too. And, while that had been hard, it had also been worth it.

He was worth it. He always had been.

'Little one,' he said quietly. 'You make me so very happy. Every single day.'

* * * * *

THE ONLY KING
TO CLAIM HER

MILLIE ADAMS

MILLS & BOON

For all who need strength to tackle the next battle:
'There are far, far better things ahead
than any we leave behind.'
—C.S. Lewis

CHAPTER ONE

MAXIMUS KING LOOKED across the ballroom at Arianna Lopez, who up until tonight had been a disgraced starlet working her way back into the good graces of society. Optics were everything in this age of social media. Constant visibility.

Arianna had made the terrible mistake of being beautiful, rich, and seeming selfish. And so, had fallen out of favor with the clambering masses on the internet who saw her as a property belonging to them.

And rehabilitating image was his business. Tonight had been a sterling success. The charity event was sparkling, and perfect. And she now looked more Madonna than whore.

His job was done.

She was the same shallow, ridiculous creature she'd been when they'd met two weeks ago. But now the world had forgotten her tantrum about the roses she was given not being entirely white, and so it didn't matter what was in her heart.

Only what people saw.

Optics, after all, were everything.

With every aspect of a person's life available for public consumption nowadays, it had to be so.

Perhaps it was why he took such great, perverse delight in using optics as his cover.

For no one, not even his family, knew the truth about Maximus King.

He straightened his tie and turned, beginning to walk out of the room. He heard the click of high heels behind him.

He paused. He knew that it was Arianna; he had noted the sound her shoes made against the marble floor. No one ever took him off guard.

"Are you leaving?"

"Yes," he said.

"I thought that we might…leave together. After all, our working relationship was so satisfactory. I thought we might be able to…transition it." She put one delicate, manicured hand on his shoulder, and her touch left him cold.

But he smiled. That charming grin of the playboy that all the world took him to be. "Not tonight."

"Not tonight?" Her eyes widened. "I was under the impression you're up for it every night."

He gave her his best, most practiced grin. Nothing to see here, just a playboy. Not a care in the world. "There's already a woman waiting in my bed, sweetheart." He winked for good measure. "You have to book early."

He turned and continued to walk out of the ballroom. His car was there at the front of the hotel waiting for him. He scanned the street, a habit. Then got into the vehicle, maneuvering through the San Diego streets, making his way back to his glittering mansion in the hills. He had a spectacular view of the ocean from the front, and the protection of the mountains in the back. Lots of windows.

With bulletproof glass.

Again, part of the facade. An appearance of vulnerability, of openness. Without actually offering it.

He parked his car in front of the house and got out, using the fingerprint sensor to allow him entry into the home.

And the moment he stepped into the darkened room, he felt something was off.

He paused and reached into his suit jacket. He had a small gun there with a silencer. He always carried it.

As he walked deeper into the house, he heard nothing. Rather, he sensed a ripple of disturbance in the air. He had learned to listen to his gut. It was the difference between life and death. And he was still alive.

"I would quite rather you did not shoot me."

The voice coming from the darkness was feminine, accented and sweet.

"Who are you?" he asked.

He heard a rustle of movement, coming from inside the living room, and then he saw a figure, dressed in white, moving toward him. She stepped into a shaft of moonlight that filtered in from the windows that faced the sea. Small, with long blond hair and a round, pale face, he could not make her features out in the dim light.

"I am Princess Annick, formerly of the lower dungeon. Lately of the palace proper."

Something echoed inside of him.

"Annick," he repeated.

He knew the name Annick. *Princess* Annick.

"Who sent you?"

"*I* sent me," she said. "A perk, I suppose, of being free. And I am free." She made a small sound that might've been a laugh. "Peculiar, that. I am not accustomed to it."

"You're the Princess of Aillette, correct?" He knew.

He didn't need her to confirm. He'd taken an assignment there only a year ago. That meant he'd learned the history of the country and he would not forget it. He took his work seriously, and that meant he didn't go in and perform the task unless he was quite clear on what was being done.

As far as the US government was concerned, there was no Maximus King enlisted in their ranks. His work, and any trail that could be traced back to him, was so coded it would take a mastermind to track him down.

Granted, he had always known it was possible. Hence the bulletproof glass.

But he still could not quite figure out how this woman was here, now, and with full knowledge of both his lives.

"Oui," she said. "It is me."

"I have already done a service for your country, Annick. I'm not certain why you are here."

"Oh, it is in regard to that service, Mr. King."

"I don't do follow-up visits."

"Ah, but you see, you have created a problem."

"Removing dictators from power is the solution. Not the problem."

"What of the vacuum that is left behind?"

"Not my responsibility."

"Eh," she said. "Then what is?"

"Just as I said. I receive orders from military intelligence. I gather a team, or simply myself, depending on the situation. I carry out orders. I leave. I assume that the government sends a crew in after to handle the rest."

"Ha! Lip service at best," she said. "Three months of transitional assistance and then what? Gone. I am left with few resources, and little path to rule a country that still scarcely believes I am mentally well enough to rule. Though I believe I have been perfectly wonderful in the year since I have begun to rule."

"You claim to have few resources, and yet here you are."

"I am very sneaky," she said. "And that comes from many years of imprisonment and secret plotting for how I might make amends when I was released."

"Were you not complicit in the regime?"

"I was certainly *not*. As I said, I was primarily ensconced in the lower dungeon. I was trotted out as a figurehead on rare occasions. Proof of life and all. And I confess, if I have one weakness it is that I do care a bit for my life. I did not wish to be dead."

"A common wish," he said.

"Quite."

"So what is it you want, Annick? Other than to not be dead."

She looked up at him, and for a moment, he thought he saw her falter. For a moment, he saw vulnerability. "I would like for you to come back to Aillette with me."

"No."

"You have not even heard my proposition."

"I don't need to."

"You should hear my proposition, I think."

"You are perhaps overrating your proposition. I have so much here," he said, indicating the mansion that he did not care about at all. He was dead inside. And when you were dead inside, you did not fear death, not overmuch. But Annick did not need to know that. Annick only needed to know what the rest of the world knew about him. Though she did know a few things, which he found disturbing. She knew that he was responsible for the death of the dictator of Aillette.

Annick had joined his two lives together.

A problem.

But he was not in the business of dispatching small women.

It was only ever those who deserved it. Only ever those who had committed great and terrible atrocities. He did not consider himself to be a good man, but he was a man looking for a way to balance the scales in the world.

To try and fix what he had not managed to fix all those many years ago.

And nothing would bring Stella back.

He remained, she was gone and it did not fix itself, no matter how many deserving people he took out of the world. But he considered it his payment.

A way to try and at least put some sort of balance out into the universe.

Annick looked at him and lifted a shoulder. "I require a small thing. I need you to return to my country with me. To act as my guard."

She had successfully silenced the brute.

She had done a decent amount of research into Maximus King before stealing away to San Diego to confront him. He was a fascinating character. She found she was not frightened of him, though she perhaps should be. But she was not easily frightened.

For her entire family had been lost to her as a child, and she had been trotted in and out of the dungeon ever since. Educated, made to appear somewhat civilized.

They thought she had been made loyal.

But she had been lying, for all her life, out of a sense of self-preservation. And now she finally had a chance to make up for it all. Now she had a chance to finally make a difference. To make the years of farce worthwhile.

She just had to convince this playboy, who she was given to believe was a secret assassin, to become her protector.

She needed a man by her side. This was the problem.

Annick was a realist. You could not live ten years as a prisoner without being a realist. The world was harsh. And nobody cared if you were a child. Nobody cared when there was power to be had.

Annick had been forced to play the part of silent figurehead to a country that she loved, to stand beside men who made her burn with hatred and smile. So that for all the world to see, Aillette was a functioning government.

It was not.

Her people were badly treated.

Reform. Revolution.

Those had been the rallying cries of the men who had stormed the palace and destroyed her family.

It had been none of those things.

And now that she was back in power she would see that her people were never harmed again. She needed his protection. For her people, not so much for her.

Dangerous men did not scare her.

She had made a bargain with herself when dealing with such men for many years now. Making a bargain with a man such as this bothered her not at all.

"You wish me to return to Aillette with you?"

"I more than wish it. I command it."

"Or?"

"I will think nothing of exposing your identity."

"You see, in order for that to concern me," he said, his voice hard, "I would have to care a great deal more for my life than I do."

He was bluffing. At least, she was counting on this being a bluff. If it was not, then she might have a little trouble.

But he was. Surely.

This was the part she'd known she must steel herself for. Threats made her stomach shake. She did not wish to issue them. But she would do what she must.

"Your sister Violet? Who is a Princess, I believe, in Monte Blanco. What would become of her and her country, of her husband, if the world found out that her brother was an assassin?"

His eyes went sharp. Good. "You are playing a dangerous game, Annick."

"Life is a dangerous game, is it not? And what of Minerva. Your sweet sister and her lovely children. Her husband. Your mother and father. What of them? If your identity was known, then their safety would be at risk."

"You dare threaten my family?"

"They are not threats." She shook her head. "I am merely presenting you with a piece of reality. It is not a threat—it is just true."

"The end result of your truth is that innocent people, innocent children, may die."

"Innocent people, innocent children, have died in my country already," she said. "And if I cannot successfully wrest control here, do I not risk another revolution? An invasion from my neighbors? Yes, I think I do. I *know* I do. I am not open to such risk-taking."

"And yet you have taken a risk coming here." He reached into his pocket and took a device out, and with a flick of his wrist, the lights came on.

She blinked against the invasive brightness. She had seen pictures of him, but they did not do him justice. He was a very large man, broad, with dark brown hair.

His face was handsome. Uncommonly so. She had never seen a man with quite such a competent scaffolding. A strange thing, human beauty. For it was just an arrangement of features and skin placed over bone in a particular fashion.

Yet his was quite striking.

And it made a sensation stir low in her belly. One that was foreign to her. It reminded her a great deal of fear, but it was not that. She was not afraid. Then she noticed that in one of his hands he still held the gun. The light revealed the weapon she had known was there all along.

Though she had the sense just then that the true weapon was the man himself.

"Please do not shoot me."

"I've no desire to shoot you. Therefore, to please us both—you and your desire to not be dead, me and my desire to not shoot a woman—I suggest you leave, and forget this conversation ever occurred."

"I cannot. I *cannot*, because it is what must be done for my people. I have been over many solutions. *Many.* Are you a man who desires power? As my guard, as my...my right-hand man, you would be very powerful."

"No. If I desired power, don't you think I would have filled one of the vacant positions I left behind already?"

"And that is a strange thing," she said. "Because most men do desire power, do they not?"

"I suppose, to an extent. But then, I often wonder if such men have ever been up close to it."

"Yes, a good observation, I think. For power does not entice me, personally. It is only that I must take it, as is my responsibility. My birthright. All my family are dead."

"I'm sorry. But you have presented a scenario wherein *my* family might all be dead."

"It is not what I want, Maximus King. I hope you understand. What I want is for the safety of my country to be secured. What I want is for you to help steady the situation that you have created."

"Again, the situation was not mine."

"Whose?"

"Your neighbors to the east, in Lackland. I believe they thought it better to depose the despot in power for their own reasons."

"Yes, for reasons likely of taking over. Which I do not want either. So, you can see the situation I find myself in. I need money. Would you not like to have this power?"

"As I said, I am not overly enamored of power."

"Then why do you do it? Why do you do this…this insipid job you pretend to do? What is it, repairing the reputations of Hollywood stars? And you kill people for money."

"I carry out missions assigned to me. And often that results in the deaths of men who would kill countless others. Countless innocents."

"You and the government then decide who is good and who is bad? What is that, if not an exercise in power? Playing God. Playing God with public opinion, playing God with life. Do not tell me you don't wish for power. I am not stupid, me."

She wondered, for a moment, if she had gone too far. He did not frighten her, not really. But she was very aware of the fact that if she pushed him too far, she would not get what she wanted, and that did frighten her. For she had no other plan. No other idea for how she might bail her country out of the disaster it found itself in.

"What other enticements have you to offer?"

She fortified herself with a breath. For she had been prepared for this moment. "Me. My body."

He looked her up and down. "Please do not take this the wrong way, but I have no need."

She narrowed her eyes, feeling insulted. "What does that mean?"

"I do not need to take a woman in trade for anything. If I want a woman, I simply have her."

"Not me."

"And that is supposed to be of particular enticement to me?"

She lifted a shoulder. "*No* man has had me. A shock, I would think, given that I have been kept prisoner for so long. But I think it was quite a game, right? To keep me untouched. For future leverage. Virginity is valuable."

His gaze flickered dispassionately over her again. "Is it? Here it is quite disposable. Something to throw away at the earliest of conveniences."

"Well, not for me. For every indignity I have suffered, for all that has been taken, not that. But I will give it to you."

"I don't have a need of your virginity, Princess. I didn't even need my own. It's been gone for twenty years and I haven't missed it."

"Money, then. What I have is a land rich with minerals. Gold and oil. Untapped. The dictators, they were not so smart, I think. But I learned a great many things, because I had nothing but time. So, I read. And what I discovered is that there is much unexplored in my country. But I need the investment to see it done. And I need to live. I need to keep living, or none of it matters. And for that I need you."

"You think you can buy me?"

"You are bought. Repeatedly. Do not pretend to be

a man of great principle now. If you are a man of great principle, then you would perform your task for free, but you do not."

"No one works for free."

"Yes, see? That is what I'm saying. No one works for free, and I do not expect you to. You protect me, and I will reward you in the end. Consider it a new mission, but this time you fix what it is you broke."

"You believe you need a guard? That you are in danger? And for how long do you foresee needing this?"

"I am to be crowned Queen soon, and I think…some time. It has been held off by the council, my coronation, to see if I am fit after my time as prisoner. And I worry the neighboring countries…lie in wait. It will take time."

"How much time?" he asked, impatient now.

"My neighbors in Lackland are a threat to me," she said. "I have intelligence that says they will overthrow me."

"From where?"

"Your government," she said, waving a hand. "Such a help they were, ridding us of dictator extraordinaire Pierre Doucet, and such aid was given! For all of three months and now I am threatened and on my own. So you see, I get insurance of my own. Protection of my own. And it is fair I confiscate one of their resources to do it."

"The resource being me?"

"Oui."

"You're trying to play the victim here, Annick, and yet you lead with a threat to my family?"

"You lead with a gun. So, seems fair."

She steeled herself, for she knew what was coming.

She knew what she had to do. She had planned for this. She had prepared for it.

"We will be quite close in the palace, while you protect me. I am ready to give you a preview of what we might share."

"Really?"

He stared at her stone-faced, and she took a step toward him. She had practiced this. Her hips swaying with each movement, eye contact with him never wavering. Of course, eye contact with herself in a mirror was a damn sight different than contact with the man himself. His eyes were blue. It was shocking on one with such dark hair. They were piercing, as if they could see into her soul. But he did not move.

His face was like rock. And his undoing would be that he underestimated her. His undoing would be that he did not think her an enemy.

She sighed, reached into her pocket and leaned in as if to kiss him.

Then she pulled the handkerchief out of her pocket and clapped it over his face. He removed her hand immediately, but it was too late. She had anticipated that. That he would be stronger. That his reflexes would be faster. That she would have to overdose him.

He growled and lunged toward her, knocking her back, and he came down on top of her, his hard body a heavy weight she could scarcely wiggle free of, until…

Until his muscles relaxed. Until it was clear that the chloroform had done its job.

"It is good that I planned for this."

But a one-woman kidnapping job of a very large man was not easy. Again, she had anticipated that and had brought with her a hospital gurney. In addition to a van she could load him in.

By the time she had driven to the airfield and unloaded him onto the private plane, she was feeling nearly cheerful. Had she known kidnapping her personal assassin would be quite so simple, she would have done it many years ago.

Now all that was left to do was…wait.

CHAPTER TWO

MAXIMUS WOKE READY to kill. He reached for his gun and found it wasn't there.

"I took it, obviously," came a now familiar voice.

Annick.

He immediately remembered everything that had transpired. And he had...

He was a fool. One of the most beautiful women in all the world had attempted to seduce him earlier tonight, and he had brushed her off without so much as a second glance. Annick looked at him with her round, pale eyes and had begun to walk toward him after offering her virginity, and he had stood still. He had told himself it was to see simply what she would do next, but the fact of the matter was, he had let his guard down. Which was not something he had done in his life. Not ever.

If he had, he would be dead.

No. He had done it once before. And a woman was dead because of it. But never since.

Until now.

"What the hell did you do?"

"Chloroform," she said, as if he were very stupid. "An old, but effective method to subdue. And now you are on my private plane."

"I thought you had no money."

"Not exactly. We have a limited economy in bad need of overhauling. And if selling a private plane would fix the problems I have, I would. This was obviously left over from the previous regime. The regime that no longer exists. Thank you for that. But like I said, you made this problem. I am pressed on all sides. It is not just Lackland who seeks to take advantage of my weaknesses."

"This is kidnapping," he said.

She spread her hands. "So it is. But I find I had no choice."

"I hate to tell you this, Princess, but you can't make me do what you want me to. I don't answer to anyone." He leaned back in his chair. "I'm no one's bitch. Least of all yours."

"What does this mean? *Bitch?* I do not wish you to be my 'bitch.' I wish you to be my guard and my counselor. Very clever of me. You can be *all* these things."

"Why me?"

"You know why. You are sent out by your government to depose men. Bad men. You have never once carried out an operation against the innocent, and that is not a credit to any nation, but to you."

"No," he said. "I leave the atrocities to others."

"But you don't. You don't *leave atrocities*. You handle them. You are Maximus King, this famous consultant and maker of social darlings. And you are The King, the military operative who has performed the most clean and precise removals of barbaric governments in modern history, whispered about and yet never really seen. Part of a branch of the military that may not truly exist. So many cover-ups, and coincidences, yes? And so you, specifically, are perfect for me. You will take a public position as my adviser, and given that I spent many years in a dungeon, it is perfect sense that I take an adviser. Adviser in public, guard in private. You are scary."

"Not to you, it seems."

"No, but," she said, "you are to others. And anyway, don't take it personally that you don't scare me. I am not scared by much."

She should be. She was small. Thin.

Her cheeks were round, but only because she was young. If he hadn't known about her history, then he wouldn't be able to guess. He knew about the royal family in Aillette. Their murders had been highly publicized at the time. Killed by a man who had their trust. An adviser to the King. That Princess Annick had been spared had been headline news. He had done even more digging into the royal family before he had gone to handle that bastard of a dictator last year. He knew that Annick was only twenty-two.

She was very pretty. Owed to a fine, aristocratic bone structure, and impossibly pale features. Her nose was small and pointed, her lips pale like the rest of her. Her lashes were nearly white, her eyes the softest of robin's-egg blue. She looked fragile in every way. Like contact with the sun would make her burst into flame. And she was telling him that she did not fear him.

"I lost my whole family. I lost my way of living. I was a prisoner, knowing that my only hope in all the world was, someday, for someone with more power than I to change things. Now I have power. I have a plane. I have a title. That means something. I will not sit back. Not ever again. And if I must die for my actions, then I will. But I will not wait. Not anymore. I am not a coward. And I am very angry that I have had to act the coward in order to wait until I might be most effective. You, I do not fear. I fear a life spent free where I still behave as if I am in a dungeon. That is what I fear."

He found the most grudging respect burned inside of him for Annick. Grown men feared him. As well they should. And this little Princess had kidnapped him. Something stirred inside of him, and the reaction gave him pause.

For he was not immune to feeling here.

Though for years now he had been.

Like tonight. Nothing, not a single thing, had stirred inside of him when Arianna had touched him. He couldn't get a thrill out of the job he did in the public eye. He could not even get an adrenaline rush out of pulling a gun on anyone. But this, this was interesting. This was something new.

What angered him was the fact that she thought she was in control.

"If we are to work together," he said, "you do not get the control. You cannot force me to do anything."

"Eh, but I can," she said. "With chloroform."

"You cannot possibly lug me around to every event you have planned."

She nodded her head slightly. "It is impractical, yes."

"At a certain point you will need my cooperation. And let us dispense with your threats to my family. I don't believe that you would do anything to put innocent lives in danger."

She looked regretful. "I would not *want* to."

"I don't think you will. Because that would be the real tragedy, wouldn't it? That they were able to make you into a monster such as them. Monsters who care only for their own goals."

"My goals are the welfare of my people."

"Every villain thinks they're a hero."

"Unfair," she said.

"I didn't realize we were playing fair."

"We are not playing at all," she said.

"I lie to the public to protect the images of shallow, silly people. I work in secret to rid the world of the truly vile," he said. "So the bottom line is, I'll do pretty much anything to line my pockets."

She looked at him, her eyes glittering.

"Not true," she said. "Or you would kill a bit more indiscriminately."

"I follow orders, but I make sure that I am fighting for the good of humanity. I'm not loyal to any one country, but to freedom. Human freedom. Human dignity."

"And that is what I want. Bring that to Aillette. Bring it to my people. And I will give you money."

A chance to liberate an entire country in this way was an interesting one. And in truth… He was getting tired. He was getting tired of all of it. Of the farce that he ran every day of his life. Of the wars he was waging behind the scenes.

Of seeking out atonement when he knew he could never have it.

When it came to dealing with the military, his tenure with them was much more on his own terms now than it had been in the beginning. And the unit he was part of didn't exist in an official capacity.

It was up to him what missions he did and did not take. If he wished to make Annick his mission for a time, that was up to him.

After all, if he left Annick in peril, everything he'd done up until now was a lie.

"There was an attempt on my life," she said softly. "I worry. And coming up is my coronation. I am to become Queen, not just a Princess. What will happen then, I do not know."

"You're worried they'll try again." Instantly, all of his instincts sharpened.

An attempt on her life, he could not allow. Not because he had—as she'd said—played God and upset the balance without ensuring she had adequate protection. But because if he did, then what would the point of any of it be?

To spend a life avenging one woman, while causing the harm of another.

It was everything he despised. Powerful men playing games with the world and women falling victim to them. Not because they weren't important, or smart, or strong at their core. But for want of that elusive power granted by society and the physical strength needed to fight off an enemy.

Annick needed muscle.

It could easily be him.

"Yes. The question is who do I trust, eh? I am left with a military, but who is loyal to me, really? I do not think I have the skills to ferret that out."

She didn't. Not like he did. She was small and pale and determined as hell, but she was not a military tactician. But he couldn't help her like she truly needed him to. Not with limited power.

There was a path forward that seemed clear to him, immediately.

"You might have yourself a deal," he said. "But I will have conditions."

"Yes," she said, waving a hand. "You would not be a good mercenary if you didn't have conditions."

"I'm not *a* mercenary," he said. "Not technically. And anyway, aren't you mercenary?" he asked.

"Clearly. To an extent. Would you like a drink?" She maneuvered around the cabin of the plane, the white outfit she was wearing flowing around her body, revealing curves that he had not realized were there. She had a generous behind, and her breasts were nicely rounded.

But that didn't mean he'd take her up on her offer. There were always women.

He did not need this one.

"How do I know you won't poison it?"

"I have already proven I have a willingness to poison you. It is whether or not you decide to trust me that I can help you with. I'm willing to do what I must to get you back to my country. You are already on the plane. So, why would I bother to do anything extreme now?"

"Whiskey."

"That is this?" She held up a bottle with amber liquid inside.

"Yes."

"I have never been allowed to drink," she said. "It would not do. For I had to maintain a visage of…purity. That's what it is. Pure, snow-white Princess." She indicated her outfit. "The symbol of the spirit of Aillette." She made a tutting sound. "Such lies."

"Why did they do that?"

"Why? Because the people were restless with the monarchy, but it was not ever popular to kill my family, even in the name of a revolution. It was not that my father was such a great King, but tradition matters. And so demonstrating that I was still there, and keeping me as some kind of symbol, I think it was to give people a good feeling. Limited though my outings were. I am far too talkative."

"Shocking."

"And I suppose sometimes it worked. Though now

the people are convinced I'm fragile. Even though I outlived the men who took over the country. So, who is fragile?"

"You're not fragile," he said. "Clearly."

That pleased her, he could tell. Though she tried not to smile, she fairly beamed from the inside out.

"I'm not," she agreed. "I'm quite ruthless."

"That is apparent."

"I do what I must. I am what I've had to become to survive. You understand." The creature thought she was a sight more frightening than she was, that was obvious.

Though he did understand her. That was the problem he could understand all too well. What happened when you were left behind.

When a bullet meant for him had instead struck the woman he loved, everything had shifted. He had not been able to save Stella.

He looked at Annick. And he felt a grudging tug in his chest. As if Stella were there asking if all he could do was kill for her.

It's so easy, isn't it? To take out bad men and imagine the face of her killer every time. But that's revenge. This is a chance to actually save someone.

A vulnerable woman.

"I think we can help each other," he said.

"I knew you would see," she said, brightening.

"Yes. I see. I don't want your body," he said.

She wrinkled her nose. "Well, that is fine in any case."

She looked vaguely insulted.

"But I will take a share of what I'm investing in here." In fact, he would welcome the chance to be rid of that farce he conducted in Hollywood. It had never been a game he'd enjoyed, but lately it had grown more and more tiresome. There was a limit to how much amusement he could extract from fooling the world.

The double life he lived was wearing on him. It offended him. To go and play at rehabbing images and then go off and take down another totalitarian regime.

And all he ever did was make the smallest dent in the world. Rolling a stone up a hill forever.

And here she was, offering him a chance at redemption.

Offering him power.

"I'll help you, Annick." And he was formulating an idea of just how she could help him. She wouldn't like it. He didn't care. "You don't need my image. You need to create one of your own. I would be willing to help you with that."

"Just for money?"

He inclined his head. She didn't need to know about Stella. That was his business. His wound.

His debt.

"I am skeptical."

"I will transform you into the leader your country needs. I will cow your enemies. Better yet, you will."

He straightened as she handed him the whiskey. He swirled the liquid in the glass, doing his part to channel the Maximus King that everyone knew. It was easier. A more comfortable skin for him to act in. Annick had come face-to-face with the soldier. Few people knew of him. Even fewer who had *met* the soldier now lived to speak of it. But everyone knew this version of Maximus King. The Playboy. The one who took no one and nothing overly seriously. And why would he not take this job? It was a lark, after all.

"And if it is not fixed then? Then what? You leave—"

she waved her hand "—and I am back where I was. No. I need more. I need you to stand in. I need you to keep my enemies at bay."

"Trust me, I will make Aillette into a fortress of wealth and perceived power. I will ensure you are safe, Annick. You have my word on that."

"I lived for too long, I survived for too long, to lose it all now. You cannot let it happen."

She faltered, truly faltered, and he could see now that everything Annick had done up until this point had been driven by terror. By fear. And if he were a different man, he might've felt some guilt. Might have felt some pity. Instead, he felt anger. Anger was about the only emotion he knew. It was about the only thing he could manage. Otherwise… Otherwise his chest felt hollow. Dead. It was the rage that kept him going.

His grief had burned out years ago. Like the blood that had drained from Stella as he held her in his arms. As she had died. That grief was gone.

Replaced by the poison of hatred. It fueled him. It spurred him on. It had made him lethal. It had made him useful.

The sad thing was, he knew how to play the role of Maximus King so well, because it was who he had spent the first twenty-two years of his life as. A debauched playboy. A debauched playboy who had loved precisely one person in his life more than he loved himself. And she had died in his arms.

He had been Annick's age then. And it had changed him forever.

And here Annick was, never having been silly or young. She had been a prisoner. And now she was being asked to lead a country.

"I won't. I'll protect you."

And he didn't need ask anymore why it was his responsibility. It clearly was. Nothing to be done about it.

He wasn't a good man. And he was nobody's superhero.

But when he made a promise, he kept it.

It was why he didn't make very many.

"Good." She seemed happy.

"Did you want some whiskey?"

She wrinkled her nose. "No. I think perhaps it is best that I keep my wits about me. That is a bad thing about alcohol. It takes your wits."

He chuckled. "Not a problem I have."

"Why?"

"I drink too much. And it has ceased to affect me."

She frowned. "Why?"

"Don't you have things you like to forget?"

She nodded, her expression getting very sad. "I have so many things I would like to forget. But I spent a great many years with only my own company, and I have been forced to go over the very bad things in my mind far too many times. Now… There is little point. It is too late. I have relived the past over and over again."

"I'm sorry."

Her lips curved upward. "I almost believe you."

"I am," he said, taking another drink of the whiskey.

"Do you feel it?" She touched her chest. "Here. Your sorry."

He wished he could tell her he did. That, in and of itself, was a novelty. "No. But I don't feel anything there. Except for maybe anger."

She nodded. "I am well familiar with that. It burns. I have been so angry, for so many years. Sometimes anger is the only thing that keeps you alive. And everything else… It just hurts too badly."

"Yes, you're right. Anger is easy. Anger gets things done."

"Pity is a pointless one. I tried that when I was twelve. Felt an endless amount of self-pity to go along with my grief. But then I remember, I'm the one that's alive. Not my family. So pity is not something I should feel for myself. Angry is better."

"Angry is better." He lifted his glass. "And if you would drink, we could say cheers to that."

"Say cheers?" She squinted and looked at him.

"A toast," he clarified.

"It is not toast."

"No. It's… *Salud.*"

"Right," she said, understanding.

"Where did you learn English?" he asked, intrigued by this woman who was such a strange mix of naivete and cynicism.

"From my governess. When I was a girl. So I had a lot of years when I did not use it. But I made a game in my head. To remember to speak French, and English, and German. So that I don't forget any."

"What was your life like?"

"Oh, it was not *so* bad. Except the loneliness. I had school. They could not risk me being stupid. But they also did not want me to be too educated, so they did not show me news from the world outside. I have spent the last year reading about everything that happened. Everything that happened in the world. It has been a strange and depressing time for me. But also, good."

"I imagine. That many years of world history all in one go seems a little bit extreme."

She smiled. "My life is nothing but extreme. That I can say."

"How long until we arrive in Aillette?"

"Soon. Only maybe a half hour now. I had to give you a lot of chloroform. You're very large."

He laughed. "And you are certain you wouldn't kill me?"

"I truly hope to not kill you, Maximus King. I need you too badly."

And something reached down deep in his chest just then, something he hadn't expected. Because he could not remember the last time someone had looked at him quite like that. He had been told a number of times by women that they needed him. They needed him to rehabilitate their image, which was essentially what he was going to do for Annick. That they needed him sexually. Yes, that was one of his favorites. His chest might be dead, but the rest of his body was not, and he did enjoy beautiful women. One of the perks of selecting the persona that he had chosen to carry on with his normal life.

Maximus King, the image consultant in San Diego, could have any woman he wanted. He took nothing seriously. He was charming and good in conversation. And he was even better in bed.

So yes, he was accustomed to women saying they needed him.

But not like this.

There was no greed in her eyes. No avarice.

There was an honesty there, that was what called to him. An honesty that was so different from anything he had been exposed to for an age.

It was simple. And clear.

She said that she needed him, and she meant it.

She also wouldn't hesitate to use chloroform on him if she needed to.

He didn't doubt that either. She'd do it again.

"But you were willing to risk it."

"Well, if I could not bring you back to Aillette, then I would not have had you anyway."

"Very practical."

"I told you. I had a lot of time to think. I have had a lot of time."

"And how did you find out that I was the one who performed the assassination?" That was very important. Because if he had been made by one of his contacts, then it was going to be a problem. There were very few people who knew his identity. As Annick had already said, those people had a vested interest in the outside world not knowing that they knew who he was. Or why they knew him.

"I'll never tell anyone about you," she said. "I swear it. And it is not important how I know."

"It is," he said. "I need to make sure there aren't enemies out there we both need to know about."

"No! It's only me. And I needed you. It was what I had to use against you, so I did."

"Good. You were desperate, and I will forgive you for that. But if you ever threaten my family again..."

"It is not a thing I want to do. I don't want to threaten your family. I don't wish it."

"Good."

"Ah," she said. "We are descending. I look forward to welcoming you to Aillette."

CHAPTER THREE

SHE DIDN'T KNOW why she was nervous. It was a very strange thing. To feel nervous. He was not a prisoner anymore. Sometime during the flight they had made the transition from prisoner and jail keeper into allies. And she was much more comfortable with that. She had no wish to become a jailer. Not simply because she'd had one her entire life. It was far too much work. She needed help. She did not need another project. If he had continued to resist her…

It would have been a problem.

Of course, his denial that he wanted her body had wounded her slightly, but she would not dwell on that. There was no reason for her to feel out of sorts over that exchange.

They walked into the palace, and she found she wanted him to like it. Which was quite strange. But she had changed the palace quite a bit since the other regime had fallen, and she was proud of the changes she'd made. The modernizations.

"It is a bit different since you were here last," she said, feeling proud.

He flicked a glance around the space. "I suppose it is."

"You do not remember."

"I have one job when I am sent on these missions. It is to get in and out without being detected until it is too late. That's it."

"You're cold, aren't you?"

"I have to be."

"To have a secret life? Or just to live?"

"Either. Both. Don't you think?"

"I wish I could be cold," she said, feeling a bit flat. "But I'm not. I never have been."

"Only a while ago you claimed to be ruthless," he pointed out.

It was quite annoying.

"I think they are different things. I am willing to do whatever I must for Aillette. For my people. They have suffered enough. I have suffered enough. We all have lived a collective hell. And yes, I have been willing to do what needed to be done in order to pull us from it. But there is no… There is no coldness in me. I burned with it. Like I said."

"I burn when I'm angry."

She stared at him, and suddenly, she felt warm. There was something about the look on his face, about the keenness in his blue eyes, that made her feel unsettled. That made her feel…strangely hungry. She did not like it. Did not understand it.

She squinted. "But you're cold mostly?"

Amusement tipped his mouth upward. "Mostly."

One of the women who worked on her staff, Elise, rushed up to them. "You've returned," she said, speaking in their native language, which was a dialect of French that the Parisians insisted was not French at all.

"Oui," Annick confirmed. "With Maximus King. He is my new…guard. Adviser."

"Good?" she said, phrasing it as a question.

"For the whole country," Annick said, switching to English. "He will be a great asset to Aillette. He is a businessman. And he will know how to help with the finances. He will also be exactly what we need to be taken seriously."

He chuckled. "I can't say that the world takes me seriously."

He had slipped into some sort of character. She had noticed it on the plane. Their interactions at his house and the initial interactions when he woke up were markedly different to the interactions they had after she'd given him his whiskey. She didn't know why. Except...

She knew that he had a double life. She knew that the man that he pretended to be was not the man he actually was. She knew that he was lethal. Dangerous. And that the majority of the world had no idea.

Perhaps he was playing that up, even now. And she could see why. He played an interesting and dangerous game. Being as visible as he was, conducting missions that required the utmost in discretion.

"Ready him a room," she said, and all of the women that were present in the antechamber nodded and scurried about their business. She looked to him, to see if he was impressed with the organization of the palace.

"You have a lot of women working here," he said.

"I do," she said happily. "That was one of the first changes I made, you know. For when I was here before, it was all men. Except those doing menial positions. I made a change. Women in this country who desperately needed money... I hired them. Now they can take care of themselves. If they have husbands that are cruel to them, they can leave. This is a very good thing."

"It is a good thing," he confirmed.

"I would hire men if I needed them. I am hiring you. But for the most part I find women do the work just fine."

He chuckled. "Sadly, you need a man to protect you?"

"It's sad, this thing in the world. I am not so strong."

She looked up at the ceiling. It was midnight blue marble, swirled through with bright colors. It reminded her of the painting *The Starry Night*, and she had always thought it beautiful. She had made changes to the palace, but what she'd said was true. They were not flush with money. These things were not changes she had bought. These stones had been here for centuries. The only things that remained of her family. She had always found them soothing.

"I do not care much for men."

She had not meant to say that out loud. He was, after all, a man, and she needed his help, so perhaps it was not in her best interest to say mean things about his gender.

"You don't?"

She would have to answer for that now. "*Non*. It was not women, after all, who seized power in my country and killed my family."

"No, I suppose it wasn't. If it helps, I'm not a big fan either. I have seen a great many atrocities in this world. Most of them committed by men. So I'm with you."

"Well. I'm glad we can at least agree on that. Though I hear tell that your sex has a few things to recommend it."

"Do you?"

"I have heard. I surround myself now with many women, and we have conversations. Most of them have a fondness for at least one man in their lives. That is fair, I think. But... I do not know enough of men."

"Is that why you offered me your body?"

Heat flooded her face. "It is not a gentlemanly thing to remind me of that, I think."

"Is that so?"

She frowned deeply. "You turned me down."

"I was not aware it was a proposition, so much as a form of payment." He looked her over, his expression dispassionate. "Payment I don't require."

"Yes. That is what it was. Payment. If you don't want it, it's okay with me."

"Then you don't need to be so angry about it."

"I'm not angry," she said. "I have no anger to waste on you, in truth."

"Another very good thing, because I have a feeling that anyone who is on the receiving end of your anger is going to find himself very unhappy."

"Yes. This is true." She looked at him out of the corner of her eye. "It was a good thing they did not wish me dead. Pierre Doucet, he was a friend of my father's, and yet he killed my father, his wife and son. By order, at least. He did not spare me due to any sentimentality. I tell you this. He only wished to use me when it was convenient to show my face, and I made it hellish hard for him. I do not hold my tongue well." Anger, sadness and old fear welled up in her chest. "I might have suffered when I misbehaved, but it was worth it. A reminder that I was still me."

"They hurt you?"

She lifted a shoulder. "They killed my whole family. Stole my life. A beating here and there was nothing." She felt moisture in her eyes and hated it.

He stopped her. He did not touch her, but his gaze stopped her. And she saw there... The predator.

"I am very glad I was put on the mission to kill Pierre Doucet. I am glad I ended him."

She was not used to this. Not used to someone being so firmly on her side. "As am I."

She led him through the palace and toward the rooms that she had chosen to be his. "Here you are," she said, thankful to leave the previous subject and its accompanying heaviness in the past. "I think you will be comfortable. I have given you extra blankets."

That earned her a very long stare. "Thank you. In your chloroform kidnap, you didn't by chance happen to pick up a razor, did you? Because if not, I find myself inconvenienced."

"It is there," she said, feeling proud. "Everything you need. I anticipated that we might have difficulty. You know, I came prepared with chloroform. And I was prepared to have this room fitted out for you. With razors and anything else you might need."

"I see. And how did you, a woman who admittedly knows nothing of men, accomplish that?"

"I told you. I have women I work with who know. I do not need to know." She stepped into the room, pleased with the grandness of it. Surely he would be too. Shortly, he would be happy with this place. She might need his help, and she might need an investment, but with what she had she could offer much. The room was large, and though everything in it was old, it was competently outfitted. And she was quite pleased with it. "You will find suits."

"I don't wear suits that you buy in a store."

"We did not buy these in a store. They are made for you."

"And how," he said, "did you accomplish that?"

"I was very proud of this. I called your sister."

He frowned. "You called my sister? Which sister?"

"Minerva. I called Minerva, and I told her that I was designing you a suit, but could not get a hold of you, and that I needed information from your tailor, which she gave to me. And then I got your measurements."

"You are a stunning little weasel—do you know that?"

"What does this mean? *A weasel*. I'm not a weasel."

"Sneaky. Weasels are sneaky."

"Oh, yes," she said, feeling pleased with that. "I am sneaky. So. A weasel it is."

"You know," he said, pausing at the center of the room. "You're the only one who knows. The only one who knows who I am. Everyone else in this world knows Maximus King, and some might know about The King, that much-whispered-about super soldier. But they don't know both."

"*I* know both. Though what I do wonder is if actually no one knows either one. Do you know?"

"What kind of question is that?"

She shrugged. She shouldn't keep staring at him. He really was desperately handsome, and it was throwing her off-balance.

He was the kind of man who made a woman do foolish things. Those were the kinds of things she knew about from her staff. They had become her friends. And she could admit she had hired women her age so that she might have some friends.

She had missed a lot of life.

And she listened as they sighed and moaned and talked about all the ways they were fools for the men they claimed to love. Annick had found it incredibly off-putting. But she was also curious; she couldn't deny it. She did not know men. And that was... It was a difficult realization.

She had lived around them and been kept by them, but men to her were nothing more than imposing physical presences. Every one of her captors had disgusted her. Every one. But what she felt when she looked at Maximus was not disgust. Not even close. She had a feeling it connected up to all that long-suffering sighing of the women she knew. But she also could not quite imagine what it would mean. Physical intimacy like that. She knew what it was, in the practical sense. Knew what it was physically. But she did not really understand why a person would do it.

She looked at him, and heat stole over her body.

Do you really not understand?

"An honest one," she said. "The man you were at your house, the man when you woke up on the plane, the man you are now, they are not all the same man. So I wonder. Do you know which is real? Are any of them real?"

"Here's a hint. I was *this* man once. This one. Maximus King. Charming and easy to be around. With absolutely no blood on his hands." He paused for a moment. "Until I wasn't."

"I see. Something happened to you."

"Yes. Something happened to me."

Except, she had the sense that that wasn't strictly true either. That he was holding something back, even saying that much.

"Get your suit," she said. "And dress for dinner. You will join me and we will go over the timeline for my plans. I am eager to speak of such things."

Then she turned and left him there, feeling trembly and shaky and not entirely certain what was happening inside of her.

But it didn't matter. What mattered was that in just two weeks, she would be Queen. And Maximus King was here to protect her.

She had done it.

That was all that mattered.

CHAPTER FOUR

THE SUIT FIT, which irritated him more than he would like to admit. That the little devil surprised him was also more irritating than he would like to admit.

There was something about her. About the way she asked questions. The way she talked about her life. He found it difficult to be unaffected by her.

What he was good at was showing no emotion at all. Betraying nothing of what was going on inside of him. And so, when she had spoken again of offering her body, he had been able to remain outwardly impassive.

Even while inside he had felt more than a stirring of interest.

Come to dinner.

She was issuing commands that he had no reason to deny. Which would most certainly put her in a false mind of just how in control she was.

He could walk away from all of this at any time. This insanity. This farce.

But nothing has held your interest this long for…

Well, that was the issue. Nothing had. He often wondered if it was even possible for him to feel anything again. And then she had shown up. She had made him feel… Well, she had made him feel.

And she had managed to fill a closet up with custom suits that fit.

That in and of itself earned his acceptance of the dinner invitation, he should think.

The palace itself was old. Not crumbling, but definitely showing its age. Fortunately, it was put together with precious stones and metals, and those things tended to gather color and richness as they aged. Tended to find a new sort of life.

The palace was no exception. The jade and amethyst, emerald and ruby, was only that much more entrancing now.

And if he were a man whose head was turned by such things, he would be in awe.

But no. The gemstones did not do it. However, when he walked into the dining room and saw her, he felt his blood begin to heat.

She was different than when he had seen her last. She had been dressed all in white before, a flowing pantsuit, with her pale blond hair caught in a knot at the base of her neck.

Now she was wearing a green gown cut to show off her curves. Her blond hair was loose, spilling over bare shoulders, falling like corn silk over her breasts. Everything about her looked soft. And he knew that wasn't the case. So the artistry that must've gone into making her appear that way was surely a thing of great mastery.

The makeup around her eyes was gold, her lips crimson.

"I'm glad you could join me," she said.

"You will recall it was more a demand than a request."

"I did half expect to have to drag you out of your bedroom."

"I was banking on you not wishing to chloroform me in order to accomplish the task. But then, I also don't see the point of turning down a free meal."

"A smart man. Very smart. And good."

"No," he said. "Not good."

"I meant only that it is good you are smart. I did not mean you were good. You are, I know, a killer."

"Yes," he said.

"Your family does not know."

"No," he said, taking a seat at the head of the long table. "My family does not know. Nor will they."

"Perhaps we could invite some of them to my coronation. Under the pretense you are my consultant. It will be advantageous for me to have a connection to Monte Blanco. And to your brother-in-law, Prince Javier."

"Yes. I'm sure it will be advantageous for you. It's a shame he's so busy with his new wife, or you could've kidnapped him."

"It is true," she said. "He would have been most convenient. A spare, no official position in his country, but raised to be royal. Also, he is the captain of the guard." She frowned. "His brother, though, I hear has an ill humor. He would not have liked me to kidnap him."

"You know a lot about my brother-in-law."

"Of course. It pays to know these things. As I said, I have spent the last year going over everything."

"What have you learned?"

"Everything about world events." She squared her small shoulders. "You know they shielded me from many things. What was happening out there. And I wanted to learn all of it, and I did. And I thought…it would make the blank spaces in my mind feel full." She blinked. "It did not." She didn't speak for a long moment. "I wonder… I wonder. I would like…some time to learn more about myself."

"What do you mean by that?"

She shrugged, in that rather careless way she had. "You know, I have had so much decided for me. And even now, I know so little. I wish to do things like choose my own clothes. As an example. I hate everything that was bought for me. So, when the regime fell, I had my staff choose clothes for me. But I don't know if it is what I like. I don't know how to know what it is I like. Same with food. I did not keep the same menus, but I went back to what my mother and father made. Some I like. Some…"

"So what you're telling me is you know a lot about the state of the world, but not what you want to eat for dinner."

"It is exactly this," she said. "Some things I know… Some things I don't."

"I…" He found himself speechless, which was…not something that he could remember happening. Except he suddenly realized that he wasn't sure what he liked anymore either. He played a part. Slipped that role on like a second skin. He drank to excess in public because Maximus King would. He had supermodels on his arm because it was what Maximus King would do. Some grotesque version of himself that he imagined might have existed had he never known Stella. Had he never been in love.

A reckless playboy who cared only about appeasing his own appetites. But for someone who indulged as richly as he did in the hedonistic things of this world, he could not say that he loved them. He drank whiskey on the plane because whiskey was what he drank, not because he loved whiskey particularly. And he found the sort of beauty Annick possessed to be far more compelling than the beauty on any of those supermodels. As for food…

He ate what was served to him. He did not consider it much.

"What is it?"

"That will be our first step, Annick. We will find out what you like to eat. How do you summon your staff?"

"A bell," she said. She looked very pleased, and she produced a small silver bell.

"Ring it."

She did so. And three women appeared, with their hair in low, neat ponytails, their clothing all the same, black from head to toe.

"We need food. Food from restaurants in the city. Whatever was being cooked tonight, bring that too, but bring a variety. Annick—Princess Annick—needs to try some things."

"What are you doing?" she asked.

"It does not do, Annick, for a Queen to not know her own mind. You need to know what you like. Everything you like. Because it is the job of those around you to make you happy, to make you comfortable, and if you do not know what you want, how can you give easy commands? If you cannot give easy commands… you don't look like you're in charge."

She looked like she was considering this. "Okay."

"Mostly," he said, "if you don't enjoy things, you will become cold and hard and dead inside."

"What? Like you?" She asked it with some humor, but she had no idea.

"Yes," he said. "Like me."

She looked slightly abashed. "Sorry," she said.

"Are you going to say that you didn't mean it?"

"Oh, no," she said. "I very much meant it. Only I am sorry that I said it. I'm very out of practice with talking to people I don't hate."

He laughed, the bubble of humor in his chest entirely unexpected.

"Are you?"

"I have made friends," she said. "Here on my staff. But it is a learning process."

"I see."

"Yes, I think you do."

"Regrettably, talking to people that you hate will be part of the position that you occupy. I have to talk to people I hate all the time."

"As a hit man or as an image consultant?"

"As an image consultant. I don't talk to anyone in my other job. And you had better be careful about where and how you speak of such things. I'll ask again—how did you find out about me?"

She shifted. "No one knows who 'The King' is. I know. They know you are coming for them, but they did not know from where. Me, I listen. I have nothing else to do but listen. I collect information as I can. And somehow, it all just fit."

"How did you know about me at all?"

"Your sister Violet. I was fascinated by her. By this woman from California, who married a Prince and helped reform a country. After all, is that not what I must do?"

"Yes. Though I think you must give her husband and his brother some of the credit for the reformation of their country."

"Yes. I did not say they don't get credit. But I was intrigued by the way bringing in an outsider could help. That is when I started looking at you. And that is when I realized. That you are The King."

"Again, how?"

"Connecting dots."

"No one else has connected those dots."

"When you are a prisoner for so very long, and cut off from so many things, your other senses become heightened. And you learn how not to be stupid. And so, I am not stupid."

"Tell me."

"I saw you."

His breath left his body. She looked up at him, her pale eyes glittering. "I was hiding. In the dungeon. I heard footsteps. And I am not a fool. When you are kept locked away, you have very few options when it comes to deciding when you want to speak to someone or not. So, often, I'm quiet. I hid in the corner. I heard you. And I saw you. But you did not see me. I was in the darkness, and I saw you. Your eyes."

"My face was covered."

She shook her head. "Doesn't matter. I saw your eyes, and though you did not see me, I felt it. Like lightning here," she said, touching her stomach. "When I saw you in your house, it was the same. I've never seen eyes like lightning."

He gritted his teeth, holding back what he thought might be the truth. It wasn't so much that she *recognized* him as she was attracted to him. And who would have ever thought that his undoing would become some virgin trapped in a dungeon *recognizing* him because he made her heart beat faster.

"But you must have known before you came."

"I suspected. I suspected from seeing pictures, yes. But I knew for sure when I went to your house."

"And if you had been wrong?" he asked.

"I might have kidnapped you anyway. Either way, either persona, is of use to me."

"You *are* ruthless, aren't you?"

His proclamation seemed to cheer her immensely. "I said so. I don't lie, Maximus. I tried. It would have been easier were I proficient at it. I might have been let out of the dungeon more. I might have been beaten less. And now here I am, free. I *hate* lies. If I am to be the best Queen, then I cannot lie."

"Life is a bit grayer than that, Annick. I hate to inform you."

"Eh…" she said, that nasal sound of dismissal she seemed quite fond of. "I'm tired of gray. I'm tired of the dark."

She would not like, then, what he was planning. But she would have no choice.

She'd brought him here.

But he would be the one to decide how it went.

Then the doors to the dining hall flung open and in came trays laden down with food.

For now, he would let her eat.

"And here we are," he said. "Your dinner is served."

Annick stared at the food that had now been laid out on the table, and then she looked back at the man who was responsible for ordering it.

"This is nice."

She foolishly found that she wanted to cry.

She had read once, in her studies, that small kittens that were kept in cages from the time they were born still saw the bars in front of them even when they were removed, and staring at this feast laid out in front of her, she had to wonder if she had been seeing bars where there were none.

If she still treated herself as a prisoner. She often kept to corners of the palace. She did not indulge herself overmuch. Some of it was wanting to preserve that which she felt was important. Her integrity. Some of it was being afraid that wanting too much would make her little more than a dictator.

But… He had brought all this food from restaurants run by her people. It surely benefited them that this money had been spent.

Her stomach growled. She was hungry. And she was…delighted.

"I have never seen so much food." She frowned. "Except I must have. In the early days of the palace. I was twelve when that ended. And I know I have memories from before. But…"

"It's hard," he said, his voice surprisingly tender. "When memories from before are too good."

She nodded. "Yes, it is not bad memories that I turn away from. The bad reminds me why I keep going. It always has. It is a terrible thing to think of my parents dying. But their deaths reminded me of why I lived. But remembering how happy we were…that was too painful. Well and truly."

"Annick," he said. "You can enjoy the food."

She practically fell upon it then. She was starving. But it had more to do with everything else than it did actual physical hunger.

She piled the plate high with salad, french fries, bread, pastry. Steak.

"Quite an assortment."

"It is what I want. Isn't that what this is about? What I want?"

"Yes."

She suddenly felt a bit bratty and quite self-indulgent. But she wanted it. For just these few moments.

"Eat pastries first," she said.

"Is that by royal command?"

"Unless you don't want to. Eat what it is you want. But do not let protocol stop you from eating the pastries."

"Annick, protocol never stops me from anything."

She studied him. "No. I expect not."

She had done so much reading about him. About The King and about Maximus. And she wondered which bits and pieces were true. She wondered if he was half so... wicked as the tabloids claimed.

And then she wondered why she was quite so interested. Yes, she had been prepared to offer her body to him. The very idea made her warm now. What would she have been? If she had been free? What foods would she have liked? Would she have had a score of lovers by now?

She very much liked the look of this man. She wanted to touch him. It stood to reason that if she were around other men who possessed a certain level of attractiveness, she might wish to touch them too. And if she had full freedom...she might have.

She turned her focus back to the food, but she could feel his eyes on her.

"You must realize, Annick, that your plan will not work."

She looked at him again. "What?"

"Adviser. Guard. These are not official titles. It is not a statement. It is not strong."

"And you think you can do better than this plan?"

"I know I can. It isn't enough to have me by your side. You want 'The King'? I will be the King, Annick. But you will be my wife."

CHAPTER FIVE

"FOOLISHNESS!" SHE SAID, without even thinking. "I cannot *marry* you."

"And why not?"

"You said you didn't want power," she said, narrowing her eyes. "A lie. You are making the ultimate power grab now that you are here."

"You brought me here—you can hardly accuse me of engineering it. But think about it. What stronger stance will you take as a Queen than having a King beside you? And I can protect you, truly protect you. I can be in your chamber at night."

Heat crackled up her spine. "You said you did not want my body."

"I do not. But this is a traditional country. Do you think you won't create rumors by bringing me here? Me? With my reputation?"

Her eyes went narrow and bright. "Okay. I see. But... but to what end?"

"*Any* end. The end that makes the most sense."

"And what do you get out of it?"

"The good I can do commanding an army outstrips what I can do alone. Don't you think?"

"For how long?" she asked, her chest squeezing tight. "How long would we have to...?"

"For life. A royal marriage cannot be anything else, but we can live separate lives."

"And…and children?" she asked, her throat dry as sandpaper.

"There will have to be children. For your kingdom." His words were like stone. "But no need to concern ourselves with them for now, don't you think?"

She shook her head, her ears buzzing like they were filled with bees. "Years."

"Years," he agreed.

"I am angry with you," she said, her heart thundering hard. "Because this is not stupid. Not foolish. But I do not want it."

"I didn't want to come here in the first place, but you brought me. If you bring a lion into your house, you cannot be angry when he goes on the hunt, can you?"

She sat there, her scalp and cheeks burning with shame.

"What are you thinking about?"

"Sex," she responded.

"A topic you seem invested in."

Her face was like fire now. "Well, you asked me for marriage, and that means it matters. Is what they say about you true?"

"Who, and what?"

"The papers. They say you're very wicked. That you…that you have an insatiable appetite for women. In a sexual sense."

"I understood what you meant."

"Well, I find that I'm curious. If it is true."

"No."

Her stomach felt something strange. It was a lot like disappointment, though it shouldn't have been. "Oh."

"I'm not insatiable. I suppose, if you ask some, I'm

wicked. But…insatiable implies a bit more passion than perhaps I feel."

"You are not passionate?"

He looked down the table. "You're hungry, yes?"

"Yes, I am hungry. Maybe five times a day. I eat small amounts at a time typically."

"Sex is another appetite," he said.

The words were flat, and practically spoken. And she did not think they should make her stomach go tight.

"When I am hungry, I eat. When I want a woman, I seek one out. I do not see the point in denying hungers. But I'm not a glutton."

"Hmm," she mulled. "Perhaps I am."

"Do you think?"

She looked at her plate of food, which was half-demolished. And she looked at what remained. "Yes. I think I might be. I have been denied, and this is all here. And I want it all. Everything I have missed."

"You think it will be the same with other things?"

"I'm beginning to wonder." She frowned. "Will you have love affairs?"

"I do not intend that we should be beholden to only each other," he said. "Be as gluttonous as you wish."

"So, you would have me take lovers, then?"

"Eat your food, Annick."

His patience with her was wearing very thin. She could see.

"I suppose I must learn to be less forthright."

"Probably."

"It's just I'm very tired of this."

"I'm sorry, but a life in the public eye is to an extent signing up for a *life* of subterfuge. This is something I know a lot about. And you did not answer me."

"This is not fair. I want to be *me*, and I want to be free, but that is not… It is not possible, is it?"

"No. For a life of public service means always carrying yourself with a certain amount of diplomacy."

"Yes. Though…"

"There is no *though*," he said. "If you wish to be taken seriously as a leader, if you wish to be seen as something other than a child, caught in the center of all this, if you wish to be a Queen, to escape the tragedy that has happened to you, then you have to behave like any leader would be expected to behave."

"I have done," she said, feeling irritated now. And exceptionally hard done by. "I went and kidnapped you, did I not? I behaved as a leader would. I refused to subject my country to further unrest by keeping us at risk. I am strong."

"Then you will learn to show it in a way that the world recognizes. You asked me to come and help you. I have offered marriage. Now, don't resist me."

She let out a particularly delicious French curse and then took another bite of delicious pastry. At least her fury paired well with butter.

"Don't take it personally."

"I'm tired," she said. "That is all."

"Go to bed."

"No. I'm tired of my life. For a moment, I looked at all this food and I thought, why should I not have everything I want? But then you reminded me. You reminded me that I must be, in some way, still not me."

"You can be you. With the friends that you have here in the palace. It's just that with diplomats you are going to have to endeavor to behave in a certain fashion."

"All right. I endured prison these many years. Why not more?"

"It is prison?" he asked. "To be married to me?"

"I do not know." She looked at the table laid out before her. She would have had to choose a husband someday. And he was a good choice. The idea made her skin feel oversensitive. "No. I suppose it's not."

"And a gentle reminder, that you have taken me prisoner."

"You have agreed," she said.

"In the way that you agreed?"

She waved a hand at him. "Don't do that. Don't try to paint yourself as some sort of victim, when we both know you're not. You would not stand for it. You have agreed to help me, and I cannot say that I know why, but I do know this—you have chosen to. I was prepared to fight to bring you over to my side, but I did *know* that I needed to bring you to my side. I knew that I was not going to be able to hold you as a prisoner."

"Indeed, Annick."

"Don't you ever feel tired? Two lives. It's too many lives. I did not even do it so successfully, and it was too many for me."

"It is not," he said. "Because I am living one of them for someone who cannot live at all. Perhaps if you thought of it that way, it would help."

Her heart twisted, the sympathy that she felt surprising her. She had lost so much it was rare that anyone else's loss touched her. Then again, she didn't often sit and speak to another person. Not like this.

"Who did you lose?"

"It doesn't matter. *Who* doesn't matter—not anymore. But dedicating my life to removing men from the world who create destruction? That is a fitting tribute to their memory. Trust me on that."

"It is strange, is it not? That sometimes to become

avengers of atrocities we must commit some of the same. You know, me kidnapping you."

"We do what we must. I cannot despise you too greatly because of that."

"I find I cannot despise you, this marriage bargain notwithstanding. But then, it was never my goal."

"What is your favorite?"

She looked at all the food. "I couldn't choose."

"You must have a favorite."

"Choice. That's my favorite."

He smiled and nodded slowly. "That is a good answer."

CHAPTER SIX

HE SLEPT WELL in the palace, and there was something surprising about that. It was strange to be here as himself, when the last time, he had been here as The King.

He looked in the closet, shaking his head. The way that Annick had gone about procuring a wardrobe for him was one of the most ridiculous things he'd ever heard. But also, ingenious, and it was true what he'd said to her last night. He had to respect her determination. She was a strong, feral creature, and if Stella had wanted him to pour his energy into anything, it would've been helping Annick.

It was not all truism that drove him, not really. There was something more difficult to pin down. He had been working for years now to try and make Stella's death mean something. The problem was, there was not much in the way of meaning to be found in the death of a beautiful young woman caught in a firefight between businessmen that she should've had nothing to do with. He was not a man who sat. He was not a man who stood idly by and let things happen, and he had been unable to do anything when it had mattered most.

He dressed in a suit and marveled at the fact that it really did fit perfectly.

He paused for a moment, guessing where he thought Annick might be.

And for some reason, he knew she would still be in her room.

There'd been something watchful about her in the large dining room. She had said she was not accustomed to big meals like that, and what he wondered was if Annick was still uncomfortable in large spaces. She had been kept in a dungeon most of her life, so he could see why. He paused in front of a woman wearing what he took to be the palace uniform. "Princess Annick's room?"

She eyed him warily. "If Annick has not given you the location of her chambers…"

"I will find it, thank you."

If he were Annick, he would have put him close by. She would want him to be near enough to be convenient. Perhaps far enough to feel safe.

Then there was the simple question of where the primary bedchamber in the house was most likely to be located. He paused at the end of the corridor. At the double doors there.

"There you are." And then he flung them open.

"Eh!" She made a sharp exclamation and scrambled back on the bed, covering herself with her sheets. Annick had her hair in a braid and was wearing what appeared to be an extremely virginal white nightgown. She had coffee and pastries around her.

"Good morning," he said.

"I did not say you could come in."

"No. You didn't." He shrugged carelessly. "But I didn't ask."

"Treason," she said.

"To enter the Princess's bedchamber unannounced? My *fiancée's* bedchamber."

"I may have agreed," she said, sniffing loudly. "But it is not announced."

"I assume you will announce it soon."

"Indeed," she said. "At the coronation. I made a plan of it last night." She gestured toward a notebook on the bed, and he could not explain it, but his stomach went hollow.

She was…*cute.* And he could not remember the last time he'd found anything or anyone *cute.*

"Why do you eat in here?"

"I like it. I did not have a real bed for a great many years. This is one of my favorite places to be. Bed."

She looked at him, and then suddenly color flooded her face.

And he felt an answering desire tug low in his gut.

What he'd said to her last night was true.

Sex for him was simply an appetite to be sated.

He was not the prowling, ravenous wolf that the tabloids made him out to be.

He had loved only one woman in his life, and he had loved her very dearly. They had been young, and while sex had been a part of their relationship, it had been… sweet. He had not been Stella's first lover, but her second, and she his. Their lovemaking had hardly been the kind that rattled the walls.

But they had cared for each other. At first, he had thought that maybe women just wouldn't be a part of his life, but it had gotten to a point where it didn't seem like there was any reason to not have sex. His heart could not be touched. That was simply a fact. His body, though…

There was no point making it an issue. No point making it much of anything.

Annick unfortunately engaged, not his heart, but his

sense of obligation. And along with it, desire. This was not as simple as he liked his attractions to be.

They would have to have children, for the sake of the kingdom. And what was marriage to him? Nothing.

But he would have her gently. With care for what she'd suffered. And it wouldn't be about desire.

He would have control.

"Is that so?"

"Yes. Would you like a pastry?"

"Thank you," he said. "Though I would prefer coffee."

"I have that as well."

"An extra cup?"

"I have that too," she said. "Coffee service can be made in my room." She looked very pleased with that.

He crossed the space and found the coffee station. Where he poured himself a cup of black brew, then went and sat on the end of her bed.

She turned pink, all the way to the roots of her hair. "What is my lesson today, then?"

"What lesson do you feel is the most important?"

"Well. At the coronation, I will need to know dancing. I do not know dancing. I will also have to carry on conversation with people I don't know. And... I will need clothes."

"A stylist can be employed for that, and they will help you figure out what it is you like. And combine it with what it is you want to say."

"What does this mean?"

"Your clothes send a message. As you mentioned to me earlier, they liked to dress you in white because it sent the message that you were pure. An unsullied figurehead. In that same way, you will be making statements now."

"I need to look powerful. Confident. I don't want to look pure. I want to look like a warrior."

"Then all you need to do it is to speak to the stylist about it."

"All right. Dancing, can you help me with that?"

"Yes. More than that, I can help you project the right feelings. In the world we live in now, where pictures are taken constantly, if you're going to be pretending to be something you're not, you have to be very good at it."

"Is that how you ended up consulting people on image?"

"No. It could've been anything. It is something I slipped into and I am good at it. Very good. I've spent my life in Southern California, around people who are nothing but image conscious. And yes, I had to learn to fit in. I had to learn to pretend that I was one of them." His chest went tight. "That I was like my father."

"Your father..."

"Robert King. Self-made businessman extraordinaire. Not as entirely on the up-and-up as he would like the world to believe." His father had secrets. Secrets he knew would hurt his whole family. Secrets that had already hurt the innocent. "My father is an expert at looking like he belongs."

"Is that where you learned it from?"

Perhaps it was simply in his blood. "I don't know that I learned it from him, but I discovered what a necessity it was by being his son."

"I see." He did not think she did. But it didn't matter. She didn't need to see.

"Get dressed," he said.

"I do not take orders," she said, narrowing her eyes and curling her fingers around her coffee cup like claws. "I'm to be Queen."

Half his mouth lifted. It might have been a smile, though he hadn't decided to do it, which was strange. "A boon for you, surely."

"Indeed."

"But for now, you are only a Princess. And I," he said, turning that half smile into his best grin, the one that he knew made women flutter. The one that spurred every tabloid to print photos of him. "I am The King and you will do what I say. That is what you brought me here for, am I correct?"

"To do *my* bidding," she said, pulling her knees up to her chest, the thin white material on her gown pulling down, exposing the plump, firm lines of her breasts.

He could see her nipples through the fabric. He would've said that he was a damn sight too jaded to get excited over a shadow of areola, but apparently when it came to Annick he was anything but immune.

He straightened the cuffs on his suit jacket. "Annick, I do no one's bidding. I do not take jobs I don't see as important. Now, you listen to me. I am not staying in Aillette forever. We might marry, but I will go on with my life. I will not be here to prop you up forever. That means you must learn to stand on your own feet. Congratulations, you managed to get me to the palace. Now make use of me. Do not be stubborn. Do not fight simply because you spent years being unable to fight. Because you felt weak. You weren't weak. If you were weak, you would be dead. You wouldn't be here. You hate that you had to hide pieces of yourself, but it kept you alive. You hate that you had to play a game, but it's why you're here. So now you will play a new game. And you will let me teach you the rules."

"I don't like this," she said, looking at him out of the sides of her eyes.

Wretched creature that she was, he imagined she had disliked a great deal in her life. "I don't care. If you will not work with me, if you will not do what I say, then I will walk out right now."

"I will have the guards seize you."

"I would hate to hurt your guards."

"You have no weapons," she said.

He fixed his gaze on her. "Annick, do you honestly think that I require weapons? A gun is a useful prop, but a man must know how to take care of himself. A man must know how to contain all the danger he possesses in his own body. Myself, I can seduce or I can kill…with just my hands. I don't require weapons. As you observed, I am both Maximus King and The King. I could be anything I choose."

"You will *not* kill my guards," she said.

"I certainly wouldn't want to. But if I decide to leave, I will leave. And only God will be able to help those who stand in my way." He looked at her. "Now, get dressed."

CHAPTER SEVEN

ANNICK WAS STILL stewing by the time she made her way downstairs. She had put on a pair of black wide-legged trousers and a navy blue shirt. Mostly because she knew that he expected her to come down in a dress, given that he was already clad in a suit in the early hours of the morning speaking of dance lessons.

So, she did not comply, because it was the only power she could find in the moment.

She had the terrible feeling that she was outclassed in about a thousand ways as she walked down the stairs that led to the ballroom.

Perhaps it was all a false sense of security. Being able to take him from California in the first place. She had gotten the upper hand, but she had the sense that she hadn't had the true scope of what was happening. She had engaged in a battle and won a tentative victory. But this was a war, and Maximus had the controlling power.

She'd wanted that power. Finally. To be in total control of all that happened around her, and by engaging Maximus, she'd entered into a devil's bargain where control wasn't possible. Even though he was fighting for her, he had still superseded her.

So, small rebellions it would be.

Her heart fluttered strangely as she approached the

ballroom, and she took a breath, pushing both doors open and making a rather dramatic entrance. He did not even give her the satisfaction of looking surprised.

"It took you long enough. Come over here."

"I don't think you understand. I don't like orders," she said, fixing him with her most narrow stare.

"I don't think *you* understand. I don't care what you like. You asked for a very specific thing—in fact, you demanded it. Now you must face the consequences of your own actions. You were a prisoner for a great many years, subject to the whims of other people, so perhaps you have forgotten what it means to have agency."

"I have always had it. No one could ever get in here," she said, tapping her temple.

"Perhaps. But I meant in the real world, where real actions take place outside of here." He tapped the same spot she had just tapped. And she flinched. His touch aroused strange sensations between her legs, and she didn't like it. "There are real consequences. If you are going to run around acting tough enough to take me on, then you have to be prepared for what comes of it."

"Threats," she said. "Many, many threats. And yet here you are, standing in the middle of my ballroom."

"It would not do to let you die. It would not do to let you fail."

"Why?" she asked, feeling emboldened. "What is this sudden caring that you have for if I live or die?"

"I'm not a monster," he said.

"Are you not? For I was under the impression that you were."

"There is one code that I have, one thing I live by. I will not let innocent women be destroyed. I will not do it. I will not take part in it. I will not allow it. If there is a chance for me to stop atrocities being committed against the innocent, then I will. It is the only thing that keeps me from being a monster. And you should be grateful that it's a vow I've taken. It's why I won't just leave you. It's why I have agreed to help."

"Why?"

"That, my dear, is none of your blessed business."

"And why not?"

"You might have discovered some of my secrets, but you don't get to know me." He leaned in, and the scent of him wound itself around her, made it difficult for her to breathe or think. Made her head fuzzy. "No one knows me."

He moved away from her, and she did not find it any easier to breathe now. She could still smell the vague impression of him. Skin and cologne and something very uniquely him.

"You don't get to know me either," she said.

He chuckled, and then he wrapped his arms around her and pulled her up against his hard chest. "You don't know yourself, darling." He moved one hand to her lower back and grabbed her hand in his other, holding it outstretched. "Now, we learn to dance."

He moved her over the ground like she weighed nothing, his strength calling to something inside of her that she could not quite grasp. His strength making her feel vulnerable and empowered all at once.

She had never felt anything quite like this before. The sensations of being held in a man's arms. She resented that he made her feel this.

But then…

She met his gaze and her stomach turned over.

She could read nothing there. It was impossible. His mouth was set into a grim line, his jaw forbidding and square, the stubble that darkened it making him look even more dangerous and disreputable.

She sort of wished he were the ravening wolf she'd been led to believe he was from the tabloid stories. Because if he were, then he might have done something to answer the restless calling that rose up between her thighs. If he were, then maybe none of these strange feelings inside of her would be questions. They would simply be action.

She was supposed to be learning to dance, but what she was learning was the unexpected joy in feeling feminine and fragile. It had always been something she despised.

She was small, and it meant she could not fight back physically against the men who kept her imprisoned. The men who oppressed her people and her country.

She had taken no joy in the things that made her a woman. In her softness. Had never found her breasts to be at all useful.

But he made them feel heavy. Aching with desire to be touched.

Suddenly, their existence seemed to make sense, and that was a wholly awing and unexpected sensation.

But he was controlled. Dispassionate. And he seemed not to feel any of the things that she did. None of the sparks that rioted over her skin as he shifted his hold on her.

She had forgotten she was learning to dance. She was simply following his movements. Her feet somehow naturally gliding over the floor in a rhythm, following along with his own.

"You've done this before," he said.

She shook her head. "No."

Yet as he said that, she had a memory. A faint one. A small one.

Of laughing and twirling in the ballroom, standing on her father's feet.

She pushed it away.

"No," she said, her throat going tight. "No. There was never any dancing."

"Well, you are very good at it."

"Why compliment me?" She looked at him, feeling angry. Angry that he was trying to bring memories up inside of her when she would just as soon not have any. "You hate me."

"I don't hate you. I find that I hate the world that brought you to the place you're in now. But not you."

"Disappointing."

She didn't know why that made her angry. Only that it did. Perhaps because it would be satisfying if he felt something as hard-edged for her as hatred.

Because she felt like she was being cut open from the inside, being held in his arms, and he was like marble. Unmoved. In...everything.

"Don't be petulant, Annick. It does not suit you."

"Don't try to be kind, Maximus. It does not suit *you*."

"I have never met a woman filled with so much spite when she's getting exactly what she wants."

"And I have never met a man who so determinedly did not live up to his reputation. *Disappointing*."

He cocked his head to the side, his eyes keen. And suddenly she felt naked in a way that was disconcerting but not entirely unpleasant. "What exactly is disappointing you?"

"I don't know, but you are legendary. Playboy. Soldier. Either identity. I would have expected you to be something a bit more... I don't know. *Dangerous*."

And suddenly, she found herself being propelled back, her shoulders butting up against the wall of the ballroom. "Am I not dangerous enough for you?"

She huffed. "I have subdued you."

And that was when she felt the air between them change. His lips curved into a half smile, the light in his eyes turning into a blue flame.

His hand drifted from where it held hers, slowly, the tips of his fingers gliding over the tender skin of her wrist, up to the curve of her elbow. "Subdued?"

They drifted along to her shoulder, across the line of her collarbone, to the base of her throat. And then he raised his hand slowly and rested it on her neck. He did not squeeze. Did not tighten his hold at all—rather, he simply let it rest there. But she could feel the danger. The threat.

And winding through it, as if it were a threefold cord, eroticism.

Something that made her skin crackle. That made her nipples tighten and that place between her legs go soft and damp.

"You only think that because you still labor under the delusion that you have captured me. You invited me in. I am in your palace. Ready to take the position of power that you have offered to me. Nothing will happen here that I do not decide. Do not mistake control for subjugation, Annick. It would be a grave mistake on your part."

Then he released his hold on her, and she found herself still there, pinned to the wall, her heart beating wildly.

She didn't know what had just happened.

She had made a study out of engaging in power plays that the other party did not know they were involved in. But this was an open war for power, naked and on display.

He was right. She had invited him into the palace. She had offered him carte blanche. And she didn't actually know what he would do with it.

He claimed that he would protect her. That he would help her.

But he was clearly going to do it only on his terms.

And for the first time she did wonder if she were foolish.

If she had sought emancipation at the hands of a man who only knew how to control.

His business training women how to control their images—that was a facade. That was a piece of him that wasn't real or true.

So who knew what he was actually doing. What the end result truly was.

Remember what you want. Remember what you need.

Yes. She would do well to remember that. Who she was. What she had come to him for.

And suddenly, she was not content to allow him to have the final say in this interaction.

And so she flung herself away from the wall, wrapped her arms around his neck and crashed her lips against his.

And the world burst into flame.

CHAPTER EIGHT

HER KISS WAS unpracticed. Unskilled.

She kissed him like a girl might kiss her very first crush. With desperation and earnestness, closed mouth and frozen, even while her body vibrated with energy.

And he...

He felt a molten flame melting in his stomach that was unlike anything he could remember experiencing.

Her breasts were firm and lush, pressed against the hardness of his chest, and his hand found its way down to the rounded curve of her ass, squeezing tight as she continued to kiss him.

"Open for me," he growled, angling his head and pushing his tongue between her lips.

She gasped, but the gasp accomplished his command. Turned shock into obedience. And he took advantage of it.

A whimpering cry rose up in her throat as he slid his tongue slowly against hers, teaching her the deep, slick rhythm that could exist at the center of a kiss.

Even if she had not already told him she was an innocent, he would know.

There was no disguising it. She had been angry when she'd thrown herself at him, but the anger had evaporated. Replaced by wonder, curiosity and arousal that she did not have the skills to hide.

But there was something about that. About the genuine nature of her reaction that made it impossible for him to resist.

And if he should, he could not remember why.

Really? This woman, this sad, desperate woman, who has been kept captive all these years, and you can't think of a single reason why you shouldn't be kissing her right now?

Control.

The word penetrated his lust-fueled haze. And for the first time in longer than he could remember he felt ashamed.

Ashamed of what he had done, ashamed of what he had been about to do, and the novelty of that was almost greater than that of the arousal he felt over the kiss.

Guilt. Guilt and uncontrollable lust. He couldn't remember when he had felt either thing.

It was a heady cocktail, and one that did nothing to dampen the desire that he felt.

He wanted to luxuriate in that shame.

Because there was something about it that made him feel…human.

It had been a very long time since he had felt human.

"Enough," he said, setting her back away from him.

"Why?" she asked, her eyes wide, her breathing fast and hard. "Why is it enough? It seems as if it is very clearly not enough."

"Annick," he said. "This was a dancing lesson, nothing more."

"I don't want just dancing. Show me this."

"No," he said, his voice hard, rough. A stranger's voice.

He was choked on his need for her, and he felt nearly dizzy with it. She was…

She was practically glowing, like a magical creature the likes of which he did not believe really existed.

But then, anyone who could make him feel…anything on par with what he did now was… Something he had not expected.

"I wish to know myself. You said that I should. How can I know myself if I don't know what it is to be a woman?"

"When you choose a man to teach you," he said, his voice rough, "he will be one who can give you what you want. Who can be gentle with you. To be slow and teach you all the things your body can do."

"Are you saying you could not?"

"I could do things to you that would make you scream. I can make you forget your name. But I'm not gentle. And I'm not patient. I'm not the kind of lover a virgin should have."

"Then I will find a man. And have him dispense of my virginity at once. So that I might have you before you leave. For I find I wish to know what it is to be naked with you."

"The hell you will," he said, the possessive statement coming out of his mouth before he could stop it.

"It is…that thing. Catch Thirty-Two."

"Twenty-Two."

"You will not have me if I'm a virgin." She spread her hands. "You do not wish me to go become *not* a virgin."

"You're losing focus. Your virginity has nothing to do with whether or not you're good at running a country."

"I want to *live*," she said. "And until I get past all these confusions, I don't know how I'm going to. How will I be Queen? Tell me this, Maximus King. Because I do not know how to be a person. I was a child, and then I was a prisoner. I became a woman physically while locked in a cell. But I have not learned to dress myself. I have not learned to dance. I have not learned what to do when I feel these things."

"A tip for you," he said. "You enjoy spending time in bed. Make work of exploring your body while you do so. It might help take the edge off."

She stared at him, her eyes owlish. "I would not know where to begin with such an endeavor."

"Annick," he said, his voice rough. "Trust me when I say you don't want to explore these things with me."

"You are to be my husband, eh? *Your* big idea! So, we will eventually."

"All right, then," he said, forcing his voice into a neutral space, not allowing the red flame of rage he felt at the very idea to take hold. "Take another lover first."

"Why?"

"I told you, you are too innocent."

"Eh. *Innocence.*" She said it like something filthy. "The way that they define innocence. Yes? This... *Virginity.*" She laughed. "As if a man's anatomy is the bringer of knowledge and corruption. *Men.* They think far too highly of themselves. I saw my parents murdered. That is what a man stole from me. I have not been *innocent* for a very long time."

Her words struck at a strange place inside of him, and he found that the real reason he wanted to turn away was not the differences between them, but that common bond.

For he did not wish to discuss that. Not ever. Did not wish to face the darkness inside of them that might just match.

He was more comfortable alone.

For the kind of man he was, it was better. It was the only way.

And he knew full well that it wasn't entirely for her benefit that he turned away. Yes, he needed to protect her. Because there was no point, no point at all in pretending that what he was doing was to keep her safe if he became the one to cause her harm. But there were things that were better left uncovered inside of him. And protecting her came hand in hand with protecting himself. At least, in this instance it did.

She had been made victim enough. She didn't need to be exposed to the demons, to the darkness that she seemed to have the power to unleash inside of him.

There were any number of women who didn't call to that thing, that creature that lived down in the deepest recesses of his fractured soul. But he could feel Annick scraping at the bonds of it.

And he wouldn't do that to either of them.

He wasn't a good man. But he worked at not embracing the monster.

And so, he would walk away now. It was the best thing. It was the only thing.

"When is your coronation?"

"We have a week. And then we will announce our engagement."

"Good."

"What does that mean? Good?"

"We have a goal. We have a plan." He looked her over. "I would thank you not to go off script again."

"Oh," she said. "Are my virginal fumblings too much for you to resist? I can't think why else you would need to warn me away so."

"It's for your own good. Trust me."

A small smile curved her lips. "This is the problem. I do not trust anyone."

And he left with the distinct feeling that he had not succeeded in gaining the upper hand.

He was avoiding her. It was an irritation. Ever since their kiss in the ballroom, he had made himself scarce.

They had conducted lessons of a kind, but often they involved other people. He had brought in a body language expert; he had brought in stylists. And from that point on she had been surrounded by women who had spoken to her about being her true self and other things that seemed somewhat ridiculous to her.

None of this was actually about being her true self. It was all strange lies, a rallying cry she could not get her head around.

She did not need to be her true self.

She needed to be a woman who looked like she could be Queen.

It made a mockery of what she wanted, which was actually to know who she truly was. She wanted to understand. Wanted to be something other than a useful tool. She just couldn't see a future where that was possible.

She had hoped. For a grim little while, she had hoped.

And that hope now felt sharp. Made her feel ill-used.

It would have been better to have no hope at all.

Still, she had succeeded in putting together a wardrobe that pleased her. The clothes that she had chosen were exactly as she had told Maximus she wanted them to be. They felt like armor.

The red dress that she would wear tonight on the eve of her coronation had long sleeves, a plunging neckline that revealed a wide V of pale skin. The fabric was stitched into clever panels that looked a bit like individual pieces of armor. It was a thick weighted fabric that held that shape even as she moved. And yet there was something incredibly feminine about it. And it made her feel strong.

She had been paraded around in soft white things for years. Her blond hair loose, as soft as everything else. Barely any makeup.

She looked in the mirror now. At the woman who would be Queen, and she was satisfied that it was a transformation.

Her hair was down, but slicked back, behind her ears and flowing down her back, a golden waterfall. Her lipstick was the same red as the dress, her eye makeup a pale bronze. She looked like she could just as easily lead troops into battle as she could dance the waltz.

And that seemed a triumph in and of itself.

At this event, she would also be introducing Maximus as her fiancé.

And she tried not to curl in on herself with embarrassment over everything that had transpired between them.

It wasn't like she hadn't seen him.

It was just… She wanted him.

And the fact that he was so immune to her…

It was an interesting thing.

Being beholden to such…typical feelings. Embarrassment and jealousy over his past lovers. Insecurity about her own appeal as a woman. She had never worried about that. In fact, she had always hoped that she was not overly appealing as a woman. She didn't want to fend men off. She didn't want to be seen as beautiful. It was a dangerous thing. Just like her softness and her femininity was not something to enjoy.

So, feeling a different relationship to those sensations was…

It was all very strange.

As was the embarrassment.

She looked at herself in the mirror one last time and found that she could not feel embarrassed when she remembered what she looked like. Not tonight.

For tonight, she looked like everything she could hope to be. Strong, a warrior. And beautiful besides. Like something that Maximus would have to notice. Though she should not care if he did.

She lifted her chin high and walked out into the corridor. And there he was. Looking resplendent in a perfectly fitted suit. He was clean-shaven, his dark hair looking disreputable. As if someone had just run their fingers through it.

No wonder the media wrote such things about him. He always looked like he was both perfectly put together and like he had just exited a lover's bed.

Even she took in those undertones from his appearance, and she could not recall having ever seen a person who had recently left a lover's bed. She had certainly never left one.

"What?" he asked, lifting a brow. "You look angry."

"I'm not."

She frowned even deeper.

"And beautiful."

"Well, thank you," she said, smiling in a way that bared her teeth. "I do not know what I should have done if you, the man who has rejected my advances, did not find me beautiful. I might curl in on myself and implode into a glorious ash pile of sadness."

"That is quite acidic, even for you."

"Perhaps I feel acidic. But here we are, ready to make our debut to the world as a couple. So I suppose we had better look as if you're not disgusted by my touch."

That flame flickered in his eyes, and she felt echoing tension inside her in response.

"Who said your touch disgusted me?" he asked.

"You recoiled from me quickly enough last week, and besides, you have avoided being alone with me ever since."

"I'm not here to prop up your self-esteem."

"No, indeed not."

"Which means I should not answer your provocations," he said.

"Why should you now?" she said darkly. "You haven't before."

He took hold of her wrist and turned her to face him. "You should thank God I have not answered your provocations," he said. "And that I have kept barriers between us."

"Right. Because you are protecting me? From the things that I want?"

"From distractions. From harm."

"You forget," she whispered. "You forget what I have been through."

"I don't forget. It's why I won't do anything."

They quit speaking after that. Instead, they walked toward the ballroom, and when they arrived at the door, he took her arm. But no sooner.

Everything that happened after that was a blur. They and their engagement were announced by her right-hand woman, her adviser. And the ripple that went through the room was undeniable.

The stir that they created was unlike anything Annick had ever experienced before, and she found it difficult to separate her response to what was happening around them and to touching him.

Mostly, she was angry. That no matter how she put this armor on, no matter how she worked to ready herself for this, no matter that it was her plan, she still felt...

She still felt like a woman who had been imprisoned for the better part of a decade. A woman who didn't actually know enough about life to understand what she was feeling. And now she had announced her engagement to this man. Announced her intent to make him King.

There was nothing real here, no feeling. No love.

She was always an emblem, never a human.

Even in this. In her impending marriage.

She had not given thought to marriage, and then it had seemed as if a marriage to him would be a solution and not a lance of pain in her chest. Not a further bit of recognition that she was only now, and would always be, sad little Annick whose trappings mattered, never her heart.

She would have to make a speech. She was being propelled up to the podium. It was what she had known would happen. She had words prepared, but suddenly she wasn't sure if they would come out right.

"Good evening," she said. "I thank you all for taking the time to come here for my coronation. It is officially a new day for our country. For too long we were kept under the rule of an oppressive regime. And many of you felt as if I may have played a part in it. But over the last year, I hope that what I have done is earn your trust. And now, as I prepare to ascend the throne as Queen, I offer you this assurance. That I have chosen a King, who will rule as Kings have done here for centuries. Maximus King is just the sort of modern man you can trust as your ruler. He will be fair. I will carry out the legacy of my family, not ruling in the same way as my father, but hopefully realizing the progress that would have been made had things gone as they should have. And I will have Maximus, and his influence and strength to guide Aillette. He will bring with him the modern sensibility that many of you would like to see enacted here. While providing the traditionalists with the figurehead they wish to see. He will also bring business acumen. And we have been in discussions for how to increase industry here and strengthen the reserves of this country, and the riches of its people. It is a new dawn for us. A new day. And I am happy to ascend the throne as Queen Annick, with King Maximus by my side."

She nodded, and the room erupted into applause. Maximus stood beside her, tall and strong, and saying nothing. And for once, it felt like her plan had worked.

It was just that inside she still felt a little bit broken. A little bit lost. Uncertain about what to do. But he was there, and he was steady. And nothing about him seemed uncertain at all. And so there was that. There was that. Which was a great blessing.

She didn't understand herself. That she was irritated that he provided her with the strength that she had wanted him to provide her with. That the people had reacted to him with such great satisfaction. Which proved that he was what she needed all along. But she'd known that. Why should she be upset about it?

Because somewhere deep down she had hoped she would be enough, she supposed.

Because what she had begun to tell him days ago

was that part of her had hoped that she could overcome her people's doubts by being a woman who led with her heart. Who found a level of honesty with her people that those before her had not.

Because she wanted to be different, and she realized that, given the circumstances, she had to be the same.

That she could find a balance, find some progress, but she wouldn't be able to be fully her own person, not really.

Because things were too tentative. And it was more important she looked solid than that she be loved.

And it was the source of her dissatisfaction now.

Ridiculous.

But then, she felt slightly ridiculous.

To care so deeply about this now, when she'd been handed what she needed to be protected. When he was living no more authentically than she.

He was helping her. Shouldn't that be enough?

"Shall we dance?"

And she didn't have a chance to respond. And truly, there was no response to make other than yes. For he was now her fiancé in public, even if he was still her adversary in private.

And there was nothing she could do about it. It was a scheme of her own making, a plan she had seen as a necessity.

You have to see it through. Your feelings don't matter.

Her feelings never mattered.

There was no use becoming morose about it now.

He took her in his arms, and she found herself returning to that floating sensation. That strange place where she was caught between memory, dreams and reality. Suspended between all three.

And held fast only by him.

'She felt unbearably fragile in that moment when she should've felt strong.

She was doing it. Her plan was working. And yet she felt reduced.

Yet she felt…

And she could see it, hear an old song rising up inside of her. One that she tried not to remember.

Her father's soft voice singing as he danced her around the ballroom.

When the memories started, she could not stop them. No matter how hard she tried.

CHAPTER NINE

SHE PULLED HERSELF free of his arms. "I must excuse myself," she said, smiling, because people were watching. The whole gilded, glittering ballroom was filled with people, like it had not been since she was a girl. And tomorrow, she would be crowned Queen. And all of it was simply too much.

She remembered this room full of her family.

And they weren't here.

She remembered dancing now. Dancing with her father.

As she never would again.

"Excuse me," she said again, and took as many dignified steps out of the ballroom as she could manage. Before she started to run. To flee out into the garden, praying that the night sky that enveloped her now would simply swallow her whole. Open up and pull her into the black velvet, cover her with the diamond stars. Conceal her. Conceal this weakness from her people. Even from herself.

She had thought, given a year of time away from everything, that she would be stronger. That she would be braver. That she would be prepared to cope with all of this, but instead, the changes that were being instigated around her only reminded her of everything she'd lost.

She did not feel a whole year advanced from her captivity. Rather, she felt like she had been brought back to the stage when she had been taken. When her world had been shattered.

She ran down the garden path until she saw a stone bench. Then she flung herself over the bench, curling around the stone and weeping.

She never wept.

Queen Annick of Aillette could not afford to show such weakness.

And so she'd hidden it. Hidden it because what other choice did she have?

And then she felt strong, warm hands on her waist, lifting her up off the ground, pulling her from the depths of her misery. And she fought. Like a hissing, spitting cat, because how dare he? She was angry. And she was upset. Devastated. And half of it was his fault. She did not deserve to be pulled out of her darkness. Rather, she wanted to pull him down into it.

And so she fought him. Until he grabbed her wrists, steadying her, pinning her against his chest. He moved her arms down, fixing them low at her back, her breasts brought up against the wall of his chest.

"What the hell are you doing?"

"I hate you," she said, seeing him suddenly as the emblem of everything that was bad. "I don't feel strong. This was supposed to make me strong. I feel a failure. That I need you to stand beside me to keep me safe. That I am not enough. That I do not magically know everything, that I cannot stand on my own strength because it is not there. That I feel alone in a ballroom full of people, where the ghosts feel more real than those who actually stand next to me. I feel like a twelve-year-old girl who was shut away, locked in time, and yet I know I am not a girl. Because a girl would not want the things that I do. With you. I cannot even have that. I cannot lead my country without you, and I cannot stand to be with you."

"I am an enemy of your own making, Annick," he said, his voice rough. "Your anger with me is not my fault."

"It is," she hissed, wiggling against him. "You were supposed to help. You were supposed to help, and instead you've made me even more confused. And you make me feel all these things. Me, I do not like it."

She could feel her grasp on her English slipping as emotion rose inside of her. "This was supposed to be a special night for me, and it is nothing. Nothing but... Nothing but a reminder. It is all wrong."

"Do you know what this is?"

"What?"

"Grief," he said, his voice a fractured pane of glass. "It's grief. You've been locked away for so long that you never got to have it. You had to protect yourself. You had to save yourself. But all those memories that you put away are out here. And believe me, I get it."

"Why? Because you too have grief?"

"Yes. And because I too have been running from it."

He stared at her, his eyes burning into hers. And that flame wasn't banked. Wasn't low or subtle now. Was more than a flicker.

It was an inferno.

"Then what do we do? How do we keep running?"

"I know," he said, his thumb dragging along her lower lip. "I know just how to keep it away."

"Please," she whispered.

And then he was kissing her, her wrists still pinned

against her lower back, caught in one of his large hands, as he tasted her with a ferocity that shocked her.

He had been so adamant that they could not. So adamant that it was bad, and now, he was kissing her with an immediacy that made a complete mockery of everything he'd said before.

"Why?" she whispered, in the brief moment when their lips parted, so that they could both draw breath.

"Maybe because I am a monster," he said. "And maybe you are too. My darkness sees yours. And I cannot resist it."

Her heart pounded faster, harder. Because that at least seemed true.

All the rest of this, all the rest was a farce. Playing a game so that the people of her country would accept her. Playing a game so that she would look strong while she felt like she was breaking apart. Allowing him to assume some kind of control when she didn't want him to have any. But she also wanted him. And there was an honesty to that.

She had no expectations of what things between men and women were like. Though the way that the women who worked for her spoke of it, she did not know if it was commonly such a dark and terrifying thing. A monster all of its own.

But she wasn't like them.

She wasn't like anyone.

She'd known that for years. Lying in her dungeon room, she'd known it. There weren't a lot of other girls who had spent their formative years like she had. It had made her feel terribly lonely to realize that. Made her feel very alone.

Except, looking at him, she realized that he wasn't like anyone either.

This man who was capable of being so charming. Who was so beautiful, but at the same time so very deadly.

Who was brilliant and charming, and also dark and terrifying.

Who could give pleasure with his hands, and take life with them too.

He was like no one. And neither was she.

And in that singularity, they met.

In their darkness, there was a bond.

And so they didn't speak again. She simply kissed him. Learning the movements. Learning the way that his tongue felt best sliding against hers. Learning to glory in the strength of his hold.

Learning to love the way she was delicate, the way he was strong. She had never in her wildest dreams thought that she would like that.

In fact, when she had first begun to fantasize about finding a lover, she had imagined that she might like one she felt most easily in control of, but from the beginning she had been enticed by Maximus's strength. By the danger in him.

What she really wondered was if she would ever truly be aroused if she did not feel she was overcome.

Because there was some strange and wicked strength to be found in this. In the fact that she seemed strong even while he had her arms trapped.

Because she could see that he had been pushed to the edge. That he was pushed to his limits. That in many ways, she had control over him.

It was a magical thing. Mystical and quite beyond her understanding. So she didn't try to understand.

She simply kissed him. Simply reveled in the deep desire that coursed through her body as his tongue played games with hers.

As her heart tried to beat its way out of her chest.

She struggled, her breasts rubbing against the hard wall of muscle that had her trapped there. And a pulse throbbed between her legs.

Oh, how she wanted him.

She was mindless with it.

And this felt right. In this sea of confusion, amid all the things she didn't know, she knew this.

That she was a woman, and he was a man. And this was everything that was good about those facts. This desire, this need and the sparks that it created between them, with everything wonderful about what it meant.

And the idea that she might be closer to knowing one more thing about herself, to finding a sense of completion, gave her peace even in this storm.

And so she kissed him.

Finally, finally, he released his hold on her wrists, and she was free. She moved her hands to his face, to his shoulders, down the front of his chest. She grabbed hold of his tie and began to loosen the knot with clumsy fingers. She had no idea about the mechanics of a man's tie. Did not have a clue how to begin undressing him, only that she wanted him undressed.

He might not be her true King. But here, now, she wanted him to have this dominion over her body.

Here and now, in the middle of all the lies, this was real. It was true. There was no one here to see. It was not a show.

It was just her. And him.

And there were very few moments in her life that had this kind of honesty. If any.

And this was what she needed. Something real to hold on to. Something that felt good and not just sad.

Not just like a tragedy that left a yawning, darkened void behind.

Maximus was creating a need inside of her, while the sweep of his hands over her body was answering that need.

He was making her want, but he wasn't leaving her wanting. And it was magical to discover these sensations.

He had told her to go to her room and explore her own body, and she hadn't even tried. It wasn't her own touch she wanted. It was his.

She wouldn't have known where to begin. Because she wanted what he was doing. And she was so ignorant she didn't even know how to fantasize about it. But this…

This was it.

And it wasn't all fairy dust and gossamer. There was an edge to it. Like the black velvet of the night sky had wrapped itself around them, cloaking them in darkness. A soft, brilliant darkness that enticed them both to sin.

That enticed them both to satisfaction.

She got that tie free and began to undo the buttons on his shirt.

Oh, she wished she could see better. Because his chest felt magnificent.

And she felt insatiable.

"What is this?" she asked, panting heavily. "I don't know if I want to lick you or bite you."

"Do either," he said, his voice rough. "Both."

And so she did. She leaned in, and she bit his pectoral muscle, and then she soothed it with the flat of her tongue.

"Is this normal? I am hungry for you." She pressed her face to his body and inhaled deeply. The scent of him only made her that much more aroused. "I think it might be madness."

"It is madness," he said. "And this is why I told you to stay away from me."

"You said you were not insatiable."

"But I looked at you and knew that I could be. And I don't think even a woman with years of experience can handle me insatiable. I should not be asking you to."

"But I need it," she said, tears gathering in her eyes. "I need something strong enough to block out the memories. To block out the bad things. I need something strong enough to make me feel good, because there is so much sadness. There is so much. And sometimes I feel like I might be crushed beneath the weight of it. But not when you kiss me. Because whatever this feeling is that you create inside of me, it is enough. It is strong enough... It is strong enough to make it feel good."

Because the pain was still there. The weight was still there. And this was not a light trip through a field of daisies. But it created in her pleasure at an intensity that matched the difficult things, and if that wasn't a gift, she didn't know what was.

She moved back to him, burying her face in the curve of his neck and kissing him. Licking him.

This was real.

The whole facade of the marriage, of the two of them together, might be for show, but this was not.

She was so very hungry for real.

More even than pastries.

"Don't hold back," she said.

Because she had a feeling he would try. She had a feeling he would try, and she didn't want him to. Didn't want him to be able to.

She wanted him to be as lost as she was. Utterly and

completely, in the madness of this sensual haze. In this dark intensity of need.

She pushed his shirt and jacket from his body, leaving him naked from the waist up. The moonlight shone over his muscles, and she could see that he was indeed a weapon. A lethal, masculine weapon filled with great and terrible beauty. It was exactly the sort of beauty that she coveted. For it was frightening and made her heart stutter, but it also made her feel strong. Safe.

And she was a warrior woman in a red dress made of armor, and whatever they were about to do, the battle they were about to engage in, the war for pleasure, she knew they were both going to be well able to withstand it.

She unzipped her gown, let it fall down to the floor, and suddenly she felt vulnerable. Standing out there naked in the moonlight. Wearing nothing more than a pair of red lace panties that scarcely covered anything.

She was bare to him.

His hands moved to his belt, to the closure on his slacks, and he took the rest of his clothes off. Even in the dim light, she could see that he was thick and strong, larger than she had imagined a man might be there. But it also thrilled her. Because she was not afraid of this. She had withstood a great many things. Had endured atrocities she had not wished to endure. And this was her choice.

A great mystery of life that had not been taken from her forcibly, something she had always been grateful for. And she was choosing it. Here with this man who made her wild with desire. Who made her feel something better than normal.

And then that big, warrior man knelt down before her, and she found his strong arms wrapping themselves around her waist and lowering her slowly to the stone bench as he leaned in, pressing his mouth against the needy heart of her, lapping at her with intensity that gave no quarter to her inexperience. Just as he had warned.

She did not have the time to express shock. She could only hold tightly to his head as he feasted upon her. As the aggressive strokes of his tongue pushed her to that promised place that had been created in her with the touch of his lips to hers.

Then he pushed a finger deep inside of her, stroking at her core, at a place inside of her that incited a riot of need. The invasion was foreign, but wonderful, and when he added a second finger, she gasped. It was too much, but it couldn't be. For if she hoped to have that most masculine part of him inside of her, she would have to get used to this.

And quickly, she did. Quickly, the intrusion, the friction, became welcome, as he lapped at her more firmly with his tongue.

And then little ripples began to spread inside of her. Her need growing, opening up. Expanding, until she was made almost entirely of it. Until she thought she might die of it.

And then he sucked that sensitized bundle of nerves into his mouth, the suction making her crazy. Causing her pleasure to break over her like a wave. She cried out, her legs draped over his shoulders, her heels digging into his back. And she didn't care if anyone heard. She cared about nothing. Nothing but this.

And then he was there. She was still seated on the edge of the bench, the thick head of his arousal pressing against her. He gripped her behind and impaled her with his length, and she gasped, the searing pain she felt a shock, particularly on the heels of such great pleasure.

But he didn't stop.

He thrust into her like a mad animal, his teeth scraping against her collarbone.

And somewhere, in the pain and uncertainty, a thread of pleasure began to wrap itself around both, binding them up. Until she couldn't tell which was which. Until she couldn't make out what was him, what was her. What was pain, what was need. Until they were both made of stars. And she could tell when he reached the edge, when he began to shatter as she had done. "Come for me," he growled, and just like that, she did. Just like that, she broke again.

Only a moment before she had been consumed by the amount of unknowns in the world. By how adrift she felt. By how not her she was.

But lying there, sprawled indecently in the darkness of the garden with Maximus inside of her, she felt like she had an answer.

She did not know what it was for.

But as she held on to him, she felt rooted to the earth. Grounded in a way she could not remember ever feeling before. And it was...a revelation.

"I'm sorry," he said, gruff as he removed himself from her.

"Don't," she said, feeling like she was made of spun glass. Not sure if she loved or hated it. "Don't apologize."

"Why not?" he asked, his shoulders tight, his whole body gone stiff like a stone.

"I don't want you to. I don't want you to apologize. It was wonderful."

He looked away, his face shrouded in shadow. "I was rough with you. I hurt you."

"Life has hurt me worse than you ever could. At least you made pleasure out of the pain. I did not know such a thing was possible. And there, I have learned a lesson."

"Don't," he bit out. "Don't excuse me."

"Me, I am not forgiving," she said. "If I wished to be angry at you I would be. But I wanted this. Choice is one of the most beautiful things in this world," she said. "It is our own choices that spin together the being that we are, and I have had so many years of choice being taken from me. And the position I find myself in now, one where I must be a good Queen. One where I must protect myself… My enemies still take choices from me, Maximus. Back me into corners where only one option remains. To fight as I can. It is why I took you. It is why I agreed to this marriage. But this…*this* I chose. Do not take this from me too. I wanted to know. I… Sometimes I feel crushed beneath the weight of the things I don't know, but at least I know this. At least I chose this."

"You don't understand," he said. "I was close to being out of control and…"

"And what?"

"I can't afford to lose myself. There is a darkness in me that I keep on a leash."

"And you only let it out to play when you take a job that allows it? When you decide that you are engaging in a quest for vengeance? Is that it?"

"You can't possibly understand," he said.

"Alors!" She made a face of mock horror. "Of course I cannot. I'm just a virgin. And you know so much more than me."

"We must go back to the ball."

He dressed her, the movements perfunctory, and she felt herself beginning to crack. But she would not allow him to see. "There are some things you are going to have to trust me about," he said.

She stared at him, trying to figure this man out. What he wanted. Why he seemed so filled with regret. He was supposed to be a playboy who had sex as easily as most people breathed. And this was not easy.

She did not like it.

"Yes, I will allow for that when it comes to you teaching me how to look strong. But I will not allow for that when it comes to you teaching me what my body wants. When it comes to teaching me what my heart wants. If that was darkness, then I want more of it. For, me, I am a little bit dark myself." She tried to smile.

He was dressing, and he didn't look at her. So, her show of bravado didn't seem to matter.

"I can't love you," he said.

She jerked back. "No one loves me," she said. "Why should you matter?"

He looked like she'd struck him with her words. But they were a truth. Why should she know them and he be spared them?

"No one?" he asked.

"No. My family are dead. My people... They certainly don't love me. Look at the great lengths I'm having to go to in order to be accepted. And then there is my staff. They have become friends of a sort. But it is not love. No one loves me. It is no matter to me if you are added to the great list of those on this earth who do not."

"It's not..."

"People love you, though, don't they? Your sisters. Your mother and father. Your friend Dante. Yes, I have done research on all those in your life. He loves you too. He's like a brother. Is he not?"

"Well, yes," Maximus said. "Though him sleeping with my sister has complicated some things."

"He married your sister."

"Semantics."

She tilted her head to the side. "You are an image maker—aren't semantics your business?"

"To an extent," he said.

She swallowed hard, a sense of unfairness building inside her she could not quite come to grips with. Of course she didn't want him to be unloved. But he did not seem to know how to accept love, and she would very much like some love. "How very good it must be to be loved by so many. Do they know…do they know how dark you are inside?"

"No," he said. "And I would do just about anything to keep the truth from them."

"It would hurt them."

"Yes."

This honesty was rare for him, she knew. And as gifts went, a small one she would take. An intimacy that somehow felt deeper than what they'd shared with their bodies. Though perhaps one had led to the other. Stripped barriers away that might otherwise have stood.

"Why don't you tell them?"

He paused for a long moment. "There are some things you don't want to burden other people with."

"I see." She looked at him and recognized at that moment the weight he carried. It was not unlike hers. Not so different. "You can burden me. For I do not love you either. You do not love me. That is simple, eh? We help each other."

"You've been through enough."

"Yes. Just enough to be strong. To be strong enough that even when you hurt me it does not hurt so much."

She found that she liked much better being trusted to take the strength of his darkness, the strength of his need, than being told she was too weak when she had endured so much and had stayed standing. When she had endured the kinds of things that would have reduced lesser people to rubble.

She would rather stand here with him. Her body buzzing, throbbing, feeling fragile and strong all at once. Like the thinnest of unbreakable glass.

"Let us go," he said, offering her his arm.

"You're going to leave me alone tonight, aren't you? You're not going to listen."

"You were a virgin," he said, his voice rough. "Surely even you can see that you might need a little bit of time to recover."

She would have laughed if she hadn't felt so fragile. Something as big as a laugh might make her crumble. "Life has never given me a moment to recover."

"Then consider it the first sensitive thing life has done for you."

"Eh." She waved her hand. "Nobody wants a sensitive penis, Maximus. One prefers them hard."

"You talk a big game for a woman who has seen precisely one."

"A good one, I think."

"Annick…"

She saw this moment then, for what it was. He was acting as if she was the innocent, the one who needed protection.

But for whatever reason, it was her soldier who needed this. Who needed this distance.

"Fine. I will let you play the part of gentleman tonight. But only because *you* need to. *I* do not need you to. But if you need to feel good, if you need to feel redeemed for what you have done to me, then I allow it. But tomorrow…tomorrow is my coronation. And you must stand up with me. And then tomorrow night… I will be a Queen. And don't you think then I might be strong enough for you?"

"Remember what this is."

She lifted a shoulder. "There is no name for what this is. You cannot play the part of a more experienced man. Not now. Not with this. We are both virgins in this, I think."

She walked on ahead of him, and she knew that her hair might look mussed, that she might not look the perfectly put together warrior woman she had looked when she had first gone into the ballroom tonight. But she felt stronger. Somehow, now, she felt that the armor was underneath her skin, rather than just draped over her body in red fabric.

And there was something to be said for that.

For laying claim to at least one of the mysteries in the universe.

Yes, there was something to be said for that as well.

And even if she still felt raw, and a little bit vulnerable, she also felt strong.

And she would happily take that and lay claim to it.

CHAPTER TEN

"WHAT EXACTLY IS going on?"

Maximus was the unhappy recipient the next morning of a group video call from both of his sisters, and his friend Dante, who was also now his brother-in-law.

He was rocked by the previous night. By his encounter with Annick, and even more so by the conversation after.

I will let you play the part of gentleman tonight. But only because you need to.

He was a man who lived a life in the shadows, and Annick seemed to have the ability to drag him into the light.

If you need to feel redeemed for what you have done to me...

Oh, Annick. If only she knew, there was no redemption, not for a man like him.

"Obviously my engagement has been announced?" he said, shutting his thoughts down and grinning into the screen, as was expected of him.

"Your engagement. To the Princess of a principality that until very recently was run by a crazed despot," his friend Dante said.

"Yes. The very one."

"How did that...?" It was Violet who asked that question, though she wasn't able to finish it. She was staring into the camera, looking comically confused.

"How these things normally work, Violet," he said, as if his sister was terribly slow. "Kidnap."

"Kidnap," she said. "You're not telling me that tiny little creature kidnapped you. That's embarrassing. At least *I* was kidnapped by a very large man."

She reclined in her chair, round with her pregnancy and looking amusingly embarrassed on his behalf.

"Don't underestimate a small woman with a large amount of determination, Violet," he said. "I've decided to go ahead and allow the kidnap. Just as I decided to go ahead and pursue an engagement with my beautiful captor. Why wouldn't I?" He affected the most charming smile he could. "Think of all the things I've done. There isn't a very long list of things I haven't. Virgin Princesses? Well, that was a stone left unturned. And the opportunity to be King? She's being crowned Queen today. And in Aillette that makes me King."

"Seems unearned," Violet said.

"And strange," Dante added.

"But you should at least admire her industriousness in procuring herself the husband she wanted. She chloroformed me."

"Did she?" Minerva looked positively delighted by this news.

"Of course you would like it," Dante said. "Given you ended up engaged to me because of a rather grand lie you told on TV. It was very nearly kidnap."

"I *did* do that," Minerva said. "I really do admire women who go after what they want. If I would've thought of chloroform, I would've used that."

"And to think," Dante said, addressing Maximus.

"You worried about your sister when I married her. You should've been worried for me."

"Don't worry about me," Maximus said. "Everything is well in hand. You can tell Dad and Mom that they can come visit the palace sometime."

"Well, Mom will like that," Violet said. "Two children married into royalty. And you only married a billionaire, Minerva. You look like the slouch out of the group."

Minerva did look angry about that, since she historically felt left behind. "But I gave them their first grandchild," she said.

Regret kicked against his stomach. Because he had not used birth control with Annick last night. And though children between them was somewhat inevitable, she was young and it did not have to be now. He did his best to push the thought aside. What was done was done. He had a feeling there would be no asking Annick to procure any sort of emergency contraceptives. He could only imagine the scathing that would earn him. She would do precisely what she pleased and nothing else. That much he knew.

"You will all be invited to the wedding, of course." To do anything else would be strange. He was almost troubled by how easily he lied to his family. But he'd been doing it for so many years that it was second nature. Second nature to smile like this, to make jokes about how he was doing this simply to enrich the portfolio of all that he'd done. Yes, this kind of subterfuge was easy. He didn't even feel guilty about it.

No, what he felt guilty about was taking Annick's virginity. A novelty within a novelty. He had been... rough. He should not have taken her on a stone bench without a care for the pain she might've experienced. But he had.

He thought back to what she'd said.

You need this...

He pushed it aside. He didn't *need* anything. And he didn't need to have her again.

Control was his.

He would not give in to the beast inside of him.

To do otherwise made him no different than the men he took out of this world. The men he hated above all else.

If he could not protect her, then his life was forfeit.

And so, today he would go to her coronation, and tonight, he would reinstitute the distance between them.

There really was nothing else to be done.

She was to be Queen today.

Annick looked in the mirror at her sleek reflection. Her hair was piled up atop her head, ready for a crown. For coronation. She wondered what it would have been like if life had gone the way it was supposed to.

Her parents would still be dead. That was the nature of coronations. It was why they were, in her opinion, sort of a terribly barbarous thing. A ceremony. Passing the torch. But only when the flame of your loved one was extinguished.

And Annick... Well, she never should've been Queen.

She squeezed her eyes shut and tried her best not to think of Marcus, her older brother. The one who should have been standing here today. The one who should have always been here.

And then she tried not to think of Maximus. Of the way her body burned when she remembered what had transpired between them last night.

This day was to be a ceremony, celebrating her becoming Queen. A coronation. Essentially, she was being recognized as a woman. At the moment, it all felt a bit too literal. For last night, she had been introduced to another dimension of what it meant to be a woman. For last night, she had...

And he had turned away from her.

She had never felt half so alone as she did going back into that ballroom without him. As she did for the whole rest of the evening, in a space filled with hundreds of people.

She had given a good speech, had found a strength in herself that she had not known was there, but it had done nothing to ease the loneliness in her.

She was good at standing alone.

But she was tired of it.

And she had not yet seen him today.

Today she was wearing emerald green. A brocade fabric made up the gown, which was shaped like a large bell, the fabric making dramatic folds, billowing out around her feet.

The door to her chamber opened, and there he was. He looked stern and striking in a black suit with a black shirt and tie. He looked... Well, he looked like the King. Of her country. And of death.

He looked every inch the assassin that he was.

How did other people not see this? How did they see him and think that he was nothing more than a feckless playboy? It was so patently untrue. So clearly not all he was. Not even remotely.

"The guard has been vetted, checked over and completely cleared. The perimeter is secure. You have nothing to worry about tonight, Annick. I have seen it is safe."

"Well. You had better," she said, keeping her eyes on her own reflection, only glancing at him in the mirror. "It is, after all, why you are here."

"Yes. It is."

"To do anything else would be an abject failure. Are you a failure, Maximus?"

"I think you know that I'm not." He straightened the cuffs on his sleeves, the movement inescapably catching her eye. She looked away as quickly as possible.

"You will escort me to the front of the room for the ceremony today. And when the country pledges their allegiance to me, you will also."

"Will I?"

"Yes," she said. "You know you cannot be King of this country and not be a citizen thereof."

"And is a King beneath his Queen here?"

That brought to mind images of his strong, hard body beneath hers. All that power trapped between her thighs. And in her image, he looked up at her, his eyes fierce, and she knew that to imagine that she might be in control if she were on top was a fiction.

She blinked, ignoring the scorching heat in her cheeks.

"I believe you know he's not," she said, feeling particularly scabby. "But that does not mean I must submit to your nonsense."

"I would never ask you to submit to such a thing."

"Why did you leave me?"

Why could she not keep these sorts of questions inside? Why was she incapable of holding her tongue around him?

It was the strangest thing, for with him she found the core of what she claimed to want: a space where she could be wholly herself.

It was just she could not seem to entirely control it. And that was... Well, that was a double-edged sword.

What they had was nothing more than a mercenary arrangement. He was only able to be King because he would be married to her. And she needed his protection. She would've had to marry someday anyway, so it had been the smartest thing to agree to his demand. Of course it had been. To do anything else would've been stupid. He was the one securing her forces. He was the one making sure she was safe.

Any other man would have far too much power and she would have to be certain she could trust him. There was no reason not to marry Maximus. And there was no reason to be soft and tender about what had occurred between them in the garden. It would have happened eventually. An inevitability. And yet she felt soft and tender, and it didn't matter if it was inevitable.

She wanted to rest her head against his chest.

You are a fool, Annick. You never went soft in all your years of captivity, and now you wish to snuggle up against this hunk of stone?

"I left because it was the best thing to do," he said. "You asked me here to protect you, not to defile you."

"Did we not agree that defiling would happen at a certain point?"

"I believe I told you to take another lover first."

"And what about what I wanted? I didn't want another lover."

"You said that you suspected you were a glutton. That you might wish to make love to any number of men in your lifetime. Why should you settle for having me first?"

"I wanted you. Why should I do anything but have what I want? If I want a pastry for dinner, why should

I not have it? If I want you as a lover, why should I not have you?"

"I was not able to be as gentle with you as I should've been."

"I did not ask for gentle," she said. "The world has not been gentle with me, Maximus King. The world has treated me roughly. And here, I find something that I want. Your body and your mind. Why should I not have this? Because you say so? Because you think you know me? You do not know me. You do not know me any more than I know you. Sharing pastries before dinner together and speaking of sex and gluttony is not knowing me. You do not get to decide how strong I am."

"I would never seek to make decisions about what you can handle. But you don't know me. And you know nothing of sex."

"I know some of it now. That men are hard. And that it hurts when you are inside at first. But then it feels wonderful."

"It won't hurt every time."

"How can it not? You are so very vast."

His lips twitched. "You have a way with words."

"I say it as it is," she said. "And I know my mind."

"We can help each other."

"Can we? Tell me how we can. And tell me why sex would get in the way."

"It's because of me. I need control. Especially on a day like today. I am helping you. *Protecting* you. Keeping you safe. I can't afford to be distracted."

"And why? I feel I have a right to know. What is this distraction you feel you might face? For I have never seen you distracted."

"In the garden last night, an assassin could've come upon us and I would never have known." He touched her chin then, his hands rough. "Until an assassin's bullet pierced your skin."

She shivered. But not with fear.

It was desire, but then... It was a deep, searing pain as she looked into his eyes and saw the echo of old demons there.

This was not a fear rooted in the abstract.

He was afraid. He was angry, at himself.

"But he did not," she said, her tone gentle.

"It could've happened. I let my guard down once, and the consequences were severe."

"Tell me." This was the loss he'd suffered. She knew well that he had.

"This is not a topic of discussion open between us," he said.

"Why?"

"Don't test me."

And like that it was over.

He resisted this honesty between them and she could not help it.

He extended his arm, and she took it and he led her out of the chamber.

"Why? I'm not a prisoner anymore. This is not a dungeon, and you are not a dictator. You don't get to tell me what I'm curious about."

"And it is my life. I don't have to share it with you if I don't want to. You are the reason I'm here. You brought us together. You presented a case that was so compelling I couldn't turn away from you. And I have found ways that you could be of use to me. That this *arrangement* could be of use to me. I'm tired," he said, his eyes nearly black now, "of going on missions, of trying to rid the world of evil, one man at a time. It is... It is a dark pursuit. On that you can trust me. If I had a soul, it was shed somewhere along that road in the past fifteen years. And I have not seen it since."

"Then why bother to help me at all? Why bother to try and rid the world of terrible men? If you do not care, if you have no soul inside of your chest, then why are you here at all?"

"Because there was a woman," he said, the words immediately sending a chill through her body. "And she did have a soul. A lovely one. More beautiful than you could imagine. And when she died, I vowed that I would do something about the injustice in the world. Because if I did, then…more people like her would not die."

"Who was she?"

"It doesn't matter. Now you know. Now you understand."

That was not understanding, and his skeleton of a story was not telling. She was reeling, trying to piece the details together, but too soon they arrived at the small chapel where her coronation would be held.

And she had to push aside all thoughts that were not about this moment.

It was a smaller gathering than at the ball last night. Nobility and dignitaries from the country, who had been driven underground during the previous regime, were all there and resplendent in their finery. There were leaders from around the world and a select group of citizens who had been chosen to attend.

It was wonderful. A look at her country in the best light possible. Free and happy and ready to move into the future.

She suddenly felt small and unequal to the task. And as much as it angered her, she was glad that Maximus was there beside her. She was glad that she wasn't doing this alone. Glad that he had offered to marry her, even if she should be appalled to have considered such a thing. Even if she should be angry that she felt she needed a man to assist with her ascension to the throne.

It's nothing to do with being a woman. Or him being a man. And everything to do with spending so much of your life locked in a dungeon...

Yes. She had.

Hadn't Maximus begun teaching her new things? And that made her feel too raw. She couldn't think about that. Not at the moment. She could only focus on putting one foot in front of the other. Could only focus on the solidity of his strength to her right.

It was nearly like a wedding. They walked up the aisle together, but then he left. For it was not him she would be making vows to, not today. It was her country. Her people.

While the priest handed her a scepter, and a robe was draped over her shoulders, she stood. A blessing was spoken over her, and then she spoke the words of affirmation back, vows promising stability. To honor the people, the country, its traditions. To make progress where it needed to be made. To protect and support and heal. And she meant the words. Every last one of them. Because she had survived for this. Had lived for her country. And when the heavy, golden crown was placed on her head, she felt it fully. For this was her cause.

Not pastries and finding out whatever it was she preferred best to eat, and not sex in the garden. This.

The responsibility hurt. Making her heart ache.

But nonetheless, she finished the ceremony and looked out at her people.

"With all that I am," she said. "With my life. I will serve." She swallowed hard, and she pressed on, with words from her heart and not words from a rehearsed script.

For she understood, suddenly. That while she might have to present a certain front, it was her core, who she truly was, that had brought her to this moment.

That had helped her to survive, and to keep her spirit through those long years of captivity.

That had driven her to seek help from Maximus.

Yes, in some cases her choices had felt forced upon her by those who sought to harm her. But it was her strength that allowed her to withstand them.

Not just anyone would have chosen to fly across the world, find the super soldier who had led the mission against her country's dictator, chloroformed him and forced him back to her country.

Not just anyone could stand here in this moment, after being a prisoner. After withstanding an assassination attempt only a month earlier.

Only her.

Queen Annick.

"We lost much when we lost my parents. You lost a King, and with the death of my brother, the future King. And I know that I, as Queen, am an unknown. But with all the strength I possess, I will lead you. I will honor my father, but we will also push forward. This is a new era. We will not hide here in the mountains, a kingdom isolated. We will embrace technology, connecting with the world as we haven't done before. We will grow in strength. Not me, not Annick. But all of us. This strength will not be to subdue, but to stand on our own. All of us. Together."

And then it was done.

"And here now is presented to you," the priest said, "Queen Annick Lestrade of Aillette."

She was met with applause, and she nodded serenely, walking back out of the chapel with Maximus meeting her at the door.

There would be a large luncheon after, tables set up in the gardens outside, but she was not sure she could stomach any food. Or being in the gardens. Considering what had happened the last time she was there.

No. She would be strong. She would not trip at this first hurdle that was not even a hurdle.

And so she spent the rest of the day smiling and speaking to whomever wished to speak to her. By the end of it all she felt every inch the symbol. As if there was nothing of the woman left at all. It was an odd sensation.

And then she looked back at Maximus, and she felt… That she couldn't breathe.

She wanted him. She wanted him again. And it didn't matter that he had been unkind to her. Didn't matter that he had abandoned her. That he had said it was for the best. That he had made it plain that he was not going to share with her or be intimate with her again because of…control. Or whatever else he'd spoken of.

What did you survive the dungeon for?

Wasn't *she* enough of a reason?

Finding this core of herself, recognizing it, made her ask new questions even now.

Did their arrangement have to be solely for her country?

Oh, she cared about it a great deal. She would serve her country, give her life for it. It was true. But couldn't she also want something for herself? Couldn't she have also lived…simply to live? To be touched by a man. As she had been last night. To be able to get married. To be able to have children. To enjoy dresses and makeup.

To enjoy pastries.

She wanted those things. She did not think that it made her bad or selfish. Yet he was all about control. But he would not tell her why.

Here again, she was to be a figurehead.

His wife, but not for real. He would not share with her. He would not sleep with her, because he'd been undone by what had happened between them. She knew it. She'd seen it. Her honesty was a devastating weapon to him. And she would have to hide herself from him. As he would continue to conceal his own secrets.

It would be far too similar to living that dungeon life she had been in for this many years.

She was sad for it.

When the luncheon finished, and the guests had cleared away, she found that Maximus had vanished as well. She gathered her skirts, lifting them up from the ground, and swept back into the palace, moving down the corridor, heading toward his chamber.

Then she walked in. Without knocking, because why would she? He had come into her room without so much courtesy the morning of their dance lesson.

And she was not disappointed. For he was there, his jacket discarded, his shirt partly open, showing a beautiful slice of his chest. That she had licked. Bit. She wanted more of him. She was just so...hungry.

And she wanted someone to share that with.

"I am a woman," she said.

"Yes," he answered. "You are not a coffeepot. That much is certain."

Perhaps her honesty was her greatest weapon, and why should she shield him from it? He was hurting her with his distance. Why should she protect him?

"I am a woman, and a Queen. I am both. And I had

the terrible sensation today as I stood up there before the crowd that I would lose myself as the crown was placed upon my head. I thought to myself…this is why I lived. This is. This coronation. This moment. The opportunity to take care of my people. But then I thought…it is not why I lived. I would have lived if I would've lost the country. I would have lived, and it would've mattered. Does it matter?"

"Of course it does," he said. But his face gave nothing away, and he stood rigid.

Though it was that blankness that spoke volumes, at least as far as she was concerned.

"It does," she said. "It matters that I breathe. It *does* matter."

How she wished she could break down his walls. But maybe the fact that she had broken them was evident here. Maybe she had, and that was why he was so horribly blank. So she pressed on. "I am not a person who died." Tears pushed against her eyes. "My family died. There was nothing to be done. My family died, and it is… True sadness. But I'm not dead. I'm not dead and I am more than a figurehead to be trotted out at the whims of…of those men. Those men who saw me as nothing more than…" She blinked back tears. "I would go days sometimes without seeing the sun. All that time I spent in a dark dungeon. And they would let me out, only to serve them. And in my heart I thought that if I could survive, then I would fix things. And sometimes it gave me the strength to keep going. But sometimes I just thought of being held again. Being loved. Sometimes I just thought that maybe someday there would be a man who would hold me in his arms. And sometimes that was enough."

She waited. She waited, but he did not surprise her. Instead, he did what she'd feared.

"I'm not that man," he said.

"I don't need you to be," she said, desperate now and not caring if he knew it. "But I would like for you to be *you*. I would like for you to not hide what you are—*who* you are—from me. When I am the one who has seen you. I am just so very tired. And so..." She reached behind her back and grabbed the zipper tab of her green dress and released it, letting it fall to the floor. And then stared at him. He looked at her, hunger in his dark gaze, and she felt an intense tug of satisfaction. She was wearing nothing but a strapless lace bra and matching panties. And the shoes that she had not bothered to take off.

"I cannot explain," she said. "I can only feel. Feel the desperate weight of that darkness closing in around me. It was so horrible. I was nothing. Nothing. A tool to be used. And that was what decided if I lived or died, and that is what I had to be. And you can see now why it angers me. To have to say the right things, to do the right things. To dress the right way. When I want me to matter. Me. What I want. And it never will. Not out there. Because you're right. I must be appropriate. I must be what my country needs. But I am also a woman. I am not just a Queen. And I want you. Whether you are rough or not. I want you, the real you. The real... Feelings for me."

"I do not have feelings," he said, his voice going pitch-dark.

"I don't have the words," she said, feeling full to the top with frustration. "Learn French if you want good words. I don't have them in English. Or learn my language. Learn my language if you want to hear something better. Only... I am tired of being contained. I am tired of easy. I want *hurt*. Because hurt is better than nothing at all. The gray and darkness and numbness. Do you have any idea? Do you have any idea what it's like to be locked away like that? No, you don't. Because you were raised rich and with freedom."

He moved toward her, and she could feel the crackle of intensity beneath his skin, could feel it barely contained inside of him, fighting to escape. "I know what it is to be trapped," he ground out. "To be trapped inside a darkness that you cannot fight. To be trapped inside something you cannot even see. Don't tell me that I don't understand."

Her frustration boiled over then, because she was standing there, bared in every way, and he was still resisting this and she simply could not. "Then if you understand, fight against it *with me. Feel* with me."

"There's no reason," he said, his voice as rough as gravel. "And it benefits no one to care."

"Lies," she whispered, the word choked by emotion. "You care. Whether you want to or not, whether you want it to be about the sainted woman that you speak of or not, you must care about the world."

"Or maybe I'm simply a killer." He took hold of her arm, drew her to him. She responded. Her nipples going tight, her heart thundering harder. She did not fear him. She felt for him. So much, she might burst with it. "Have you ever thought of that? Maybe I'm filled with hate, and *killing* is the only thing that makes that feel better. Maybe I dress it up in missions and assignments and all of those cold clinical words we use to justify government-sanctioned death. What if I like it? What if I care about that more than I care about fighting for justice?"

"It is not true," she said. "Whatever you say, it is not true. Or you would not have offered to be the King here. You would have simply gone about finding a person to assassinate in order to protect me. You would not have allied yourself with me as you did."

He released his hold on her. "Or perhaps you prove your point. Perhaps you prove your point that killing sometimes creates more problems."

"I don't know." She turned from him, pacing away from him. "I don't know about any of this. But tonight…"

She took the crown from the top of her head and placed it on the dresser by the door.

"Can I be Annick? And you be Maximus? Not the King, not the Queen. But just us. As we are. Can we be simply feeling? It doesn't have to be feelings for me. It can be feelings for her. It doesn't have to be anything easy. It can be sharp. It can be painful. But this… Last night. When I bit you. When I tasted you. I am just starving. I am just starving for all that I could have. For all that I have missed."

He didn't say a word. Instead, he stepped forward, grabbing hold of her hips and dragging her up against his body. She could feel his desire there. His hardness. The need that he felt for her, and he could not deny it. No matter how much he might want to. She pushed at his shirt, shoving it from his shoulders and tearing buttons off it as she did. They scattered across the floor, and then his chest was bare. Just as she liked it.

And she found herself dropping down to her knees before him, undoing the belt on his pants and opening them, reaching her hand inside his underwear and revealing that thick length of him that had felt so incredible inside her the night before. And she was ready. Ready for him. Ready for this. She was ready for everything that he might have for her. But first. She wanted this. This moment to luxuriate in the feel of him. The taste of him. She wanted this moment for them. For her. She wanted this moment to simply be.

She leaned in, sliding her tongue along his length.

"Annick," he growled, taking a handful of her hair, and she felt the pins there biting into her scalp.

Does a King submit to his Queen here?

You know that he does not.

And here she was, on her knees, submitting to her King.

Except, it was not so simple. For he was at his end; she could see that. The fierce light in his eyes, the strength with which he held her in his grip. He was beyond himself, and she was... She was powerful. In this moment, on her knees before him, she was everything. Woman. Queen. Submissive. Powerful. In this moment. Finally, she could feel all the light that she had been denied for all of those years. In his strength. His heat. His taste.

She didn't obey him. Rather, she leaned her head forward, pulling against his hold, loving the way the pain dovetailed with the pleasure that pierced her like an arrow between her legs. And she took him in deep. Tasted him, took him in so deep that he touched the back of her throat. And he growled, bucking his hips upward. And she took it. All of it.

"Annick." He said her name, rough and raw and ragged, and it was everything that she needed it to be.

She lost herself then. In pleasuring him.

In this endless circle of need. It filled her. It emptied her. Giving him pleasure gave her her own, and she could not have explained that if she had been asked to. All she knew was that she wanted it. Wanted him.

All she knew was that she was a slave to this. As much as she was the master of it.

And she had come to him across the world, not because she had thought they might find this, simply because she thought they might be able to help.

But this was more than help. And it was more than simply for her. It was something...

A gift.

Annick had spare few gifts in her life.

A spare few.

He jerked her away from him suddenly, and she could see that he was pushed to his limits, his muscle shaking.

"Not like this," he said, his words a fractured example of the control within.

"Why not? You made me shatter that way last night."

"But I want to be in you, my Queen. I wish to feel how tight you are. How wet. I wish for you to come apart in my arms while I shatter against you."

"Yes," she whispered.

And she would. She would.

"Take your clothes off," he ordered.

And she could hear it. That his restraint had slipped its leash.

That she'd gotten her wish.

And now she would pay the price.

Oh, she craved that price.

He freed himself from the rest of his garments while she undid her bra, drew her panties down her legs. While she kicked her shoes off.

"Yes," he said. "There you are. Not a Queen, are you? Just mine."

"Yes," she whispered.

And she did not know why she found such a great comfort in that. In being his. Except he would never take her to a dungeon. He would never lock her away. He wanted to make her feel good.

As long as she belonged to Maximus, she would be safe.

Suddenly, she wanted to weep. Safe.

She could not remember ever feeling safe. *Safe*.

Safe with him. If she was his, that was how it would be. And he could be hers. She could...

And then she couldn't think anymore, because he closed the distance between them and kissed her. Hard and fierce and long. Kissed her until she couldn't think. Until her world was reduced to the way his hard body felt naked against hers. Then he lifted her up and carried her to the bed.

He was over her, those eyes gleaming and intense. The eyes of a man who had sat there with his finger steady on the trigger, waiting to take a life. Who had done so to save lives. Who claimed he had no conscience and no soul but held her like she mattered.

And he positioned himself at the entrance of her body, and when he thrust into her, she gasped.

For there was no control, no finesse. All the things he'd said he needed were gone. And she reveled in it. Gloried in it.

For this was what she needed.

This. This moment of abandon. Each thrust was so intense it was nearly painful. Pleasure. Pain. Lights flashing across her closed eyes. Every sensation she could possibly have hoped for cascading over her in the moment. Her need building to such heights she didn't know if she could withstand it.

And yet she would. Because she knew what true hell was. Having nothing. Having no one. Feeling nothing.

Not even knowing what to dream for, so you had to dream of what you might do for your country, and nothing else.

For thinking that the only reason you might matter was to serve the greater good, and not to simply be.

But in his arms, she could be.

In his arms, the years of deprivation, the years of nothing, melted away.

And when she shattered, she was the stars again. Every starry night she hadn't been allowed to see, as the dungeon ceiling had been her view. She became all she had lost.

When it was over, she lay with him. Let him hold her. Until the sounds of their hearts beating quieted. Until she could breathe again.

"No more prisons," she whispered.

"I do not seek to put you in a prison," he said.

"You may not seek to," she said, tracing a finger over his forearm, "but the end result is the same. By denying me... It is the same." She breathed out slowly. "It is not the same. I know it is not. But sometimes I feel full to bursting with these emotions... I don't ever want to go back. To being nothing and feeling nothing. When I saw my parents... My brother."

He tightened his hold on her. "How did you escape?"

She spread her hands. "I didn't escape, eh?"

His lips curved upward. Only barely. "You lived."

"Yes," she agreed. "I lived. They made sure that I saw the executions of my family." She shook her head, sadness building inside of her. "It is the deepest of sorrows. To have lost them that way. To know that everything in my country would change as well. That it was not just I who lost, but everyone. All of Aillette. And I could do nothing to stop it."

"That's why you kept going."

She nodded. "It was easier that way at first. To think

only of my people. To think only of the things that they had suffered, because the things that I suffered…"

"Do not tell me what you suffered," he said. "Tell me of how they lived, not how they died."

She was choked with gratitude. For no one had ever asked for that. No one had given her the opportunity to speak of it. She had denied herself the gift of remembering for too long. Because it was easier. Because it felt simpler to focus only on the fact they were gone, rather than remembering how sweet it was when they were there.

"My older brother liked to tease me. He also gave me sweets. Always. When he and my father would travel together, he would always bring me back something nice. To commemorate the other country. A fruit candy, or a chocolate. Pastries. Cakes." She smiled. "Perhaps that is why I liked eating dessert first so much at dinner those nights ago. It reminded me of him. Of Marcus. He was a good brother."

"And your father?"

"Fair and strong. And very traditional. A man who did not believe in progress for the sake of it. But I admired him greatly. He was very kind. To everyone who worked in the palace. He was fair, even though he could be strict. He was never cruel. He taught me to dance," she said, her voice breaking. "Standing on his feet. I did dance. I lied to you. But it was an easy lie, eh? These truths hurt. These memories."

"He sounds like a good man."

"You would never have had to assassinate him." She laughed. "Though in the end he was, I suppose. His goodness did not save him. It was a terrible lesson. Knowing that being strong and good could not keep you safe. I hated that lesson."

The time it took him to respond spoke volumes of how he listened. It was such a wonderful, strange thing. To share with another person like this.

Yes, she had made friends with her staff at the palace, but they worked for her. It was not the same as this.

"The world is a broken place," he said. "Good people die."

The words were heavy and fragile all at once. And she knew she had been trusted with a truth that resided deep within his soul.

"I know well. My mother, she was… She was beautiful. Tall and elegant. And her hair always looked perfect. She smelled like lilacs and sunshine. A particular perfume, but I do not know it. All memory of my family was eradicated from here. None of their things were kept if they did not have value. Value to *them*. But what had value to them is different than what would've had value to me and…"

"Of course."

"All I have are memories. I remember one time we all went on a picnic. We sat by the lake, and we were happy. We were so happy. Happy to eat together and be together. I will not forget that. It was a gift. It was not long before the coup. I think that is what strikes me now as so desperately unfair. My father was a King. My brother was the heir. My mother was a Queen. But they were just my family. And if we had just been a family they would never have been killed."

"All too often innocents are caught in the cross fire." He shifted, holding her more tightly. "It is a fact of this world that I despise, and one I have fought for years. It does not do good to dwell on the things that you cannot change. Or to ask *what if.* For I have done that. I have done it exhaustively. I have asked why many times and was never met with an answer. Sometimes things simply are."

"Yes. But it is hard not to wonder. How things could be different."

"But that is the path to insanity. Or at least revenge."

"Is that the path you've been on?"

"Yes," he said.

"What happened? I spoke of my family to you... I gave myself to you. Tell me. What is it?"

"My story is not of help to anyone."

"Well," she said, "I don't know that my story is particularly helpful to anyone either. But someone should remember my family. And only I remember them in this way. It is an honor to their memory to speak of them, isn't it?" She waited. Only for a beat. "Maybe you should speak of the woman you lost."

There was a breath. Then her name.

"Stella."

"Stella," she said, testing the name.

She felt a surge of jealousy, and she felt also that it was unfair. She didn't know why she should have it either. He was in her bed, and that was enough. She didn't need anything more.

She only needed to listen. As he had done for her.

As they built a web of intimacy together.

"I fell in love with Stella when I was very young. I had no aversion to marrying. My parents had a wonderful marriage. *Have* a wonderful marriage. Long and healthy. Functional. I always thought... I would find the right woman, and I would marry her. Quickly and easily. For love always seemed quick and easy to me. Why wouldn't it? After all, my parents lived a fantasy. Why wouldn't I live the very same fantasy? Love came quickly. It came easily. And it was lost just as quickly and easily. And my life… My life was never what I thought it would be."

"Sorry," she said, her heart squeezing tight. It was not language barriers that made words ineffectual, not now. It was the fact there were no words for these things. For the deep sadness and unfairness in the world. She hated this. Hated that he had been through so much pain. Why did it feel like this?

She didn't think she could recall ever feeling quite so sorry for another person's tragedy. And at the same time she felt…angry. Angry because part of her wished that she could have been loved half so dearly as this Stella woman had been. But Stella was gone, and Annick lived.

What a very strange thing. Everyone who had ever loved Annick was gone. And this man loved a woman who was not here. It left behind a broken Annick. A broken Maximus. How much more right the world would have been if Annick were gone and Stella were here.

But Annick wanted to be here. Wanted to be in Maximus's arms, in his bed. Annick wanted to be the one who was here, breathing next to him, touching him.

Yes, that was what she wanted. Even if it meant the world remained broken and out of sorts.

She was sorry, though. That a man so beautiful should be so haunted.

She wondered if anyone felt so sorry for her. If anyone looked at her and thought it sad that someone so young had been robbed of so much life.

She didn't know that they did. But either way, she cared for him. Cared for his brokenness. Even if no one much minded her own.

Even if he didn't.

"What happened?"

"My father is not quite the self-made businessman he appears to be. Oh, he is responsible for the way that his life has gone, but he's done things…"

"What things?"

"He engaged in a host of shady business practices initially. My father is a good man in many ways. You have to understand that. As a boy, Dante was living on the streets, tried to rob my father and kill him. And rather than extracting punishment from him, my father sent Dante to a school where he was educated. Took care of him. Introduced him to me. Gave me a lifelong friend who is truly more like a brother. My father also promised my sister to a King in return for aid to his business. And he made bad bargains with the wrong people. And those people sought their revenge when my father thought he could outrun them. When he thought he could cheat them. My father is a family man. He has never been unfaithful to my mother. He raised us well. But he waded into dark waters to create his fortune. And those things have a way of coming back to haunt you. And they did. They did. There was a man sent to punish my father. Sent to kill his son."

"Maximus…"

"But the assassin's bullet did not hit his son." The word broke, along with his voice.

"It hit Stella. I didn't protect her. I couldn't protect her. I didn't know. I was naive. Ignorant. Innocent in a way. I believed that my father was a good man. I believed that he would never do anything to put his children in harm's way. But he did. And worst of all, we didn't know it. Because I didn't know it, I didn't know that Stella was ever in danger by being with me. Her murder remains listed as unsolved. Because the man was an international hit man. And she was just… She was just a girl. A young, beautiful girl who had the misfortune to fall in love with the wrong man, who was connected to the wrong people. She deserved more. She deserved better. She sure as hell deserved to live."

"And all this is for her. All of this," Annick said. "Even protecting me."

"I could see her face when you told me about your plight. She would've been angry with me for abandoning you. She was a good person."

"And you loved her."

"Yes. Of course, then I thought… I thought that love was simple. And that people were exactly who they appeared to be. That love was easy and life was charmed. That my father's legend was real. None of it was real."

"You have a family," she said. "A family who loves you."

He nodded slowly. "That's the truth of it. I do. I have a family—you don't. It must be difficult to have lost your family. Though in some ways I felt that day that I lost mine. At least, my illusion of what it was."

"Me," she said, "I would rather have an illusion than nothing. Than a life spent in the dungeon. I'm not saying it is easy, this. This thing that happened to you. This thing that you learned about your father. But I know what it is to be left with no one. No one to care about your pain. Did your father at least care?"

"He was broken by it. I've never seen a man weep like he did, not even me. Not even me when she died. But he made me swear that I wouldn't tell. Not my mother. Not Min or Violet. And not Dante."

"So they could keep the family they always thought they had."

"My kindness was not for him. But for them."

"It makes sense, this. But then, you're all alone. Maximus King to them. They don't know you. They don't know who you are."

"No. They don't."

"You are in a dungeon. One that you have fashioned for yourself from the stone blocks of your secrets. Maximus King, you fill me with great sadness."

"Don't be so dramatic. I'm not in any kind of prison. I'm here of my own free will. No one has forced me into anything."

"I did. With chloroform."

"You are far too proud of your chloroform, Annick. I could have left at any time if I wanted to."

"Can you? Would you always see bars?"

"See bars?"

"It is reading I did," she said. "About kittens."

"And what do kittens have to do with bars?"

"It is what kittens have to do with us, I think. If they are raised in cages, even when they are freed they see the bars before their eyes. They do not truly ever see themselves as free. They know captivity. They exist in it even after the walls are removed. Do we do that? I wonder."

"People? Or us specifically?"

"You and me." She put her hand first on her chest, then on his. "Maximus and Annick."

"I'm just doing what I can to make the imbalance of the world right again. It takes a lot of bad being removed to begin to make up for Stella being gone."

Annick nodded gravely. "She must've been very good, your Stella. To lay claim to your heart once and forever."

"She was."

"She is not using your heart, though. And you could maybe use the return of it."

"It isn't that simple."

She shrugged. "Me, I find most things are actually quite simple."

"Yes, but that simplicity is unique to you, Annick. You act as if you can just say whatever you want. Do whatever you want. Chloroform whoever you want, and it will fix your problems."

"Ah, my life is not so complicated. I might have felt like I could not be myself, but at least I knew what to do. Survive. That is a very simple life. To survive. It is this wanting that I find complicated, Maximus King."

"What is it you want?"

There were many things she wanted, but few of them were possible. For now, she would stick with possible. "I think…more pastries. And then I will have some more of your body."

"Is that so?"

"It is so," she said, nodding definitively.

She couldn't fix the past, not for either of them. But for the moment she felt soothed. For the moment she felt like she might even have a real friend. She was sad for him. For all that he had lost. But it made him kindred in a way. In a way that no one else she knew was or could be. He was broken. Missing pieces of himself. And so was she.

"Then that is what you shall have."

CHAPTER ELEVEN

THEY WERE TO be married the next day. Neither of them had seen the point in tarrying over the planning of the wedding. It was for security. And it needed to be done. Whatever else she might think about necessity, he knew that she understood that. His family had also arrived. They would be staying for a time after the ceremony, and there really was nothing he could do to persuade them otherwise. Annick, for her part, was pleased. And if he were a different man, he might find it charming.

"It is just that there has not been family in this palace for a very long time," she explained, when expressing her delight about his family coming to visit. And he found he could not begrudge it to her.

She was so fragile. And yet so determinedly strong all at once. Annick and her chloroform. He had never intended to get himself embroiled in this sort of thing. Had never thought that he would get married. Most especially not after Stella. His love for her had been branded on his soul. Initially. Now what he did was not out of blind grief. It had left him in doubt of eternal love.

Because he didn't feel that love anymore. He didn't feel her close to him. That year he had spent loving her could do nothing to close the gap of the sixteen years spent without her. And so, revenge, balancing the scales, that was his quest. It was nothing to do with love. And the things he had learned about his father in the aftermath of it all...

It had twisted everything he thought about the world. Losing Stella had been more than simply losing her. It had meant a change to the way that he saw absolutely everything.

Annick made him feel something.

He did not care for it.

He had shared with her, though, and that had... It had moved things onto strange and shaking ground. There was a connection that he felt with her unlike anything he had experienced before, and that had not been the way this was meant to be.

He was supposed to protect her.

He was supposed to be helping her.

He was not supposed to be affected by her.

"Well, this really is quite something."

He turned where he stood in the entry to the castle, just in time for his sister Violet and her husband, Javier, to walk through the door. Violet was pregnant and looking glowing. It did something strange to him, to see his younger sister grown in this way. He'd been through it already with Minerva, though it had come out later that the child she had come home from a semester abroad with was not actually her child, but the child of a friend who had needed rescuing. As if thinking of her conjured her up, Minerva came in as well, also pregnant. Dante was with her, carrying their adopted daughter in his arms. And behind them came Robert and Elizabeth King, his parents, who looked tan, fit and remarkably well-preserved. As always.

"This is incredible," Minerva said. "You both live in such splendid palaces."

"Cara," Dante said. "Are you disappointed that I have not bought you a palace? Because I could. Would you prefer an atmospheric ruin in the Highlands? One with a very large library..."

"Yes," she said. "Would you really buy me a castle?"

"And a pony if you so wish."

His eyes glittered with humor. And Maximus was surprised to discover how pleased he was with that. His friend had been beset by darkness for years. And Minerva seemed to have brought him out of it. He never would've thought that. He would have said that Min was too shy. Too bookish. But she had done wonders for him. He didn't know the Prince that Violet had married, but he had it on good authority that sunny, flashy Violet had done much the same for him.

He thought of his own fiancée. Wide-eyed, determined, and no less tortured than he was.

His sisters had brought with them a sense that the world could be right. And they had given it to those men that cared for them so.

He could bring nothing of the kind to Annick. And she would hold no magic elixir of healing for him.

They had seen too many dark things. They knew too many hideous truths about the world.

"Well, it's good to see all of you," Maximus said, working to put his mask in place. He wouldn't have to explain that to Annick, which was a blessing. Because Annick understood. Annick knew.

He felt a ripple go through his family, and he turned. Annick was standing in the doorway, wearing her crown and a silver gown that wrapped around her curves.

Annick had taken this dressing-for-how-she-wanted-to-appear thing to heart. Intensely. She was nothing if not blatantly over-the-top at every opportunity.

"Hello," she said.

"Your Majesty." His mother curtsied.

"Your Highness," came from his father.

Minerva curtsied and Dante inclined his head. Javier and Violet stepped forward, shaking Annick's hand. "Your Highnesses," Annick said. "It is good of you to come and grace my country."

"A pleasure," Javier said. "For I know full well how good it is to be able to share your country with the world after many years of it being on the brink of devastation. My own brother has just reformed our native land of Monte Blanco to a glorious state. And you are more than welcome to come for a visit."

"I should like that," Annick said. "I should love to speak to you about all the things that you have done to fix the…atrocities that were visited upon your people. I am working diligently to try and make right what has happened to mine. But it is not so simple always."

"It never is."

"Indeed not," Violet chimed in. "Sometimes they must kidnap someone to accomplish their ends."

"It makes for an interesting story at parties," Annick said. "A slightly more interesting story about how we met than many others have, don't you think?"

Violet laughed, and the rest of his family too. Clearly utterly charmed by this rather serene version of Annick that stood before them.

It was not a part she was playing. And yet she was also not the urchin he'd held in his arms the night before, who had told him dirty jokes, then happily ate pastries in bed and wiped her buttery fingers against his bare chest.

It was all of her, fused into one formidable being.

And it was a sight to behold.

"That is true." Violet shrugged. "And I have the added bonus of being able to tell people that I was kidnapped specifically so that I could marry his brother. And ended up marrying him myself."

"We're interesting if nothing else," Javier said.

"Quite," Annick agreed.

"We shall have dinner," Maximus said. "First, you may all find your bedrooms and put your things away."

"Will you come with me?" Violet said, smiling. "It's just that I have packed so many things, and I would hate to inconvenience your staff."

"What about your husband?"

"Oh, I'll inconvenience him plenty. It's only that I still need more arms than that."

Leave it to Violet to have packed an entire castle.

He followed his sister back out to the front of the palace, and she rounded on him.

"Are you in trouble? Blink twice if you need to leave."

"It was my idea," he said.

"Marriage was your idea?"

"Yes," he said. "It was. She needs help. I'm not marrying her under sufferance."

"Well, you can leave. We'll get you diplomatic immunity. Whatever you need."

"Whatever you need," Javier agreed.

"I don't *need* anything. I promise. Anyway, it's entirely possible Annick is pregnant with my child. So I should probably stick around." He knew the act he put on contributed to his family's response to this. Had they truly known him, they wouldn't have been half so worried.

"Oh, good God," Violet said. "You are such a man

whore that you had to have sex with the woman who kidnapped you?"

He looked pointedly at his sister's baby bump. "What kind of person would do such a thing?"

"It's different," Violet said. "Isn't it?"

"I don't know."

"Do you love her?"

He looked at his sister. "No."

"Then why are you doing this?"

"I don't need to be in love, Violet. I don't want to be."

"Is this because of Stella?"

He knew his sister couldn't remember Stella well. She'd been too young. But Violet knew that their father wasn't perfect. He'd sold her in marriage, after all. But she didn't know about this. And he wasn't going to explain.

"That was sixteen years ago. And things have changed. I am who I am."

"So you're going to marry that beautiful creature and never love her?"

That stung. But this wasn't the moment to worry about Annick's emotions. He was here to protect her. He was marrying her to protect her. That was it.

"Annick has a life to get to living. I'm not going to hold her back. Not when it's her chance to be free."

"And your chance to maintain the status quo. Congratulations."

He rounded on his sister. "And what do you mean by that exactly?"

"I think you know. You found yourself a stunning woman who isn't going to demand fidelity of you. And you get to be a King. Must be fun. And the bonus is that you get to rehab the image of the country. But what about you? Do you ever get deeper than image?"

"And where exactly is all this coming from?" he asked.

"It just seems to me that you found yourself a sort of ideal situation."

"And yet you don't sound happy for me."

"Well, no. Because actually… I hoped for better for you."

"You don't know me, Violet. Not as well as you think."

"Whose fault is that?"

"It wasn't an accusation," he said. "Merely an observation."

His sister produced a purple velvet trunk, which he picked up off the ground and slung over his shoulder, walking back toward the palace. He didn't need lectures from Violet on how he might proceed with his life. She didn't know the half of it. Didn't know the half of him. He strolled back into the palace and saw Annick standing there. Their eyes met. Annick was the only person who did know. His whole family, the people he had grown up with. His parents who had raised him… They didn't know. Only this woman knew. This woman he had known for a couple of weeks. He didn't quite know what to do with that realization. So he simply walked on. Tonight, they would have dinner. Tomorrow, they would be married. And it didn't matter what Violet had to say about it. It was set in stone. It would not change.

CHAPTER TWELVE

ANNICK FELT STRANGE, sitting there with his family. Knowing what she did about his father, and that no one else knew it. And just…being around the family. It was a strange and layered thing. Shot through with moments of exhilaration and happiness and deep, unsettling grief. She felt quite unlike herself.

Unable to find a retreat inside of herself to go to as she normally did. Unable to protect herself against the sheer domesticity of what was happening in the palace.

A palace that had not seen such a thing since the death of her family.

"Violet and Maximus have always been the excessive ones," Min was saying. "And I was the one that everyone overlooked."

"Not everyone, *cara.*"

Minerva laughed at her husband. "Oh, you most of all. Don't try to rewrite history now, Dante. Anyway, if you would have noticed me a moment before it was appropriate, my father would've had you killed."

"Unless I did it first," Maximus said, smiling that charming grin that she knew was fake. What was real was the threat underlying his words. She knew that he wasn't lying. Or exaggerating. Except that… He would've done it himself. If a man had done anything to harm one of his sisters, she had full confidence that Maximus would be the one to handle the insults all on his own.

"It's good you have Maximus here with you, Annick," Robert King said. "He's always been brilliant. Since you're trying to accomplish reform here in the country, I know he'll do right by you and your people."

Annick studied him closely. He did seem a very nice man, as Maximus had said he was. He was of indeterminate age, obviously old enough to have Maximus as a son, but still difficult to pinpoint. His wife even more so, her face dramatically lacking in lines. They were a beautiful family. Violet stunning, Minerva an understated mourning dove. Elizabeth King the sort of blonde beauty that all celebrities aspired to.

She could see how Maximus had felt like he lived a charmed life. And how badly it would've hurt to have had that challenged. To have lost that in any regard.

"Yes," Annick said, looking directly at the older man. "He's quite brilliant. And I think…much more than anyone realizes." She could feel his warning glare burning into the side of her face. "I'm quite lucky to have him."

"Anyone would be," Robert King agreed.

Dinner was served then, a basket of pastries coming out before the meal. Annick smiled.

"Is this a tradition here?" Minerva asked.

"No," Annick said happily. "Well, I suppose it will be."

By the end of it all, the tension she felt toward even his father was forgotten, because she felt surrounded by this love that she had not been near for years.

And she wanted so desperately to be part of it. She wanted so desperately to belong to someone. Wanted so much to be…

She cut that thought off. It did no good to dwell on the things she did not have control over. It did no good to wish for the clock to reverse. To wish for life to be different. She had done it hundreds of times. She knew it did no good.

She had lived the life she did. That was all.

Tomorrow she would marry into this family. Something that she could never have foreseen. Something entirely different to the life she had imagined loomed ahead of her. Tomorrow, things would change.

When dinner was done, she excused herself, and she didn't even wait for Maximus. She found herself wandering away from the bedrooms. Away from the ballroom. Away from every civilized part of the castle, to a place that she hadn't been back to since the day that she had been set free.

Her heart constricted in her chest as she made her way down the dark, narrow steps. As she descended down a level, and then another. All the way to the lower dungeon.

This place was a reminder. Of where she had come from. Of what really mattered. It wasn't her feelings or his family or...

Her dungeon lay untouched since she'd been freed.

It needed to stand. As it was. At least, it felt to her it did.

It was not a grimy jail cell. It was a room. With a bed in the corner. No windows. It was dingy, not clean. Atop her small nightstand a copy of the Bible and *Anne of Green Gables* sat there still, the two books that she had read the most during her isolation, as they were the only ones perennially left behind by her tutor. There was a small desk in the corner, which had also been there since the beginning. And nothing more. She felt small here. That trembling sensation that she'd always battled in her chest loomed large.

"What are you doing down here?"

"I... I might ask you the same thing?"

"I followed you."

"I did not give you permission to do so."

"Since when have I needed your permission for anything?"

"This is not to share." Tears filled her eyes. "I want you to go away."

"Is this where they kept you?"

"It is not your..."

"Is this where they kept you, Annick? In this room like a...like a patient at a mental ward?"

"Yes," she said.

"This is...disgusting."

"It is," she agreed.

"I would go back and kill them all over again if I had not already done so," he said, his tone black as night. "How dare they do this to you."

"It is so. They did it. I suppose it does not matter how."

"It matters to me."

"I felt so different sitting around your family, I thought perhaps I would come down here and see if I was. But I'm the same. I tremble standing here. Afraid that I will not be able to choose to leave." She turned around. "But the bars are not there. You are." He filled the doorway, his large frame taking up all that space once occupied by the locking door.

"How did you survive it?"

"The way we all survive such things. We go to whatever place inside of ourselves we can find that will protect us. Keep us safe. You have this place. This place you go to when you smile with charm to your parents. Or maybe it is the place you go when you pick up your gun to kill the men who you imagine are the ones who killed Stella. It is what you do, yes? Every time. That man becomes the man who killed her."

"This is not about me."

"It is about those of us who live on. When we sometimes wish we had not. That is what this is. We are not so different, Maximus King."

"This prison cell is a damn horror," he said, looking around.

"My life was a 'damn horror,' as you say. And yet somehow I am here. As are you."

"Let's go upstairs."

"We are to be married tomorrow. And I am Queen." Unexpectedly, a tear slid down her cheek. "I did not ever think I would live to see this day. A wedding day. The day that I wore the crown. It is all hitting me now. After all these years of hiding. All these years of feeling nothing. It is all hitting me now. All these feelings that were locked away here. How can you even have feelings in here?"

"You can't," he said. "This place is torture all on its own."

"Yes. It is so. But it is a torture I survived. To come out of this place. To this moment." She looked at him and her heart ached. It felt too heavy. Much too heavy. And suddenly, she wanted to run from him as badly as she wanted to run from the cell. Because… What she really wanted, standing there, raw from that dinner she had just shared with his family, she could admit wounded her just as much.

She wished that she could be loved. It was a terrible thing that Maximus grieved Stella so much. But… But what a wonderful thing to be grieved. What a wonderful thing to have someone love you quite so much that they turned their life inside out, that they became a mythical beast on your behalf, attempting to rid the world of injustice just so you might be avenged.

She had no idea what that sort of love must be like.

Years. She had spent years in this room. With captors who were utterly and completely dispassionate about her. Captors who didn't care if she lived or died. Who trotted her out when it was necessary. Who used her to support their great and terrible acts. Who only educated her, even just the slightest, so that she could put on a performance of being cared for.

She was so hungry for love. There were so many things to grieve about the loss of her family, but the deepest one, the deepest one that she had not wanted to acknowledge for all this time, was that when she lost them she had also lost the only people who cared about her.

The only people in the world who loved her.

And she had him, this dark avenging angel, but he was not *her* dark avenging angel.

He was avenging the wrongs committed against another. And he was using her as a token for that, but it still wasn't the same.

It still wasn't…love.

"I am tired," she said. "And I must ready myself for our wedding. I should not like to be a hideous bride."

"You could never be hideous," he said.

"I am, I think, cursed with faint praise, eh?"

"You will be nothing but beautiful," he said, his voice too smooth, his smile too easy. He was playing a part again.

Why? Because all of this was too real for him?

He ran, when things were intense. When they shared. Even if his body was here, his soul was running and she knew it.

"Says Maximus King? Or the King?"

"I don't know what you're talking about."

"Ah, the Playboy. How nice for me. I will meet him again at the altar tomorrow. And he had better look exceptionally sharp. Had better do me proud. In my country."

"As trophy husbands go, you have a very good one."

"And one who could ward off the threat without so much as breaking a sweat. I am quite fortunate, I think."

"You look angry."

"I am angry. All the time. Aren't you?"

And tired. Just so damn tired.

"I'll see you in the morning. My very angry bride."

"See you then."

But when she went to sleep, she no longer felt filled with that momentary joy she'd experienced. That sense of wonder that she was getting more than she had ever imagined she might. Now she felt overwhelmed by the realization that what she wanted was the love of the man who had no heart left to give. The love of a man who did not even know who he was.

And wanting Maximus's love was as impossible as wanting the love of her parents.

For when he said that his love, his heart, was gone, she believed it.

So she wrapped herself up in a blanket on her bed and then wrapped herself even deeper in a blanket of impossibility and futility, and she would not allow herself to weep.

CHAPTER THIRTEEN

IT WAS A beautiful day for a wedding. Too bad she still felt so terribly sad. But her gown was sensational, and even though her heart was sore, she looked like she ought to.

It was only her feelings that were not quite where she hoped they would be.

She had thought a lot about those feelings. Love. Of course, it was natural that she wanted love. But that did not mean she was *in* love with him.

That would be the saddest thing of all. It was only that she was lonely. And when he held her, it felt like something special. It was good she had not let him hold her last night. His arms contained a kind of magic that made her feel happy, but also sadder all at once.

And now they would be married.

She walked down to the chapel all on her own. It was different than the day of the coronation, when she had had Maximus to escort her. She held the bouquet of flowers that had been provided for her and looked down at the blossoms. A curl of blond hair fell into her face as she did, and she felt a strange cracking sensation about her heart. Her father should have been here. He should have been here to give her away. To place her on the arm of Maximus King, a man who would care for her. She felt a presence behind her. And she turned. It was Maximus.

"Are you ready?"

"Aren't you meant to be inside?"

"Probably. But I came to find you."

Her heart nearly flew from her chest. He came to find her.

She remembered being in that dungeon room. Being in the dark. Seeing him.

Knowing somehow that he would be her salvation, but she had not known it would be this.

Even though she had been too afraid to do it at the time, she reached her hand out for him, and he took it.

He was here.

He had come to find her, just now.

He would be her husband and she… She was happy about that.

"I was only thinking of my father," she said softly. "It is not so much that I need a man to give me away. I do not. It is that a father cares for his children. For his daughter. And when he gives her to a man, he is giving her to a man he believes will care for her, if all is well. My father died in fear of the safety of his children. I am safe. I wish he could see. I wish that he could have given me to you, rather than seeing me stolen away by the men who then killed him. Though perhaps in his last moments it was not his concern."

"The ones you love are always your concern," Maximus said.

There was a flower pinned to the lapel of his suit jacket, and he snapped it off then. Then he placed it down on the stone wall right beside the entry to the church. "For your father."

Tears filled her eyes and she broke a blossom off the

top of her bouquet, then another. And she set them beside the first. "My mother and Marcus."

"Do you know," he said. "I never was a big believer in the afterlife. And spirits. And living on. But I know that it is Stella who guides me sometimes. My memory of her, her spirit, whichever you like to call it. They see you."

She closed her eyes and nodded slowly. "Thank you."

Maximus looked to the flowers. "I will keep her safe. I swear it with my life. If you were here, you would approve this match. You would know that I was sincere. That when I make vows I keep them. And I make this a vow. Annick will come to no harm as long as I am here. I would give my life for hers."

Annick shivered. But she couldn't speak.

"Shall we go in?" he asked.

"Yes," she said.

He took her arm, and he led her up the aisle, as he had done for the coronation. The priest was there waiting, just as he had been then too, but Maximus stood with her. And these vows were not to the country, but to each other. The traditional vows always spoken at weddings in Aillette.

"The world is full of hard places," she said slowly, reading from the paper she held in her hands. "But I will be soft for you. The world is full of uncertainty, but I will be constant. The world is out there, and we are here. And in my heart, you have become the world."

When Maximus spoke, his rich voice filled the room, vibrated with her soul.

"The world is filled with danger, and I will be your strength. Your weapon. Your sword and your shield. I will be your guard. I will be your warrior. I will protect you and preserve you, for my life is yours. And my world is here."

She was not supposed to believe it. It was not supposed to matter. Not quite to the degree that it did. But oh, how she wished she could. How she wished she could freeze all of this and hold it to her chest.

And when they were introduced as the sovereign rulers of Aillette, King Maximus and Queen Annick, she felt the strangest sense of wholeness. Of unity. She looked at him, and she looked out in the crowd, at the King family watching them, clapping for them. Applauding as if this was a common American affair.

And she felt...part of something. Part of a family. And Maximus had even included her parents. Had spoken vows to their spirits. And suddenly she didn't feel so alone. And it was that hope inside of her that frightened her the most. That need.

Oh, how could she have ever talked herself into believing she did not love him? This beautiful, broken man who she had spirited away with the aid of chloroform, but who had turned the power around when he demanded marriage. This man who was trying to right wrongs that simply could not be fixed. This man made from lies and vengeance and a deep, unending love for another woman.

She loved him.

She did. There was nothing to be done for it. Nothing that could make it go away. And she didn't even want it to. Because last night she had revisited that dungeon, and it was isolation. The bars were gone, and Maximus was there instead. Though he might be his own kind of prison. Yes, loving him might be its own kind of hell.

They were swept off to the reception. A large white tent lay out on the lawn. And she had never felt quite so broken or quite so happy in all of her life.

Her people were here, eating and smiling and free.

It all made sense then. How she could live for them and herself. How those two things were not at odds. How she could love Maximus with deep ferocity and love them as well. How she could love him and expect nothing in return, but also want it desperately. How she could wish to devote herself to this country, but also wish to be a wife, and a mother to whatever children they had. Children who would also be both property of the country, and property of themselves. It was a difficult life, this. And one thing she was certain of when she stood there watching it all was that it took more courage and more love, and not less. You could not lead if you did not contain all these things. Not well. Not right.

And so it might be dangerous. To care like this. But if she did not, if she held back, if she tried to protect herself, then it would be like living in a dungeon. For then, in that life, she had held back everything that she believed, everything that she felt, simply because she had to protect herself. That had been a matter of life and death, but this was not. She could not hold back these feelings. To do so would make her a lesser Queen. To do so would make her less than Maximus deserved.

He had believed in love at one time. And all that he thought about the world had been destroyed. Cruelly. Could she not give him a piece of it back? She wanted to. Oh, how she desperately wanted to. For her Maximus King. Her King. Her husband.

Her love.

And she somehow knew innately that after today he would try to resist her. Because of course he would. It was the way of him. He drew close, and then away. What was he afraid of?

Feeling. She knew.

He was adamant that he had no heart left, but everything she had seen of him suggested otherwise.

The way that he stayed with his family, even with the issues he had with his father... No, he was not a man with no heart. Not a man with no soul.

He was a man with so much love to give, so bright and brilliant, like the sun that had been hidden from her for all those years. And it was nearly too much for her to bear. But also, she was sensitive to it. More perhaps than most because she had been kept in the darkness for so long. Because she had been kept away from people. And this thing between them... It was magic. It was more than necessity.

More than sex. She was certain of it.

She tried to remember back to when she had thought that sex was merely an appetite, as he had said. That he was a pastry she could go about sampling before she had another, and she realized what a foolish thing that was. There would never be another. Not for her. It was this broken man. With her. All broken. Together.

Yes, life was filled with tragedies, but looking at him now, she felt all of the miracles it contained as well. For he was a miracle to her.

She only hoped that she could be one for him.

And she would not let him pull away. Not tonight. Not on the night of their wedding.

She might have been a virgin only recently, but she was not afraid to seduce him.

She was not afraid to show him what was in her heart.

He had taught her about food, and the pleasure she might find there. His body, and all the joys that it contained. And now perhaps she would teach him about love. In the way that she understood it.

Love after brokenness.

After all these gifts he had given to her... Could she do anything less for him?

The wedding had left him feeling grim. Yes, it had been his idea, and yes, he had made many a bold declaration inside of himself that a wedding meant nothing, but he found it seemed less true than he would like.

By the end of the evening Annick was tired, he could tell. So when all the guests had left, he took himself off to his own chamber. He had a need for distance. His family was still in residence, and interacting with them was always a chore. Being that charming playboy that he was so accustomed to being... It was becoming a chore.

So what are you, then? The soldier?

He feared that it might be true.

That everything about Maximus King was simply a shell. That the one who was real was a man who took orders, carried out missions other men shied away from.

The one who pulled the trigger without mercy when necessary. The one who existed in a space between revenge and vigilante justice.

He had done good, but the question was, how much did he even care about it anymore?

If he were honest, he had lost that connection to Stella at some point over the years.

He no longer felt that deep, aching grief that he once had for her. No longer felt as if she was some sort of eternal love, a guiding light.

No. All had become darkness at a certain stage. Except Annick.

When he had walked Annick down the aisle today, when he had seen her in her gown, she had been light.

And he felt…reluctant to touch her. Like if he put his hands on her snow-white dress he would leave behind oily dark fingerprints. Or perhaps blood.

There was blood on his hands and he couldn't even bring himself to feel guilty about it. And that bothered him more than anything.

At first… At first it had had a cost. Killing. At first, he had felt the weight of every life he had taken. Yes, it was no different than war. These military operations. He knew that; he understood it. Many men did such things. They fought for the safety of their country, the lives of their countrymen, and what he was doing was that. He killed dictators' investments. Assassins. Murderers. None of them were innocent. But at a certain point, he had lost his own claim to innocence. He might be able to justify each and every thing he had done, might be able to weigh it against the lives those men would have eventually taken. But it did not make him a saint. It did not make him right.

He wondered sometimes if he was simply a man in darkness, the same as all of them. Choosing a side, and deciding it was right.

If the right evidence had been presented to him, would he have been involved in the removal of Annick's father?

He wanted to say no. But there had come a point where he had chosen who he believed. About who was good and who was evil.

No, he never, ever would have harmed a woman or child, but even so.

He had questions about his own frailty.

And he wished to drown those questions away in alcohol tonight. Not in Annick.

There was a knock at his chamber door, and she appeared. As if he had conjured her up with the pour of the whiskey. Whiskey like he had on the plane.

Whiskey, which Annick claimed she never had.

Oh, Annick, far too innocent for him. Far too much of a soft, undeniable beauty. That was, he supposed, the trade-off of her being locked away in that abysmal room. She had not been able to touch the outside world, and it had not been able to touch her.

"What are you doing here?"

"What is this? This stupid question. Why do you think I'm here?"

"For a drink?"

"No. An insult, Maximus, that you think I'm here for anything other than my wedding night."

"Such a traditionalist," he said, fighting against the rising tide of lust that was taking hold. Doing away with any kind of defenses he'd put up.

He had promised her family he would care for her, and this vow he'd made to the dead felt binding. But it was heavy. For how could he be sure he would not fail her? How?

"Don't take it as an insult."

"I have."

"I'm not in the mood."

She looked at him, all narrowed eyes and indignation. "Me, I think you're a liar."

"Of course I'm a liar. A liar," he said, advancing on her. "A liar who shows a mask to the whole world." He took another step closer to her, a dangerous heat rising up inside of him. "A drunk." He lifted his glass. Then he took another step toward his bride, so close that he could smell the lovely, enticingly feminine scent that he associated only and ever with her. "A killer."

"Yes," she said softly. "All these things. And me? I

am broken. Grieving. Tragic. Ruthless. Innocent. Guilty. We are all a great many things, are we not?"

"Don't test me tonight," he said.

"It is for just that reason that I test you. Because you don't wish it. Who wants to test a man who is prepared for that test? Boring."

"Are you in danger of being bored?"

"Not with you. Never with you." She closed the door behind her. "Also, I am not leaving. You do not scare me, Maximus King. I suppose I am now Annick King. You have made me a King as well." Her lips tugged into a smile. "And a Queen. A strange thing."

"I did not think a Queen would take the name of the man she married."

"Maybe not in public. But in private, I would like to do so. I have no family. I like very much the idea of being part of yours."

That brushed against that raw, deadly thing inside of him. "Whatever you wish."

"And if I wish for my wedding night?"

"Unwise," he said, tipping back the last of his whiskey.

"You keep saying this. As if there is a monster in you, waiting to savage me at the first available moment. But I have not met this monster. What would you say if I told you that I would like to meet him?"

"You don't."

"Why not? Did your Stella meet the monster?"

"Stella," he said, his voice rough, "didn't meet the monster because I was just a man when I was with her. Just one man. Not…whatever I have become."

"Good," Annick said. "I want to be the first. You were my first. Let me be yours."

"There have been many women."

"But none of them have met the real you, have they? No one has. Not your family…and even with me you hold back."

"I saw the dungeon that you lived in for all of your life. I feel sorry for you. I pity you. I would never put you in an even more pitiable position by exposing you to everything I am."

"And me, I'm not fragile. You know what I've seen. The same things you have. The life of the ones I love drained away right before my eyes. How could you think that I am someone who needs to be protected from monsters? Maybe I am a monster as well. Maybe we all are, given the right circumstances. Maybe that is the real secret. That we are all of us capable of anything if pushed. I kidnapped a man and dragged him across the world in spite of the fact that I spent many years being held prisoner. You would think I would not be able to do so, but I did. When feeling desperate. Because we are all human. We just lie, all the time, about what it means to be human."

"This is your final warning."

He could feel the beast within pulling at the chains. He would give her something to be afraid of if she wasn't careful.

"I do not do what I'm told anymore." And then she unzipped that wedding gown and let it fall to the floor, revealing her bare, pale body, so fragile and lovely. Soft. Calling to everything that was dark and rough and hideous within him.

He wanted to devour her. Consume her. Make her his own. Utterly and completely. His captive.

His Queen. Did she understand that he was no better than those men that had held her for all those years? She didn't seem to care. She was foolish for him, and it made him angry as much as it satisfied him. He had no real consistency when it came to her, and that bothered him most of all. He didn't know what face to wear, what mask. And that resulted in this feeling that he had no mask at all. A fate that terrified him most of all.

"Give me your darkness."

"No."

"It is in our vows. And I will add to them. Give me your darkness and I will be your light."

"You need all the light you have. If you have any yet remaining inside of you…"

"I will give it how I wish. It is not exhaustible." She reached out and touched his face. "And when it is put up against the darkness, the light wins, Maximus. Every time."

"Annick…"

She pressed her body against his, her face determined. "Take me. Make me yours. You. Whoever he is. The King. Maximus. Someone in between. Or someone much further in the dark. I want to be yours. In a way that no one else ever has been. I want to know you. All of you."

"I have blood on my hands," he said.

"If that is so, let me see it. If that is so, let me decide if I'm strong enough."

"I would spare you."

"Life has not spared me. I was never innocent. You know this. I was created as something strong enough to handle you. Do not dishonor that. Do not dishonor my pain by trying to protect that which is not there."

He growled, unable to resist. Unable to stop himself now. It was done. The thing inside of him loosed. And he grabbed her face, gripped her chin and held her steady as he lowered his head for a kiss. As he consumed her. Claimed her as his own. As he made her his.

She gasped, arching against him as they kissed.

"I want you to be my prisoner now," he said. "How do you like that? How would you like it?" He kissed her neck, all the way down her delicate throat, where he bit her. And she gasped. "Mine. What does that make me? A man who would take you prisoner all over again."

"But I would choose it." She put her hands in front of her, holding her wrists together. And he wrenched his tie from his neck and bound her quickly. Efficiently. A kick of desire ran through him as he saw her like that. A willing supplicant bound for his every desire.

"To your knees."

She obeyed, and he felt... Like there was a knife pressed against his flesh. Pushing deep. Pushing him to see how far he could go. How far he could take this. He began to disrobe. Removing his shirt. Removing the rest of his clothes slowly. Determinedly.

And she knelt there, a pair of white lace panties across her hips, and that black tie a dark slash against her pale wrists.

"Take me into your mouth."

She straightened up, obeying, using her mouth to pleasure him.

"Come now. You can still use your hands."

She raised her bound wrists, cupping his length with her hands as she continued to pleasure him with her tongue.

"Yes, this is what I will do with my prisoner. She will see to my pleasure. To my moods. What do you think of that? Will you enjoy that, my Queen? Being available for my every need? My every desire?"

"I'm yours," she said. "Gladly." And she continued on. Giving to him all that he asked, all that he demanded. He put his hand on the back of her head and began to thrust his hips forward in time with her movements. She made a small sound, but continued to pleasure him. And when he felt his own desire rise to the point that he could no longer hold back, he knew that he should leave her be.

He should not finish it this way. But she wanted the beast. She wanted all of him. She would have him.

He growled, releasing then, and when it was over, she looked up at him, a light of satisfaction in her eyes. "What else do you desire of me?"

He picked her up, carried her to the bed then, laid her out before him, spreading her like she was a delicious feast. It would not take him long to be ready again. That release had not been sufficient to drown out the ache in his gut that existed only for Annick.

"A glutton for punishment?"

"I told you I was a glutton," she said. "It is not my fault you do not believe. Not my fault that you insist on treating me as if I am fragile. Perhaps, had I not been kept in a dungeon, there would've been a great many lovers before you."

He growled, pinning her to the bed. "But I would've been your last."

"Would you?"

"Yes," he said, looking at her with all the ferocity that he felt building in his soul. "And you know what? I'm glad there were no others. Because you are mine." He put his hand between her legs. "Mine."

"Then the return is true. Me, I am possessive. And if this possession is good for you, then it is also good for me."

"Very good." He parted her slick lips with his fingers and pushed one deep inside of her. Watching as her face contorted with pleasure. As he teased her. Loving the silken feel of her. Loving that he was the only man ever to touch her like this. That he would be the only one ever.

He let that sense of possession run wild inside of him. Oh, this woman. How she called to him. How she tempted him, teased and tormented him. He wished to bury himself in her and never come back from it. He wanted to send them both into oblivion. Where there was nothing else and no one else. Nothing but them. Ever.

But he wished to extract every last drop of pleasure from her body first. He lowered himself down between her legs, tasting her as he continued to stroke the inside of her body. As he went on a search for that pleasure point he knew was deep inside, all the while moving his tongue over that sensitized bundle of nerves.

She twisted, arched beneath him, and he used his free arm to hold her to the bed. Her hands were still bound, but that didn't stop her from trying to claw at him.

"Behave yourself," he said, biting her inner thigh, earning himself a sharp cry. He pushed her. Further. Higher. Faster. Until she was sobbing his name. Until the beast within began to roar. Wanting to extract all that he could from her. To make her weak with ecstasy. It would never be enough. This. How could it ever be? He felt the deep, cavernous hole inside of him, and he did not know how he was supposed to fill it. Ever. And so he aided her until she was shaking. Quivering violently against his mouth. Until she shattered around his fingers, until he was so hard he hurt with it, but would not allow himself to sink into her honey depths. Not yet.

He lifted himself, pressing his hardness against that unbearable softness, dragging himself back and forth between her folds. She gasped, reaching toward him with her bound hands, and he took hold of her and forced those hands above her head. "Stay still." He rocked his hips back and forth over her, that slick friction torturous. A tease of what he truly wanted. To be deep inside of her, surrounded by her, rather than just moving against her desire.

"You do not get to take control here. This pace is not for you to set."

She shattered again. And again. So many times that he lost count. And he kept going until she was limp in his arms. Then he took her, turning her onto her stomach, propping her hips up, leaving her face buried in the bedspread, her arms thrown out in front of her, still bound. The image that she made there, a woman in the throes of surrender, to him. It was the most erotic thing he'd ever seen. And he could no longer claim to be dead inside, because his heart beat so fast he thought it might drill a hole through the front of his chest.

He felt too much here. And there were no lines between the two men that he saw himself as. Between Maximus and The King. Between the man and the killer. He just was. He just was, and he felt dirty and monstrous and free all at once. Shame, greater than anything he'd ever known, welled up inside of him. And nearly as quickly, a sense of being home assaulted him as he touched her lower back, dragged his palm over her perfect ass and brought his fingers down between her thighs to rub her gently. She whimpered.

"Is it too much for you?"

"Never," she said, her voice muffled but defiant. "I am not weak. Me, I am not easily brought down."

"Good."

He positioned himself at her slick entrance and thrust home. He was blinded by it. And he could no longer play games. He gripped her hips hard as he pounded himself inside of her. Lost himself completely in the sweetness of her body. In the rhythm of her cries of pleasure.

"Maximus," she whispered. "I love you."

He nearly stopped then, but it was too late. Those words grabbed hold of him. His throat, his heart, and dragged his release from his body. He cried out as his release overtook him. As his need became the only thing. He spilled himself deep inside of her, the roaring in his blood like the howling of wolves. And in that moment, there was nothing. Nothing but her.

He was only one man. The one who had lost himself in her. The man who was surrounded by Annick. The man that Annick said she loved. And for a blistering, blinding moment there was nothing else. Nothing but his release and hers blending together. Into one seamless moment. A perfect feeling.

"Annick," he growled.

And when it was over, he reversed their positions, brought her on top of him and tried to find his breath. Somewhere in all of that, her words had shifted to a white light. And he could not hear them again, could not see them. He could only feel them. He was in a daze. Like nothing he'd ever experienced before.

"I love you," she said again.

And that time, he moved away from her. His heart turned to stone. For it was something he could not bear and he had no choice. He had to harden himself against it.

"No," he said.

"Why not?"

"It can't be like that between us. How can you say that? After what I've done to you." He reached out and grabbed hold of the bonds on her wrists, removing them.

"How can I say that after you have made me come more times than I can even count? What does this mean? This insanity coming from you?"

"There's more to life than orgasm, Annick, and you should realize that I've used you pretty appallingly."

"In all the ways I have asked," she said, sounding almost triumphant. "I am not foolish, Maximus. And I am not weak. I like these games. Because in them I'm a prisoner, but I am strong. Do you not see how that is powerful? And in these games, you are a monster, but you are a man. You bite me. You push me. But it only gives me pleasure, not pain. Do you not see the freedom we find here in this?"

"Sex games are not real."

"*Games?* It is not games. And it is not different from talking. From being. It is the same. We are what we do here in this bed. It is part of us. And it cannot be separate. We were playing stupid games to pretend that it could be. Me, and all of my talk of desires. About how I would be with many men. I could not. For I am playing a game inside where I pretend that any man could arouse such passions. But I know they could not. It is you. It is you, and the strength that you have brought to me. These changes that you have given me. It is who you are."

Her words hit him hard, with the force of a bullet. How could she speak with such certainty about him when he felt no such certainty about himself?

"Who am I? Do you know the answer to that?"

"It is simple. You are charming. And good. And bad. Very bad. A killer, you are right. Though for good reasons. I am not ignoring pieces of you to construct love. I know it is there. Just as I know your heart is there, whatever you might think."

"You really don't know any of that for a fact. You don't actually know what you're talking about."

"Am I stupid?"

"You know I don't think you are."

"Then why act like I'm stupid when it is you who are scared?"

"I'm a killer, Annick, and I don't regret it. That's who I am. I was a different man once. I loved someone once. And I won't do it again."

"Lies. You love. And you believe in good. You want to say that you don't. You want to believe that you don't, because it is scary to you. I scare you. You don't scare me, Maximus King, and you need to. Because *you* need to scare me away. But I won't be. Because I'm not weak. Because I know what it is when men love only power, and that is not you."

"But I love my anger," he said. "And I love that I have had the freedom to let it run free."

"Fine. But you did not do bad things with it. You did good for the world. Yes, these are unsavory things, but there is war in this world, is there not? You cannot make yourself out to be a villain any more than a general might be. You do more than simply follow orders—you are willing to do what must be done. No, I will not let you recast yourself as a villain simply because it keeps you safe. Simply because you fear what it might mean to let yourself feel."

"I told you, I'm a monster."

"Yes, and I believe you. But I love this monster. All the pain that you have been through. All the things that have broken you. The things that have left you sharp and jagged and difficult. For I am no different. Broken and sad in some ways, but filled with hope. And I want, more than anything, to live." She looked at him, her eyes filled with sadness. "You have spent years killing for a woman. Will you not live for one?"

"I can only live a half life. And you deserve more than that."

"You go back on our bargain? Now that you have had your way? Now you have married me?"

He looked her in the eyes. "I vowed to stay with you. I vowed to protect you, and I won't break those vows."

"No. Just bind us both in a life where you refuse to love me but accept my love for yourself."

"I would never have asked for it," he said, the words scraping his throat raw. "You're the one who seems insistent on giving it."

"More fool me."

"I can't give more than this." How could he? His heart was a stone, and what was beneath...

He was battered. Wounded beyond repair.

She deserved someone more. She deserved something more, but the world had given her a broken and lacking life, and him, a broken and lacking man to go with it.

"No. You won't," she said. "Because you are afraid. A coward. So brave. So brave when it comes to doing things. So afraid when it comes to the feeling of them. Don't think I cannot see. I told you. I do not need a bitch. I need a guard. I need my cane."

"Careful," he said, grabbing her wrist then. "Careful before you insult me."

"You insult us both."

She got off the bed and began to gather her things. She dressed slowly, the anger and hurt radiating off her in waves. But she would know someday that he was doing her a kindness by not prolonging this. By not lying. For his part, he wouldn't lie.

"It is an offense, this," she said. "That we have both survived so much, and both traveled through so much darkness, for you to run away from the light when it is offered."

"Annick…"

"I thought you could rescue me, Maximus. But you are the one who needs rescuing. And if you will not take my hand, then I cannot help."

And then Annick slipped from the room, closing the door behind her. And he was left alone.

As it should be.

CHAPTER FOURTEEN

RAGE SWIRLED THROUGH Annick as she went down the halls, heading back toward her room. She felt mortally wounded. She had known that it would be a fight. That all of this would be so much work. But she had thought... She had thought that she would be able to reach him. Truly, she had. She felt nothing but deep regret over this.

It wasn't her own pain. Not so much. It was his.

He still saw the bars. And until he decided not to, there was nothing she could do.

She heard a sound. A sound that was almost no sound, and then the brick beside her head split apart. She screamed, dropping low and crawling to her bedchamber, slamming the door behind her. She didn't know where it had come from. And it was likely that whoever...

Suddenly, there was a hole in her bedroom door.

She lay flat, as flat as she could. Someone was actually trying to assassinate her.

It was happening. And Maximus wasn't here. He wasn't... She heard the sound of a struggle on the other side of the door. A roar, thunderous and terrible. Clattering and banging about. And then it was silent.

"Annick," came the sound of a rough voice.

"Maximus," she said.

"Open the door. It's safe."

She scrambled to her feet and went to the door. And there he was. Half-dressed, a wound on his face. "An assassin. From Lackland. So now you have your answer as to who is your enemy. It wasn't just the other regime they wanted removed. They'll be dealt with. Harshly."

"Maximus…"

"You forget that I know secrets about them. I didn't take the job to get rid of the dictator of this country without getting insurance. It will be dealt with. And you will be safe."

"I…"

"I was distracted, Annick. Because of that, you nearly paid the price. It will not happen again. Never."

"It was not… It was not anyone's fault—it was only that…"

"It was my fault," he said, his voice rough. "My fault. I will remain here. I will be your guard, but that is all it can be. A husband in name, but not…not in truth. All of tonight I should have been watching. I should have been prepared. But I was not. And you…you nearly died for it."

"I wouldn't trade anything about tonight."

"I would trade everything," he said. "It's nice for you that you're willing to sacrifice yourself, but I never will."

"Maximus…this has nothing to do with anything that—"

"It does. It has everything to do with it. This is finished. We will not discuss it any further."

"You don't get to decide. You don't get to decide everything about my life."

His rejection was so final. So complete. He was still

standing in the room but she could feel the separation. Could feel how absolute it was.

His face was stone. And in that moment, he was The King, and none of the man remained.

She did not know how to reach him. Didn't know how to touch him.

And he was no longer going to allow it.

"Then you put us both in prison."

"Better in prison alive and free than dead."

He turned away from her and went back into the corridor. He was barking orders. Demanding to know how this had happened. There was practically a full-scale military operation happening in the front of the palace by the time she took her next breath.

And she just sat on the bed. She started to tremble. She should be most upset about the fact that she had nearly been killed, but she was mostly frightened of what the future looked like without Maximus. He had retreated. Gone away behind this war-general facade.

She knew that she would not be able to take him now. Chloroform would not be sufficient to subdue him. To bring him to her.

No.

If she was ever going to have him, he would have to choose. And she didn't know if he ever would.

Annick had spent all of her life in a state of hope. She'd had to. If not for the hope inside of her, she would have lost herself completely while she had been captive. But now she could not find it.

Because how could you hope for a man who had no hope for himself?

She had been wrong, perhaps. Perhaps his darkness was so black it drowned out her light.

Annick had never felt so hopeless before.

In the moment, Annick felt like she was Queen of nothing except her own broken heart.

And there was simply no triumph to be had in that.

In the weeks since the attempt on Annick's life, Maximus had waged a full-scale tactical war against any forces that might seek to oppose his Queen. He had made sufficient threats toward Lackland, and he knew that they would not be pursuing her ever again. Already, he had banded together with Monte Blanco to ensure that the Lacklanders would be punished. That steep sanctions would be introduced.

The alliance that he had with his brother-in-law was strong, and he was grateful for it. He had hardened his heart against everything. Everything but seeing to Annick's safety. Shoring up the borders of the country. Nothing else mattered. Nothing.

And he… He had been a fool. A fool to believe that he could let the beast out. That he could somehow let his guard down for even a moment. Yes, he had been a fool.

He was not even bothering to pretend that he was the man he'd been in California, not anymore. He had transformed. And there was something comfortable about the position. About being a war general.

He was grateful his family had not remained in the country to see the shift, for his energy had to be devoted to this, to her, and he did not have time to waste answering their questions.

Someday, he supposed, they would have to talk.

What mattered now was Annick.

And it distracted him from the tearing weight in his chest over the distance between himself and his Queen.

It was essential. There was nothing else to be done.

He had used not only the political connections that he

had through his brother-in-law, but also business connections that he had through his other brother-in-law and best friend. If he could truly call anyone a friend.

Dante must have sensed his black mood, and those sentiments, because it wasn't long before he showed up at the palace unannounced.

"And where have you left my sister?" Maximus asked, looking at his friend.

"At her new castle. With her pony. She's very happy."

"You indulge Minerva."

"I live to indulge Minerva. She was not indulged enough in her life, and frankly, neither was I. Between the two of us, we live an extravagantly spoiled life. She has books and libraries and runs her charity. I have access to her body whenever I want…"

"You seem a smart man, Dante, and yet you have not picked up on the fact that it is not a good time to test me in any regard."

"Oh, no, I did. It is only that I want to know why. Black moods are typically reserved for me."

"No, it's just that I usually hide mine."

"Fair. What is going on? I don't blame you for tearing a swath through the world after that attempt on your wife's life. But what I do want to know is why you're behaving in quite this way."

"It's none of your business."

"Isn't it? I am your oldest friend. Your only friend. Don't think I haven't watched you fake your way through life all these years. I know that you changed when Stella died. And I might not know all the particulars of it, but you lost yourself. You became only that shallow playboy. Though you were never only that. This… This is actually more the real you. You being an asshole, that is."

"A very good friend you are."

"It's true. So tell me. What is it that's going on?"

"She brought me here to protect her. This is not a love match."

"Well, I say bullshit to that. It's obvious that she loves you."

He gritted his teeth. "She does."

"Then what's the problem?"

"I can't love her."

"You can't love her? This is your version of not loving somebody?" Dante chuckled. "I'm surprised literal heads haven't rolled over this. You're on a warpath, my friend. If this isn't love, what is?"

"Justice," he bit out. "Nothing more than justice."

"Is that so?"

"You're reading into things that are not there."

"Why not love her?"

"Because it's too dangerous. I let my guard down with her. She was nearly killed because I…because I spent the night with her hands tied over her head driving her mindless with pleasure, and then she said she loved me and I was consumed in my own feelings, too much so to pay attention to what was happening."

"I'm sorry—are you blaming sex and feelings for the fact that someone tried to assassinate her? Because her feelings are not what caused someone to attempt that."

"You don't understand."

"No, I don't."

"I was complacent the day that Stella died too."

"You could not have protected Stella. You didn't know what was coming."

"I should have," he said. "I should have known. I should've done something to save her."

"But you didn't. You couldn't have. Hindsight is

all well and good, Maximus, but it doesn't change the past."

"People lie to you about who they are," he said. "They lie to you and then…and then it only puts those you care about in danger."

"What are you talking about?"

"My father…he's not everything he appears to be."

"Your father rescued me from a life of… I would be dead by now if it weren't for your father."

"I know. But Stella is dead because of him. Because of his choices."

"If you have a problem with your father, you should talk to him."

"There's nothing to say. There is nothing to say except that actions he made in business created enemies who destroyed my life. And I could never… I could never look at him the same way again."

"Is this about your grief over Stella's death? Or is it about anger toward him? Him disappointing you and abusing your love?"

That made him stop. "It's not."

"I don't know that I believe that. You should talk to him," Dante said.

"We're not a family that talks about their feelings."

"Well, maybe it's high time we did. Because I can see now, Maximus, that you have been living in some kind of private hell and I let you. What kind of friendship is that?"

"Your friendship is not the issue here."

"Well, perhaps it should be."

"This is not your concern. I can handle this alone."

"Clearly you can't. And speaking as someone who lived under a shroud of their own darkness for a very long time, I can tell you that you shouldn't have to. Minerva saved me. Loving her saved me. You can laugh all you want about castles and ponies, and you can recoil in horror at the fact that I'm sleeping with your sister, but I love her. I love everything about her. And she forced me to change. She forced me to heal. And it was the cruelest, kindest thing anyone has ever done for me. She did not leave me to die in my brokenness. Your family gave me so much, Maximus, but not even your father's caring, your mother's love or your friendship healed me. It was Minerva, and the way that she demanded I love her back. She was the one that changed everything. That fixed everything. It was her love. So if you found a woman that is demanding you give her your heart, then you damn well do it. And if something stands in your way, that is the thing that you should destroy, not the love that could be between you."

"You don't understand what kind of man I am."

"I don't need to. Does *she* understand what kind of man you are?"

"She says she does."

"So listen. Believe her."

"Why should I?"

"Because the other choice is a life lived alone. And believe me when I tell you it's not even a half life. Because I'm standing on the other side of it, and I'm telling you."

"Her whole family died. And she says she loves me. The world treated her in the worst possible way, and she still loves me. And I… I was betrayed and I just… I spiraled into darkness, and I think I might like it there. I think I might not have the strength to walk back out. Because when you live in the darkness, nobody sees what you do. You don't have to be accountable for anything. For anyone."

"I can see the appeal. But what's the point of it?" He looked around the room. "Why did you come here in the first place?"

"Because she needed help."

"And that mattered."

"I don't know why in hell it did. Only that it did."

"I think you do know. It's because even then she called to your heart. Because even then you cared, whether you wanted to or not." Dante stared at him. "Talk to your father."

And then his friend was gone, as if he had not flown across the world to see him. A part of Maximus wondered if he had hallucinated the entire thing.

He poured himself a glass of whiskey, and he started to take a drink. But then stopped. He stared down at the amber liquid. And then he reached for his phone and called his father.

"Hello?"

"I blame you for Stella's death."

There was a long pause on the other end of the line. "I know you do. I blame myself. Because it was my fault."

"But worst of all, I hate that I idolized you and you didn't live up to it. I don't know how I can ever trust anyone or anything ever again. Especially because… in the end, I'm not any different than you. I'm two different men. I don't know how to reconcile that with anything."

There was nothing but the sound of broken breathing on the other end of the line. And when his father spoke, his voice was heavy.

"I failed you, Maximus, and nothing has ever brought me greater pain. Everything I did was for our family. For our betterment. And I'm responsible for the death of the woman you loved. I hate that. I hate how short my focus was. How arrogant I was about my own resilience. How I might've felt like I was untouchable, but didn't take into account the fact that my family was not. And that my family made me vulnerable. But… I'm not two different men. I am one. I'm very flawed. I care about the people in my life, but I can get blinded by my greed. By opportunity. I have a difficult time saying no. It's why I've engaged in business deals I should've walked away from. It's why I… That in the moment sometimes I forget my own principles. Because it's easier to say yes to what's right in front of me. Since Stella's death I've been better. But it doesn't take away what I did. It would be comforting to think that I was two men. But I'm just one broken one."

It was the strangest thing. That realization. Maximus remembered how he had felt in Annick's arms. Like he was one. The man and the beast. It had been comforting in a way. Even though in another it was easier to believe that one man was real and the other was a facade. Whichever felt better at the time.

Annick was the only one who knew. She saw him as one, and she claimed to love him anyway. She saw him. And she made him want to know what it would be like if he let go of everything that had happened in the past. Of the betrayal of his father, the loss of Stella and every black act he'd committed along the road to this point and accepted it. If he let go of the flaws in the world.

And knew the fact that he could never really quite balance the scales.

He had killed the man who had imprisoned Annick. Had removed him from power. Had set her free, but it didn't erase what had happened to her.

You could never erase the bad things in the past.

You could only go forward. Otherwise... It was like Annick had said.

Seeing bars where there weren't any.

"How do you live with it? How do you live with the flaws inside of you? How do you move forward?"

"I didn't have a choice. I love you. And Minerva and Violet. And I love your mother more than anything. And I have to live with myself. So there comes a point where you simply have to do just that. Live. Even if things don't seem fair. Even if the world is broken. Even if *you* are."

"I don't deserve her."

"I don't deserve your mother. I don't deserve the fact that you still speak to me, Maximus. I never have, and I don't take that for granted. I don't deserve Dante's loyalty, or Min and Violet's devotion. I can only accept your love. Because it's the only thing that makes living worth it. It's not the money. It's you."

It was the strangest thing. Because the world was still as it was, and his father had still made the mistakes he had. But there was a deep acceptance inside of him now that hadn't existed before. The world was broken and he couldn't fix it.

But he could love a woman who lived in this world. And she could love him. And with that love it was possible that they would make things better than he ever had with vengeance. Than he ever had with darkness.

There were no scales.

There was no cosmic scoresheet. There were tragedies. And there were triumphs. And there was right and wrong, and justice to be sure.

But mostly, there was love. And with love you could blot out a multitude of sins. If you were only brave enough to try.

"Thank you," Maximus said. "For helping me see." He hesitated for a moment. "I'm not who anyone in this family thinks I am."

"We should talk about it. Sometime. When you've settled things with your wife."

Maximus nodded. "All right. But I warn you that when you know the truth, you might not want me as a son anymore."

"Maximus, you have wanted me as a father in spite of my frailties. I could never not want you as a son."

Maximus hung up the phone and sat there for a long moment. Then the strongest, sharpest pain he'd ever felt pierced his chest. It was like dying. But he was still alive. Everything that he had tried not to feel since the attempt on Annick's life assaulted him then. It was no longer just anger. No longer a desperate need for revenge. He had nearly lost her. He had nearly lost her without ever truly having her. He had nearly lost her without ever telling her that he loved her. Without ever letting himself feel it. It was not protection. It was foolishness. It was fear.

And fear was a great liar.

He was gasping for breath now, barely able to.

He had told her he didn't love her. His Annick. He had hurt her. She had already been hurt so many times.

He did not deserve her. He didn't.

He doubled over with that knowledge. With that pain.

But she had said that she accepted him. All of him. Everything that he was.

Why? *How?*

He didn't have the answer.

But as he lay there, stunned by the full force of these emotions, he knew that it didn't matter why.

Because it wasn't fair.

Nothing about life was.

Not the childhood Annick had spent in the dungeon, the death of Stella or the fact that Annick loved him. Knowing all that he was.

None of it was fair.

It was better than fair.

It was love.

Annick was fed up with her own frailty at this point. She had lived through unimaginable cruelties, and she had not fallen apart. But that was the problem.She had not had the time then. Now she was safe, well taken care of and feeling quite ill-used. And she now had the luxury of reveling in it.

She missed Maximus. She missed everything about him. And she was ready to bind her own wrists and present herself in his bedchamber as a gift. For him to unwrap.

"Have a bit of pride," she said to herself.

She did not want pride. She wanted Maximus.

She lay across her bed, and as if her dreams had conjured him, there he suddenly was. Strong and silent and standing in the doorway, and she remembered what she had thought when she had seen him there in the dungeon. It was no longer bars, but him. He was not a prison, but a strange sort of freedom. A path to the center of herself. To all of her desires.

A man who was strong enough to take her anger, her grief, her joy, her pleasure.

A man who felt created most especially for her, but he did not seem to want to see it.

"What is this?" she asked, sitting up. "Are you here to brief me on military procedure?"

He shook his head. "No. I'm here to tell you... I'm

not worthy of you. And I'm… I'm not two separate men. There's no monster in me. Just me. And it's been easier to pretend that I had a life in one place that was all its own, and a life in another that belonged to someone different. But it's all me. I took those missions because it was easier to do something than sit in grief. Because I was afraid of what I might do with my anger if I didn't channel it into something specific. I kept my old life because I still wanted to be near my family. Because I still loved my father even though I was angry with him. And I never chose another person to love because I never even knew what love was.

"I was young and life was easy, and I fell into something good with a woman who was as light and happy as I was. And now I've seen dark things in the world. Atrocities. And knowing about all of that and having the strength to love anyway… Well, I wasn't strong enough to do that. Or brave enough. It took a woman who had seen as many terrible things as I had to make me want that again. Annick, from the moment I saw you it was something different. It was like you united both pieces of me. You made me have to figure out what it meant to be me. The Maximus King who cared about things. Who enjoyed pleasure. Who enjoyed life. And the Maximus King who was lost in a world of darkness and revenge. Wanting to protect you gave me purpose. And knowing you made me feel things again. Watching you live… I thought I was dead inside, but no. You made me into something so much better than I was even before."

"We are both broken, eh?"

"It's not being broken that defines us. It's love, don't you think?"

"Do you love me, Maximus?"

"Yes, Annick. I love you. Not like anyone ever before. Not like anything. I love you in a way I didn't think was possible."

"Maximus," she said, flinging herself up off the bed and wrapping her arms around his neck. Kissing him with everything she had inside of her.

"Thank you," he said. "For kidnapping me. I think you might've rescued me."

"Well, I know for certain that you rescued me. Maximus, whatever you want to call yourself, you are mine. Nothing else matters. I know what you've done." She spread her hands. "But you do not have blood on your hands. Many people were saved because of what you did. You had anger in your heart, yes. But you're a good man, and you always were. Your anger never took you to a place where you might harm an innocent. You were never a monster. Just wounded."

"Without all my mistakes, without all the pain, without all that I lost, I would never have made it to you. Whatever else I know to be true, I know that. You rescued me. You rescued me because of what you did. Set me free."

"And you set me free."

She had a strange, heavy sensation in her chest and looked toward the dresser. Her wedding bouquet was still there. She went over to it and grabbed hold of one of the flowers, breaking another blossom off. "For Stella," she said. "You would be proud of him. You would be proud of who he is. And I will take care of him. And love him."

"I hope you know," he said, putting his hand over hers, "that what I feel for you isn't the same. I loved her as a boy. I love you as a man."

Her heart lifted. "And I hope sometimes as a monster. Because I did quite like the monster."

"I will be whatever you wish. Your captor. Your protector. Your man. Your monster."

"You are all those things, I think. There is no pretending. Not with me."

"Never. And you don't need to pretend anymore either."

"No," she said. And she flung herself into his arms, feeling every big thing she had done since he'd first come into her life. Hungry and happy and filled with a sharp, aching joy that made her vibrate. She wanted to lick him and fight him and kiss him all at once, and she would. She would.

"Me, I love you. And that is quite a brilliant thing."

He cupped her chin, his eyes touching her soul. "There are no bars, Annick, not now. All I see is you."

It was true—there were no words for the sort of pain she and Maximus had endured in their lives.

But there was love and joy that transcended language too. That could only be felt and breathed and lived. And they had that.

It made the world beautiful and magical, and bright enough to drown out all the darkness that had come before.

Always.

Forever.

EPILOGUE

MAXIMUS AND ANNICK built the most beautiful life out of the broken pieces they'd been given. It was not less. It was not secondary. It was everything. And when they welcomed their first child into the world, a boy, and Annick named him Marcus after her brother, Maximus felt joy like he'd never known before.

"You know," Annick said, looking at him as he held his son, "you were never dead inside, Maximus. You were just protecting yourself."

"Yes. To an extent. But I also didn't know. There was nothing in me that could ever have been prepared for the joy that was coming."

"Thank God for chloroform, eh?"

He chuckled, looking down at that tiny perfect life they had created, and all around at the beautiful, glittering life they had created in this world that was their own.

"Yes, Annick. Thank God for chloroform."

And for the small, determined woman who had believed in love, happy endings and kidnap, who had been strong enough and determined enough to redeem him and to save them both.

* * * * *

MILLS & BOON

THE HEART OF ROMANCE

A ROMANCE FOR EVERY READER

MODERN
Prepare to be swept off your feet by sophisticated, sexy and seductive heroes, in some of the world's most glamourous and romantic locations, where power and passion collide.

HISTORICAL
Escape with historical heroes from time gone by. Whether your passion for wicked Regency Rakes, muscled Vikings or rugged Highlanders, awa the romance of the past.

MEDICAL
Set your pulse racing with dedicated, delectable doctors in the high-pre sure world of medicine, where emotions run high and passion, comfort love are the best medicine.

True Love
Celebrate true love with tender stories of heartfelt romance, from the rush of falling in love to the joy a new baby can bring, and a focus on emotional heart of a relationship.

Desire
Indulge in secrets and scandal, intense drama and plenty of sizzling ho action with powerful and passionate heroes who have it all: wealth, sta good looks…everything but the right woman.

HEROES
Experience all the excitement of a gripping thriller, with an intense ro mance at its heart. Resourceful, true-to-life women and strong, fearless face danger and desire - a killer combination!

To see which titles are coming soon, please visit

millsandboon.co.uk/nextmonth

MILLS & BOON

Coming next month

REDEEMED BY HIS NEW YORK CINDERELLA
Jadesola James

"I'll speak plainly." The way he should have in the beginning, before she had him ruminating.

"All right."

"I'm close to signing the man you met. Giles Mueller. He's the owner of the Mueller Racetrack."

She nodded.

"You know it?"

"It's out on Long Island. I attended an event close to it once."

He grunted. "The woman you filled in for on Friday is— *was*—my set date for several events over the next month. Since Giles already thinks you're her, I'd like you to step in. In exchange, I'll make a handsome donation to your charity—"

"Foundation."

"Whatever you like."

There was silence between them for a moment, and Katherine looked at him again. It made him uncomfortable at once. He knew she couldn't see into his mind, but there was something very perceptive about that look. She said nothing, and he continued talking to cover the silence.

"You see, Katherine, I owe you a debt." Laurence's voice was dry. "You saved my life, and in turn I'll save your business."

She snorted. "What makes you think my business needs saving?"

Laurence laughed incredulously. "You're a one-person operation. You don't even have an *office*. Your website is one of those ghastly pay-by-month templates, you live in a boarding house—"

"I don't need an office," Katherine said proudly. "I meet

clients in restaurants and coffee shops. An office is an old-fashioned and frankly completely unneeded expense. I'm not looking to make money off this, Laurence. I want to help people. Not everyone is like you."

Laurence chose not to pursue the insult; what mattered was getting Katherine to sign. "As you like," he said dismissively, then reached for his phone. "My driver has the paperwork waiting in the car. I'll have him bring it round now—"

"No."

It took a moment for the word to register. "Excuse me?"

Katherine did not repeat herself, but she did shake her head. "It's a kind offer, Laurence," she said firmly, "but the thought of playing your girlfriend is at least as absurd as your lie was."

Laurence realized after several seconds had passed that he was gaping, and he closed his mouth rapidly. He'd anticipated many different counteroffers—all that had been provided for in the partnership proposal that was ready for her to sign—but a refusal was something he was wholly unprepared for.

"You're saying no?" he said, to clarify.

She nodded.

"Why the hell would you say no?" The question came out far more harshly than he would have liked, but he was genuinely shocked. "You have everything to gain."

She tucked a lock of dark hair behind her ear, and he was momentarily distracted by the smooth slide of it over her skin. The change in her was truly remarkable. In her element, she was an entirely different person than the frightened teenager he remembered, and she carried herself with a quiet dignity that was very attractive.

Continue reading
REDEEMED BY HIS NEW YORK CINDERELLA
Jadesola James

Available next month
www.millsandboon.co.uk

LET'S TALK

Romance

For exclusive extracts, competitions
and special offers, find us online:

[f] facebook.com/millsandboon

[y] @MillsandBoon

[o] @MillsandBoonUK

Get in touch on 01413 063232

Available at
weloveromance.com

MILLS & BOON
Desire

Indulge in secrets and scandal, intense drama and plenty of sizzling hot action with powerful and passionate heroes who have it all: wealth, status, good looks…everything but the right woman.